COMMODITY

Shay Savage

Acknowledgements

Special thanks to Anthony for all your bodyguard and military expertise as well as your constant willingness to provide me with interesting stories. You always entertain! Also, thanks to Caesar and Jim for answering my countless questions about varying topics and to Christine and Chuck for being such an adorable couple. All of you helped me to bring the *Commodity* characters to life!

As always, thanks to my team for their encouragement and support. Because of you, this book is done in record time!

Prologue

No one ever saw them.

We didn't know where they came from or why they came here. We only knew that in one blast, the planet was left in ruins. For weeks, the bodies of men rotted in the streets.

Men. Not women. Not children.

The women and children were gone.

With the cities destroyed and communication impossible, we could only guess what happened. Men gathered in loose tribes, trying to get answers, but there were none to be found.

As the weeks turned into months, survivors emerged from secluded, rural areas, underground shelters, and subway systems in the larger cities. Only a handful of women were among them. Men outnumbered them a thousand to one.

During the first year, the weather warmed. Rainfall nearly stopped. Lights began to appear in the sky, moving slowly over our heads, but they never came down. We had no face for our enemy, so we turned against each other.

Fights broke out as survivors struggled for limited resources. Clean water and food were at the top of the list and would only be traded for fuel, guns, or ammunition.

The few, unfortunate females still to be found became the most prized commodity.

COMMODITY
Part One

Chapter 1

Life has given me shit.

Maybe I should take that sage advice and make some damn lemonade, but I'm pretty sure any lemons I choose at the grocery will have already turned. Maybe it's my own fault.

Life didn't start off all that bad. I can't complain about my parents too much—they did what they could, given the circumstances. They just had things on their minds that took precedence over me. It's all okay; I understand why they were like that. At least they weren't abusive, and they did pay for my college education. I should thank them for that since I have a good job.

Well, had.

I changed all that in only one afternoon.

I lean my head against the window of the plane and stare at the clouds below. I've been left alone with my thoughts for too long again, and even though I'm exhausted, I doubt I'll sleep.

I reach down and scratch my knee. I hate wearing panty hose. In fact, the entire getup I'm in makes me feel even more on edge that I am already. Navy blue skirt and matching dress jacket over a frilly white blouse—it's definitely not my style, if I even have one. I can barely walk in the heels though they aren't that high. Even at work, we only had to dress in business casual clothes. On my own time, blue jeans and T-shirts are definitely more me.

Closing my eyes, I breathe deeply and try to focus on something inside my mind that brings me some peace. It's always the same image—a meadow full of sunshine and bright yellow dandelions. I've never been to such a meadow, but I imagine it would be peaceful.

The meadow changes. The dandelions go to seed, and the seeds float on the wind, leaving nothing but naked stems. The meadow morphs and bends until it's a metal shell. The scent of spring blossoms is gone, and instead, I smell sweat and feel the pressure of bodies all around me.

"For those of you who checked luggage, your bags will be waiting on carousel six. We hope you have enjoyed your flight, and thank you for flying Air Choice."

I startle awake at the sound of the voice. I can't remember exactly the dream I had been having, but the feeling of being immobilized lingers in my head. I take a deep breath and look around at the other passengers for a moment before quickly checking around my seat for any items that may have fallen out of my purse.

I shamble into the aisle, making sure to place one foot in front of the other so I don't trip in the damn shoes. As I try to make my way out of the plane, my eyelids droop against my will. I stop and have to wait for the guy in front of me to get his bag out of the overhead bin. Despite the brief doze against the window of the plane, I hadn't slept much over the past two days. I want to lean a hand against the seat in front of me to keep from falling over, but it would likely put me in contact with the man struggling with his carry-on. I shake my head a little to clear it and glance over my shoulder.

There is a woman a few rows back with long, dark hair. She's holding up her phone and taking a picture of me. I almost smile out of habit and then consider flipping her off. I do neither. The last thing I need right now is more press. Instead, I turn back around quickly, wondering what happened to subtlety, and bump the man in front of me as he finally retrieves his luggage.

I flinch from the contact. At least it had only been through my sleeve, but I can still feel the spot where the pressure of contact was made. I close my eyes for a moment and try to push away the thoughts in my head, but they come at me anyway.

Hands pushing me down, holding me in place. Hot breath on my neck. Pain.

I bite my lip, and the sting brings me back to the moment. It's the same spot I've been biting on a lot, and it's already sore. I'm sweating along the underside of my bra and down the small of my back. I had never had any claustrophobic inclinations before, but they've emerged over the last few months and seem to be getting worse. I need to get out of this plane.

Placing my oversized sunglasses on and pulling my shoulders up close to my ears, I exit the plane. I look at my feet as I walk up the ramp, dodging other passengers as I go.

"Hey! Aren't you the lady from Archive Industries? I saw you on T.V.!"

I don't respond. Instead, I walk a little faster, suddenly very aware of how alone and unprotected I am right now. All the people around me are too close; any of them could reach out and grab me at any moment. I taste bile in the back of my throat and walk faster.

Maybe I shouldn't have refused the escort for the first flight.

Paxton and I had fought about it at some length. At the moment, I'm not even sure why I was so adamant about being on the plane alone. I think I just wanted a little bit of time pretending I was just me again, not some hunted corporate spy or whatever the media is calling me today.

I hear additional whispered comments, but I don't look toward whomever is speaking.

As I head through the doorway, an airsick passenger from another flight sits listlessly in a wheelchair as paramedics check her over. They've got her right in the middle of traffic flow, and everyone has to step around the hindrance. I don't mind; it's given everyone something else to look at and allows me to get around the crowd at the gate. As the space opens up, I see a line of men dressed in black suits and wearing earpieces with small wires curling around their ears. In dress and demeanor, they look exactly like the team that escorted me to the plane in Chicago.

I look away from them, down and to the side. I don't need to look to know that they're coming for me. I've had a group of them around since the death threat.

They should have been with Daniel.

"Ms. Savinski?"

I see the shiny black shoes first and let out the breath I've been holding before I look up to face my escort. I blink several times before I realize my mouth is hanging open.

The man is tall—at least six feet, maybe a little more. His hair is blond and closely cut. His eyes are intense and give me the impression that he sees everything. He's older than me by several years—maybe in his early thirties—and has a military bearing.

I take in the rest of him as my heart starts to beat faster in my chest. He's all muscle underneath the suit jacket that doesn't fit quite right around his biceps. His dark eyes don't exactly match his complexion, and he has a strong jawline and high cheekbones. There's a thin scar near his temple. He looks like he just walked out of a black-and-white movie, maybe something from the twenties or thirties. He just needs a fedora and maybe a tommy gun in a violin case.

"My name is Falk Eckhart," the tall, blond man says. He doesn't offer me his hand to shake but keeps staring at me with those piercing eyes. It's unnerving and sends a shiver down my spine. "My team will escort you, ma'am."

Falk. What the hell kind of name is that, and why am I reacting to him this way? I haven't thought about men in months, not since…since…

I bite my lip again, effectively erasing the thought as the sharp pain hits me. While I'm at it, I dismiss my reaction to him as well. He's not classically attractive or even cute though I have to admit there is definitely something to his look. He's strong, composed, and a little intimidating in size and demeanor. I'm unnerved by my response to him.

"Ms. Savinski?" he says again, and I realize I haven't answered him at all.

He bows slightly toward me as I nod in acknowledgement and quickly glance around to see if anyone's heard him say my name. There are a few people who slow to look toward us.

One of them—a young, rotund man—stops in his tracks and stares at me for a minute before taking out his phone.

"Hannah Savinski!" he calls out. "Hey! Are you going to Washington to testify?"

Before I can even begin to form a response, Eckhart is in his face.

"Back off," he says sternly as he towers over the man. He's just an inch away, but he doesn't touch him. "Put that phone away, and get to wherever you're going. You hear me?"

"Yeah, whatever. Asshole." The guy shoves his phone back in his pocket as he backs away and heads toward the tram.

"Ms. Savinski, are you all right?"

"Yes, sorry," I reply as I try to remember what I should say next. "It's good to meet you. Please, call me Hannah."

His eyes widen minutely, and I see the corner of his mouth twitch.

7

"No, ma'am," he says softly. "I couldn't do that."

I narrow my eyes at Eckhart as I meet his eyes again and realize he's been watching me look him over. His lips remain in a line, but his eyes twinkle a little. He's not laughing though—just a slight smile that sets me at ease even as I feel heat rise to my cheeks.

I consider insisting he call me by my first name, but the set of his shoulders makes me think that any effort to change his mind would be wasted. It's hard not to be annoyed by the way people treat me now as if I weren't the same person I was before. I tell myself that it doesn't really matter, that this team is only supposed to keep me out of harm's way until Monday and that I can put up with the formality for that amount of time, but it's difficult.

Well, I can be formal and stick with last names as well and refer to him as Mr. Eckhart. Maybe that will keep my mind from wandering too much. I won't have to try to remember *Falk* at all.

"This way, please." He holds out his arm to direct me toward the rest of his team, and I tense slightly, but he doesn't touch me. The last security head kept grabbing a hold of my arm until I finally screamed at him not to touch me. I can still feel the heat from Eckhart's body close behind me, but I'm okay with that. It reminds me that he's keeping others away.

There are five additional men in the entourage. Two walk ahead of me, one on each side, and two behind, but none of them makes physical contact, and I manage to relax a bit more. There is a crowd starting to form, and I can hear the clicking of people's phones as they snap pictures, but I feel reassured by the protective shell the men around me create.

It's strange that these men in suits aren't making me panic. Maybe it's because I know they're being well paid to protect me. Otherwise, what sets them apart from the others I'll be testifying against?

"The flight's been delayed." The guard in front of me turns around to speak to Eckhart.

"How long?" Eckhart asks.

"Forty-five minutes."

"Weather related?"

"Apparently."

Glancing toward the windows, I see the downpour of rain and flashes of lightning, but I can't hear any thunder from inside the Atlanta Airport. As we close in on the gate for the next flight, hundreds of people are standing around, all waiting for their flights to be called. I want to sit down, but there isn't an empty seat to be found.

"They're changing the gate."

Feeling like a cow in a slaughterhouse, I'm led to the end of the concourse and eventually get on the next plane headed for Washington, D.C. Eckhart is in the seat beside me—the first row of first class. We'll meet another team from his company when we land.

As we settle in, the flight attendant offers us a drink. Falk refuses, but I'm not too proud to admit it sounds pretty good, and I order a rum and coke. I figure the caffeine could do me some good. I glance out the window as I sip at the drink. It's still raining but not like it had been before. I look at Eckhart, but he's checking out the passengers to our left out of the corner of his eye.

"How long have you being doing this?" I ask him.

"Four years," Eckhart replies as he looks back in my direction.

"Is everyone you escort being hunted like I am?"

"No, ma'am."

"Who else?"

"Mostly government officials," he says, "senators, representatives, and cabinet members."

"Have you ever escorted the president?"

"Once."

I'm impressed. If Falk Eckhart is good enough for the president, maybe I should relax a little and get some sleep. He certainly seems to be aware enough of everything going on around us, so I should be safe.

Safe.

Such a simple little word. I haven't felt safe since I was nine. That's when my fourteen-year-old sister, Heather, disappeared. We had no idea what had happened to her. It wasn't until I was at work years later when someone in accounting asked me to check on a data discrepancy that I discovered the truth. One little transaction lead to so much more, and my life has been upside down ever since.

The captain's voice comes over the intercom.

"Apologies everyone, but I'm afraid we've got some bad news. We've hit our maximum flight time, and we'll have to head back to the gate."

"What does that mean?" I ask.

"Flight crews have a maximum number of hours they can work," Eckhart explains. "If we take off now, they'll go over the limit. We'll have to wait for another crew."

"How long will that take?"

"They'll have to locate a fresh crew. It will be hours."

I check my phone for the time. It's already after nine o'clock. It will be the middle of the night before we reach our destination.

I listen to the grumbling and exasperated sighs of other passengers as they drag out cell phones and start contacting loved ones to inform them of the delay. Eckhart taps on his phone and sends a message to the rest of his group to come back to the gate.

Back inside the airport, it's a madhouse. Multiple flights have been cancelled, and there are lines of people all waiting to get new flight information and a hotel room for the night.

"I just contacted this hotel, and they don't have any more rooms for the night! How can you give me a voucher for a hotel that doesn't have any rooms left?"

"Who's going to pay for the hotel I already have booked for tonight, huh?"

"All my luggage is checked! What am I supposed to do about clothes for tomorrow?"

Eckhart sends one of his crew with our boarding passes and passports to collect vouchers as he keeps me away from the crowd. Everyone is so angry with the airline that they aren't paying attention to me, which is good.

"They put you in different hotels," the security escort says when he returns with vouchers for me and Eckhart.

"That's ridiculous."

"They said there wasn't anything they could do—it's all automated."

Eckhart takes a step away from me, clenching his hands into fists for a brief moment before he stretches his neck to the left and then the right. His chest expands as he takes in a deep breath, causing the button of his jacket to tighten against the fabric.

"Stay with her." Eckhart glares at the information counter as he stomps up to the front line, ignoring the other passengers. I can't hear anything he's saying, but he's leaning over the desk and flashing his identification. The person behind the desk is wide-eyed and nodding a lot. She hands him something, and he returns to the group.

"We're in the Hilton," he announces. "You have the penthouse."

He hands me a small plastic case with the airline's logo imprinted on it.

"What's this?"

"Toiletry bag," he says gruffly. He turns to one of the other guards. "Is there a car waiting?"

"Yes, sir."

"Let's go."

I finger the little vinyl bag and let myself be led out of the airport to a black SUV parked next to the curb. Eckhart opens the back door and I settle into the middle of the seat. He speaks to one of the other men before sliding into the front.

I am left alone in the back of the car as the others climb into different vehicles. Leaning back and closing my eyes, I try to pretend that none of this is happening. I think back to one of the first interviews with the police and how they called me brave for coming forward. I didn't understand what they meant then, but I do now.

This sucks.

I stare out the window as light rain coats the glass. Inside the car is warm, but gooseflesh still prickles over my arms as I remember another ride where I was tossed into the back of a windowless van.

Hudson is incarcerated right now. No bond set. They can't get to you.

As many times as Paxton, my attorney, has told me this, I know it isn't true. The group that would like to silence me permanently has power and people. If they weren't so powerful, Paxton wouldn't have insisted on the security detail. I knew it wasn't just to keep the media and curious people at bay though it did help with that as well.

I just want it to be over and done.

The car stops outside the hotel, and a valet comes to open my door. There are people everywhere—how does the media know where I am all the time? I'm ushered into the lobby, and Eckhart's hand presses lightly against my back as he maneuvers me through the crowd. I try not to flinch, knowing he's only trying to do his job. It doesn't matter how attractive I find him; I don't want his hands on me.

I glance over my shoulder at his face, trying to convey my thoughts with a look. He glances at me and quickly drops his hand, and my back chills as the contact is lost. Up closer now, I can see his eyes are deep blue, and he scans everything around us as we head for the elevator. I shiver as the express elevator moves quickly to the top floor.

The room is huge and completely ridiculous for a single person's one-night stay. It's not even the whole night—we have to

12

be back at the airport in five hours. I've always stayed at reasonably priced hotels, usually finding the best deal possible after consulting a host of internet travel sites. I'm used to the kinds of rooms where normal people spend their nights away from home. This seems more like something out of a dream.

A nightmare is more like it.

"Someone will be posted outside your room at all times," Eckhart says. He hands me a business card with his name and a phone number scrawled over the front of it. "If you need anything, please let us know. Contact me directly if you run into any issues."

"Thank you."

The door closes and I am blissfully alone. I don't partake of the in-room bar, but I do turn the television on. The deep bathtub looks like it has jets built in, and a soak is tempting, but I'm afraid I'd pass out in the water and drown. Instead, I kick my shoes off, drop to the bed, and open up the toiletry bag.

Inside is the tiniest tube of toothpaste I have ever seen, a plastic brush that will never get through my thick hair, a razor, and a miniscule tube of shaving cream. There is also an extra-large, white T-shirt that is so thin, it is completely see-through. I shake my head and snicker at the whole assortment.

Dropping my head to the pillow, I stare at the shirt, wondering if I should put it on just to keep my other clothes from getting sweaty while I sleep. The suit I'm wearing is going to be all wrinkled if I don't, so I push myself out of bed and hang up my clothes, ditch the panty hose and my bra, and pull the thin, white fabric over my head. I glance in the mirror, and there is absolutely nothing left to the imagination.

"Great look," I mutter to myself.

"You got nice titties, girl! Really nice titties! Bigger than the ones we usually get to see around here! Heh! Heh! Heh!"

Bile rises into my throat, and I rush to the bathroom, but nothing comes up. I grab one of the soft, white towels and shove it under my knees as my stomach rolls around.

Paxton said I only have to get through this one more time…one more time, telling it all. It shouldn't take more than a day or two, and then I can put it all behind me.

Bullshit.

It's never going to be over. What exactly am I supposed to do afterward? Find another job? Who the fuck is going to hire the snitch? What else does that leave me? Stuck with selling the book and movie rights. Or maybe just hiding out somewhere, away from the public, watching my picture appear in Facebook memes.

I squeeze my eyes shut and lay the side of my head on the rim of the toilet, refusing to cry. Even though there's no one here to see me, I don't want to give the bastards the satisfaction. I'm just going to wash my face and go get a couple of hours sleep. Tomorrow is going to be a busy, busy day.

But before I can act on the thought, my vision blurs, and I'm out.

I'm awakened by a knock at the door early in the morning. I'm still slumped against the commode, and my knees ache. I pull myself off the floor and go to the door. It's Eckhart.

His eyes nearly bulge out of his head as he stands there with a small bag in his hand. There's a guy from the hotel behind him with a cart full of food. I look at him for a moment, trying to understand why he's looking at me so strangely, and then I remember how I'm dressed.

"Shit!" I wrap one arm across my tits and use the other to push the door mostly closed, so I'm only looking at him through the crack. "Sorry! I…I…"

I don't know what to say.

"We'll need to leave in about twenty minutes," Eckhart says. "I thought you could use these."

He shoves the small plastic bag through the barely open door. I look inside to find a package of women's underwear and a pink sweatshirt with "Atlanta" scrawled across the front of it.

14

"Sorry," he mumbles, "they didn't have a lot of choices in the gift shop downstairs. I thought you'd be hungry as well, but I didn't know what you might like."

"That's fine," I say quickly as I turn away from the opening to hide the blush I'm sure is covering my cheeks. "I appreciate it."

I hide in the bathroom so the cart can be brought inside, then pick at the pancakes on the cart and sip at strong coffee while Eckhart waits outside with the rest of his group. There's no time to shower, but I brush my teeth and manage to wash all the important parts with a washcloth and soap, conscious of the men just outside my door. I stare at myself in the bathroom mirror and wonder if this is worth it.

Doesn't matter if it is or not—it's too late now.

"It's only a short flight to D.C.," Eckhart informs me as I leave the sanctuary of the hotel room behind. I can't look him in the face now that he saw me in that sheer getup, but at least he's acting like nothing happened. "We'll have you there quickly."

"Fantastic." I don't even bother to hide my morose mood. The closer I get to the destination, the more surreal it all feels. My heart is beating too fast in my chest, and I feel like I'm going to start hyperventilating. I consider asking Eckhart for a paper bag, but I don't think he'd find the humor in it. This guy is all business.

The elevator shakes once during the fast descent from the twenty-first floor, and I have to grab onto the railing of the car to keep my balance. Eckhart starts to reach out for me but pulls his hand back when he sees I have a hold of the railing. He looks from me to the lighted display at the top of the elevator car and scowls.

As soon as the elevator doors open, it's obvious something is going on. In my paranoia, I think it's about me, but I quickly see that it's not.

There are about thirty people in the lobby, all pressed up against the glass doors.

"It must have been an earthquake," someone in the crowd says. Others seem to agree.

"That wasn't an earthquake," a man argues. "Not enough to shake the building. Not around here."

"A fire?" a woman questions as she holds a school-aged boy's hand tightly. "Did a plane crash?"

"I don't see anything outside."

"Get out of the way and let me look!"

Hotel security appears and tries to move everyone away from the doors as they quote fire codes. Eckhart sends one of his guys to get information from the hotel security group before he brings me off to the side.

"What's going on?" I ask.

"No idea," Eckhart says with a sharp shake of his head. "Let's just give everyone a minute to clear."

He takes position behind me and slightly to the right. He keeps his right hand hanging close to his hip, and when I look down, I can see the bulge of a gun there.

I close my eyes. I have never liked guns, have never been around them, and don't know anything about them. Knowing one is so close to me makes my skin crawl, and I can't help but wonder how many times Eckhart's used it.

There's a rumble from outside, and the floor shakes. It is what I would imagine an earthquake feels like, but in Atlanta? Don't those only happen on the coast or something?

"Do you think it's an earthquake?" I ask dumbly. Eckhart obviously has no more of an idea than I do and doesn't bother to respond. He keeps his eyes forward, watching the short interaction between hotel security and the man he sent over to talk to them.

The conversation ends, and the security guard from Eckhart's team turns to head toward us. As he turns, he makes eye contact with Eckhart and shakes his head slightly. Eckhart starts to speak, but I never hear his words. They are drowned out as a massive explosion rocks the building and sends me crashing into him.

Chapter 2

My ears ring and my head throbs. I'm barely aware of Eckhart's arms around me as he helps me back to my feet. I hear screams, but they're muffled. People are pushing past us, and Eckhart's team is trying to steer them all away from me as they scramble past.

A large wooden support beam falls from the ceiling of the lobby, crashing onto the marble floor. More people scream, and I think I see someone trapped underneath the rubble.

What the hell is going on?

"Outside!" I hear Eckhart say as he pushes at my back, directing me toward a shattered glass door. "Be careful."

He keeps his hands close to me but not quite touching as I step over the glass and out of the hotel. Eckhart stays near me as we head out into the street with many of the other hotel patrons. There are people everywhere, running around the cars and heading to our left. Eckhart looks to the right and the mass of people running in our direction. There's another blast from that vicinity though it's not as close as the previous one.

In the distance, there's a massive rumbling sound, and we all look up as a twenty story building collapses a few blocks away. There are more screams from the crowd, and Eckhart grabs my arm.

As soon as he comes in contact with me, I tense everywhere. He had only touched me lightly on the back before, but now his fingers grip my arm as he pulls me off to the side near the brick wall of the hotel.

"Sorry," he mutters as he releases my arm. "Just stay close to me."

I nod, unable to answer with words. People are running everywhere—screaming. There's another explosion in the distance, and the ground beneath me shakes.

"Brand! Offner! Head north and report back. Miller and Hester—south towards that last blast."

"On it."

Each pair heads off in the given direction. As they disappear into the surge of panicking people, Eckhart holds his hand up to his ear and listens intently. He scans the area, taking everything in as he listens.

Several police officers try to organize people, telling them not to panic. It's not working. The police officers look as confused as everyone else. There's another blast close to our right. From the alley between buildings, a man runs into the street. His clothing is on fire, and he screams as he burns. One of the police officers runs toward him, but they disappear behind a car, and I can't see what's happening. The building on the far side of the alley suddenly collapses into rubble, sending bricks and glass everywhere.

"Oh my God!"

"Air or ground? Well, figure it out!" Eckhart turns to the last remaining member of his security team. "Keep contact with both groups. I want to get Ms. Savinski out of the way."

"What's happening?" My voice is shaking as I speak. I look up into the air, not sure what I'm hoping to find. "Are we under attack?"

My question is ignored.

"We're headed in there," Eckhart says as he points to a wide staircase leading down inside one of the buildings.

"You taking her underground?"

"You see a better option?"

"No, sir."

"Come with me," Eckhart orders as he turns me around and directs me to the long staircase heading down below the main floor of a shopping center. There are signs all around, but he whisks me away too fast to read them. The stairs lead down into darkness, and my chest tightens.

"Where are we going?"

He doesn't answer—just urges me forward. He stays behind me and to my right as we head down the stairs against a sea of people heading up. When we reach the bottom, the lights are flickering, and a train is stopped next to a concrete platform.

"I don't think the trains are running," I start to say, but my words are interrupted by the loudest explosion yet. I'm thrown forward, and I feel Eckhart's arm around my waist as he stops me from landing head first on the concrete.

"Move!" he orders as soon as I'm upright.

I have no idea where he's taking me, and I can't think straight. The explosion still rings in my ears, and my feet are cramping up in my heels. I can't make sense out of anything that is happening and can only follow unwittingly as Eckhart brings me to the edge of the platform in front of the train and jumps down to the tracks.

"Come on!" he orders as he reaches for my hands. "Don't think! Just do what I tell you!"

I glance over my shoulder once, hesitating.

"Move!" he screams.

My hands are shaking so badly, I can hardly hold on as I crouch down and sit on the edge of the platform. Eckhart takes my hands to help me down. His skin is warm and his grip is sure, but it doesn't comfort me. For a moment, I consider getting caught in the explosions behind me might be better than being touched by this man I don't know at all.

I tense, my muscles frozen. Suddenly, all I can see is the stained, metal ceiling of a van, and tears burn my eyes. I can hear Eckhart speaking softly to me, but it takes a minute to hear what he's saying.

"Come on, Hannah," Eckhart says quietly. "You can do it. I've got to get you somewhere safe."

"Safe?" I echo.

"Come on now."

I swallow once and push myself off the ledge with my heels against the concrete. I land steadily next to the track, and the ground crunches under my heels. Eckhart releases my hands immediately.

"There you go," Eckhart says. "Just head that way, and don't get close to the center rail."

I balance on the slender walkway that goes into the subway tunnel. Eckhart keeps close to me as we go deeper into the passage. I hear more explosions, but they're muted. Dust falls all around us as the ceiling shakes.

"It's going to collapse!"

"Not on us, it won't." Eckhart's voice is so calm and sure, I can't help but believe him. "Just keep moving."

Eckhart speaks into his radio, but there's no answer.

"Are we too far away to reach them?" I ask.

"There must be something in the tunnel that's blocking the signal."

"Maybe we should go back."

"Not until the explosions stop," he says. "You're safer here."

As soon as the words are out of his mouth, the tunnel starts to shake all around us. The lights flicker and then go out, but Eckhart

20

produces a flashlight from God-knows-where and shines it ahead of us.

"Run!" Eckhart grabs my hand and pulls me alongside him as he hastens farther down the tunnel. The ground is sloped, and I can barely walk in these shoes, let alone run. I stumble, and Eckhart holds tightly to my hand, but I still fall to my knees.

"Kick them off!" he orders. "Get rid of the fucking shoes!"

I look around at the ground where the light shines, trying to figure out how I'd be able to step anywhere without cutting my feet.

"There are rocks down here!"

Another loud crash from further up the tunnel is followed by a low, escalating hum. As we look in the direction of the train, part of the tunnel begins to collapse. Chunks of cement and metal begin to fall from the ceiling.

The hum increases, and I hunch my shoulders to block the sound as I try to keep up with the man in front of me. It doesn't help. The noise grows louder and louder until my head pounds, and I can't think. My skin vibrates. For a moment, it feels as if I'm being lifted off the ground by the sound itself.

The sound cuts off abruptly, and my knees suddenly buckle under me. As my hand slips from Eckhart's, I fall against the rocks near the track. He has to stop and come back for me.

"What was that?" I cry out.

He ignores my question as he yells, "Come on!" and pulls me back to my feet.

I hear a sharp pop from above my head. I start to glance upward, but Eckhart grabs me around the waist and hauls me off to the side. The movement isn't fast enough, and a large chunk of concrete hits my leg, tearing through the panty hose and the skin beneath.

I scream as searing pain runs up and down my leg. I can't see how bad it is in the dark, but I can feel blood running down my ankle. Eckhart grabs me by the waist and holds me sideways as he pulls off my shoes. He sets me back down again and yells.

"Run, dammit!"

"I can't! My leg!"

He flicks the light to my calf but moves the light away again before I can really see it.

"Shit!"

Chunks of concrete fall behind us as he suddenly grabs me around the waist and throws me over his shoulder. I can barely breathe with his shoulder pressed into my diaphragm. There's dust in my lungs, and the pain in my leg is nearly unbearable. Another piece from the ceiling plummets right behind us, shattering and sending shards into my arms as they dangle at Eckhart's back.

I jiggle and bounce as Eckhart runs, dodging falling chunks of the tunnel. He skips over the tracks to the other side, and my chin bangs painfully against his back. I try to grip the back of his jacket, but it doesn't help. All I can do is close my eyes and press my lips together to keep from screaming.

Thankfully, we only go a little farther before Eckhart slows and then stops. The tunnel behind us is silent now as he lowers me to the ground and shines the light from his flashlight back toward the way we came. There's dust obscuring the view, but I can't hear any additional sounds of collapse.

"Did it stop?" I ask.

"Shh." He cocks his head to one side and listens intently.

There's nothing to be heard but our own panting breaths. We stand there motionless, me on one leg, using him for support for what feels like forever before Eckhart silently takes my hand and helps me limp farther away from where we came. I follow, occasionally glancing back into the darkness, but I hear nothing. After several more minutes of walking, the tunnel begins to slope upward, and Eckhart stops.

"Sit," he says, using his flashlight to indicate the indentation in the concrete next to the track. "I need to look at your leg."

"We're not going to keep going?" My body wants to comply with his demand, but my mind is racing.

22

"This is the lowest point of the tunnel," he says. "It's the best place to be right now."

"How are we going to get out?"

"I'll worry about that after I check you out." He looks me over. "Are you hurt anywhere besides your leg?"

He shines the light at me, and I look over my arms. There are only a few scrapes there.

"I don't think so."

"Let me look." Eckhart crouches beside me and holds my ankle gently in his hand. I tense at the touch, and he looks into my eyes and speaks softly. "I'm not going to hurt you."

I swallow and nod, allowing him to examine my leg. There's a long, bloody gash over half of my calf. The skin is split wide open and dried blood surrounds the opening, but fresh blood seeps out of it slowly, too.

The sight nauseates me.

"I don't have anything with me to treat this," he says after a moment, "but it's not too deep. Your leg is going to tighten up on you, though."

He sits back on his heels and pulls the end of his shirt out of his suit pants. He undoes a couple of the buttons at the bottom and then pulls the shirt up to his mouth, tearing the fabric with his teeth. He rips off a strand of fabric and quickly wraps it around my leg.

"Just to keep it from bleeding more," he says. "We'll need to get it properly bandaged when we get back to the surface."

He releases me and stands as I rub the skin near the wound.

"How long will we stay here?" I ask.

"Until the explosions have definitely stopped," he says, "or until I hear from one of the other guys."

"The radio still isn't working?"

"No, but it really should be."

"Phone?"

"No signal down here even on a good day," he says. "We're going to have to wait it out."

23

"What if a train comes?"

He raises his eyebrows at me, and I realize how ridiculous my question is. Without bothering to answer, he sits beside me and leans against the cold wall. I glance over and see the light reflecting off the sweat on his temple.

"What do you think is happening up there?"

"I don't know," he says slowly. "I can only speculate."

"Guess, then."

"Invasion," he says. "I don't know who, but that was definitely an attack. A big one."

"But who?" I press. "Terrorists?"

"I don't know who has that kind of power. I never saw any planes, and I didn't hear any tanks. I don't know how anyone would get that far into the middle of the country without some kind of warning."

"What else could it be?"

He turns his head to look at me. His eyes are dark and solemn.

"I don't even want to guess."

Chapter 3

My throat is dry and scratchy, and my neck hurts. My ass hurts, too. Actually, most everything hurts. I open my eyes and try to get my bearings, but it's completely dark, and I gasp.

"I'm right here." The deep voice next to me is quickly followed by a click, and a small amount of light illuminates the area around me. "Just conserving the batteries."

A sharp pain in my leg brings everything back to me—Eckhart, the hotel, the explosions, and the people running in the street.

"How long was I out?"

"A little over an hour."

"Anything on your radio?"

"Nothing." Eckhart shifts beside me. "No more explosions either."

"Is it safe to go back?" I rub my hands over my dusty skirt and check my phone. There's no signal, and the battery is nearly dead.

"The only way to know is to try," he says. "It's been quiet for a while now."

"Should we go?" I know I'm peppering him with questions that he can't answer, but I don't know what else to say.

"I want you to stay right here," Eckhart tells me. "I'm going to head back the way we came to see if we can get out that way."

"Why can't I come with you?"

"Because I can move faster on my own. Your leg is going to feel pretty painful when you put weight on it, and I'm fairly certain you're safe here for now."

"What if someone comes?"

"Scream," he says. "The tunnel echoes and I'll hear you. I can be back here quickly."

"What if there are more explosions?"

"Then I'll come back."

He stands, and the light flickers around the tracks and the rocks. He dusts off his backside with one hand.

"I've got to take the light with me," he says. "I won't be gone long though. Just yell if you need me."

"What if...what if you don't come back?"

Eckhart looks down at me before crouching and looking me in the face.

"No matter what has happened up there," he says, "you are in my protection. I don't take my job lightly. I will not let anything happen to you. You, Hannah Savinski, are my one and only concern until I can get you to the Pentagon."

He keeps staring into my eyes until I nod at him, accepting his words.

"Now stay put," he orders. "I'll be back soon."

He jogs into the tunnel and around a corner, and I'm left in complete darkness with nothing but my thoughts.

Five months ago, I was just a grunt in the IT department of a company with a lot of government contracts. I worked nine-to-five, came home to a diabetic cat in a quiet apartment on the north side of Chicago, did my laundry, and watched Netflix. A single email regarding account data with some funky-looking numbers on it changed my life.

"Hannah, could you please check the discrepancy in this report? Jillian's out of town, and I know she usually does these things, but we've got people waiting on this. Mr. Hudson has already gone over everything, so it shouldn't be a big deal."

"Sure! No problem!"

"Maybe I should have just ignored it," I whisper to myself as memories return to me. If I had done just that, none of what followed would have happened.

And sixteen young girls would have been sold into sexual slavery.

I close my eyes tightly, tasting bile in my throat as other memories surface.

"You really think you can just turn us in, you stupid little girl? Don't you know who I am? Don't you know what kind of power I have? Well, I'm going to show you!"

I bite my lip to bring myself back to the present, but that doesn't set me at ease. Pulling my legs to my chest and wrapping my arms around them makes my leg throb, but it provides a little comfort anyway. I lean my chin on my knee and try to gather my thoughts.

What the hell happened? It wasn't an earthquake—I am sure of that. Every explanation that pops into my head sounds like the plot from a late-night movie on the sci-fi channel. I keep thinking about all the apocalypse-themed television shows that have been so popular over the last few years.

Maybe Doctor Who will show up and set it all right.

I tighten my grip around my knees as a light appears up the tunnel. True to his word, Eckhart returns, walking at a quick pace next to the track.

"What did you see?"

"The tunnel has completely collapsed. Whatever hit above it was big. We'll have to go the other way and hope the passage is clear. We'll take it slow so your leg doesn't get too sore. If it gets to be too much, I can carry you."

"What happened to my shoes?"

"They fell off when I was carrying you, and they're buried under a ton of rubble now. Luckily, you aren't."

A shiver runs down my spine at the thought.

Eckhart has me lead as we walk beside the tracks, and we take a slow pace as I limp along. He keeps the light ahead of us, aiming it downward occasionally as we dodge debris. The next station isn't far away, and Eckhart boosts me up onto the platform before hauling himself up. There is no one on the platform at all and no sounds to be heard from above.

"It looks like there's less damage here," he says as we start up the stairs.

I have to hold tightly to the handrail in order to raise my leg enough to navigate the stairs. It takes way too long, but eventually we emerge from the station onto the dusty sidewalk, and my breath catches in my throat.

Entire buildings are flattened to the ground. What used to be skyscraper office buildings and hotels are completely razed. Cars are crumpled together or just abandoned in the street, and they are covered in a thick layer of grey dust.

There are bodies everywhere: all over the street, in the crosswalks, and up against the buildings. Some of them are in piles, but most are just strewn about around stopped cars and delivery trucks. As I look around, I see no one else standing. Even when I look through a window into a nearby shop, all I see are more bodies.

For half a second, I stare at the corpses, reminded of every zombie movie I have ever seen. I wait for them to rise up and start coming after our brains, but none of them move. I shake my head, trying to clear the ridiculous thoughts from my head.

Are they ridiculous?

"What the hell happened?" My head is spinning. I can't think straight at all. I can't even make sense of what I'm seeing.

28

Eckhart doesn't answer. He pokes at his radio and phone but must not get any kind of response since he shoves them both back into his jacket pocket. I look at my phone as well, but there's no signal at all. Eckhart is still looking all around us, taking it all in. I try to do the same though I have no idea what might be going through his head. Then something strikes me.

"They're all men," I say.

"I noticed that."

"Where are the women?" I whisper.

Eckhart doesn't answer. He steps up and checks the body closest to us, turning it over. There's blood all over the man's face, and his eyes stare blankly into the sky as he's rolled over.

"There were children here before," I say softly. "I remember one boy with his mother back at the hotel. There had to have been children here, too."

"I know."

Everything hits me all at once.

All these men are dead.

The women and children who were here are gone.

I have no idea what's happened.

"Breathe." Eckhart is suddenly next to me, his hands on my upper arms.

"Don't touch me!" I scream and push him away, nearly falling over one of the bodies. I scramble away from it and press myself against the side of the nearest building, looking all around me but unable to comprehend what I'm seeing.

Where did they all go?

"Calm down, please." His eyes implore me along with his words. "I won't hurt you. I'm going to protect you, but I need you to stay with me here. Stay calm. I need to think."

"They're....they're...they're all dead!"

"I know. Don't look at them."

"They're everywhere!"

29

"Don't look!" He stands in front of me, blocking my view of the street. "Turn around, face the building, and get yourself together."

I shake my head but do as he says. I stare at the slight imperfections in the mortar and even trace them with my finger, trying to keep my thoughts away from the bodies all around me. My finger trembles as I slide it through the rectangular grooves. I continue the action until my heart slows, and I can breathe normally again.

"What happened to them all?" I whisper, but I don't get a response. I turn my head to find Eckhart and see him examining one of the bodies. He comes back to where I'm leaning against the wall and hands me a pair of sneakers.

"Where did you get these?"

"Don't ask," he says quietly. "Just put them on and don't think about it."

I take a deep breath and do as he says. My hands shake as I lace the shoes up, but I manage to keep my thoughts off of the previous owner. The shoes are a little big on me, but I can walk better now.

"We should keep moving," Eckhart says.

"Where do we go?" I watch him take a deep breath and figure all my questions are probably annoying him.

"I need more information," he says, "but we need supplies first. You need water, and you have to be hungry by now."

I haven't even thought about it.

"You okay to walk?" he asks as he looks down at my foot. "It's only a short way."

I nod. If I open my mouth, I don't know what's going to come out of it. Maybe it's best I haven't eaten.

"Come on, then." He waves his hand and directs me down the sidewalk. He takes his position behind me and to the right again.

"Shouldn't you be walking in front of me then, make sure the way is clear and all?"

"No, ma'am."

"Well, why not?"

"From here I can see what's in front of you," he says, "and I'm already in position if someone comes up from behind. With you on my left, I can also draw my gun faster without you being in the line of fire."

"Oh." It does make sense when he explains it like that, and I feel like an idiot for not thinking of it myself. The man obviously knows his job. "So, where are we going?"

"My place. It's not far from here, and I need to get a few things."

"You live here in Atlanta?"

"Yes, ma'am."

"I thought you were from Washington."

"I travel back and forth," Eckhart tells me. "I have an apartment here and another one in Virginia, just outside of D.C."

Eckhart's idea of not far is not the same as mine. We only stop once at a small convenience store where Eckhart ducks through the broken front door and grabs bottles of water for each of us.

We're looters.

Eckhart looks back and forth across the street as he takes a long drink from the bottle.

"What are you looking for?" I ask.

"There have to be other survivors," he mumbles. I don't really think he's responding to my question. "Where are they?"

It takes more than an hour to get to Eckhart's apartment at the edge of downtown. It's a simple, gated community, but we don't see anyone there, either—just more bodies in the parking lot. Unlike the downtown area, most of the buildings are still standing.

Eckhart waits for me to go first as we head up a flight of stairs. At the top, he unlocks the apartment door, and we go inside. It's a small, uncluttered space. There's a couch, a chair, and a large screen television in the main room, which connects to a small

31

kitchen. There are a couple of closed doors in the hallway beyond, and Eckhart heads for one of them.

On the other side of the door is a bedroom. The only furniture inside is a bed and a small nightstand, but the room is completely full of stacked, black crates.

He opens a closet door, and I glance inside and take in a sharp breath.

There's the expected rack of clothing, but that doesn't catch my attention. Each wall of the closet is lined with all kinds of guns. There are big guns, little guns, shotguns, guns with long scopes on them, and even a sword of some kind. On a shelf, there's a collection of knives as well.

Who is this guy?

"How many guns do you have?" I ask breathlessly.

"Enough," he replies.

"What's in the crates?"

"They're footlockers."

"What's in the footlockers, then?"

"Ammunition," he says. "Also enough food for about six months and a water purification system."

I stare at him open-mouthed.

"I've got some medical supplies, too." He pulls a roll of gauze and some other items out of one of the footlockers and then retrieves a washcloth from the bathroom. "Let's take care of your leg."

He sits me beside the bed and drops down next to me. I remove the shoe he commandeered and slip off the torn pantyhose. He takes my heel in his hand, placing my foot across his thigh. I tense a little. He's barely touched me the whole time, and this contact feels more intimate to me than any contact we've had since we met. He slowly unwraps the bit of shirt he wrapped around my leg and takes a good look at the wound.

"Not gonna lie," he says, "this is gonna hurt. You want a drink first?"

"Will I need one?"

"Yeah, maybe."

"Okay."

He gets back up, heads out to the kitchen, and returns with a bottle of whiskey.

"Take a good drink," he says, and I do so. The liquid burns my throat, but I don't make a face at it. He sits back down and grabs my foot again.

He runs the pad of his thumb next to the gash, examining it closely before carefully wiping it off with a cool, wet washcloth. It stings, but it's not so bad. The whiskey is warming my stomach, and I try to concentrate on that feeling.

"The skin has pulled apart," he says. His voice is still soft and calm. "You need stitches."

"Will we have to go to an emergency room?" I ask.

Falk looks up at me and raises his eyebrows.

"We passed what used to be the closest hospital," he says. "I've got what we need here, but I'm not about to claim I'm an expert. I can get the job done, though."

"You mean, *you* are going to stitch me up?"

"Yeah."

"Are you a doctor, too?"

"I'm not," he says, "but I've seen it done before."

"No!" I pull my leg away and push the heels of my hands against the floor to scoot away from him. "No fucking way! You aren't a doctor, and there's no way in hell you are operating on my leg!"

"It's not an *operation*."

I'm not listening. I pull my legs under me and try to stand, which was a stupid thing to do. As soon as I put weight on my leg, the pain shoots from my calf all the way to my hip, and I scream.

Eckhart is right beside me, keeping me from falling. He angles me back until I sit on the edge of the bed. He leans forward and looks me right in the eye.

33

"It has to be done, Hannah," he says. "If we don't, it's going to get infected. There is no hospital and no doctor to treat you. It's me or nothing, which means it's me."

I blink back tears. I don't want to cry, not in front of Eckhart or anyone else. My leg throbs horribly, and somewhere in the back of my mind, I know it needs to be treated, but I don't want it to be done here, like this.

"So, I'm *Hannah* now?" Snark beats fear every time. "Get one good look at my leg, and we're on a first name basis?"

He sighs and stands with his arms crossed over his chest, glaring down at me.

"Ms. Savinski, you need to let me do this. You don't have any other options."

"Fuck you," I growl at him, but he doesn't change his stance.

"You are under my protection." He separates the words, making each one count. "I will not let anything happen to you. Sometimes that means going against your wishes, but it's always in your best interest. Now, we can do this with your cooperation or without. Your choice."

"What are you going to do?" I ask, challenging him. "Tie me down so you can operate on me?"

"I don't want to have to do that."

"But you would?" My heart is pounding again, and there's pressure behind my eyes.

He closes his eyes and brings one hand up to rub at his forehead. I watch his chest rise and fall as he takes a deep breath before looking back down at me.

"Please, Hannah." He drops down to his knees in front of me. "I don't want you scared. I'm not going to hurt you. I won't touch you any more than I have to in order to get your leg fixed up. *Please* let me do my job. Let me help you."

I look down at him in front of me, and I can't doubt the sincerity in his eyes. My heart is still racing, and I can feel my pulse all through my leg. When I glance down, I see it's bleeding again.

"Are you sure you know what you're doing?"

"I'm sure what I can do will be better than nothing."

I close my eyes and bite down on my lip. It hurts, but my leg hurts more. I nod quickly before I can change my mind.

"Want more whiskey?" he asks.

"Yes."

He hands me the bottle, and I take a big swig.

"Take another," he suggests, and I do.

He goes back to one of the footlockers for more supplies. I don't look at what he's bringing over and stacking on the floor next to the bed. I don't think I want to know.

"Scoot back on the bed," he says softly. "Lay on your side with your left leg up."

I do as he says. My whole body is tense despite the whiskey running through my system.

"Try to relax," he says quietly.

"I'm trying."

"I'm going to clean it out first," he says. "I need to make sure there isn't anything still stuck inside that could cause problems later."

"Do I get a bullet to bite on?"

"I can get one if you like."

I glance down to see if he's serious, and I think he is. I shake my head, and he nods slightly before looking back to my leg. I look around the room, trying to find something I can focus on while he goes to work. I end up just looking at the latch on one of the footlockers, wondering what's inside of it.

I grit my teeth as Eckhart goes to work.

"There's a little piece of something inside," he says. "Hold on."

The sudden pain runs from my leg to my hip, then up my spine. The scream that comes from me is uncontrollable, but not as loud as the next one.

Eckhart's arm crosses my stomach, holding me in place. His fingers grip my wrist as he holds me to the bed.

"No! No! NO!" I scream and thrash as everything comes back to me. I pull my knee to my chest, wedge it between my body and Eckhart's chest, and kick at him with all my strength. "Get your fucking hands off of me!"

He almost falls from the bed but manages to catch himself right at the edge. I pull my legs up to my chest and push myself backward until I'm against the headboard. Eckhart looks at me with wide eyes as he presses his hand to his sternum.

"I'm not *them*," he says. His voice is calm and soft. "There's a piece of concrete in the wound. I have to get it out, or your leg is going to get infected. If it gets infected, you are going to be in a lot of trouble."

"Keep your hands off of me." I grit my teeth as I speak each word so there's no room for misunderstanding.

"I have to touch your leg to get it out," he says.

As the pain subsides, I start thinking a little more clearly. The wound in my leg keeps throbbing, and I can feel it bleeding again before I look at it.

"Let me get it out," Eckhart says again, his voice still soft. "I'll only touch you as much as I have to, I swear."

"Don't hold me down." I slowly stretch my leg out again, wincing as the skin tightens and moves around the cut.

"This is going to hurt," he says darkly. "It's going to hurt a lot. You have to stay still, or it will be worse."

"I'll be still."

"It's not going to be easy."

"Just don't…don't hold me down."

"I won't if you can stay still."

"I will."

He takes a deep breath before moving closer to me again. He keeps his eyes on me as he reaches out slowly and places his hand on my ankle, right below the gash. I see a flash of metal as he picks up a pair of tweezers.

"I don't suggest watching."

I look away, trying to find the latch on the footlocker again. It would probably be better if I could close my eyes, but I need to see that it's Eckhart—my bodyguard—not Hudson and his cronies.

"Fuck!" I can't help it. My whole body jumps as I feel a sharp jab deep inside the wound. Eckhart's hand stays firmly on my leg, but he doesn't grasp it tightly and doesn't push down. I try not to scream as he keeps going.

"I got it out."

"Is that all there is?" My voice cracks as I speak.

"I think so."

I grab the blanket on the bed as I feel his hand on my ankle again.

"I can still get you that bullet." His voice remains quiet and calm even though I know he's got a needle and thread poised over my flesh.

I shake my head quickly, not completely sure if he's trying to make a joke or not.

"This is going to sting."

I feel cold liquid running over my skin, and I hiss as the alcohol makes its way into the wound. The whiskey has dulled the sensation a little but not nearly enough.

"You got this," Eckhart says. "I've seen guys in combat freak out more than you have. You're doing great."

I know the exact moment the needle punctures my skin. I squeeze my eyes shut, forgetting all about the spot I was going to focus on. I try to find that happy meadow in my head, but all the dandelions are dead, their seeds cast to the wind, and the sky is dark and foreboding.

Instead, I focus on my breathing. In, out. In, out. Another stab. In through my nose, out through my mouth. Another. This one feels deeper, and I hold my breath as I tense.

"Relax." Eckhart's soft words flow into my ears. "Halfway there."

"Only...half?" I can barely get the words out.

I can feel my skin being pulled and tightened with each stitch. I can't look down to see what he's doing. If I do, I know I'll throw up or pass out or worse.

"Almost there."

I swallow hard, focus on my breathing, and try to keep the tears at bay.

"One more."

"Just get it done!" I hiss through my teeth as the final stab and pull makes my head swim.

"Got it!" Eckhart leans back a little. Out of the corner of my eye, I see him grab something on the bed beside me. "Just need to finish cleaning it up and getting it covered."

I stay motionless as he opens a tube of antibiotic cream and applies a generous amount to the wound. Finally, he covers it up with gauze and tapes the bandage around the rest of my leg.

I'm still dizzy when I sit up. The white gauze looks strange wrapped around my leg, but I'm glad I can't see the actual cut any longer.

"Can I walk on it?"

"Try not to do much," Eckhart says, "but you should be all right to move a bit."

It does feel better when I stand, and I can walk on it more easily even though I'm limping. He puts all the medical supplies back in the footlocker and shuts it. I follow him into the living room, my head full of questions.

"So, what—you've been...been planning for this?" I wave a hand back in the direction of his bedroom.

"It's always good to be prepared."

"And now what?"

"Survive."

Another simple little word, but his tone and the meaning behind it...it's too much. My head fills with visions of the man burning in the street, the sounds of buildings toppling to the ground, and the screams of people all around me, and it's all too much to take.

My knees give out, and I drop to the floor. I barely recognize the sounds coming from my throat as panic takes over.

"Shit," Eckhart mutters. He walks into my view and drops down beside me. Tentatively, he touches his hand to my shoulder, and I flinch. "You're okay. You're going to be okay. Just breathe."

I double over, my stomach cramping up on me. Wrapping my arms around myself, I lean over until my head is nearly touching the floor. Eckhart is beside me, and I know he's speaking to me, but his words have no meaning.

I've had attacks like this before, shortly after my personal nightmare unfolded. There are anti-anxiety drugs in my checked luggage for whatever good that does me now. I try to remember what the doctors told me about keeping my focus on one thing until my mind and body calm down, but I have nothing to focus on.

I'm in an unfamiliar place in a situation that is beyond bizarre. I have no method for coping with this. I feel a hand on my arm. The touch is slow and gentle, and I reach to grab hold.

Eckhart's fingers circle mine. He's the only thing even remotely familiar, so I set my mind to concentrate on the feeling of his flesh against my hand. He's still speaking in soft tones, and I can feel his thumb rubbing against my palm.

Abruptly, I turn to him and reach out to clasp my hands around his neck, nearly knocking him over. The sobs come loudly as I hang onto him and press my face against his broad chest. He slowly puts his arms around my waist and settles back, pulling me with him as he leans back against the couch.

"I've got you." His voice is soft and reassuring, but I can't stop crying. "Just like I said before—you are under my watch. I'm not going to let anything happen to you."

I'm shaking all over, and I feel like a fool, but I can't pull myself together. I keep seeing the bodies in the street and feeling the tremors beneath my feet as we were running through the tunnel. I feel like I'm in a tight, enclosed space. My thoughts flash back to being grabbed outside my apartment and shoved into the back of a van.

"You stuck your nose where it didn't belong, Ms. Savinski. You're going to pay for that."

The van keeps moving as I'm held against the rough floor in the back. Hands are holding my wrists above my head as someone rubs at my thighs.

"You got my girls taken away from me, you bitch. Now it's your turn."

"Please...please, no! Don't!"

"It's okay. It's just me. You're safe." Eckhart's hand rubs up and down my back. "They're gone. They can't touch you again. Ever."

I don't know how long I've been crying. The windows are dark now, and Eckhart has me wrapped up in his arms against the couch. My cheek is pressed against the wet spot made by my tears on his shirt.

"Shit...I'm sorry," I babble as I push away.

"It's okay," he replies. He tilts his head to the side and looks at me.

As we stare at each other, the meaning of his words resonates in my brain. I pull away, unlocking my hands from his neck and pushing myself along the floor until I'm a good foot away from him.

"How much do you know?" I ask quietly.

"Some of it," he replies. "I study up on anyone I'm protecting. I have copies of the police reports and everything else I could get. I don't have any details, but I know the gist of it. I also talked to Mark Harrison from the last team, and he told me about your having a bit of a meltdown when he touched you, and you weren't expecting it."

"So that's how you knew." It made sense. He'd been very careful about not touching me unless it was absolutely necessary. Even then, he'd kept it as brief as possible.

"I didn't want to make you uncomfortable," he says with a shrug. "I still don't want you to be uncomfortable, but this situation is different. I don't know much about what's happened here, but I do know this—something killed all those men, and something took the women and children."

"Do you think whoever it was is still around?"

"I'm not going to take a chance with your safety," he responds. "They might still be out there. If they are, I want you protected. Like I said—you are in my care until I get you where you are supposed to go. Until then, you're under my watch."

"All right." I take in a long breath and let it out slowly. "What do we do now?"

"You get that all out of your system?"

"I think so." I sniff and wipe my eyes with the back of my hand.

"Good." He turns toward me and places his hands on either side of my face. "That's the end of that now, you hear me? I need you to focus. I need you to think clearly. I need you to be strong and do what I tell you to do, or I'm not going to be able to keep you alive. Do you understand me?"

"I'll try," I say with another sniff.

"No, you fucking will not *try!*" He narrows his blazing eyes at me. "You are going to do everything I say. Got it?"

I stiffen, but it's not from his touch this time. He hasn't spoken like this before, and I don't know how to react. He huffs out his nose and tosses his arm over the couch cushion.

"I'm not trying to scare you, ma'am," Eckhart says. His voice is calmer now. "I don't know what's going on here either, but in order to figure it out, I have to be able to focus. I can't have you falling apart on me. If you do, you're going to be dead, and I told you I wasn't going to let that happen."

I take a deep breath. Everything he says makes sense, but there's a big difference between understanding the reason for doing something and actually being able to bring yourself to do it.

"All right," I say. "I'll stay calm."

"Thank you."

I look to his eyes for a moment.

"Will you at least call me Hannah now?"

"Yeah, I suppose I could do that." He cracks a half smile.

"And I can call you Falk?"

"That would make sense." He pushes himself off the floor and heads toward the kitchen. "Let's get something to eat and then sleep. We'll go out tomorrow and see if we can find any other survivors."

I stand up just long enough to sit on the couch. I feel like I should offer to help him, but he seems pretty confident as he starts taking things out of the refrigerator to determine if they are still all right since the electricity has been out.

"At least the gas works," he says, testing the stove. "I'm not much of a cook, but there's plenty to keep us going here for a while."

"Falk?"

"Yeah?"

"What do we do if we find someone?" I ask. "I mean, we can't exactly bring people back here, can we? You wouldn't have enough supplies for a lot of people."

Falk laughs.

"I have no fucking idea, Hannah."

Chapter 4

I wake disoriented.

It takes only a few moments of glancing around the sunlit bedroom to remember where I am—Falk Eckhart's apartment and doomsday preparation center. The brightness in the room tells me I've slept late into the morning. After a pretty decent meal, Falk had insisted I sleep in the bed, and he had stayed on the couch. I'd passed out almost immediately after crawling under the blankets.

I hear the water running in the bathroom and realize that Falk must be taking a shower. I remember how it felt to have him hold me, and I'm more than a little embarrassed by my reaction to the circumstances I have found myself in.

Then again, I don't suppose there is a handbook to follow when the city has been flattened and virtually everyone has been killed.

I shiver as I untangle myself from the blankets and drop my feet to the floor. I'm wearing the underwear Falk bought in the hotel shop along with the thin, white T-shirt supplied by the airline. I change into the Atlanta-themed sweatshirt and pull my skirt back on.

I'm going to need more clothes.

Staring out the window, I notice there are no bodies in the little green area behind Falk's apartment, and I wonder if we should go door-to-door to see if there is anyone around. The water shuts off in the bathroom, and I turn away from the view out the window.

I open the door from the bedroom into the living room just as Falk steps out of the bathroom, wrapped only in a towel.

My eyes probably bulge out of my head. I knew he didn't quite fit into that suit jacket, but seeing him like this—mostly naked with water still dripping from his hair, over his shoulders, and making a trail right past one of his nipples—I can see exactly why. The guy is built. Seriously, majorly built. Not in an over-the-top-I-never-leave-the-gym kind of way, but with a chiseled and sculpted sort of look.

He's absolute perfection from his surprised and intense eyes to the plain, white towel wrapped around his waist.

"Oh, shit!" Falk takes a step back, tightening his grip on the towel. "I thought you were still asleep."

"Sorry," I mumble, tearing my eyes away from his glistening chest and abs. "I didn't mean to…"

…to stare…to ogle…to practically drool on you.

"Sorry," I say again as I make my way over to the couch and sit down with my hands over my face. He ducks into the bedroom and closes the door quickly while I try to compose myself.

I can hear him rummaging around in the closet. I don't want to think about how he's probably standing there, sans towel, as he picks out something to wear for the day. I try not to wonder what the rest of him looks like as my heart beats quickly in my chest.

I must be losing my mind.

Since the day I was abducted, I haven't had a single sexual thought. I haven't fantasized about my favorite actors, watched a romantic comedy, or read an erotic book. I haven't even masturbated. Men have been the farthest thing from my mind.

It's just the situation.

Everything around me is in chaos, and he's here, trying to keep me calm and safe. He let me break down, but he's remained levelheaded. He's comforted me. It's natural to feel some kind of attraction. It doesn't mean anything.

Closing my eyes, I lean back on the couch and try to clear my mind. Right now, I should be in front of a slew of government officials, giving my testimony for the fifteenth time. I should be pointing to the documented data where I first found the discrepancies, how I traced those through the computer system and found a holding company with a name that wasn't on the books. I'd be explaining how I'd enlisted Daniel's help in researching the holding company and describing the websites he'd found with pictures and video of underage girls.

"How do you know that Mr. Hudson was involved?"

"He was one of the men who assaulted me."

"Are you sure?"

"I'm positive."

"You never saw him though?"

"I heard his voice."

"But you never actually saw *Mr. Hudson, did you, Ms. Savinski?"*

"No, sir, but it is his DNA they found on me."

"Hannah?"

I flinch and open my eyes. It takes me a moment to respond. "Yes?"

"I think I have some clothes that will fit you if you want them."

I head back into the bedroom slowly, limping. Falk is dressed in blue jeans and a dull green T-shirt. It's a stark contrast to the suit he's been wearing. There's one handgun in a holster at his hip and another in a holster around his shoulder.

"My sister left some of her laundry in my dryer the last time she visited," he says as he holds up a pair of sweatpants and a long-sleeved T-shirt. He points to a laundry bag on the bed. "There are

45

jeans and a couple other shirts in there as well. They might be a little big on you, but they're better than nothing."

"Definitely better than nothing," I say. "Thank you."

"I'm going to gather a few things up and load them into the car," Falk says. "I think the first thing we need to do is look for other survivors. There has to be someone else around. We can also go back to the airport to see if we can locate our luggage as well."

"What are you going to put in the car?"

"Food and water," he says. He takes a packet of what appears to be some kind of ready-to-eat meal and stacks it with a few others on the floor. "Also some ammo and a couple of the rifles."

My skin tingles.

"Is that going to be necessary?"

"I don't know," he admits, "but I'm going to have it with me in case it is."

"How did you know to do all this?" I wave my hand in the direction of the footlockers lining Falk's bedroom. "I mean, why did you collect all of this?"

"In case of a zombie apocalypse." Falk gives me a wry smile, and I just stare at him, trying to figure out if he's joking or not. He stops. "I just like to be prepared for anything. It could be a storm that takes out the electricity for days, the country getting attacked, or some natural disaster. It's good to have certain things on hand. Honestly, I never expected to need any of it."

"You have a big collection of guns."

"It's not a *collection*."

I look to the lineup of rifles on the closet wall and raise an eyebrow.

"Yeah, it is."

"It isn't. It's just enough."

"If I could get to the internet right now, I'd be looking up the definition of the word *collection* just to prove my point."

He eyes me for a minute.

"Do you know how to use one?" he asks.

"No." I shake my head. "I've never even held one."

"I can teach you."

I look at him sideways, trying to decide if he's being serious or not. There's nothing in his expression to indicate that he's joking.

"Do you think that's necessary?"

"Don't you?"

He is serious. I can't imagine myself holding a gun, let alone firing it. The idea of aiming at some living thing and firing a gun is completely incomprehensible.

"I really don't think I could do that."

Falk takes one of the handguns out of its holster, holds it pointed toward the ceiling, and pulls the clip out of the handle. He pulls back on the top of it, dropping a bullet into his palm, and then looks inside the chamber before holding the weapon out to me.

I take the heavy, metal object in my hand, holding it loosely.

"Don't put your finger on the trigger," Falk says.

"I thought you unloaded it."

"I did," he says, "but only put your finger on the trigger if you intend to fire it."

He shows me how to place my finger along the body of the gun, right above the trigger. I hold the weapon for a moment before handing it back.

"Not so bad, is it?" he says.

"It's heavy," I respond. "I still don't think I could use one."

"What if you had been armed when those men came for you?" Falk asks quietly. "What if you had been able to protect yourself?"

"I don't know…" My voice cracks. I can't think about this. I won't. I do anyway. "Maybe they would have killed me."

"They were going to kill you when they were done regardless. If you had been armed, maybe you would have gotten away sooner."

My throat is burning. I can barely get the words out. He's right about one thing—they were planning to kill me. I don't have any doubt about that. Maybe if I had a gun with me, things could have been different. Maybe if Daniel had one, he would still be alive.

"I don't want to talk about this." I turn away from him and stare at one of the footlockers, wondering if it's the one full of ammunition for all those guns.

"I'm going to teach you to use one."

"Fine." I can't argue with him about it. Arguing means thinking and remembering, and I don't want to think about it anymore. "Are we still going to go to Washington?"

"Once I get a better idea of what's happened around here, then yes. I think that's our best course of action. D.C. has a lot of shelters in place. There are bound to be more survivors there."

"How will we get there?"

"By car," he says simply. "We'll see what we can figure out locally, collect what we'll need for a few days, get in my car, and I'll drive you there."

"What about gas? The pumps aren't going to work without electricity."

"I can siphon gas from other cars," he says. "Newer models are a little tricky, but there are plenty of older ones around. Don't worry about things like that. I got it."

I nod, accepting what he says as truth.

"Shall I make breakfast?"

"Sure," Falk says. "The eggs in the fridge should be fine, and there's bacon in the freezer that needs to be cooked and eaten, too. Feel free to cook anything and everything that might go bad."

"I'll pack up some things for later, too."

"Perfect."

An hour later, I've cooked nearly everything from the refrigerator and half the things from the freezer and packed them into a cooler. Falk didn't have a lot of fresh food on hand, but it's enough for a couple of days, and the idea of his freeze-dried meals isn't all that appealing to me. I've also brewed some iced tea and poured it into thermoses.

As we make the final trip to the parking lot and Falk's Subaru Forrester, I wonder how long it will take to get to Washington. It would be a long drive under normal circumstances, but if we have to find cars to siphon gas, it's going to take a lot longer. What if we run out of gas altogether? Would we end up stuck somewhere? Or would Falk want to walk to Washington?

Falk climbs in and turns the key, but there is only a churning sound from the engine.

"What the fuck," he mutters as he tries again with the same result. He gets out of the car, pops the hood, and pokes around.

"Is it the battery?" I ask as I open the door and peer around the hood.

"It sounds like it." His eyes are narrowed as he looks around the parking lot. "I'll have to try one of the others."

Two hours later, I'm still sitting in the passenger seat while Falk tries to get yet another car started. He'd already tried hotwiring a couple of them without success, and then he'd broken into his neighbor's apartments looking for keys. None of the cars had worked.

Falk climbs out of a Honda, slams his fist on the top of it, and then stalks back over to me.

"What do we do now?" I ask.

"No fucking idea." Falk takes a deep breath and stares off toward the road. "Give me some time to think."

He leans against the car and rubs his fingers into his eyes. After a minute, he ducks into the car, reaches around me to the glove compartment, and pulls out a pack of cigarettes. He goes back to leaning on the car as he lights up and takes a long drag.

He's silent, and I don't want to interrupt his thinking as he smokes. I try to come up with ideas of my own, but the throbbing in my leg is distracting, and I really don't have a clue what we should do. The silence in the parking lot is unnerving. There should be people walking around, kids playing at the pool, dogs barking.

"Falk?"

"Yeah?"

"Does your apartment complex allow pets?"

"Yeah."

"Well, where are they?"

He glances around the area, cocks his head for a moment, and then looks back at me.

"I have no idea."

I rub my hands up and down my arms as a chill runs through me. No women, children, or dogs. What about cats or other pets? I could hear the faint chirping of birds in the trees and the constant buzzing of insects, so there were some animals around. Why not dogs?

"There's a shopping center less than a mile from here," Falk says as he tosses the cigarette butt away. "Let me check on your leg—do you think you can walk that far? Then we can go stock up and see if we can find anyone."

"I think I can," I say. "How will we bring stuff back?"

"We'll have to just bring what we can carry for now," he says. "There are bound to be shopping carts or something we can use. I'll figure out a better way later."

Falk and I go back inside where he unwraps the bandage from my leg, cleans the wound again, and bandages it back up. It's painful but not unbearable, so I decide I can make the trip. Despite Falk's rather foul mood, I don't like the idea of being left alone in his apartment.

We head off down the street with one of Falk's rifles strapped over his shoulder. He keeps a slow pace so I can keep up as we make our way to the shopping center.

There is no sign of another living being, not even when we get to the main road. It's slow going with my limping, and we have to dodge a lot of cars that have smashed into utility poles or are just

50

parked up on the sidewalk, and there are bodies of men everywhere. I keep my eyes on the ground as we pass the cars. I don't want to see the passengers inside—or worse yet—no one inside.

Falk takes the side streets, looking for signs of life. There are none. Every time we pass another neighborhood, I keep thinking we'll see someone this time, but we don't. We only see more bodies—all men.

The empty cars in the street bother me the most. I can't help but wonder who was in them. I also can't stop myself from checking the back seats for child restraints. Every time I see one, I shudder.

Still no signs of women or children.

Falk leads me to a strip mall parking lot. One half of the mall is completely destroyed, right down to the ground. The only stores standing are a nail salon and a sandwich shop, and the windows are broken out of both of them. The bodies of two men hang out of the smashed building, their blank eyes staring at the sky.

"What's going to happen to them all?" I ask.

"Cleaning up would be a big job," Falk says. "In a couple of days, it's going to be a lot worse."

"Did you have to go there?"

"It's true." He shrugs as he climbs through the broken window of the sandwich shop, carefully avoiding the bodies. "Hopefully, someone will start organizing—putting things back together."

"We haven't seen anyone at all." I follow him inside but don't get past the entrance. There's nothing but rubble inside.

"Maybe they're in hiding." He doesn't sound convinced or convincing as he maneuvers around debris trying to get back behind the counter. Everything inside is smashed and useless, so we go back outside.

"Maybe we're the only survivors." I can only whisper the words, barely able to comprehend the thought.

I look up at Falk as his face tightens and his lips smash together. He looks like he's about so say something right before he focuses in the distance.

"We're not," Falk says. "Look."

I follow his nod with my gaze and see three men in dirty jeans and flannel shirts appear from around the corner of the strip mall. One of them points to us, and they all start heading in our direction, waving. As they approach, I can see they're all in their early thirties, and their clothing is filthy.

Falk stands up straight and touches the gun at his hip briefly before letting his hand fall back to his side. He's tense and alert, like he was when we first stepped out of the hotel.

"Don't say anything." Falk looks at me with those intense eyes as he speaks.

"Why not?"

"I'll explain later."

The three men stop as they get close to us, and Falk takes a step in front of me. I watch him closely as they interact.

"Hey there!" One of the men in the group moves ahead and addresses Falk. "What the fuck happened around here?"

"I was hoping you would know." Falk takes a step forward and offers his hand. "Falk Eckhart. We haven't seen anyone since it happened."

"Beck," the dark-haired man says. "Beck Majors."

Beck is slightly taller than Falk with a more slender build. He's got that rough-and-ready look I associate with old cigarette or whiskey commercials. He would have looked completely in place if he had ridden up on horseback. He points to the other two men as he introduces them.

"This is Caesar and Ryan Tucker."

"My brother and I just came here for the weekend," Caesar says. He's a medium-sized, broad shouldered guy with a shaved head. "Beck had gone on about how we needed to visit, but I think we picked the wrong time."

"Phones aren't working at all," Ryan says. He's much smaller than his brother and obviously younger by several years, and they look nothing alike. He's got a scruffy beard, round eyeglasses, and a beret on his head, giving him a hipster vibe. "I've got a short wave radio that isn't picking up anything, either. I'm not so sure this is isolated to Atlanta."

"Where were you when it happened?" Falk asks. "How did you keep from getting caught up in it?"

"We were exploring the storm drains near Decatur," Beck says. He rubs at a smudge on his jeans, and I wonder just what they've been walking through. A distinctly unpleasant smell comes from the group. "Caesar and Ryan are big into spelunking, so I said they ought to see what the city has to offer. Felt the ground shaking, but we were pretty deep in, and it took a while to get out. Some of the exits were blocked by rubble from the street. When we got back to the surface...well, we saw all this."

Beck waves his arm in the direction of the street.

"Where were you?" Caesar asks. "Any idea what happened?"

"None," Falk admits with a shake of his head. "We were downtown at the time. Took shelter in a MARTA tunnel. When we came back out, everyone was dead."

"How did you end up out here?" Beck asks.

"I live near here," Falk replies.

"Who's this?" Beck asks, indicating me. He runs his tongue over his lips and gives me a smile. "I feel like I know you from somewhere."

I swallow and start to respond, but Falk beats me to the punch.

"Hannah," Falk says tersely. "Where are you headed now?"

Beck glances back and forth between me and Falk and raises his eyebrows. Ryan shuffles his feet, and Caesar stares at me closely. He widens his eyes, and I know he's recognized me, but he doesn't say anything.

"I was going to head home," Beck says. "Try the landline."

"Mine was dead," Falk says. "What area are you in?"

"Near Emory."

"You a student?"

"Faculty," Beck says. "I teach anthropology. Caesar and Ryan live in Valdosta, right by the Florida border."

"What do you do there?" Falk asks as he turns to the other two men. His questions are starting to sound like an interrogation, and Beck's eyes narrow as his friends respond.

"I'm a state trooper," Caesar says. "Ryan's been working at the local airport, saving money for school."

"I'm going for a law degree," Ryan says, but Falk doesn't look at him. His eyes are on Beck, and the two men are staring each other down. The silent interaction is unnerving.

"You were military," Falk says with a very matter-of-fact tone.

"Yeah, briefly." Beck's throat bobs as he swallows.

"What branch?"

"Air Force. I was in communications."

"Deployed?"

"No. Never called up."

Falk nods slowly.

"What about you?" Beck asks.

"Army. Infantry." Falk doesn't offer any additional details. They continue to stare at each other until Caesar speaks up again.

"If the landlines are dead, we'll have to gather more information another way," he says. "We've got a car nearby."

"I've tried several," Falk replies. "All of the batteries are dead."

"We're parked just a couple of blocks from here," Beck says. "Let's at least give it a try."

After listening to Beck's car try to turn over for a couple of minutes without starting, everyone gathers in the street to discuss our next move.

54

"We should stick together," Beck says, "at least until we figure out what's going on."

Falk glances at me, but I'm not sure if he's looking for my opinion or not.

"We did come out looking for people," I say quietly.

"Yeah, it makes sense," he says after a moment of silence. He looks back to Beck. "Do you have any supplies?"

"Just what's in the car," Beck says. "Back at the house I have more."

"Weapons?" Falk isn't messing around.

"Just a couple," Beck says.

"My Glock is back there, too," Caesar offers. "I didn't bring extra ammo, though."

"Should we go get them?" Ryan asks.

"Yes," Beck says. "Let's collect what we can and search for more people. Emory's campus might be a good place to look."

"We'll follow you," Falk says with a nod.

The three men walk off down the street, and Falk and I trail behind. My leg is cramping up a bit, but I try not to let it slow me down.

"How did you know that guy was in the military?" I ask.

"The smell." Falk glances at me out of the corner of his eye and his mouth twitches into a slight smile. "Knew he wasn't army."

"But you were?"

"Yes. Did four tours overseas."

He doesn't seem interested in offering more information, and I don't ask. Maybe he'll tell me more about it later. The rest of the trip is silent as we walk to Beck's house, just south of the Emory campus. It looks like it was a nice, suburban community with a Panera and a Chipotle, but the entire area has been leveled.

Beck stands in front of what I assume used to be his house, staring toward the university. I can only determine what used to be there by the piles of red brick. Otherwise, it's flattened.

"Holy shit," Beck mumbles.

Caesar is poking around inside a black Toyota pickup parked at the curb. The back end has been smashed by a blue compact car, but the front seems to be intact. He ducks out of the vehicle with his hands full.

"I don't think my truck is going anywhere, battery or not," he says, "but the important stuff survived."

He holds up a gun in a holster and a bottle of amber liquid.

"Is that the Glenlivet?" Ryan asks.

"Fifteen years."

"First positive thing I've heard all day!"

All three of them laugh, and I find myself cracking a smile as well. I guess it really is the simple things when it comes right down to it. Falk doesn't seem entertained by the idea, and he gestures to me to join him.

Caesar hands the bottle to Beck and follows.

"Are you still planning on heading to Washington?" Caesar asks. His voice is low, and I'm fairly sure Beck and Ryan don't hear his question. Falk stares at Caesar for a moment without a response. "I've read the reports. I know who she is. I assume you are part of her security detail."

I bite down on my lip, remembering that Falk didn't want me talking to these guys too much. I should have asked him why when we were walking, but I didn't. I look over to him for direction and see him nod at Caesar once.

"It makes sense to head that way," Falk says. "It's the most protected place in the country, and they're bound to have more information than anyone we find here. Getting there is obviously an issue now. Whatever took out the electricity and everything else must have impacted lead-acid batteries. If I can find a vehicle that uses lithium-ion batteries, it might work."

"What do you think happened?"

Falk glances at the sky but doesn't offer a verbal opinion.

Caesar looks over to me.

"I assume you'd like to keep your identity under wraps."

56

"I'd prefer it, yes," I respond. "It's just easier that way."

"I'm not going to say anything," he says, trying to reassure me. "I don't think either of those guys would care, but there's no telling who else we might run into."

"I would appreciate it if you don't say anything." Falk's voice is steady and stern. "She's still under my protection until I can get her to the right people in Washington."

"You've got more faith than I do," Caesar mumbles.

"It's good to have a direction," Falk responds coldly, "with or without faith."

I look back and forth between the two of them, trying to make sense of their conversation. Falk doesn't seem interested in explaining, and I figure I'm going to have a lot of questions for him when we're alone again.

Beck approaches, abruptly ending the discussion.

"There isn't a whole lot inside the house that's salvageable," he says. "I did pull out my Berretta and my AR plus two boxes of ammo. I can't get to the kitchen safely, but there is a Publix nearby. We'd have better luck finding food there anyway."

"Why don't you go check it out," Falk says, "and bring back whatever you can carry."

"Are you giving me orders already?" Beck's got a half grin on his face as he looks at Falk, his head tilted to one side.

Falk doesn't move or respond, and the air around us suddenly seems electrified.

"I could go," I say quietly. It's the first thought that comes to my mind to try to diminish the tension between the two. The look on Falk's face is making me nervous, and Beck seems happy to keep poking the bear.

"You're staying here," Falk says definitively.

"Well, that was certainly an order!" Beck says with a laugh. "Why don't you let the lady make her own choices?"

"It's fine, really," I say quickly. "I don't care one way or the other. I was just saying I could—"

57

"You're staying here," Falk says again. He looks over to me and gives me a stern look. "You need to rest your leg, and we're going to find decent shelter for the night. I don't want to waste the time getting back to my place until I know for sure what else I need."

"Seems like that's something you could do on your own," Beck says.

"I'll go," Caesar pipes up. "God knows what you'd consider nutrition anyway. Ryan and I can check it out and bring back what we need for a couple of days. Maybe we'll find more survivors as well."

"Better ask him if that's okay," Beck says with a snort. "Maybe he's already got you pegged for wood gathering."

Beck stomps back off toward his house, and Caesar sighs.

"Don't mind him," he says quietly. "Everything he's ever owned was in that place. He's just in shock."

I look down at the ground, unsure what to do or say next. Conflict has always made me uncomfortable, but recently my life has revolved around it, and I don't like it. Whenever I witness people arguing, it reminds me of how my parents would fight when I was young.

"I'll get him to go with me," Caesar says. "Is there anything you need?"

"See if there are any camping supplies," Falk says, "especially lanterns and batteries. Flashlights, too."

"Will those batteries work?" Caesar asks.

"They worked in my flashlight. Maybe the alkaline ones are fine. We'll just have to figure it out as we go."

"Will do." Caesar heads off.

A crash from near Beck's house catches our attention. Beck is kicking at the rubble and screaming obscenities while Caesar tries to calm him down.

"Asshole," Falk mutters under his breath.

"Beck?"

He glances over at me, his eyes dark, but doesn't speak.

"You don't like him."

"No, I don't."

"Why not?"

"Because in the infantry, we hate everyone else." Falk hefts the rifle over his shoulder. "Also, because he's a liar."

"How do you know that?"

"He's an anthropology professor with an assault rifle. You don't find that odd?"

"I didn't really think about it. You have a lot more guns than he does."

"I have a reason for it."

"Maybe he's been waiting for the zombies, too." I smile, trying to make light of the antagonism, but Falk isn't amused.

"Stay clear of him," Falk says with a growl.

"How am I going to do that?"

"Just stick by me."

"Fine." I'm frustrated by the nature of Falk's answers.

Falk doesn't get a chance to respond. Beck and Caesar walk back to us.

"We're heading to the store," Caesar says. "Ryan's going to stick around and help find a good place to set up camp for the night. We can talk about what to do tomorrow when we get back."

"All right," Falk says without looking up. "Check the cars in the area. Look for something new enough and sporty enough to have a lithium battery. We're going to need transportation options."

Beck's jaw tenses and he glares at Falk. Caesar reaches out and pushes against Beck's arm before he says anything.

"I can do that," he says as he pulls Beck away.

Falk watches them walk off. Caesar puts his arm around Beck's shoulders, and I think he's speaking into his ear. Beck glances over his shoulder a couple of times before they move around a corner and out of sight.

"What is it?" I ask quietly.

59

Falk's eyes stay on the men as they walk off. His expression is still dark and tense.

"Just a feeling," he finally says.

"Do you trust them?" I look to Ryan, but he's sifting through rubble near Beck's house and not paying attention to us.

"No, Hannah. I don't."

Chapter 5

"Should have just taken you back to my place," Falk mumbles.

He has set up a campsite away from the buildings, saying it's safer in case there is more collapse, but he doesn't seem to like the location. I can't tell if I'm supposed to respond to his mutterings or not, so I say nothing.

I think I'm still in shock.

Caesar and Beck return with a load of supplies pilfered from the local supermarket, loaded into a large garden cart. They've got sleeping bags and tents, food, and a couple of camp stoves. Falk sets up one of the tents before coming over to me.

"This is awkward, so I'm just going to come out with it," he says. "I want you in the same tent with me. I don't trust these guys, and I don't want you alone. I hope that's all right with you."

"It's all right," I say. If I am being honest with myself, I don't want to be alone, and I know Falk better than anyone else here. "But you have to explain to me why you don't trust them."

He looks into my eyes for a long moment, and his face finally relaxes a little.

"I will," he says, "after they go to sleep."

"Deal." I smile at him, but it's not returned.

Falk goes to the cart to get some of the supplies for the tent, refusing my offers to help him, so I go and sit down near a small fire Ryan has going. I'm not cold at all—the sweatshirt Falk found for me is quite warm—but the fire is still nice.

"So, how long you two been together?" Ryan asks.

"What?" It takes me a moment to realize what he's assumed, and I quickly shake my head. "We're not together like that. We were just...traveling together. Our flight was cancelled, and we ended up in the city an extra night."

I glance in Falk's direction, but the sun has set, and all I can see is the flicker of his flashlight. He never did explain why he didn't want me talking to anyone, but I can hardly avoid it now. Besides, Ryan seems harmless enough.

"Damn." Ryan whistles. He shuffles a couple of rocks around the edge of the fire to keep it enclosed. "Maybe you could have avoided all this if you had gotten out in time."

"It's not just here." Caesar joins us and tosses more wood on the fire, sending sparks flying.

"How do you know that?" Ryan asks.

"If it was limited to the Atlanta area, someone would have come by now," he explains. "State authorities, the National Guard—someone. We'd see planes overhead, but there haven't been any. Not a single jet trail."

I look up at the sky, and there isn't a single blinking light up there. No signs of life at all. I curl my legs underneath me and bite at the edge of my thumb.

"That makes sense," Ryan says with a nod. "So how widespread do you think it is?"

"There's no real way to tell." Caesar picks up a stick and pokes at the embers. "I don't think you'd like my opinion."

"What is it?" I ask.

The beam from Falk's flashlight crosses in front of me, and I turn my head as he sits on the ground next to me. He looks over at Caesar and gives him a little nod.

"Go on," Falk says. "Let's hear it."

"Same thing you're thinking," Caesar says. "This hasn't been an invasion by anyone close by."

"What do you mean 'close by'?" Ryan grabs the bottle of scotch and opens it as Caesar hands him a couple of red plastic cups.

"This wasn't some terrorist group. They don't have that kind of firepower. They couldn't have taken out one city like that, and this goes way beyond Atlanta."

"What was it then?" I ask.

"There's really only one plausible answer," Falk says slowly.

I look back and forth between him and Caesar, but neither offers any further explanation. They're being obtuse, and it's pissing me off, and I finally snap at them both.

"Whatever the hell you two are thinking, spit it out!" I address them both, but my eyes are on Falk.

"Alien invasion," he says.

"Alien?" I repeat. "You mean, like aliens from outer space?"

He nods, and I laugh out loud, but everyone just looks at me until I stop.

"Are you serious?" He can't be. The whole idea is ludicrous.

"You have a better idea?"

"Anything but that!"

"It's the only thing that fits what we know," Caesar says. "The most destructive force we have is nukes. If Atlanta had been nuked, it would have taken everyone with it, not just men. There's no explanation for the women and children disappearing."

"Dogs, too," I add. "Maybe cats."

"I hadn't thought about it," Caesar says, "but you're right. I haven't seen a single dog or cat."

63

"Humans don't have the kind of technology to do something like this," Falk says as he scratches the back of his head. "There's nothing that kills exposed men and evaporates women, children, and domestic animals."

"So your first thought is little green men?" Ryan questions. "Isn't there some other possibility?"

"You think the plants have risen up, pissed about the ozone layer?" Beck joins the circle between Caesar and Ryan.

"There weren't any spaceships." I point this out in hopes of another idea coming into someone's head.

"If they were up far enough, we wouldn't have seen them," Caesar says. "Whatever happened wasn't the result of technology that comes from here. If it's not from here, that makes it extraterrestrial."

"There could be something we don't know about," I say. "A secret weapon."

"A weapon that makes women and children disappear? What year do you think you live in?" Beck snickers.

Everyone is silent for a few minutes, sipping their scotch and staring at the fire.

"What do they want?" I ask.

"My best guess," Caesar says, "it that they're here for you."

I grasp my biceps with my hands and suck in a breath.

"Let go of me! What do you want?"

"We want you, baby. We're here for you!"

"Hannah." Falk's voice is in my ear and his hand is on my leg. "Caesar's speaking figuratively."

"Wha-what?"

"I meant for women in general," Caesar says. "And children, apparently. That's what they took, so I assume that's what they're here for."

"Not you specifically," Falk says, clarifying.

"So, you both think that some green, bug-eyed monsters came down and took all the women? Am I supposed to believe that?" Ryan huffs a laugh out his nose and leans back to finish his drink.

"It makes sense." Beck grabs the bottle of scotch. He fills one of the plastic cups and takes a big gulp. "But how come she's still here, and are there any other women left?"

"It took a day just to find you three," Falk says. "There are others out there, and some of them are bound to be women or children. Seems like being underground kept all of us safe. There have to have been others in similar shelters."

"This is ridiculous," I say softly.

"Which part of it?" Falk asks.

"All of it."

"I'm still waiting for your better explanation." He raises his eyebrows at me.

"I can't talk about this." I stand up and hold my hand out for Falk's flashlight. "I'm going to sleep. You all can continue to talk nonsense if you want. Maybe we'll find someone tomorrow— maybe a whole National Guard unit is right around the corner."

Falk hands me the flashlight without another word, and I stomp to the tent.

Aliens. How fucking insane is that?

I kick my shoes off outside the tent and pull back the flap to duck inside. I use the flashlight to look around, seeing the two sleeping bags laid out side-by-side, a small cooler in the corner, and a battery powered lantern nearby. I turn the lantern on and switch off the flashlight.

I can still hear mumbled talking outside but try to ignore it as best I can. I pull off my sweats and socks and shove my legs into the sleeping bag. The sleeping bag feels cold against my bare skin, but the material is that funky fabric that's supposed to hold your body heat, so I'm sure it will warm up soon.

I sit with my head in my hands, rubbing at my eyes. I know I told Falk I was going to keep it together, but I think I'm allowed a little bit of a private breakdown.

What if he's right?

If it is an alien invasion, Washington, D.C. would certainly have been hit. Is there any point in going there now?

There's a rustle near the door of the tent, and I almost expect to see a grey-green creature with big eyes and an egg-shaped head come through the flap, but it's only Falk.

"Didn't mean to startle you," he says.

"You didn't," I lie. I pull the sleeping bag up a little farther.

Falk steps over me to sit on the sleeping bag at the back of the tent. He pulls off his socks and shirt before crawling inside, and I stare at the tent door to avoid looking at his chest. I'm very aware of how small the tent is and how close Falk's body is to mine as he lies down beside me.

"Should I turn off the light?" I ask quietly.

"Yes. Don't want to waste batteries."

I nod and push the button that shuts off the lantern. I scoot farther into the sleeping bag and pull it up to my chin as I lie down. I can hear the fire crackling outside and my own breathing, but that's it.

"Do you really believe all that?" I ask into the darkness. "All that shit about aliens?"

"I don't have a better theory."

"Do you think they're going to come back?"

"Hard to speculate," he says. "If they came here for women and children…well, they got those. If that's all they wanted, they don't have a reason to come back. If that was just the first wave of an attack…"

His voice trails off, and I think about what he's saying. Is it possible? If not aliens, then what? Caesar was right—we don't have the kind of technology that explains what happened.

"I felt something," I say quietly. "I felt something when we were in the tunnel by the train—right before things started collapsing."

"What do you mean?"

66

"There was a...a sound. Did you hear it? It was really low pitched. It hurt my ears."

"Yeah, I heard it."

"When I heard that sound, it felt like...like I was being lifted off the ground. When the sound stopped, that's when I fell."

Falk is quiet for a minute.

"That's when they took the others," he says finally. "You were too far underground for them to get to you, but you could still feel it."

"I don't know...maybe. I can't wrap my head around all of this, Falk. I was prepared to talk to the government about what Hudson was doing. I wasn't prepared for...for whatever the hell is going on here."

"I thought you might be relieved you don't have to testify," Falk says.

"Yeah, well..." I let out a long breath and chuckle to myself. "I have to admit, I wasn't looking forward to it. With all the threats, I really didn't think I would make it all the way to the Pentagon to even give my statement."

"I wasn't going to let them get to you."

"I know you were going to try, but..." A shiver runs through me. "Did you hear what he said? What Hudson said when they took him away? It was in the transcripts."

"Only that he threatened you."

"He said I was as good as dead. It didn't matter where I went or who I had around me. They were going to find me, and when they did, I was going to die. He didn't even stop yelling when they dragged him off. He was completely serious, and I believed him."

"He's probably dead now," Falk says. "You don't have to think about him anymore."

"It's not that easy."

In the dark silence, I can hear Falk's steady breathing along with my own. There's a crackle from the fire outside, and I imagine someone has added more wood to it though the voices have stopped.

"Do you want to tell me about what happened?" Falk asks.

I tense as memories begin to flash through my mind. I shake my head sharply.

"No," I tell him. "Not now. Maybe someday."

"All right." He shifts, and I think he's rolled from his back to his side. "If you ever decide you want to, I'm here."

"Thanks." I'm not sure the time will ever come even though I've told the story a dozen times. Falk said he had read up on me, so he probably knows most of it anyway. I don't know why he would want to hear more of it.

"I asked for this assignment," Falk suddenly admits.

"You did? Why?"

"You impressed me."

"How so?"

"Tyler Hudson is one of the most influential people in the country," Falk says. "I met him years ago when he first started working with government contracts. I didn't like him from the moment I saw him. Everyone knew he was shifty, but no one ever stood up to him. His money always talked louder than anything anyone ever said about him. Then I heard about this young woman who found something, dug in, and reported it. Then she didn't just report it, but when he tried to take her out, she escaped and reported him again. She had enough sense to go straight to the hospital and get his DNA collected. She never backed down even though she knew her life was in danger. That's impressive, Hannah."

"It feels more stupid to me now."

"It wasn't. It was brave. Incredibly fucking brave. I haven't heard of courage like that outside of combat."

"What else was I supposed to do?" I ask. "Just let him get away with it? I didn't really think about who he was. When I found the pictures...I couldn't just let that happen, could I?"

"A lot of people would. In fact, a lot of people did."

"I saw their faces," I say. "I saw how scared they were in the pictures. I knew what he planned to do to them."

"So did others. He didn't act alone."

"They all planned to profit from it."

"Do you really think they were the only ones who knew what was going on?"

"No." I take a deep breath. "I think there were others. Jillian in accounting—she must have seen the discrepancies before I did."

"But you did something about it."

"When I was in college, I took a class in modern crisis." I stop for a moment and twist my fingers together underneath the edge of the sleeping bag, remembering. "It was offered by the philosophy department. I did a paper on human trafficking. I talked to a family whose daughter had disappeared when they were traveling. They never heard from her again, and it tore the family apart. The couple got divorced, and their younger daughter ended up on drugs. She even tried to kill herself. That was all I could think about. What if one of those girls had been her? Not exactly her, but someone just like her. All those girls got back to their families."

My body shudders, and I close my eyes. The memories of the family—*my* family—flood back into my head.

"And you were abducted later and nearly met the same fate in store for those girls."

"It didn't happen, though. I got away from them."

"That's how I know you are strong enough to deal with all of this. You're going to have to be. It's going to get worse."

I roll to my back to try to see his expression, but in the dark, I can only see the outline of his face.

"What do you mean?"

"Think about it, Hannah." Falk props himself up on his elbow, and some of the light from the fire filters through the tent and creates eerie shadows on his face. "The women and children are gone. We know the men on the surface are all dead. We know those people who were underground survived. Who do you think is more likely to have been underground, men or women?"

"Men, I suppose."

"You've become a very rare asset, Ms. Savinski. If I'm right, and I think I am, that makes you valuable. People act very differently when they think there is something valuable around them."

"What are you saying?"

"I'm saying that we're in a unique situation and that people do things you don't expect them to do when they feel their survival is at stake. Those guys out there may seem like they're friendly, but that can change in a heartbeat."

"Is that why you didn't want me to talk to them?"

"In a sense, yes." Falk clears his throat. "I don't want you to get too friendly with them. I don't want you to give the impression that you are available. At some point, someone's going to take advantage of that."

I narrow my eyes as I take in what he's saying. I am the only woman in this group. Chances are, we'll find other survivors, and chances are those survivors are going to be additional men. At some point, mob mentality takes over.

"Like what Hudson was going to do with those girls."

"A lot like that, yes."

What exactly does that mean for me?

I haven't thought about the future since the day I took the information I had and sent it to the authorities. Everything has been very moment-to-moment as I was dragged from the local police department to the prosecutor in the county courthouse to the governor's office. Then those people from Washington showed up, and I was further tossed back and forth as they gathered more information.

Then the assault.

More police. More government officials. I didn't have time to think about the future or what it held for me. After the arraignment and Hudson's threats, I'd taken him at his word. I didn't expect to have a future.

Now no one knows what the future holds, but I know one thing—I'm not going to be doing any computer work any time soon. I also know my survival skills aren't exactly at the same level as Falk's. Eventually, I'm either going to have to prove my worth in other ways, or I am going to be seen as good for only one thing.

"I'm scared."

I hear Falk roll over and feel his body heat closer to my back. A moment later, he snakes his arm around my waist. I tense at first, but when he doesn't move any closer—just leaves his arm there around me—I relax against the ground. I can feel the exhaustion in my limbs creep up into my head, and I yawn.

"Is this okay?" Falk asks quietly. He tightens his arm around my middle.

"Yeah, it's okay."

"I know you're scared," he says. "That's one of the reasons I'm keeping you close."

"What are the other reasons?" I yawn again. I can't keep my eyes open any longer.

"A topic for another time."

Chapter 6

"If you'll just take a look at this television. It's on sale right now, and I think it will be perfect for you," the salesman says.

"Sorry, but I'm in a rush, late for work, and my boss will kill me if I'm late again."

Another salesman approaches. Then another.

"We have fabulous sales for you."

"I can't right now, really."

"I'm sorry, ma'am." The head salesman comes up to me, and the others shift back. "Please forgive them, but they just found out they are all going to lose their jobs. The store is closing. They have to sell all the inventory before they can leave."

I'm getting angry.

"That's too bad," I say, "but I'm late. I have to get to work, or my boss will kill me."

I push my way through the men and into my closet. I'm only wearing a towel, and I have to get dressed for work. I turn to lock the closet door behind me, but the lock isn't working. One of the salesmen pushes his way inside.

73

"You want to buy something from me," he says as he approaches. I can't make out his face, but there's a scar on it, just below his eye. "You know you do."

"No..." I can barely utter the word. He's pushing me against the rack of clothes behind me, and he reaches between my legs, fingering me. I turn my head to the side. I just want him to go away and leave me alone, but he doesn't.

"Please," I whisper. "I'm late. My boss will kill me."

I wake alone in the damp tent. The remnants of the nightmare buzz around in my head, and I feel queasy. My leg throbs painfully, and my hip is sore from sleeping on the ground. I can hear voices outside, speaking in hushed tones as I sit up and rub my eyes.

When I try to stand, I drop back to the sleeping bag, grunting from the pain in my leg. It's stiffened up a lot overnight, and putting weight on it hurts like a bitch. I press my hands against it, as if I can hold in the pain.

Falk appears at the tent entrance.

"You all right?"

"I'm okay," I say through clenched teeth.

"Bullshit." He smiles slightly at me. "I know that has to hurt."

"It's just a little stiff."

Falk kicks off his shoes and enters the tent, going to one of the bags set off to the side. He pulls out a bottle of ibuprofen and hands me three of them along with a bottle of water from the cooler.

"Take them. It will help a little."

I nod and take the pills.

"Want some help getting up?" Falk asks. "Walking around may loosen it up again. You should eat, too, so those pills don't upset your stomach. After you eat, I'll check it out and put a new bandage on it."

"I can do it." Using my hands for support, I manage to get myself to my feet. Falk takes a step forward, offering his hand to me, but I don't take it. He leaves it there anyway in case I change my mind.

I hobble out of the tent. Caesar and Beck are out by the fire, trying to cook something in aluminum foil over the coals. Nearby, one of the camp stoves holds a bubbling pot of coffee.

"Want some?" Beck says with a smile as he holds up a coffee mug.

"Please," I respond.

"I'll get it." Falk walks around the fire, ignoring Beck's offered cup, and grabs a different mug to fill with coffee.

Beck glares and is about to say something when Caesar speaks up.

"We need to figure out what's next," he says. "Are we going to stay here or find more habitable ground?"

"We're going to a group of apartments near here," Falk says. He fills the mug from the pot and brings it to me.

"Says who?" Beck asks as he crosses his arms in front of his chest.

"It makes the most sense," Falk replies. "One of the buildings isn't damaged at all, and I have supplies there. It offers protection, and everyone can have their own living space but remain close to the group. There's still running water there—enough to give us time to dig a well if we need to. It's the best option for now."

"It does make sense," Caesar says.

Beck narrows his eyes at his friend.

"That's not the point," Beck mutters. "We're just going to go to *his* apartment complex because *he* says so? That's bullshit. There are other options."

"It's as good a plan as any," Caesar says. "It's not like we're stuck there. If we come up with better arrangements later, we can change."

"It's bullshit," Beck repeats.

Falk ignores their exchange and starts breaking down our tent. Ryan steps out of his own tent a minute later, stretching and rubbing his temple.

"How much of that scotch did we drink last night?" he asks.

"All of it," Caesar responds.

"That's what my head is telling me." Ryan reaches his hand out, and he and Beck bump their fists together. "How about you, bro?"

"About the same," Beck replies. "Want coffee?"

"Hell, yeah!" Ryan smiles, stretches again, and looks over at me. "Good morning!"

"Good morning," I reply, smiling. Even hungover, Ryan is in a better mood than the rest of them.

Falk flashes me a look of warning, which I assume has to do with me speaking to the others. I raise my eyebrows at him. I know he doesn't trust them, but it's not like I can completely avoid talking.

Despite Beck's complaining, we move what we have back to the apartment complex before midday. Caesar and Ryan opt to share the apartment below Falk's while Beck takes the one across from them on the ground floor. The lanterns and some of the other necessities are distributed, and the brothers head off to look for more supplies. There's discussion about what to do with all the bodies in the nearby area, and Ryan offers to start digging graves.

Falk insists I stay with him in his apartment. I debate arguing with him about it—there are plenty of other apartments, and I'm used to having my own space—but one look from him, and I realize it will be pointless. I have to admit, I do feel safer with him close to me.

"I can't properly watch out for you if you are in your own place," he says. "You can have the bed. I'll sleep on the couch. I'm going to start teaching you to shoot, too."

"I'm still not so sure about that." I start taking supplies from a backpack and look for a place in the kitchen to store them.

"You're going to learn anyway." Falk brings another backpack over and places it near my feet. "Once we have everything set up here, we'll start your training."

"You are very bossy, you know." I put my hands on my hips and tilt my head to look up at him.

"I have to be," he says simply. "That's the only way I can protect you. I need to know where you are at all times. I also need to know that you can protect yourself if I'm not there."

His shoulders are straight and his expression tells me that he's not going to change his mind. I shake my head and go back to organizing.

There's definitely a part of me that appreciates his take-charge attitude. If he weren't here, I have no idea what I would do. I wouldn't know what sort of items we'd need to survive or what type of environment would offer us the best chances. I'd be without direction and probably scared out of my mind.

Given that, maybe I can put up with his bossiness.

For now, at least.

Once we have everything stored, we go outside and assist Caesar in building a large fire pit. He and Ryan have already gathered a good number of stones to surround it while Beck digs a large, round depression.

"It will be a good place to cook once the gas runs out," Caesar says. "It'll be easier to cook out here anyway as long as the weather is good. We should find a suitable place to keep communal property."

"There's a shed nearby," Falk says. "I think the landlord keeps lawn equipment in it, but it would be a good place to store kindling to keep it dry. It's big enough for other stuff, too."

"Good idea," Caesar says. "Let's check it out."

The shed is full of lawnmowers, leaf-blowers, shovels and other landscaping items. Ryan moves them out to the parking lot so we can make room for the things we'll need close to us. Falk heads off to find more stones to line the pit, promising me he wouldn't be far away. I decide to busy myself collecting all the nearby sticks to start a kindling pile in the shed. I don't think my leg is up for any heavy lifting.

There are plenty of small branches lying around, and I break them over my knee so they're more uniform and will stack well. I'm on my third stack when a voice startles me.

I glance over my shoulder and breathe slowly to calm my heart.

"Making yourself useful?" Beck is right behind me, causing me to jump.

"Just doing what I can."

"Uh huh." Beck leans against the trunk of a tree and watches me.

"Did you need something?" I ask when he doesn't say anything else.

"You aren't really with that asshole, are ya?"

"Falk?" I don't have to ask, but I do anyway. It's obvious who he means.

"Yeah. *Falk.*" Beck sneers the name and rolls his eyes. "The asshole who thinks he owns you."

I press my lips together and stand up, looking straight at him. I tense my fingers around the branch in my hand.

"He's just trying to keep everyone safe."

"He's on a power trip."

I watch Beck's face carefully. This isn't a topic I care to debate with him—his mind is set, and I'm not going to speak against Falk, not at this point.

"So are you with him or not?" Beck asks when I don't take the bait.

"He's my bodyguard," I say softly.

"Bodyguard?" Beck looks at me quizzically, pushes away from the tree, and moves a little closer. "Now, what would you need a bodyguard for?"

Shit. I shouldn't have said anything about it. This is likely why Falk didn't want me talking to anyone. Talking leads to questions—questions I don't want to answer. I should have kept my mouth shut.

"I don't," I say quickly. "He's not, not really. Um...he's just a friend. He likes to watch out for me."

I sound ridiculous, and I know the lie is completely transparent even as the words leave my mouth. I can tell by Beck's expression that he doesn't believe a word of it.

"You're full of shit," Beck says with a chuckle. He steps up in front of me and places his hand on my hip as he leans in close. "Now why are you lying to me?"

I freeze, my skin crawling at his touch. I can't move and I can't breathe. He places his other hand on the other side of my body, pulling me against him. I can feel each of his fingers as he splays them out on my side, pressing his fingertips into my flesh.

"I'm glad to hear he's just a friend though. Maybe you should think about expanding your other relationships."

"I'm fine." My voice is barely audible. "Really, I am."

I try to take a step back, but he keeps his grip. I turn my head away, feeling the tension running down from my neck and pooling in my feet, immobilizing me.

"You don't have to run away from me," Beck whispers as he presses his mouth into my hair near my ear. "I just want you to know—"

"Get your fucking hands off of her!"

Falk is between us before I even realize it's him. He shoves Beck backward, nearly causing him to fall.

"What the hell is your problem?" Beck screams at him. His hands come up in front of him, balled into fists.

"*You* are my problem. Pretty soon, I'm going to be your problem, you pissy little beta. Now don't fucking touch her again, or I will smack your cock-holster closed."

Jesus Christ.

79

"Falk, it's okay." I touch the back of his shirt, but he shrugs me off.

"It is *not* fucking okay!" he yells as he turns to me.

"You need to watch yourself," Beck says with a sneer. "I don't know who the fuck you think you are, but I'm not putting up with your shit, and she doesn't have to either!"

Caesar appears between them, putting a hand on each man's chest and holding them apart.

"Cool it, you two," he says. "Come on, now. We're all on edge. Let's just go back to our corners, okay?"

"I didn't fucking start it," Beck says.

"You fucking started it when you touched her." Falk steps forward, and Caesar pushes back.

"That's enough." Caesar stares at Falk, but addresses Beck. "Beck, go on, get out of here."

"This ain't over, motherfucker." Beck points his finger at Falk before stalking off toward his own apartment.

Caesar drops his hand but keeps his eyes on Falk, who watches Beck's back until he is out of sight. Once Beck is gone, Falk focuses on me.

"You all right?"

"I'm fine." My voice isn't convincing, even to me.

Falk narrows his eyes, pushes Caesar's hand away from his chest and walks to me. He reaches out slowly and traces a finger over my arm.

"Are you?" he asks again, softly.

"I will be."

He nods and holds his arm out in the direction of the apartment.

"Let me put these in the shed first," I say, picking up the branches.

Falk helps me break the last one up as we walk to the shed.

"You understand now why I don't want you talking to them?"

80

"It's not that simple," I reply. "I can't just ignore it when someone asks me a question."

"You can ignore him. Actually, if he comes near you again, just yell for me."

I roll my eyes. I've had enough conflict for one day, but I can't let Falk dictate my every action. The idea of pretending Beck doesn't exist isn't pragmatic even if it is attractive. My heart is still pounding, and though he's gone, I can somehow feel his hands on my waist, making my skin crawl. I let Falk direct me back to the apartment, and once we're there, I turn to him.

"That really wasn't necessary."

"Wasn't it?"

"No, it wasn't."

"Are you going to tell me that look on your face wasn't you remembering what happened to you? You think I don't notice when you're thinking about it? He had his fucking hands on you, and you were about to go into a panic attack."

I halt and stare at him. I hadn't realized how transparent I was.

I also don't understand my own reaction. When I was actually being attacked, I had fought. Beck hadn't attacked me—he had only touched me. Why am I freezing up now?

"How did you know?" I ask.

"It's my job to know," he says softly. "It's my job to be observant, to know everything that's going on around me. You are my focus. I rarely miss anything."

I chew on my lip, thinking. I'm still not sure I buy into the whole idea of aliens from outer space, but I'm not sure if that matters. Something catastrophic happened, and at least for now, we are on our own.

What does that mean exactly?

There's no government. No police or legal system. We are essentially in anarchy. Survival of the fittest has reverted to survival

81

of the strong—those who can protect and provide. We have plenty of supplies for now, but what will happen when we start to run out?

I shudder. I think about Beck, Caesar, and Ryan. Sure, they seem okay—even Beck hadn't really done anything wrong—but what happens as time goes by, and I'm still the only woman in the group? When Hudson attacked me, I'd been able to get away and find help. If men like Hudson prospered in a world of laws, what would they do now? There is no place for me to run—no help on the horizon.

Except Falk.

Falk wants to keep me safe. Falk not only wants to protect me, he's capable.

I glance to the bedroom door. The distance between there and the couch in the living room isn't more than a dozen feet, but it suddenly looks like a great chasm to me. Someone could come through the window of the bedroom. If I was silenced, Falk might not even know anyone was there.

I shudder.

"Falk?"

"Yeah?"

"It would be all right if…I mean…"

"What?"

I take a deep breath. I both feel and sound like a fool. Best to just spit it out.

"You don't have to sleep on the couch."

"I'm not leaving you out here and close to the door," he says with his arms crossed over his chest. "Not a chance."

"I was going to say…" I sigh loudly, place one hand over my face, and just say it. "You could sleep in the bed, too."

Falk stares at me with those intense eyes. I imagine he's watching me and waiting to see if my body language matches my words.

"You sure?" he finally says.

"I think I'd feel safer that way." Saying the words out loud relaxes me slightly.

"All right."

I nod silently before excusing myself to the bathroom to wash up and get ready for bed. I have no idea if I'm making a good decision or not, but it feels right to me. Having Falk close calms me, and I need a little calm right now. Everything else around me is insane.

I climb into bed and lay my head against the pillow. A few minutes later, Falk comes in and stares at me for a minute.

"You sure you're good with this?"

"You were sleeping right next to me last night," I say with a shrug. "This isn't all that different."

Falk nods and climbs into bed beside me. He shuffles around a bit to get comfortable, then switches from his back to his side, facing me.

"I wouldn't take advantage of you," he says abruptly.

"I know you wouldn't."

"Good. I just wanted to make sure."

My mind immediately begins to wander. I remember the view of Falk wearing nothing but a towel, dripping from his shower, and my skin tingles. He's close enough that I can feel the heat from his body through the sheet. I try to keep my breathing even, but I keep thinking about his arm wrapped around me last night, and I wonder what it would feel like to have his hands all over me.

I haven't had thoughts like this since the day I was assaulted. None. The therapist in the hospital went on and on about how I shouldn't think of the attack as sexual, but that didn't mean I had any interest in having another man touch me ever again.

Until now.

They hurt me. They battered and assaulted me. They held me down while I screamed, and they threatened to kill me. I had nightmares for weeks afterward. I couldn't walk outside by myself without looking over my shoulder.

"You've got that look on your face," Falk says.

"What look?" I ask, startled.

"The same look you had right before you broke down on me."

I reach up and quickly wipe away the tear that had escaped when I was lost in thought. I take a deep breath and center myself.

"I'm trying not to."

"He really did get to you, didn't he?"

"Maybe a little."

"Fucker," Falk snarled.

"It's not that he did anything that's so bad," I say. "It just...makes me think about everything else."

I bite at my lip to keep the memories from resurfacing, but it doesn't help. They're all flooding back anyway.

"You going to tell me what happened?" Falk asks quietly.

I swallow hard past the lump that suddenly lodges in my throat. It's already in my head now, so maybe I should tell him. If this catastrophe hadn't happened, I'd be in Washington, D.C. right now, telling it over and over again as people questioned me.

"I've relived it so many times," I whisper. "I don't know."

"You were going to tell it to a bunch of strangers," he reminds me. "I'm not a stranger anymore, am I?"

I'm starting to wonder if he can actually read my mind.

"No, you're not."

"That's good to know." Falk props himself up on one elbow and looks at me.

"All right, I'll tell you. I'm a shitty storyteller though."

"I won't hold it against you."

I lie on my back and stare at the ceiling, trying to compose my thoughts before I begin.

"It started with an accounting report," I say. "The woman who usually investigated discrepancies was out of the office. I'd been on a project a few months before, working on the programming for that system, and one of the other accountants I'd worked with

84

asked me to look at it. I followed the data through the system and found this holding company."

"Baby Blue, Limited."

"Yes, that one. I kept seeing all these small amounts—much smaller than the one I was investigating being funneled to this holding company. It looked odd, so I searched for Baby Blue on Google but couldn't find anything. That was weird, too, so I asked a friend of mine to check into it and see what he could find."

"Daniel McIntyre. The hacker."

"We were in school together," I say with a nod. "We took a lot of the same computer classes, but he was a lot better than me. He could find anything anywhere—get into any system he wanted. I didn't know he would end up…"

"He was killed in a car accident."

"He was run off the road. It wasn't an accident."

"I realize."

"He linked Baby Blue to a bunch of porn sites. Porn sites with underage girls being raped."

I take a deep breath.

"He sent me a picture from one of them," I tell Falk. "He sent it because he thought one of the girls looked like me."

"Your sister."

"Yes." I swallow again, tears welling in my eyes. "Her body was found with the others in that compound in Nevada. It brought us some closure, at least. It's the only good thing that came out of it all. At least we know what happened to her."

"That paper you talked about writing in college," Falk says, "was about your own family."

I nod, and Falk reaches over and lays his hand on top of mine where it lies on my stomach. He grips my hand for a moment and then relaxes.

"I turned it all over to the police," I tell him. "All the evidence Daniel and I found. Their investigators linked it back to

Tyler Hudson through some offshore accounts. A week after Hudson was arrested, Daniel was dead."

"The arraignment was the day before, but he was let out on bond."

"Yes."

"You were attacked the following week."

"Yes. How much of that did you read?"

"I know you were leaving your house," he says, "and you were on your way to do some shopping. It was approximately three-thirty on a Saturday afternoon. I know they were waiting for you outside and dragged you into a van."

"Yes." I clear my throat as the memories surface. "Someone came up behind me and threw a bag over my head then put his hand over my mouth. I tried to scream, but there wasn't anyone outside to hear me. I heard a sliding door open, and my leg got scraped when I was shoved inside. The van started moving right away as I was pushed down to the floor."

"I don't know exactly how many there were—at least four— plus whoever was driving. One of them held my hands up above my head, and two others held my legs."

"You don't have to give me the details," he says. "Don't put yourself through that."

I nod, feeling tears coming to my eyes as Falk's arm slips around my waist.

"I recognized Hudson's voice right away. I'd only met him in person a couple of times at the office, but he did all these employee engagement videos, so I knew his voice well. He was…he was between my legs. He kept saying how much I had fucked over what he was doing, and how he was going to fuck me over as payment."

"He was…really rough. He wanted me hurt. They said I had a lot of lacerations when I went to the hospital. A lot of bruises, too. When he was…was about done, they pulled the bag up so he could come on my face."

Falk tenses behind me. I can feel his hand shaking slightly.

"It felt like it was all over me," I say. "I kept spitting, trying to get it away from my mouth, and then someone else was holding my legs up, and he started…"

I take a gasping breath.

"He must have been the one holding my arms before. I don't know if they thought I was broken already or what, but no one grabbed my hands again. I pushed at him, but he just laughed. I reached out, just trying to find something, and came up with a piece of metal—I think it was a tire jack. It was heavy, anyway.

"I hit him with it, right across the face, I'm sure. He started screaming, and I got the bag off my head. The van wasn't moving— I think it was stopped at a traffic light. I was kicking and screaming—I know I hit more than one of them. I don't know if my reaction surprised them enough that they didn't know what to do or not. I only know I grabbed the door handle and ran off into the woods nearby, and no one followed me.

"My panties were wrapped around my ankle. I got them back up as I was running, but I only had those and my shirt. I saw those blue signs with a big H on them and followed them to the hospital. I told them I was raped and did the whole rape kit thing."

"That was almost the worst part," I say, remembering. "It was like it was happening all over again. I think I was in shock."

"You probably were."

"So, that's basically it." I take a long breath. "The police came. Hudson was found at his home with his wife and kids, and the media circus began. You probably know the rest."

Falk starts to pull his hand back, and I reflexively grab his wrist to keep it where it is. He stills for a moment, then turns his hand over, lacing our fingers together.

"Beck grabbing you made you think about it," Falk says. "That's why you were starting to panic."

"I guess so."

"The same way you did when I was trying to fix your leg." He grips my hand slightly. "I'm sorry about that. I should have thought about it. I think I was on automatic."

"I know," I say. "It's okay. You were just trying to help. Beck wasn't trying to hurt me either."

"Beck is an ass," Falk says. "He's also dangerous."

"He isn't one of the men who attacked me," I point out.

"That doesn't mean he isn't dangerous." Falk shifts, moving slightly closer to me. I can feel his leg up against mine. "He needs to be put in his place."

"'I will smack your cock-holster closed?'" I raise an eyebrow at him.

"It got my point across."

"A little homophobic, don't you think?"

"No," he replies, "it has nothing to do with being gay. It has to do with who is on top and who is on the bottom. He's military even though he lied about what he did. He's heard it before."

"What did he lie about?"

"He lied about his service."

"He wasn't in the Air Force?"

"He might have been Air Force, but he wasn't in communications. That was a crock of shit. He was special ops, same as Ryan. That's how they know each other. More likely Army than Air Force."

"How do you know?"

"The way they move, the way they talk and interact with each other. I can tell."

I shake my head. I can't argue with him on this one; I have no frame of reference. There is no doubt that Falk is observant. I could tell that from the moment I met him.

"Still," I say, slowly shaking my head, "I'm not sure if 'putting people in their place' is going to make a lot of friends."

"I'm not trying to make friends, Hannah. I really only have the one goal."

"Keep me safe?"

"Keep you safe."

"I'm not sure you have to argue with everyone around me to do that."

"Everything is different now, Hannah," he says. "There is no authority anymore. Survival depends on putting yourself at the top."

"'It's the end of the world as we know it.'" I softly quote lyrics from the REM song. I look up at Falk as I remember more of the song. "You're fine with this, aren't you?"

"Chaos is my element."

Chapter 7

"Someone has to go talk to them. We need to know what they're doing—if they're friendly or not."

"Yeah? And why does that have to be me and Caesar?"

"Because Caesar's not going alone. Not after what happened last time."

"So why don't you fucking go yourself?"

Falk and Beck are at it again.

It has been four weeks since Atlanta was leveled, and tensions are high. We settled in at Falk's apartment complex despite Beck's complaining, and things are actually going relatively smoothly. The fire pit in the grassy common area is where we get together as a group, and some of the evenings when everyone was together were quite pleasant. We've found bicycles that make it a little easier to gather supplies since two of them have been modified to drag a cart behind them.

We don't have much more information than we did when it all started. The guys like to gather around in the evenings, drink scotch, and speculate, but we really have no idea. The women, children, and domestic animals are still gone, and we don't yet know who took them. A few new people joined us, but they have more questions than answers. Two newcomers, Christine and Chuck, do a lot of the cooking for the group. They brought our number to nine.

"Do you need any help?" I ask Christine as I try to ignore Falk and Beck.

Christine, the only additional woman we have come across, and her husband, Chuck, had been in the basement of a nightclub when it all started, getting ready for Chuck's band to perform later that night. The building had collapsed above them, and they spent hours digging themselves out. Christine is a beautiful, voluptuous woman with curly red hair and a contagious smile. No matter what happens, she manages to smile through all of it.

Chuck is a character, to say the least. His long hair is braided down his back, and he has a little, white van dyke on his chin with the tip of it dyed bright red. When we found them, he'd been armed with a compound bow, and Christine kept yelling at him to stop pretending to be Legolas.

The banter between the two of them is the best entertainment around.

"I'm good with the food," Christine says, "but there are a shit-ton of dishes to be done before anyone can eat. You could work on those."

"I'd be happy to."

From the kettle on the fire, I pour some hot water over the dishes and go to work.

"What's for dinner?" I ask.

"Well, if Chuck has anything to say about it, we'll be eating the squirrel he shot out of a tree with that damn bow. However, he won't know the difference between that and canned chicken, so we'll just stick with that."

"It would be my preference," I say with a laugh.

"That's what I get for marrying someone who spent his whole childhood watching adventure movies. Now he thinks he's some damn fool elf on a quest for rodent!"

"You know what? I have an even better idea. Why don't you just fuck off?"

I look over in time to see Beck shove Falk in the chest, and I brace myself for an actual fight. They have yet to come to blows, but I'm afraid it's only a matter of time.

Falk stands up straighter but doesn't retaliate as Beck spits on the ground at his feet and stomps toward his apartment. Caesar comes up to Falk and says something quietly to him before heading off after Beck.

"Do they ever shut up?" Marco comes over to where I'm washing out pots and utensils and starts to dry them with a nearby towel.

Marco and his brother, Sam, were the first to join us after we found Caesar, Beck, and Ryan. They had been working in a field near a farm outside of town when their mother and two sisters disappeared. They had not been underground at all, but they had been far removed from any buildings. Their cattle and chickens had also disappeared. The two of them had walked all the way into town, looking for answers, and found us.

Marco had become the head of the family when their father passed away two years ago, and at only nineteen, he's very outgoing and willing to do most any task set in front of him. Sam, who is a year younger, is a quiet young man with a shy smile. Though also a hard worker, he rarely says anything, preferring to have his brother speak for them both.

"Only when they stay away from each other," I say. "I've tried to get them to play nice together, but they just set each other off."

"They're too much alike—alphas trying to be the head of the pack." Marco says.

"Is that what we are," I ask, "a pack?"

"You have a better word for it?"

"I guess not." I glance over at Falk, and he motions for me to join him. "Can you take over for a minute? I'll be right back."

"Sure." Marco grabs the dish from my hands and gets to scrubbing while I go to Falk.

"I've got to go," Falk says with a sigh. "I don't like the idea of leaving you here unprotected, but Beck just isn't going to let it go. Taking you with me is even riskier."

"Survivors spotted?"

"Yeah, near the university. Ryan saw them when he was up there. Four guys, two of them armed."

"Be careful."

"I'll be fine. I'm more concerned about leaving you here."

Falk hasn't let me out of his sight since the day Beck put his hands on me. In another situation, I would have found his presence suffocating, but it has been good to have someone looking out for me.

"I'm getting better with the handguns."

Falk raises an eyebrow at me.

"All right, I still suck, but I am better."

"You have trouble hitting dirt," Falk says. "I'm afraid you would just end up shooting yourself. I've always thought I could teach anyone in just a couple of lessons, but you, Ms. Savinski, are quite the challenge."

"Just trying to keep you on your toes."

He chuckles and shakes his head.

"Maybe we can try again when I get back."

"Sounds like a plan."

"How's your leg today?" he asks.

"It's all right. The scar is itchy."

"Yeah, sorry about that. My work isn't pretty."

"Better than getting infected." I smile at him, and he nods before staring me in the eyes.

"You be careful," he says seriously. "Find something to do in the apartment, and keep away from Beck."

"I'll be fine," I say to assure him. "I'm going to help Christine out with dinner. Beck never comes near the kitchen unless there's food being served."

"Stay close to the common area at least. Most of the guys are going to be busy digging that well, so don't go off on your own."

"I'll stay close."

He nods but doesn't look happy about it.

"I'll be back soon."

I go back to the dishes. Marco keeps washing as he hands me a towel to dry and smirks as he nods his head toward Christine.

Chuck has returned with another dead squirrel on the end of an arrow.

"I am *not* cooking that thing."

"Why the hell not? I got it for you, babe!"

"Because there's still a ton of Tyson products in a can, *babe*. You want to eat that shit, you go ahead and cook it yourself!"

"Aw, come on!" Chuck sticks out his bottom lip in an exaggerated pout and leans over so he can peer up into Christine's eyes. "I'm providing for ya, babe. This couldn't be better unless I found us a cave to live in. You could even draw on the walls!"

"Aw, darling," Christine says as she puts down a stirring spoon and takes Chuck's face in her hands. "You are my mighty hunter already, and I can draw on the apartment walls with those sharpies you found. Now get rid of that nasty thing and wash up. Dinner is almost ready."

They kiss briefly, and Chuck hangs his head a little as he takes the squirrel-laden arrow back into the nearby trees. I hold in a laugh as Christine turns back and smiles at me.

"I'll blow him later," she announces. "Everything will be fine then."

I have to cover my mouth to keep in the giggles. Marco doesn't even bother to hold back his laughter.

"Quit your belly-laughing, and grab the paper towels out of the shed." Christine points her spoon at Marco.

"I'll go," I say with another giggle. I dry my hands quickly and head off for the shed.

The shed has been completely emptied of yard equipment and is now full of community property. It's mostly consumable items like paper products and toiletries, but there are also a lot of cooking supplies and a small barrel of dry kindling. Caesar has also stashed a decent supply of whiskey on one of the many shelves.

I try to reach up to grab the paper towels, but they're on the top shelf, and I can't quite reach. I look around and find a small step stool in the back of the shed to use, and as I'm putting it back, I hear the door to the shed open.

"Well, hello there." Beck smiles at me as he closes the door behind him. His hair has gotten longer, and he is starting to look more like a gunslinger from the old west than someone from a magazine ad.

"Hi." I shove the stool back in its place and dust my hands off as I stand back up. My intent is to grab the paper towels and leave, but Beck is between me and the lower shelf where I'd put the roll, examining bottles of scotch.

"Don't think I've ever seen you without your bodyguard before," Beck says. "I barely recognized you."

My skin crawls. His words are innocent enough, but the way he says them has me on guard. There is also the knowledge that Falk would be extremely pissed off if he knew I was talking to Beck.

"Could you please hand me those paper towels?"

"I could." He smiles and moves a step to the left, further blocking me, and holds up a bottle. "You could have a drink with me first. It'll help you stomach that bitch's cooking."

I want to defend Christine's efforts, but my desire to just get out of the shed is greater. The space inside is large, but all of a sudden, it feels much smaller and cramped to me. I just want out.

"They're just behind you there," I say, pointing at the towels and ignoring his remarks.

Beck doesn't move his gaze from me.

"Just one drink," he says as he steps closer, effectively pinning me in the corner.

I look down and try to ignore the sweat that begins to gather at the back of my neck. I swallow hard and inhale, trying to keep myself calm, but I only end up smelling the whiskey that's already on Beck's breath.

"You can relax, hon," Beck says quietly. "Big brother isn't here to stop us."

"I'm not thirsty," I say.

"You aren't, huh?" He moves even closer, and I can feel his heat against my face. "Well, what are you then?"

"I'm just me," I respond quickly. "I'm just getting the…the paper towels."

"Just you." Beck snorts out a laugh. "What the fuck does that mean anyway?"

He narrows his eyes as he stares me in the face, his nose just an inch from mine as he glances up and down. My skin still crawls as I stand perfectly still and refuse to meet his look.

"Who are you, Hannah? I know you look familiar, but I haven't been able to put my finger on it. Where do I know you from?"

"We never met before all this," I tell him. "Now, really, I have to get back."

Beck slams the bottle back on the shelf, causing the whole thing to shake. I gasp and take a step back, almost tripping over the items behind me on the floor. Beck pushes his body up against mine and grabs my hair at the back of my head.

I gasp and push my palms against his chest, but he doesn't move.

"Why don't you tell me who you are, huh?" He growls right into my face as I close my eyes and try to turn my head, but I can't move. His grip on my hair is too tight. "I know Caesar knows who you are, but he's keeping his mouth shut. You can tell me, too. I'm not gonna tell anyone else."

"I'm not anyone," I insist. Panic is surging up inside of me. In my mind, I can feel hands grasping at me, holding me down. "Just…let go of me."

"Now why would I do that?"

"I need to get back to Falk," I tell him. I can hear my heart pounding, and my throat feels like it's closing up on me. "He's waiting for me."

"Falk went off to check up on those survivors," Beck says. "He's not here. Now why don't you just go ahead and fess up, baby? You know more about what's going on than you're saying, don't you?"

"I have no idea what's going on!" I twist, yank my hair from his grasp, and duck under his arm. He stumbles forward, nearly taking the shelf down. I turn to face him. "You're drunk! Now stay the fuck away from me!"

I yank open the door, listening to him laugh as I run out. I scamper up the stairs to the apartment, forgetting all about the paper towels. Once inside, I race to the bathroom and close the door behind me. It's dark inside, and though I know there's a battery-powered lantern on the counter, I don't switch it on. I just sit on the toilet with my head in my hands, shaking and trying not to cry.

~~~~~

Just as the sky gets dark, Falk and Caesar return with four new additions to our group.

I had remained in the apartment until it was time to eat and now sit on the ground with a plate on my lap. I've barely touched the food. My stomach is too queasy to eat. I haven't seen Beck since our little encounter, and I'm afraid of what he might say when he returns.

I watch as Caesar introduces the newcomers. They are also from the Atlanta area and had taken refuge in the basement of a church when the attack occurred. I only catch the names of two of them—Owen, a short, freckled guy of barely twenty years with bright, red hair, and Brett, a stocky guy in his mid-twenties with a toothy smile and a scar just below his right eye. I miss the names of the other two.

Outnumbered eleven to two now.

I swallow and wonder if Christine even counts since she's married to Chuck. I look around for her, but they must have already retired to their own place, leaving me the only woman in the area.

I guess it's really ten to one.

I don't miss how the four newbies look at me. Brett taps Caesar, leans close to say something to him, and they both look over at me. It's unnerving, especially considering my earlier encounter with Beck. He still hasn't appeared, and I figure he's sleeping it off somewhere.

I stand and stare down at my plate. Wasting food is practically criminal right now, and I wonder if I'll be able to finish it before it goes bad. While I think about what to do with it, Brett and Caesar keep talking. They're too far away from me to hear any of their words, but I see them glance over at me a couple more times, and I look away whenever they do. They're standing close together, and I wonder if they've met before. They seem very familiar with each other.

"What's wrong?" Falk is suddenly at my side, and his voice startles me. I didn't even see him approach.

"Nothing."

"Bullshit." He takes my arm and turns me to face him. His face is shadowed except for the light from the evening fire. It casts him in an orange glow. "You've barely said a word to anyone all evening, and you're not even making eye contact. All you're doing is staring at your half-eaten dinner. Now, what happened?"

"Just…just Beck being as ass." I sigh. "It's not a big deal."

"What did he do?" Falk's words are short and clipped. He scans the area, presumably looking for Beck.

"Nothing, really."

"What did he do to you, Hannah?"

99

"He was just asking who I was. I guess he picked up on something Caesar said. I don't know. He asked me who I was. That's all."

Falk stares at me for a long moment.

"Did he touch you?" he asks.

I hesitate, and Falk tightens his grip on my arm, nearly making me drop my plate.

"Did he fucking touch you?"

"No!" I pull my arm back from his grasp and glare at him. "He didn't."

The statement isn't true, but I don't want Falk to make a big deal out of it.

"You're a shitty liar." Falk runs his hand through his hair and huffs out a sharp breath. "Where were you?"

"In the shed," I tell him.

"Alone?"

"I was just getting some paper towels," I explained. "I was only in there a minute."

"I told you not to go anywhere alone!" He's not exactly yelling, but his tone is harsh.

"Well, that isn't always practical!" I stare at him as he glares at me. After a moment, he closes his eyes and takes a deep breath.

"Did he hurt you, Hannah?" Falk's voice is softer now, and he's back to his characteristic calm. I'm not buying it though. I know by his eyes that he is still burning inside.

"No, he didn't. I'm fine." I glance up to meet his gaze, hoping I am convincing enough. Beck hadn't hurt me, not really. He'd just frightened me, and that was only because he had been drinking. I just want to forget the whole thing.

Obviously, Falk isn't going to let it go.

"I'm going to talk to him."

"No, Falk!" I drop the plate, and it's my turn to grab Falk's arm. He stops and looks at my hand and then back to my face. I think it may be the only time I've initiated contact with him since the first night in his apartment when I'd had a breakdown. "Just drop it, okay? He didn't really do anything, and I don't want you two to get in yet another argument!"

"He *did* touch you." It's no longer a question.

"He didn't hurt me."

"He had his hands on you."

I can feel the muscles of his forearm flex beneath my palm.

"Come on." Falk takes my hand from his arm and holds it in his.

"Where are we going?"

"Out of here." He starts pulling me toward the apartment.

"Why?"

"Because if I see him right now, I'm going to kill him."

Something tells me Falk isn't exaggerating. Without any further argument, I let him take me back to the seclusion of the apartment. Once inside, he takes a long look at me before huffing a breath through his nose. I know he wants to say something, but he doesn't speak. Instead, he turns to the kitchen, grabs a pack of cigarettes from one of the drawers, and steps out onto his balcony.

Falk smokes very rarely, usually when he's too pissed off to speak. I've found that when he does decide to partake, it's best to just leave him be until he's returned from his adult version of time out. He usually comes back, collected and calm again.

This time, I consider following him just to make sure he isn't planning to shoot Beck right there from the balcony. I don't think Falk would do that—kill Beck in cold blood—but I realize I don't really know. He doesn't talk about himself very much, and a lot of things about him remain a mystery.

In the end, I don't follow him. I boil water for tea instead. He usually likes that in the evenings, and I hope it will improve his mood. By the time the tea is made, he returns with a declaration.

"I'm not leaving you alone again."

"You can't be at my side all the time." I hold out a cup of tea, and he takes it from me.

101

"Watch me." He sits on the couch and places the mug on the coffee table.

"Other people here need your help, too," I say as I sit beside him. "You know more than anyone about how to survive like this."

"Chuck knows some."

"Chuck knows because he's watched a lot of movies."

"Better than nothing." Falk sits back and sips the tea. "I'm not here for everyone else. I'm here for you. There are more people now anyway—they can help."

I almost forgot about the new people in the group.

"What do you think of the newcomers?"

"I don't know yet," he says. "Better than the last group."

"The last group opened fire on Caesar before he could say hello."

"Right. They're better than that."

"Aren't you worried those guys may come back? Might find us here?"

"No," he says, and there's no question about it in his voice. "I'm sure they are long gone by now."

I sigh and lean back against the couch. My mind is in turmoil, and I can't make sense of my jumbled thoughts. I keep thinking about Beck cornering me and how I nearly froze again. What if I hadn't gotten out of there when I did? What would he have done?

Probably nothing.

Not all men are like the ones who hurt me, and I know that, but being the only single woman in a group of men has me on edge most of the time. Now there are even more of them. More men I know nothing about. For all I know, one of them could have been in the group that assaulted me.

I shake my head slightly. The thought is ridiculous. I was assaulted in Chicago, not Atlanta. Everyone we've encountered has been from this area. Then again, Hudson may have known I would be changing planes here. He could have sent his connections to follow me. He said it didn't matter where I went—he would find a way to kill me.

My jumbled thoughts continue as Falk and I prepare for bed. In the dim light of a battery-powered lamp, I stare at my reflection in the bathroom mirror and tell myself I'm being paranoid. Beck isn't one of Hudson's men, and he isn't here to exact revenge. If he were, he would know exactly who I am and wouldn't have asked such questions.

Even though the men in the group probably know nothing about Tyler Hudson, they're still men. "Men with needs," my mother would have said. They are men who may eventually get tired of their own hands. They may imbibe a bit too much of Caesar's scotch supply and wait for the opportunity when Falk is otherwise occupied and I am alone and vulnerable.

"You all right in there?" Falk knocks softly at the door, and I jump.

"Yes, I'll be out in a minute."

I sigh at my reflection, rub my eyes, and finish brushing my teeth. Falk is already in bed when I come out, and I slide under the blankets with him. He rolls to his side and wraps his arm around my waist, holding me close to him. We always sleep this way though he's never once tried to take it further.

Our position is both familiar and comfortable, but I'm always tense at first. Falk thinks it's because I don't like to be touched, and he's partially right, but that's not all of it. Part of me wants to push myself against him, feel the strength of his arms and chest against my bare skin.

I clench my thighs at the thought and hope the man with the ultimate observation skills doesn't notice. Even as I think about Falk's touch, my mind pulls me back to Beck's face peering into mine. I can smell his breath, feel his fingers gripping my hair and pulling my head back, and I shudder.

"I'm scared," I whisper.

"I know you are." Falk tightens his grip and holds me closer. "I won't let anything happen to you."

"I thought I'd already had the worst thing possible happen to me," I say. "I was wrong though. This is worse."

"How is this worse?" Falk tilts his head to look at me, his expression confused. "I told you—no one is going to touch you again."

"Because it's just a matter of time. I know you want to keep me safe, but you can't watch me all the time forever. It's worse because I feel like I'm waiting for it to happen all over again."

There is one thought in my head that I don't voice because just the notion scares the shit out of me. There are too many men here now. If they wanted a piece of me, they could overwhelm Falk. He can't protect me from a mob.

Falk is quiet as he reaches over me, wrapping his arm around me gently. I take a deep breath, inhaling the scent of him. It calms me as I close my eyes and give in to the exhaustion of the day. He speaks before I drift off completely, but his words are lost in my dreams.

"He won't touch you again."

Chapter 8

I sip coffee on the balcony and watch Christine and Chuck in the common area. My head is pounding this morning, and I know my sleep was restless. Falk headed for the shower after commanding me not to leave the apartment until he was out. I don't know how he can stand the cold water. I've mostly taken to bathing at the sink with a washcloth warmed by water heated on the fire.

From the second story balcony, I can't participate in the morning conversation, but I can at least hear most of it. The couple below flow around each other with a practiced flare that only comes with years of living with the same person. They look happy and content.

"Can you hand me that…that thingy?"

"The ladle?"

"Yeah, that thingy." Chuck takes the utensil from his wife and dips it into a large pot of oatmeal. "Is there any brown sugar?"

"My white sugar ain't good enough for you anymore?"

"Oh, baby," Chuck replies with a grin, "you know I can't get enough of your sugar."

"Mmhmm." Christine saddles up to his side and reaches around to grab his ass. Chuck presses his hips up against hers and kisses her deeply.

I turn away, not wanting to be so voyeuristic. Through the balcony door, I see Falk inside and go to join him. He's in the kitchen with his back to me, pouring coffee from the pot. He's wearing only his boxer shorts, and his shoulders are still damp from the shower.

I find myself licking my lips as I take the moment to watch the muscles in his back ripple as his arms move. I am still a little confused about how I feel about him, but I can't deny that I like to look. I take a breath and try to compose myself.

"Looks like breakfast is about ready," I say.

"Good." Falk turns around and gives me an uncharacteristic smile.

"You look like you're in a good mood," I comment. "Sleep well?"

"Not complaining." He takes a sip from his coffee, and I see a long scratch on the underside of his forearm.

"What happened?" I ask, moving closer to get a better look.

Falk glances down at the mark and shrugs.

"Probably scratched it gathering wood yesterday. No big deal. You ready to get food? I'll go throw on some clothes."

He disappears into the bedroom and returns a minute later dressed in jeans and a T-shirt with a Captain America symbol on the front, and we head outside to join the rest of the group as they gather for breakfast.

My appetite has returned, and I think I might be making up for last night's slight supper as I go back for a second helping of oatmeal. Chuck must have located the brown sugar because it's positively delicious.

Ryan, Sam, and Marco sit together, chatting easily with the four new people. Falk takes me over and introduces me since I hadn't met them officially last night, and I finally catch all their names—Owen, Brian, Brett, and Wayne.

"We came down from Smyrna," Wayne says. "Been walking for the better part of two weeks, just looking for people."

Wayne's in his late fifties or early sixties. He looks like he's in pretty good shape, though. Brian is his son, and looks like the spitting image of his father. Brett and Owen are their neighbors, and they've lived near each other for many years.

"We'd about given up," Brian says. "Dad keeps blaming terrorists, but I told him that wasn't possible."

"You never know what they got hidden away," Wayne says. "You think that's better than his idea of space aliens?"

"Just pointing out the facts as I know them," Falk says. "There isn't a power in the world that could have done the kind of damage we've seen."

"What he said about the women and kids makes sense," Brett remarks.

"Where did she come from, then?" Wayne asks, nodding toward me.

"She was in the MARTA tunnel with me," Falk says as he takes a slight step closer to my side.

"Well, it ain't all women then, is it?"

Caesar joins the group and addresses me.

"Have you seen Beck around?" he asks.

"Not today," I reply. I don't make eye contact with him, and I hope he isn't going to ask me about the circumstances of my last encounter with Beck. Falk's badgering me about it last night was enough. I really don't want to talk about it.

"Well, if you do, let him know I'm looking for him." Caesar drains a cup of coffee and sets it down near the rest of the dishes. "We were supposed to head out for supplies this morning, but I can't find him anywhere."

107

"He's probably passed out cold," Ryan says. "He was pretty hammered last night. If he is awake, he's holding his head somewhere. Just listen for the moans."

"Probably," Caesar says with a nod. "I can't wait around though. Brett, you want to join me instead?"

"Sure thing." Brett stands and walks over to Caesar.

"Do you still want me to tell him you're looking for him?" I ask.

"Fuck it." Caesar and Brett head off, and I don't think much of it until later.

~~~~~

Falk steps up closer behind me.

"I'm just going to help you aim," he says softly as his arms come up around me. I can feel his chest pressed against my back. He places his hands over mine and holds the gun up a little higher. "Look right down the top of the barrel. See the notch? That's there you want to look. That's it."

I try to focus on my aim on the empty pop can sitting on a tree stump and not the feeling of him pressed up behind me.

"Take a deep breath." His words are hot in my ear. "Breathe out slowly, and pull the trigger as soon as all the breath is out."

"Why?"

"It improves your aim."

I don't understand it, but I don't question it either. Following his instructions, I fire.

The sound scares the shit out of me every time I do it. Even with the earplugs in my ears, it's deafening. I still don't hit the can, but a chunk from the stump goes flying.

"Better," Falk says. "Try again."

I do, with similar results. I go through two clips of ammo and still can't hit the damn can.

"I really am hopeless at this."

"You just need more practice," Falk says as he reloads the gun. "At this point, I think you could at least protect yourself at close range."

"Yeah, I'll just ask anyone who attacks me to stand still for a minute while I remember how to breathe."

Falk laughs.

"Eventually, it will all be second nature. I promise." He starts to put the gun back in my hands again, but we're interrupted.

"Falk!"

I glance in the direction of the common area and see Caesar and Brett coming through the trees.

"Over here!" Falk calls back. "Don't worry—Hannah doesn't have a gun in her hands right now, so you're safe!"

"Very funny."

Caesar walks up to him, glances at me quickly, then takes a deep breath.

"We have a problem."

"What's that?" Falk asks as he checks the chamber of the gun.

"It's Beck."

"What's he done now?"

"He's not doing anything," Caesar says. "He's dead."

~~~~~~

"When was the last time anyone saw him?"

We're all gathered around the cooking fire in a circle, and Caesar seems to be in full investigative mode. He even has a pad of paper and a pen, and he makes notes as he questions everyone in the group.

"Never even met the guy," Wayne says. "None of us did."

"You mentioned him," Brett says. He reaches up and rubs the little scar under his eye as he glances at me. "Never actually saw him."

Brian and Owen all nod in agreement.

"I saw him yesterday morning, but that was it." Sam says.

"He didn't come to dinner last night," Chuck says.

"I saw him coming out of the shed right before dinner," Christine adds as she glances in my direction. "Had a bottle in his hand. Headed off through the parking lot."

"Yeah, I saw him walking off," Marco says. "Didn't talk to him or anything though."

"He's got another apartment in one of the other buildings," Ryan says. "That's where I found him."

Caesar looks to me, and I feel sweat collecting on the back of my neck.

"I saw him in the shed before dinner," I say quietly. "Didn't see him after that."

"Falk?" Caesar turns to him. "When did you see him last?"

Falk stares at Caesar for a long moment, his expression passive.

"Right before you and I left to meet up with those guys," Falk finally responds, gesturing toward the four newcomers. "Never saw him after we got back."

"Where were you after dinner?" Caesar asks. "Everyone else was here."

"With Hannah in our apartment." Falk doesn't blink. "All night."

Caesar and Falk stare at each other far too long. I glance back and forth between them, but I can't read their expressions. Caesar eventually breaks the stare and writes something down on the pad of paper in his hand.

"So what happened to him?" Chuck asks. "I never heard any gunshots."

"He was strangled." Caesar looks down at the paper and taps it with his pen. "There was definitely a struggle beforehand. The place is a wreck."

"It was always a wreck," Ryan says with a snort.

"What about those men you ran into last week?" I ask. "The ones who shot at you could have followed you back here."

"I don't think they did," Caesar says. "If they had caught up to me and planned on doing something like this, it would have been days ago, not now."

"They might have been watching us," Ryan interjects, "biding their time."

"For what reason?" Caesar shakes his head. "Besides, I think I would have been a more likely target if they were going to do that. I'm the one who shot back. Beck wasn't there."

"Did you hit one of them?" I ask.

"No," Caesar responds quickly. "I only fired two shots as I ran off. It was a deterrent only. If I wanted to hit them, I would have."

"Then it has to be someone here." Ryan leans back in his lawn chair and stares directly at Falk. "Someone with a grudge."

Falk stares right back, unflinching.

"You have something you want to say to me?" Falk's voice is cold.

"You were arguing with him yesterday."

"*He* was arguing with *me*," Falk says, correcting Ryan, "just like he does every day."

"Maybe you just got tired of it."

"Maybe you need to watch your mouth."

"Enough." Caesar takes a step forward, blocking the two men's view of each other. "This isn't helping. I'm going to go back to that other apartment—see what else I can find."

"Want help?" Brett asks as he stands.

"Yeah, sure." Caesar turns around in a circle, addressing the whole group. "I think it's best if everyone stays close today. We don't know what happened, and whoever did this might still be in the area. No one should wander off alone."

Everyone gets up from their seats and heads off in different directions, talking in hushed voices. Most are heading toward their own apartments, but Christine makes her way to the kitchen area and starts washing pots and pans.

I look to Falk, expecting a lecture about staying close to him. I expect him to drag me back to the apartment and make me sit on the couch with a book while he stares at me, making sure no one gets close. I expect him to demand that I remain in the apartment for the rest of my life.

But he doesn't say a word about it.

"Want to try some more target practice?" he asks.

"Right now?"

"Yeah. Why not?"

"I'm a little shaken at the moment." I narrow my eyes at him.

He glances up at me and shrugs.

"All right. You hungry? You still haven't eaten much."

"No, but I think Christine could use some help with dinner."

"Gotcha. I'll be nearby."

I close my eyes and shake my head. I don't know how he can be so nonchalant about someone in the group apparently being murdered. I know he's seen a lot of death—he's told me a little about his combat experiences—but this is different.

It is to me, anyway.

I need to keep myself busy, so I walk over to Christine and start to help her out. She smiles and hands me a dishtowel.

"What do you think happened?" I ask quietly. I glance at Falk, but he's just sitting on the chair by the fire, using a sharpening stone on one of his knives.

"I think he pissed off the wrong person," Christine says. She finishes up a large pot and hands it to me. "I think a nice big pot of stew would work well tonight."

"Sounds good to me." I have no appetite, but I like the idea of staying busy. Chopping up whatever fresh vegetables are still left is as good as anything.

112

Christine seems to make up her recipe as we go along, adding a little of this and a little of that to some browned onions at the bottom of the huge pot near the coals of the cooking fire. I hand her whatever she asks for, and she stirs and hums a little. I don't recognize the tune, but her tone is calming.

"I saw you coming out of that shed," she says softly. She shoots a glance at Falk before continuing. "I saw him stumble out right after, looking pretty shitfaced. Beck upset you—that was pretty clear."

"He was just drunk."

"He was shitfaced," she repeats. She hands me the large spoon and instructs me to keep stirring while she opens some cans of broth. She nods in Falk's direction. "Did you tell him?"

"Falk noticed I was upset." I chew on my lip as I stir the contents of the pot. "I didn't tell him exactly what happened."

"What *did* happen?"

"It was nothing, really."

Christine stops twisting the can opener and gives me a look.

"He was drunk," I say again. "He kept asking me questions. He didn't really do anything. He was just being his obnoxious self."

"Did Falk think it was nothing when you told him?"

I look up from the pot and sigh.

"Do you think he did it?" I ask bluntly. "Do you think he went over to Beck's apartment and strangled him? Is that what you're saying?"

"I'm not saying anything," she says as she twists open another can. "Can't help but wonder though. They definitely didn't get along."

"He was with me all night." I lick my lips and wonder if I would have woken up if Falk had gotten out of bed and left the apartment. Christine is right about one thing—Falk had been mad last night—really mad. This morning he was quite chipper.

"I've seen how he looks at you, you know," Christine comments.

"What are you talking about?"

"Just like he is right now," she says. "He's always got his eye on you. Don't look. He'll change his focus if you do. I know you've said before there's nothing going on between you two, but I'm not sure he knows that."

"There isn't anything," I say. "He's just protective."

"I've been around a while, honey," Christine says, "and I know men. That man thinks a lot more of you than just someone to protect."

"It's a job to him," I insist.

"He wants you, honey. That's very clear." She dumps the last can of broth into the pot and tilts her head to look at me. "You want my advice? Let him have you. Knowing you're his might be the only thing that keeps the rest of the guys away."

I shake my head but don't get the chance to respond. Chuck comes up behind Christine and wraps his arms around her waist.

"I know what you need!" he exclaims. "Hasenpfeffer!"

"I ain't cooking a damn rabbit, and I sure as hell ain't cleaning one!"

"It's a delicacy, babe! And I'm gonna get you one!"

Chuck grabs his bow, calls to Sam to join him, and stalks off toward the trees with his head held high, humming the theme song for the Bugs Bunny cartoons. Christine shakes her head and clicks her tongue against the roof of her mouth.

"They're all about this, you know," she tells me. "They've all gone primitive. The problem is, they don't know which of them is the main dog of this pack."

"So we're all going to go back to cavemen hunting while the cavewomen cook?"

"Do you see any of the guys offering to help us?"

I can't deny what she's saying. Though it hadn't really occurred to me, she and I do most of the traditional womanly tasks, while the guys go out for supplies and build things. We gather kindling while they chop down trees for larger pieces of wood. I'd even done most of the cleaning in Falk's apartment though I assume he'd always taken care of that himself before I was in the picture.

How had I not noticed that before?

Brett and Caesar return just as dinner is ready, but they don't seem to have any more information than they had when they left. The apartment definitely had signs of a struggle, and there was blood found on the corner of the coffee table, but Beck didn't have any bloody wounds.

Caesar spends all of four minutes checking people for bloody wounds but soon discovers everyone has some kind of cut or scrape. Even I have one on my hand from where I went to place a can for target practice, slipped and scratched myself on the tree stump. We are outside more than inside, and the woods have a lot of thorny bushes.

I eat dinner in quiet contemplation, only half listening to Caesar and Brett as they discuss Caesar's notes.

How well do I know any of the people here?

It has been roughly a month since I was supposed to be on a plane to Washington, D.C. I haven't known anyone here for very long, but we've lived in such close quarters all that time, it feels like much longer. I can't imagine any of them actually doing something violent without just cause, let alone wrapping their hands around Beck's neck and choking the life out of him.

I shudder at the image that comes to my head.

Someone did it.

It has to be someone from outside, either those men Caesar encountered last week or someone we just haven't seen. We don't know how many people are out there. It could have been anyone.

But why?

What would some stranger have against Beck? He was annoying and definitely abrasive, but no one could have known that without being around him for a while. Logically, it has to be someone here.

I look around at the people in the chairs circling the fire. Marco and Sam are to my right, and I dismiss them immediately. They're both shy, country boys. I can't imagine them doing anything like that. I glance past Christine and Chuck as well—they're far too focused on each other to get in anyone else's business. Chuck would likely defend Christine to the death if he needed to, as she would for him, but Beck had never threatened either of them.

Next to the couple, I look at two of the newcomers—Wayne and Brian. As they had stated, they never even met Beck. I shake my head, annoyed that I'm not getting anywhere.

Turning my head to the left, Falk is sitting beside me. He's leaning back in his chair with an unlit cigarette in his hand, staring at the fire. His skin glows with reddish light, and his eyes sparkle with the reflection of the fire.

No—it couldn't have been Falk. Falk loves his guns. If he were going to kill Beck, he would have shot him.

Wouldn't he?

Caesar thinks Beck was killed late at night. Shooting a gun would have woken everyone up, and Falk is smarter than that. But strangling? I look toward the apartment, remembering the display of knives he has in the closet. No, he would have used a knife if not a gun.

Right?

The fire begins to die out, and I follow Falk to our apartment. Falk sits on the edge of the couch and places one of his many handguns on the coffee table. He starts taking it apart and cleaning each piece. I watch him for several minutes, pondering.

"Did you do it?"

"Do what?"

I glare at him. He's trying to give me an innocent look, but I'm not buying it. He knows exactly what I'm talking about, and he's being intentionally obtuse.

"Don't do that!"

"Hannah, I have no idea what you're talking about." He picks up pieces of the gun and starts to reassemble it.

I growl under my breath.

"Did you kill Beck?" I keep my voice low though there's no way anyone could have heard my question if they weren't inside the room.

"No." He doesn't even look up from his gun.

"Would you lie to me if you had?"

He sets the assembled gun back on the table, leans his elbows on his knees, and rubs his fingers into his eyes. I hear him sigh deeply before he looks at me.

"Yeah, I probably would," he says. "You've got enough shit on your mind. It doesn't matter though because I didn't do it."

I watch him closely, but there's nothing in his expression or posture that tells me whether or not I should believe him. His words ring true with me, and I let out a sigh.

"Okay," I say, "I believe you."

He snorts out a laugh and then stands to walk over to me. Before speaking, he reaches out and lightly touches both of my wrists with his fingertips.

"There is no way I would have left you alone last night." He runs his hands slowly from my wrists to my shoulders. "You were upset. Sometimes you have nightmares when you're upset. I wouldn't have left you."

I close my eyes and lean against him as the tension leaves my body.

"I'm sorry," I say quietly. "I didn't mean to accuse you of anything. I just…I don't know what to think of all this."

"I understand," Falk says. "I *was* pissed at him last night for getting in your face and harassing you."

"So, what do you think happened? Who would have killed him?"

"I think he pissed off most everyone," Falk says, "but to be completely honest, I don't care who killed him. If Caesar wants to

117

waste his time doing police work, well, he's welcome to do that. I wonder what the hell he's going to do if he tracks down the killer. It's not like we have any jail cells, and as far as I know, no one in our group is a judge."

"What would you do?" I ask.

"Exactly what I am doing," Falk replies as he steps back. "Nothing."

"You're all right with anarchy?"

"It's not a matter of political ideology," Falk says. "It's more about pragmatism. My focus is on survival and your safety. I don't have time to fuck around with the other shit. If someone came after you, they would have to answer to me. I wouldn't start by asking Caesar what the most law-abiding course of action might be."

"If I were threatened, would you kill over it?"

"If I had to, yes."

Chapter 9

Over the next few days, Caesar continues his investigation with no results. There are no signs of anyone outside our group having been in the area, and no one from the group arouses suspicions. Our little bunch seems to be of the same mind as Falk— just ignore that it happened.

And for the most part, it had gone away.

We'd buried Beck in the field just past the area where Falk took me for target practice. Everyone had attended the funeral, and Ryan and Caesar both said words over his grave. Afterward, on top of the dirt mound, Christine placed a ring of fall flowers she'd collected, and that had been the end of it.

Our group is now just the twelve of us.

I notice Caesar sitting near the fire, perusing his notepad. He closes his eyes and his shoulders slump. I look around quickly for Falk, but he had gone to the apartment for new batteries and must still be there. If he sees me talking to Caesar when he isn't around, he'll be pissed.

I close my eyes for a moment as my chest tightens up.

I can't keep doing this. I know Falk wants me to be careful, but I can't live with a group of people I'm not allowed to talk to. Falk is my bodyguard, not my father. I straighten my shoulders and pour the last of the coffee from the pot into a cup.

"Want some coffee?" I ask Caesar as I hold out the mug.

"Thanks." He takes the cup from my hand and takes a sip.

"Still trying to figure it out?" I gesture toward the notepad.

"Yeah, I guess so." He sighs. "I don't have the kind of resources I need to figure anything out. It's not like I can take fingerprints. I've had my share of unsolved cases, but here…well, there are only so many suspects. To top it all off, no one seems to give a shit."

"No one really knew him."

"*I* knew him." Caesar looks at me pointedly. "We'd been friends for years. Ryan knew him from when they were in the service together. I feel like I owe it to my brother to figure it out."

He looks up at me and darts his tongue across his lips.

"Is there anything else you know?" he asks. "Anything you didn't tell me already?"

"No." I shake my head emphatically. "I told you—I saw him in the shed before dinner. I didn't see him again after that."

"What happened in the shed?" He keeps staring at me, and my insides start to feel tight.

"Nothing, really," I say. "He was a little drunk. He kept asking me to tell him who I was."

"Did you?"

"No. I just got away and told him to leave me alone."

"Did you tell Falk?"

I hesitate, knowing immediately that it's a mistake to do so. I look in the direction of the apartment, and see Falk on the balcony, smoking. He's not looking in our direction, but he has likely seen us talking.

"Most of it," I finally say.

"How did he react?"

120

"He didn't do it," I blurt out. "I asked him, and he said he didn't."

"How long have you known Falk, huh?" Caesar asks. "You met him right before everything happened, right? Just another one of the guys on your security detail."

"He didn't lie to me," I say. "I trust him."

"Do you?"

I look back to the balcony, but Falk is no longer there. I catch a glimpse of him heading down the stairs, and my heart starts to beat faster.

"I've got to go," I say.

"Yeah, I'm sure you do." Caesar lets out a long breath. "Thanks for the coffee."

"You're welcome." I quickly head back to the kitchen area to prepare another pot of coffee. Falk is behind me a moment later.

"What did Caesar want?" he asks.

"I just took him some coffee." I set the pot over the grate near the coals.

"Answer the damn question, Hannah!" Falk wraps his fingers around my wrist and turns me around to face him. His grip is gentle, like it always is, but it's unexpected. For a moment, my body tenses, and in my mind there are other hands grasping my wrists. I bite my lip hard and glare at Falk.

"Just stop it!" I yank my wrist out of his hand and step back. "Falk, you can't keep doing this!"

"Doing what?"

"This!" I throw my hands up into the air and turn away from him. "You can't keep treating me like this!"

I glance behind Falk and see Caesar eyeing us. I growl under my breath, grab Falk by the hand, and haul him back to the apartment. Once inside, I stalk over to the far side of the living room and turn on him.

"This is all bad enough as it is," I say. "We still have no idea what's going on. You're still claiming it was aliens, for fuck's sake, and I can't live what life I have here if you're going to get on my ass for talking to other people!"

"You don't know anything about them," Falk say. "I'm only trying to—"

"I know, I know," I say, interrupting. "You are just trying to keep me safe, but there isn't much point in being safe if I can't act like a normal person!"

"This is far from a normal situation," Falk argues. "For that matter, you aren't a normal person anyway."

"What the hell does that mean?"

"Are you forgetting the fact that you've been hunted for months? There is a reason I was hired, you know."

"Seriously?" I stare at him with an open mouth. "You think I'd forget about that? I haven't forgotten, Falk. It just doesn't seem to matter a whole lot now!"

"If Tyler Hudson walked in here right now, would you still feel that way?"

I can't respond immediately. He's put the mental image in my head, and I can't help but let it play out. Falk and I arguing over my safety, the door opening, and Hudson being there with a gun pointed at my head. Falk wouldn't even have time to react before he pulled the trigger.

"That's not going to happen," I say softly. "Even you said he was dead."

"He's *probably* dead," Falk says, correcting me. "I still stand by that, but he had a lot of people on his payroll."

"And you think they're lurking around here?"

"I would be."

His words send a chill through me.

"What are you saying?"

Falk mumbles something under his breath, but I don't catch the words. With an exaggerated sigh, he drops down on the couch and leans his forearms on his knees.

"There were reports of people in his employ in the area," Falk says. "That's why you had six guards waiting for you instead of four. I think they were going to try to grab you at the airport."

I gasp. I always knew there was a possibility that they were coming after me, but no one had ever been caught in the act. Paxton and his uncompromising insistence on top-notch security had made sure of that.

"If the information I received was correct, there was more than one of them, too. If they were nearby when all the shit went down, they could have survived the same way we did. They could be in the area. They could even already be a part of this little camp."

"Why didn't you tell me?"

"I thought you had enough on your mind."

I cover my face with my hands. In some ways, he's right—there's more going on in my head than I know what to do with.

"I don't like being kept in the dark, Falk."

"It's enough that I know," he says. "Telling you that information only would have frightened you. I know you're a strong person, but I also know you can only take so much. I want you always thinking clearly, and that's hard to do if you're constantly watching over your shoulder. That's why I'm here—to watch over your shoulder for you."

"You mean 'to be paranoid.'"

"Call it what you want."

"I have to be able to talk to people, Falk." I want to be able to think and talk about this rationally, but the image of Hudson coming through the door keeps replaying in my mind. "I know you want me close to you all the time, and I can put up with a certain amount of that, but you can't stop me from talking to the other people here."

"How did your last talk with Beck go, huh?"

"That's not the point."

"That is exactly the point!" Falk yells, and I jump, taking a step back. Falk points a finger at me. "He was dangerous. You

123

know it and I know it. He had you cornered in the shed, and god knows what he would have done to you."

"How did you know that?" I ask. "I didn't tell you he cornered me."

"I figured it out."

"How?"

"Because you only react that way when someone's touched you!" Falk runs his hand through his hair and turns away, his jaw tight. "The shed isn't that big. I knew he'd grabbed you, and that could only have happened if you were cornered. Fuck, Hannah—it was hours later, and you were still shaken up. Are you going to tell me I'm wrong?"

He doesn't look at me as he speaks, and Caesar's words echo in my head. Do I really know Falk any better than the rest of the people here? Do I trust him?

"I have to be able to talk to people," I say again. "Unless you have something that points to one of the people here being connected to Hudson, you have to let me act like a person, and people need people. You're isolating me, Falk."

"That isn't my intent."

"But that's what's happening."

He leans back on the couch for a moment and stares toward the balcony door before he stands again, heading to the kitchen drawer where he keeps a pack of cigarettes.

"Come outside with me?" he asks.

I nod and follow him to the balcony. He lights up and leans his elbows against the rail, slowly drawing the smoke into his lungs.

"I was married," Falk suddenly blurts out.

"What?"

He closes his eyes and drops his head down so his chin is nearly touching his chest. I watch his shoulders rise and fall with a deep breath.

"Right out of high school," he says quietly. "She was two years older than me, but I'd just graduated. My parents…well, they thought we were nuts, but when you're eighteen, you know everything, right?"

He looks up at me with pleading eyes. I can only nod in response.

"We'd only been married a year," he says, continuing. "Had our anniversary the month before. I came home from work—I was flipping burgers and had to close that night—and I found her."

His body stills, and he doesn't speak again for a long time. I hold my breath, waiting, but I already know what's to come.

"The police said it was a random burglary, and I guess they were probably right. She'd been shot right in the chest. If I had been there..."

He squeezes his eyes shut again.

"Maybe," he whispers, "if I was there, I could have saved her."

"Falk..." My voice trails off. I don't know what to say.

"I can't..." He shakes his head slowly as I walk over and place my hand over his on the railing. "I can't let that happen to you, Hannah. I can't let someone get to you just because I'm not there."

"I'm sorry," I finally manage to say. "That had to have been awful."

"Yeah." He takes another long drag off the cigarette. "I enlisted right after that. Deployed right after training. It was a good distraction."

He turns his head and looks at me.

"I won't let my guard down, Hannah. Talk to people if you have to, but I'm going to be there all the time. I already let you out of my sight once. I can't fail like that again."

"I understand," I say, "and you know how much I appreciate what you're doing for me. You don't have to do any of it. It's not like you're still getting paid."

"Not sure the cash would help much right now."

"True, but still—you aren't *obligated*."

"Yes," he says simply, "I am."

~~~~~

True to his word, Falk remains at my side. He hasn't given me any shit about talking to other people and at least seems to be okay with me talking to Christine and Chuck even when he's more than ten feet away.

He's even started helping prepare meals just to stay close to me. Though he had been working hard on getting the freshwater well dug, he seems to have left the task to the other men.

"Have you ever even been inside a kitchen before?" Christine asks.

"What did I do now?" Falk drops the spoon he's holding right into the pot of vegetables, beans, and chilies. It sinks into the mixture, and Christine shoves him out of the way.

"You have to keep stirring it, or it's going to stick and get burned!"

Falk looks to me with pleading eyes, but I hold up my hands and shake my head. I'm not getting into the middle of this. The man may have been in combat, but he has nothing on the kitchen queen.

"Go get the tortillas from the fire!" she orders as she fishes the utensil from the pot.

I snicker as Falk grabs some tongs and tries to get the tortillas out one at a time without putting holes in them.

"It's a good thing you can cook," Christine says to me. "If things ever get back to normal around here, you'd starve if he was left in charge."

"He did fend for himself for several years, I believe."

"I bet he lived off carry-out and microwavable pizzas."

I have no idea, so I don't argue the point. I start gathering up plates and forks for dinner as Caesar, Brett, Ryan, Chuck, and most of the rest of the guys file out of the woods with their arms full of firewood.

126

"Smells good!" Chuck calls out as he drops a bunch of logs near the open fire. "We just need some margaritas to go with it!"

"There's rum in the shed," Ryan says.

"Close enough!"

Chuck mixes rum with a large can of pineapple juice, which works quite well. I've never been much of a drinker, but his concoction is pretty tasty. Even Falk has a small cup of the drink.

Christine has become more creative with the cooking, and the Mexican tortillas filled with canned vegetables and black beans are delicious. I'm not sure how she seasons them, but it works. It would have been nice to have some cheese sprinkled on them, but dairy products are pretty much gone now.

Christine continues to order Falk around after dinner as I move to the other side of the fire to sit. Though my leg has pretty much healed, it sometimes gets sore when I stand for too long, and I need a break. I find an empty lawn chair near the shed and back away from the fire. There's less wind here, and I'm tired of the smoke getting in my eyes.

Brett grabs a chair nearby and yanks it over so he can sit facing me.

I haven't spoken to Brett very much. I've noticed him with Caesar quite often, and he has a similar bearing. I once asked if he was also in law enforcement of some kind, but he said he had been working in manufacturing.

"You made the potatoes?" he asks. "They were damn good."

"It was actually cauliflower," I tell him. "Seasoned like mashed potatoes but supposedly better for you. They end up tasting about the same."

"Well, it was damn good, whatever it was. Not sure about that other stuff. It didn't taste like anything Mexican I've had before."

"What have you had before?"

"Taco Bell!"

We both laugh, and Brett offers me a drink from the flask he has in his pocket. I glance at Falk, knowing he won't approve, though he also won't say anything about it. He had lightened up quite a bit after our chat a few nights ago. He's not looking in my direction, but I decide to decline anyway.

"Suit yourself," Brett says as he takes a good swig.

"I was never much for scotch," I admit. "Martinis are more my style, but they're a little more complicated than just opening the bottle."

"All the complicated parts of scotch are done before it ever gets into a bottle," Brett says. "Caesar knows his scotch. He's picked up some good stuff on supply runs. It helps relieve some of the tension."

"I'm sure that's true."

"It's a little tense around here, ya know?" Brett leans forward and rests his forearms on his knees as he looks up at me with a toothy smile.

"What do you mean?" I ask.

"You know." He grins wider. "All these guys, one single chick. You realize you're quite the topic of discussion when you're not around."

The friendly chat we have been having feels abruptly different to me. I sit up a little straighter to shift my chair away, but Brett just scoots his closer. Our knees are almost touching. I swallow and grasp my upper arms with my hands.

"So, how many people here know who you really are, Hannah Savinski?"

My muscles flex, and I push back against the chair. I can feel my throat tightening up, and I glance around to see where Falk is, but he's no longer next to Christine. It's dark enough that I can't find him right away. He was here just a few minutes ago, so I know he's not far.

"I don't know what you mean."

"It's all right, babe." Brett continues to smile at me. "I won't give ya away. I'm surprised people haven't figured it out."

"They have a lot of other things on their minds."

"Still, that's a gutsy thing you did. Powerful people to go up against."

I nod. I'm not at all relaxed by his declaration to keep my identity to himself. Everything about his posture makes me think he wants something else.

"Your face was all over television in Chicago," he says with a smile. "I mean, Archive Industries is big business all over the country, ya know?"

"Um...yeah, I know." His words are increasing my discomfort. I've only talked to Falk about my past since the attacks, and he doesn't tend to ask a lot of questions.

"You were all ready to testify in front of all those government types, right?"

"Something like that," I mumble.

"Did you get a lot of names?" he asks. "Like, the other people Hudson worked with?"

I don't like where this is going at all. He sounds like someone from the media, and I wonder if he really was in manufacturing work before.

"I really don't want to talk about it," I tell him.

"Oh right," he says, his head bobbing up and down. "Yeah, yeah. Sure. I just wanted you to know you could if you wanted to."

"I don't."

"It had to have been rough on you."

I look at him sternly, annoyed more than anything now, and he seems to get the idea.

"It's okay," he says with another toothy grin. He leans forward and lays his hand on my knee. "I'll shut up about it now."

His grip tightens for a moment before he slides his hand up my leg. I can't move. My vision blurs. For a moment, I'm transported back to that van, and I feel the tight grip of fingers around my legs as they're held in place.

"Just remember, if you start getting a little tense, I'm right here for ya." He slides his hand a little further up my thigh and grips my flesh with his fingers.

Everything happens so fast.

One moment, Brett has his hand on my leg, and the next, he's flung backwards. The chair tips along with him, and Falk is on top of him, slamming a fist into his face. I jump out of my chair, yelling at Falk to stop, but he doesn't pay any attention to me.

Brett grabs hold of Falk's forearms, and the two of them roll. For a brief moment, Brett is on top, but Falk quickly jabs a fist into his side, and they roll again. I jump backward and end up against the wall of the shed.

At that point, everyone has heard the commotion, and they all run toward the fight. Falk is still hitting Brett in the chest and face, and Brett is punching Falk in the side, screaming at him to get off.

Caesar makes a grab for Falk, pulling him off of Brett and to the side. He tries to get a grip around Falk's arms to hold him back, but Falk shoves him away. As Caesar regains his balance, Falk draws the gun at his waist and points it right in Caesar's face.

"Back off." Falk's voice is perfectly calm though his eyes are wide and full of fury. He's taught me enough about guns to see that he's flicked off the safety.

"What the fuck is wrong with you!" Caesar yells. "Put that damn thing away before someone gets hurt!"

"*He* is going to get hurt," Falk says, pointing the gun to a supine Brett. "He is going to get a bullet in his fucking skull if he ever touches her again!"

"Falk! Stop!" I yell, but he keeps his eyes on Brett.

Both of them are breathing heavily. Brett places his hands behind himself on the ground and stands slowly, holding his arms out in surrender.

"I don't know what the hell is up, buddy," he says, "but I was just talking to the lady."

"Keep your fucking hands off of her," Falk says through his teeth.

Caesar steps slowly away from Falk and goes to Brett. He grabs the man by the arm and starts to drag him away. Falk lowers his weapon but steps up to Brett, causing Caesar to stop. Falk stares down into Brett's face.

"She is *mine!*" Falk growls at him.

Caesar's eyes widen as he pulls Brett away from Falk. There's blood running down Brett's face from a gash near his temple, and his lip is busted open as well.

My back is still pressed against the wall of the shed. I try to take it all in—Brett's bleeding face, Caesar's efforts to intervene, and Falk's outlandish behavior. Falk stalks toward me, his eyes blazing. He slams one hand on the wall right next to me.

"You are mine," he says gruffly. He raises his other hand and cups my cheek, tilting my head to look at him.

His eyes are bright, and he looks down at me with uncharacteristic emotion. I can feel the tension in his fingertips as they stroke slowly over my cheek. I watch his tongue dart out and moisten his lips just before he presses them firmly against mine.

I gasp against his mouth and clench my fingers around the hem of his shirt.

Despite the manner in which he approached me, his lips are soft and gentle against mine, and his fingers slowly caress the side of my face. The firm muscles in his chest are pressed against my body, and I feel the strength of his arms in every touch.

His tongue runs over my bottom lip before he pulls back, panting. He touches his forehead against mine, keeping his eyes closed. There's a scrape under his eye, but it's not bleeding. I can only barely make it out in the firelight. He turns his head slowly, placing his mouth near my ear.

131

"I swore to protect you," he whispers. His breath is hot on my neck. "In these circumstances, that makes you mine. The only way I can protect you from people like him is to lay claim to you."

I look into his deep blue eyes, wondering where my panic has gone. I should be freaking out. I should be screaming and pushing him away. I shouldn't be hoping he'll kiss me again.

"Falk..."

"I'd never hurt you, Hannah." His breath feels hot on my neck, sending shivers through my skin. "I'd never, ever force you. I know what you've been through. I wouldn't do that to you. But this…this is the only way I can keep you safe."

I'm dizzy. His words are only barely making it deep enough into my consciousness for me to understand what he means. All I can think about is the heat of his body next to mine, and the feeling of his lips on my mouth.

"Come with me now," he whispers. "Come back to the apartment with me. They're all going to see it, and they're all going to know you're mine. It's the only way to keep them all off of you."

My mind is still racing. I know I'm not thinking clearly, but everything Falk says makes sense. Brett said they've all been talking about me, and I believe him. If they think I'm with Falk, they'll leave me alone.

"Okay," I say softly. My voice is trembling.

"When we get there, nothing's changed," he says.

But it has, Falk. It changed as soon as you put your lips on mine.

"Right," I say.

He slips his hand from my cheek, down my arm, and grips my hand in his. He takes a short step back, his eyes never leaving my face, and turns to let me go first. He takes his usual stance to my right and slightly behind me, moving his hand to the small of my back.

I can feel everyone's eyes on us as we walk slowly toward the building, up the stairs, and into the apartment. Before the door closes completely, I can hear their murmured words.

"I'm sorry, Hannah," Falk says as soon as we're inside. "I'm sorry I grabbed you like that and...and everything else. I had to think fast. I had to put a stop to all of this, and it was the first thing that came to mind."

"It's okay." I back away from him. Now that I'm here and away from everyone else, I should be able to think rationally again. "But Brett...Jesus, Falk, what were you thinking?"

"I didn't see it fast enough." The tone of his voice goes up a notch. "I should have been paying closer attention. I saw him sit next to you, and I was going to come over there, but Christine distracted me, and when I looked again, he had his hand on your thigh, and you were pushing back, but you didn't have anywhere to go."

He stops speaking and stares at me.

"I snapped." His shoulders slump, and he rubs the scrape below his eye. "I snapped when I saw that, but I'm not sorry about it."

"You pointed a gun at Caesar."

"He shouldn't have gotten involved."

Chapter 10

I lay in bed as the events of the evening play over and over again in my mind. Brett's words and touch made my skin crawl, but Falk's reaction bordered on the insane. I know how much he wants to protect me and keep me safe, but what he did was completely uncalled for.

I'd fought in self-defense when I was attacked, but this isn't the same. Yes, Brett had touched me. I didn't like it, and I'm ultimately glad Falk put an end to it, but I can't agree with how he did it. Would he have shot Brett or Caesar? How far would he go to protect me?

I shudder at the thought. Circumstances aside, I'm not a violent person. Before now, I hadn't thought Falk was, either. Now I am not so sure, and my previous conversation with Caesar flows through my mind. Do I trust Falk? *Should* I trust him? Yes, he seems to have my best interests at heart, but do I know that for sure? Before meeting in the airport, I didn't know he existed.

I bring my fingers to my lips, reliving the memory of his mouth on mine. He was angry—enraged enough to pull a gun—yet he had been gentle with me. He explained why he did it and even apologized.

When I had been in college, my roommate dated a guy from her hometown. Every time she went home and visited him, she would come back with bruises. She made excuses for him—told me how he had just had a little too much to drink or that he was stressed about finals. She said he was sorry for what he had done.

Isn't that what abusive men do? Apologize after acting violently?

I take a long breath. This isn't the same at all. Falk hadn't done anything to me. In fact, everything he had done was in order to keep me safe.

I hear Falk enter the dark room and slide into bed beside me. I don't turn over to look at him but listen to his breathing as he settles behind me. I'm more aware of his body near mine than I have ever been, and I close my eyes, wishing I could just start the whole day over again.

"Hannah?" he whispers. "Are you awake?"

"Yes."

I feel his hand under the blanket, creeping around my waist the same way he did every night—protective, warm, and comforting.

"I'm sorry," he says quietly. "I'm sorry I…that I kissed you like that. I shouldn't have done that."

"The kiss didn't bother me."

"It didn't?"

"No."

"You want to tell me why you're still so angry?"

I turn my head to look at him, and it's obvious he has no idea.

"You pulled a gun, Falk. Remember what you said to me when you were first teaching me how to shoot? You said I should never draw a gun and point it at someone unless I intended to use it. Do you remember that?"

"Of course I remember."

"Were you going to shoot Caesar?"

He hesitates, pulling his hand back from my stomach and resting it on my side.

"Only if he tried to stop me," Falk says, "or if he tried to hurt you."

"Caesar wasn't involved. He wasn't going to hurt me."

"I can't be sure of that. He and Brett are friends."

"Brett has only been here for a couple of weeks."

"And they're still close," Falk says. "They know each other from before, but they haven't told anyone that."

"How do you know?"

"I'm a very good judge of character," Falk replies. "People who have known each other for a long time act differently than people who have just met. They stand closer to each other. They speak more casually. Caesar and Brett were like that as soon as we got back to camp that first night, and yet they made a show of introducing themselves when he and I met up with that group."

"Why wouldn't they just admit that they knew each other?"

"Exactly," Falk says. "Why wouldn't they? Questionable actions make me question motivation."

"You think they're hiding something?"

"I know they are."

"What?" I roll over to face him. "What would they hide from us?"

"I have no idea," he says. "They're pretty careful when they talk to one another, which is also suspicious."

I think about it for a minute.

"That's still no reason to pull a gun on him."

"If I don't know someone's motives, I'm going to err on the side of caution," Falk says, "especially when it comes to your safety. Brett attacked you."

"He only touched me."

"He grabbed your leg. You obviously didn't like it, and he obviously didn't care. He was trying to intimidate you, Hannah. That was clear."

"I'm sure he won't try that again." I grumble the words as I look away from Falk.

"No, he won't. That was rather the point."

"Your point was overstated." I roll back to my side, facing away from him.

"You didn't tell me what he said to you." Falk leans over, peering down at me.

"Nothing important," I mumble.

"He was coming on to you."

"Yeah, I guess so. He was drinking, so—"

"So, you're going to make excuses for him?" Falk reaches over and places his hand on the side of my face, turning my head to look at him. "Do I need to come out and state the obvious?"

I glance away, but he keeps his hand on my face.

"Guys are assholes, Hannah," he says. "You know this better than most. When we want a girl, we tend to go after her. We don't usually think about how you might feel about our actions unless it's made abundantly clear. I just made that clear to him."

"You claimed me."

"Yeah, I did." Falk huffs out a breath and releases my face before rolling to his back. "Guys are like any animal out there. We fight for food, territory, and mates. Put us in a situation like this, and the fight comes out a lot more often and a lot more bloody."

"So, you're all cavemen?"

"Pretty much."

"And you're going to squabble over who gets to put a baby in me?"

He looks at me darkly.

"Essentially, yes."

"Do you know how ridiculous you sound?"

"Do you realize how right I am?" He sits up in the bed and turns to face me. "I'm not kidding, here. Our minds might not actually form those words, but that's exactly what we're after. Every guy in this camp, with the possible exception of Chuck since he already has a mate, wants to fuck you. At some point, they're going to try to act on that desire, that need. You can refuse, and some of them will respect that for a while. As time goes by, fewer and fewer are going to listen to your wishes."

I swallow hard.

"You aren't making me feel better."

"I'm not trying to make you feel better," he says. "I want you to see this for what it is. I want you to understand why I did what I did."

"You made yourself the alpha in the pack. Only the alpha gets a mate."

I can't look at him when I say the words.

"I wouldn't…I'm not going to…"

"Why not?" I snap at him. My stomach clenches and my body heats up as I clench my teeth. Part of me wishes I had never asked Falk any questions—that I would have been better off not knowing or thinking about how the men in the group might see me. "Are you saying you aren't like the other guys? You don't want to fuck me?"

He flinches at my words. I'm not even sure why I'm angry—whether it's the idea that I should look at every guy in our community as a threat or that Falk doesn't want me at all.

He looks at me, obviously confused by my words. I can't blame him—I don't know what's going through my head either. First he says they all want me, and then he says he wouldn't do that to me. Rejection is outweighing relief, and I feel my eyes starting to burn.

Falk reaches over and touches my temple with the tips of his fingers, slowly pushing my hair away from my forehead. He strokes down my cheek and across my jaw. It feels electric as my skin tingles and my heart pounds in my chest.

"I've wanted you since the day I laid eyes on you."

I stop breathing and lean into his touch, my body reacting to him as if it were on autopilot. The feeling of his fingers on my skin ripples through the rest of my flesh.

"I wasn't the only one around then."

"No, you weren't. That has nothing to do with it. I want *you*."

My heart pounds and my pussy throbs at his words. I'm breathing rapidly, and I see that his chest is rising and falling quickly as well. His eyes are cast in shadow, but his dark look is still visible.

Leaning forward, I press my lips to his. He slides his hand off my face, over my shoulder, and down my arm as I reach up and wrap my hand around the back of his head. I twist strands of his hair between my fingers as I pull him closer to me, turning my head and opening my mouth to him.

I feel his hand on my waist, but it's not what I want. I reach down, cover his hand with mine, and move it up, so he's cupping my breast with his palm. He grips the soft flesh through the material of my nightshirt and runs his thumb over my nipple as his tongue slides against mine.

His lips are so warm and gentle, his tongue soft in my mouth. He runs his hand up my back, cradling my head as he turns his, kissing me deeper. It's not enough. I want more.

I don't know what I'm feeling—anger or lust. I just know that I want him.

I reach down, my hand running from his hip to his thigh, then around to the front. I trace my fingers over him, feeling the heat of his hard shaft pressing against my palm as he groans into my mouth. Sliding my hand under the band of his shorts, I wrap my fingers around his shaft. It feels hot as it flexes in my grip.

"God, Hannah…stop. Please, stop." Falk pulls back, and I look to his tense face as he squeezes his eyes shut. "I can't…not now."

"Why? What's wrong?" Slowly, I remove my fingers from his cock and out of his shorts. I don't know what to do with my hand now, so I just bring it up to my chest.

"I'm so worked up right now…" He moves his hand away from my breast, sliding it down to my stomach where he makes a fist. "I'm still pissed off. I can't right now. If I did…well, I don't think I could control myself."

"You don't have to."

"Yes," he says, "I do."

He closes his eyes again, his expression pained.

"I might not hold back. I could be too rough. I can't do that to you, Hannah. I can't take that kind of risk, not with you. If I did something…triggered some memory…"

"It wouldn't be like that," I insist. "I know the difference between what happened to me and…and *this*."

"I realize." He runs his hand over his face. "I still can't take that chance."

"I want you to." My voice sounds small and unsure. It's not like I've never been turned down before, but this feels different.

"You have no idea how glad I am to hear you say that," Falk says, "but no. Not now. Not yet. I need time. I need to figure out how to make it perfect."

He places his palm against my cheek.

"You give me a sign tomorrow night," he says. "Any sign at all. Assuming I haven't drawn a weapon within the hour, I will have you up here so fast, your feet may not touch the stairs."

I smile, the tension broken.

"Are you okay with that?" He strokes my cheek again.

"Yes," I say with a nod.

"You sure?"

"Yes, your terms are acceptable," I say, smiling at him. "Really, it's fine. I think I'm more snuggle-horny anyway."

"You're *what*?"

"You know…in the mood for kissing and cuddling."

"It's only cuddling if you have a hard-on," Falk mumbles.

"What?" I laugh, and he grins back at me.

"When I was in the infantry, it was acceptable to wrap up in your woobie and spoon with another guy when you were out on patrol. Body heat and protection, you know. Spooning is fine, but cuddling isn't. The difference is whether or not you have a hard-on."

I blink a few times.

"Did you just say 'woobie'?"

"Yeah."

"You mean, like a security blanket?"

Falk narrows his eyes.

"Don't make fun of my woobie."

I bite my lip, trying not to laugh. The mental image of Falk—muscled, armed, alpha Falk—holding a bright blue blanket with his thumb in his mouth won't leave my head. I can't help it. I laugh out loud.

"Do you still have it?"

"Of course I do." He pushes back and climbs out of the bed, fumbles in the dark of his closet for a moment, and then comes back with a camouflage blanket. He holds it up near the light of the lantern and grins. "My woobie."

"Holy shit!" I sit up and take the edge of it in my hands. The material feels light but sturdy and warm. "You really do have one!"

"It's perfect," he says. "It's lightweight, warm, and you can roll it up really small, so it even fits in a pocket if you do it right."

"So, you would wrap up in this?"

"Yep." He holds it out and pulls it around his back so it's covering his shoulders. Then he lies down behind me, wraps an arm

142

around my waist to pull me back to his chest, and coils the edge of the woobie around the rest of my body. "Pretty nice, isn't it?"

"Yeah, it is." I press my back against him and tilt my head to the side as he presses his lips to my neck.

"You're not going to knock the woobie ever again, are you?"

"Never," I say, turning to meet his lips while holding in my giggles. "I understand now."

"You'll never fully understand the power of the woobie," he says with a shake of his head, "but you have a better idea now."

His eyes glisten with humor, but I can still see something deeper inside them. I'm not sure if he's remembering something from long ago or not. I reach out and touch the side of his face, stroking my fingers across his stubbled jaw. Falk drops his gaze and moistens his lips with his tongue.

"All that shit I said before…about how those guys think of you…I'm not going to let that happen."

I nod, wanting to believe him, but I must not be very convincing. He cups my chin and brings his lips to mine briefly.

"I mean it. I won't let them touch you."

"I know you won't." I believe the words as I say them, but I also know he can't protect me from everything. "I think you probably ought to take me out for more shooting lessons though."

"I will," he promises. "You should probably start carrying a gun on you."

I take a deep breath and let it out again. If I were to be armed, he would definitely feel better about it.

"Your life would be a lot easier if you didn't have me to worry about," I say.

"Maybe." He shrugs. "It wouldn't be quite as interesting though."

"I bet you wish you never took this job."

"On the contrary," Falk says, "this job has probably saved me."

~~~~~~~

"There just isn't anything of value left there."

Falk sighs and fiddles with the unlit cigarette in his hand as Caesar pokes at his notepad with the back end of his pen.

"We're low on D-cell batteries, coffee, and canned food in general. We need more paper products as well. We've completely cleaned out the nearest stores of all those things."

"We're going to have to trek farther," Falk says. "Avondale has a Wal-Mart. We should start there. It's only a few miles."

"We should take a larger group," Caesar says. "We need as many people as possible to bring back more supplies."

"Where the fuck is the engineer?" Chuck mutters.

"What engineer?" Caesar asks, turning to him.

"In every zombie movie I've ever seen, there was always one dude who was a brainiac. He'd be working on some solar powered car or something by now. Where the hell is that guy in this group?"

"I guess we're not that lucky," Falk says. "You do make a good point though. Emory might have solar cells that survived the destruction, and it would be worth the hassle of bringing them back if we could get them to work."

"We should search through the Emory area more," Caesar agrees. "Beck spoke about that at one point. Said there were a lot of things that could help us out there—if they're still operable."

Everyone is quiet for a moment at the mention of Beck's name.

"Better transportation is something we should be working on," Falk finally says to end the silence. "I don't have any engineering experience though. We should think about other ways to mod the bicycles. There are also plenty of shopping carts to carry things back, but with either one of those, you still have to rely on human power."

"What if we worked out some kind of rail system?" Marco suggests. "Something that goes back and forth between the stores?"

144

"Too temporary," Falk says. "As soon as that store is emptied, the rail would be useless. That would be very labor intensive, too."

"If there were still horses around, we could use them," Sam pipes up.

"But there aren't," Marco snaps back at him, "so stop making stupid suggestions!"

"Hey! I'm the one that figured out where to dig the well!" Sam yells back at his brother.

"Enough." Caesar stands and stretches his back. "It's getting later as we go on about it. Let's at least start heading to that Wal-Mart and discuss other options on the way."

"Who's going and who's staying?" Chuck asks.

"Everyone who can go should," Caesar says. "If Christine and Hannah can stay behind and keep everything going here, the rest of us should go."

"We'll just hang out and do dishes, right?" I roll my eyes.

"I'm not leaving them here unprotected," Falk says. There is no room for argument in his tone. "I'll stay. I want to keep working on the well since fresh water is going to become our first major problem. If I can make decent progress today, we should be able to get it working by the end of the week."

Brett mumbles something under his breath, and Falk shoots him a sharp look.

"You have something to say to me?" Falk asks. His voice sounds calm, but I know better.

"Brett, you're coming with me," Caesar says, effectively ending the conversation. "Falk can stay and make sure nothing happens here. Wayne can stay as well since he knows more about wells than anyone else."

"Suits me," Wayne replies. "In case you were actually going to ask."

"I know you don't travel well," Caesar says gently. "I still can't believe you made it all the way to us."

"Didn't have much choice at the time." Wayne glances over at Falk. "Not sure it was a wise choice though."

Falk doesn't acknowledge the look. It's clear that Wayne isn't too happy with Falk since his run-in with Brett last night. Owen and Brian seem to share the same feelings though I can't really blame them. One thing is for sure—Falk's plan worked. Brett hasn't come near me all day, and most of the others are keeping their distance.

I'm glad for it, too. I've thought a lot about what Falk said, and I can't deny that it makes sense. Without any kind of social order, people are going to argue over fulfilling their basic needs. I'm far more aware of how the men look at me today, and I can't help but wonder exactly what they are thinking.

I'm afraid I know.

As the others head off in search of supplies, Falk continues working on the well. Wayne is far off to the side of the common area, not far from the well, though he doesn't offer to help Falk. He's got a long coil of rope that he's been knotting to use with the well's bucket.

The day goes by, and the temperature rises. Falk's been working on the well non-stop, so I pour a large cup of water to take to him. As I walk up to the hole, Falk is climbing out of it, covered in mud.

"How's it coming along?" I ask.

"Getting there," he says. "The bottom is full of water, at least."

"That's the idea."

"At least it's fresh and clean."

Falk tosses his hair out of his eyes, but it falls right back over his forehead. He pushes it away with his hand, obviously annoyed.

"Your hair is getting long," I say.

"It's driving me nuts." He pushes it away again. "I need to do something with it."

"Want me to cut it for you?"

146

"All I've got are those electric trimmers," Falk says.

"Christine has hair scissors," I tell him. "I can get those from her."

"You know how to use those?"

"I've been known to cut hair every once in a while." I smile at him.

He looks up at me, runs his hand over the top of his head, and nods.

"Yeah. All right. I need a break anyway."

Falk gets situated by the cooking fire, and I borrow Christine's scissors. Falk's hair really isn't all that long, but when I first met him, it had been very closely cut in standard military fashion. I've never attempted to do a flattop before, and I'm not sure if I can without trimmers, but I'm willing to give it a shot.

I smooth out the towel around his shoulders and go to work. The top is easy enough to get to the right length and doesn't take long. The back and sides are a little harder to get even, but it turns out pretty well by the time I'm done. I run my hand up the back of his head. It feels like a puppy's fur.

"Having fun?" Falk peers up at me with a half grin.

"I like the way it feels," I say with a shrug. "I'm all done. Want to take a look?"

He holds up the hand mirror and turns his head back and forth.

"Pretty good job," he says. "Should I tip you?"

"You can tip me later," I say with a wink.

His eyes go dark and he licks his lips.

"I'll make note of that," he says softly.

I reach out once more, stroking my fingers through the short hair at the side of his head. He leans into my hand for a moment before pressing his lips to my palm.

"I should get back to work." He stands and takes the towel from his shoulders. "Hopefully, they're going to bring back a lot of

147

water jugs, but we're still going to need this, especially when it gets cold."

Falk goes back to the well, and I go back to the apartment to gather up trash and burn it in the fire. It's nearly nightfall before everyone else returns, armed with grocery carts full of supplies. They have a good load, water included, but they cleaned out the place in one trip.

"We're going to have to venture farther for the next run," Caesar informs us. "One way or another, we're going to need better transportation."

"I ran up to the university while they went shopping," Brett says. "I did find what I think are solar cells, at least as far as I can tell. I'm not sure exactly how to use them, but maybe we can figure it out."

"There have to be some kind of diagrams or instructions, maybe in the library."

"I'm not even sure I could figure out where the library used to be," Brett says.

"I also doubt the card catalog will be a whole lot of use," Wayne says.

"Do they even have those anymore?" Caesar asks.

"What the fuck is a *card catalog*?" Brian asks with a shake of his head.

Everyone starts to take items out of the carts to get them distributed. I notice how well everyone in our small group seems to share what's been found, and I wonder how long that will continue. Will everyone be just as friendly with one another when the supplies run low?

Christine starts sorting through the canned goods while I organize the paper towels, napkins, paper plates, and toilet paper in the shed. I'm glad to see plenty of toilet paper was found since that is one thing I really don't want to run out of.

"Gonna run this stuff over by the fire," Christine says as she heads off.

I see a flash of light, calling my attention to Falk, who must have found a fresh supply of cigarettes. He leans against a nearby tree, smoking and watching me. The mud from his earlier work on the well is gone, and he looks freshly shaven, too. The sight of him sends tingles down my spine.

I lick my lips, remembering that all I have to do is give him a sign—any sign—and he is going to take me back to that apartment. The thought heats my skin and causes my thighs to clench.

I continue loading paper products into the shed, placing the things I always seem to need on the lower shelves so I don't have to drag out the stool. After unloading the last of the supplies, I step out and lean against the shed for a moment, staring into the night sky.

It's peaceful and quiet. I close my eyes and breathe in the night air, wondering how long it stays warm in Atlanta in the fall. By now, Chicago would have had its first dusting of snow, but it's quite warm and pleasant here.

As I open my eyes, a flash of bright light catches my eye. At first, I think it's Falk lighting another cigarette, causing some strange reflection up in the trees, but I quickly see that it's not.

"Falk!"

"What is it?" He heads in my direction.

"Do you see that?" I point up in the sky.

The light is brighter now, and it moves slowly across the sky. My heart beats faster as I wonder what it is. If it's a plane, that means someone is out there, rebuilding our lives. It could mean that everyone has been wrong this whole time, and the problems were isolated to this area.

Everyone else starts to gather around, shielding their eyes from the firelight and staring up into the sky.

The light suddenly turns and brightens in the sky. It looms closer, appears to grow larger, and a strange, hexagon-shaped craft suddenly glows bright orange before it zooms off to the north.

I feel my stomach drop as my breath catches in my throat. The craft continues to glow and pulse rapidly until it disappears into the night sky. Falk's arm slips around my waist right before my knees almost give out on me. He pulls me close to his side and keeps me from falling as he whispers in my ear.

"Do you still doubt me?"

Chapter 11

For the next several minutes, we all stare into the sky as similar lights appear. There isn't a pattern, and there is never more than one light in the sky at a time, but there is no longer any question about what we are facing. Falk has been right all along. We've been invaded by something extraterrestrial.

There is no sound accompanying the lights—only the occasional change in color from amber to bright orange as the craft shifts direction. As we all stand there, dumbfounded, one of the lights glows brightly and moves closer.

I can see it better now. The shape isn't quite a hexagon—it's longer on two of the sides with a point in the front. There's something jutting out from the back of it, but I can't guess what it might be. As it descends, I can see where the bright glow comes from two long strips of light running along the longer sides.

"Get the fire out!" Falk suddenly screams. He rushes from my side, grabs the huge pot of stew Christine had made for dinner, and dumps it over the burning logs. "Get it out completely! Hurry, goddammit!"

Everyone runs for water, pouring what we can find nearby over the flames. Falk runs off in the direction of the well and returns with the garden cart full of dirt from the hole and dumps it over the flames. Most of them die off, and we're able to put out the rest with the water.

"Get near the buildings!" Falk yells at everyone. "Out of sight, and don't move! Turn off your damn lanterns!"

He grabs me by the waist and pulls me over to the side of the shed. We drop to the ground and he wraps his arms around me.

"Don't move," he whispers into my ear. "Don't move at all. We don't know what kind of sensors they have."

I try to control my panting breaths, and Falk keeps shushing me in my ear. I'm not sure if he's trying to keep me quiet or keep me calm.

The craft looms over us, moving slowly. It's clearly visible now and simply huge. I have no idea exactly how large, but I don't think it could land in our common area. It looks to be as big as a football field. As it gets closer, I can hear a rhythmic humming sound, but it's at such a low register, I feel it more than hear it.

"What is it?" I whisper. I tighten my fingers around Falk's wrists where they're linked in front of my stomach.

"Shh." Falk tightens his grip on me. "I don't know."

The craft spins in a slow circle and then lifts higher as it glows bright enough to hurt my eyes. Far above the trees, it turns again and moves off to the north—the same direction as the others.

Falk let's out a long breath.

"Are they gone?"

"For now, I think." He doesn't let go of me. "Let's wait a while longer though."

We all remain still and quiet for several minutes. When nothing happens, we all slowly stand and come together near the drenched and muddy fire pit.

"What the fuck?" Brett hisses through his teeth.

"I know this is what we talked about," Caesar says, "but damn. That was…"

"Fucking insane." Chuck reaches out and pulls Christine against his chest. He leans his head on top of hers, and the red tip of his Van Dyke gets wrapped up in one of her curls.

Everyone starts asking the unanswerable questions all at once.

"Why haven't we seen them before?"

"Where did they come from?"

"Do you think they're looking for survivors?"

"No way to know for sure," Caesar says, "but it's as good a guess as any."

"We're going to have to watch the fires and lanterns," Falk says. "Lights will definitely make it obvious that there are people here."

"That's going to be a problem when it gets cold." Wayne leans against a nearby tree and stares at the mess in the fire pit.

"We'll have to worry about that when the time comes," Falk responds. "We have shelter. That will have to be enough."

"What about cooking?" Christine asks. "I can't cook for so many on the small stoves."

"We'll work that out, too," Falk says. "You won't need to cook anymore if we're all dead."

There's more talk of how we are going to get along without light at night and the heat from the fire. There are a lot more questions about the craft and what it means, but there are no answers. Hours pass, and people start heading to their own abodes.

"Frustrating," Falk mutters as Caesar walks toward his own apartment.

"What is?" I ask.

"Having some level of confirmation is good," he says, pointing his thumb toward the sky, "but it doesn't exactly make me feel any better. I don't have a face for my enemy."

"What would you do if one of them was standing in front of you?"

"Get a really, really good look at it," Falk says, "and then blow its fucking face off."

"Really?"

"They've already attacked us, Hannah. I wouldn't exactly show them any mercy."

What he says makes sense, but I'm not used to thinking of violence as the first course of action. Couldn't it all be some misunderstanding? Maybe they—whoever they are—didn't mean to do what they did. Maybe they were peaceful, and it was all a mistake.

They took the women and children.

I shudder and wrap my arms around myself as I stare back up into the sky. There haven't been any more sightings, but I wonder if they are up there anyway, just too far away to see.

"I want you to start carrying a gun all the time," Falk says seriously as he reaches out and places his hands on my shoulders. "I know you aren't completely comfortable with that, but I want you to do it anyway."

"I'm not surprised." I look up at the sky, wondering what a handgun could possibly do against such a thing.

"You'll do it?"

I close my eyes and nod. The very idea of having something like that on me all the time makes me nervous, but I can't argue with him. I open my eyes as I feel his thumb on my cheek.

"You tired?" he asks.

"No," I say as I look at him, "but I would like to go to bed."

His eyes widen slightly.

"You sure?"

"Positive."

Falk nods slowly, runs his fingers down the side of my arm, and links his hand around mine. We don't speak as we walk up the stairs to the apartment or when we get inside. My legs are shaking a little, and my heart is already pounding in my chest.

Falk turns to me, runs his thumb over my mouth, and then kisses me slowly and softly. I bring my arms up around his neck and press against him, deepening the kiss. His arms wrap around my waist, and I feel his hands just inside the hem of my shirt. He slips his fingers inside my jeans, rubbing the skin of my lower back as he hums against my lips.

"We don't have to do anything you don't want to do," he says.

"Stop worrying," I respond.

"I can't help it." He runs his hands up my arms. "I know you haven't...not since..."

"Don't say it." I place two fingers over his mouth. "There is just you and me here. I don't want to think about anything else."

"I just want this to be perfect," he says softly. "I want to be perfect for you. God, Hannah, you have no idea how much I want this to be right for you."

His words bring tears to my eyes. I can see by his expression how serious he is, how much this means to him. As a tear escapes from my lashes and falls to my cheek, he reaches up and brushes it away.

"I want you," I whisper. The words catch in my throat. "You're the only reason I've managed to stay sane through all of this. You're the only reason I'm even still alive."

"You don't owe me anything, Hannah."

"I know that." I shake my head slightly. I don't know how to express myself in a way that will make sense to him. "It's not obligation. It isn't even gratitude, though I feel both of those things as well. I feel safe with you. Even with everything that's going on, you make me feel safe. The closer I am to you, the more comfortable I am. When you hold me...I just..."

I look away as I stumble over my words, and Falk strokes my cheek again, wiping away another tear.

"I haven't felt this way in so long." I stare up at him again, hoping he can understand by my look what I can't seem to say with words.

"I will always be here," he says. "I will always protect you."

I can feel his words as he presses his lips to mine. As his hand cradles the back of my head and his tongue traces over my lips, I know he will always be beside me, keeping me from harm. It doesn't matter what happens around us—I know he will protect me with his life.

I tug at the hem of his shirt, and he lifts his arms so I can pull the garment off. My gaze travels over his torso, admiring the defined muscles of his chest and the cut of his abs. I run my hands up his arms, my fingers tracing his biceps. I stop at his shoulders briefly, then drop my hands over his chest. There's sparse, light hair over his warm skin, and my finger follows the line from his navel to the top of his jeans.

Falk stands completely still, and I run my hands over him. He doesn't even move when I unbuckle his belt and unbutton his jeans. He just looks down at me, watching my every move as I drag his jeans down his legs, and he steps out of them.

I've seen him in nothing but his boxer shorts before, but this is different. If nothing else, his dick is jutting out in front of him, making the boxers resemble a tent in the front. I stroke my hand over the bulge, enjoying the warmth in my palm before sliding my hand down the front and pushing his boxers down.

Falk closes his eyes for a moment as I stroke his bare flesh again, running my hand from his balls to the tip of his cock. It pulses in my hand as I wrap my hand around it, but he still doesn't move.

I glance up to his face and reach down to pull my shirt over my head. His gaze drops to my breasts as I reach behind myself to unclasp my bra, setting my breasts free as the bra drops to the ground. He reaches out and places his hands on my hips, rubs his thumbs over my sides, and then reaches for the button of my jeans.

He stops and looks into my eyes. I can see the desire both in his look and in the more obvious sign of his erect cock pointing right at me, but still, he hesitates. When he doesn't move for a minute, I unbutton and unzip my jeans, push them down, and kick them off.

I watch Falk's throat bob as he swallows. He stares down at the lacy pink panties I'm wearing and licks his lips.

"Hannah," he whispers. His voice is breathy and reverent. He reaches up and caresses my cheek and neck, kissing me once more. "I'll go slow—gently. If you want me to stop at any time, tell me. I will."

"I know." I run my hand from his shoulder to his chest. I can feel his heart pounding beneath my palm. "I want you, Falk. Don't worry about me. I want this."

He nods and then reaches around me, picking me up like a child and carrying me to the bedroom. He stands at the foot of the bed, kissing me again as I hold on around his neck. By the time he lays me down, I'm already breathless.

Falk kneels on the bed and runs his hands over my hips. He watches my expression as he takes the edge of my underwear in his fingers. I nod, and he drags my panties slowly down my legs, his gaze following his hands. I pull my legs up a little so he can pull the panties off my ankles, and he drops them without ceremony onto the floor as he looks up my body. He licks his lips, and his eyes darken as he runs his hands from my ankles all the way up my thighs.

Falk kisses the inside of my leg, right above my knee, and flicks his tongue over my skin. I gasp a little, and my legs tense. I can feel my pulse between my legs as he slowly makes his way up. Before he moves on, he pauses at my left calf, slowly planting kisses over the scar where he sewed my leg.

I cry out as his tongue reaches me and moan again as he licks from bottom to top, circling my clit with the tip of his tongue. He slides his hands under my ass, lifting me slightly, then wraps his arms around my thighs and pulls my legs up over his shoulders.

My ass clenches, pushing my hips up and pressing me against his mouth. I both hear and feel him groan, the vibrations from his lips rippling through my sensitive flesh. I arch my back, pressing my head and shoulders to the mattress.

He is unrelenting with his tongue—licking and sucking at me as he grips my ass, pulling me to his mouth. I glance down and see him staring up at me, his eyes dark and wanting—a parched man being offered his first drink of water.

I coil my fingers in his hair as I push up against him, my body shuddering. Crying out again, I tighten my thighs against his head as my orgasm hits me. My muscles give out for a moment, and I feel Falk's smile before I see it.

He looks up at me, still grinning, and kisses my stomach. He keeps kissing up my body, stopping to run his tongue over each nipple.

I feel his hard cock up against my thigh as his mouth covers mine. I taste myself on him, and it only makes me want more. Despite the release, my pussy is still throbbing. It's not enough just to come—I want to feel him inside me. I want to watch him lose himself in my body.

Falk wraps an arm around my shoulders and rolls, pulling me over on top of him. I have to adjust my balance as I straddle him and lean back, staring at him. He wants me on top; I can see it in his eyes. He's still hesitant and unsure, waiting for me to change my mind.

"I want this," I tell him again. "I want you."

"You have me," he says simply. "Do whatever you want."

"I want you inside me." I feel his cock flex as the base presses at my apex in answer to my desire, and I reach down to wrap my fingers around it.

It's glorious, thick, and throbbing in my hand. I run my finger along the vein at the base, and Falk shudders. I glance at him, and his eyes are closed. He runs his tongue quickly over his lips, and his chest rises and falls rapidly.

Wrapping my fingers around his shaft, I angle his cock upright and raise myself up on my knees. The head slides easily through my folds, still wet from my orgasm and his tongue. I guide his cock into position, and slowly lower myself over him.

I gasp as our bodies connect. For a moment, I can't move—I just pause and feel him inside of me. I clench around him, getting used to the pressure, and Falk runs his hands over my hips, then up to my breasts. I start to move on top of him, slowing raising myself up and then dropping back down again.

He feels so perfectly *right* inside of me—warm and sensual. He alternates between watching my face and looking down to where we're connected. Every time he looks down, I can feel him tense beneath me.

I move faster.

Falk lifts his hips, meeting each stroke, but lets me set the pace. I lean forward a little more, wanting the friction against my clit. I can feel the pressure building up inside of me again. I move faster, my eyes closed and all my focus on that one, tiny spark as it grows. I grip his shoulders, pulling on him for support as I rock at a frantic pace. His fingers dig into my hips pulling me down on him as my stomach tightens. The feeling intensifies and explodes through my body as I scream.

"Oh, God! Falk! Falk!"

My legs shake uncontrollably as the feeling pulses through my skin. I cry out again as I collapse on top of him, my chest to his. Falk's arms wrap around my shoulders, and he holds me tightly for a moment.

I feel his hand slip down my back, and he rolls us both until he's on top of me. I sink against the mattress, unable to respond even as he starts kissing up my jaw.

"Don't you pass out on me," Falk whispers into my ear. "I am far from done with you."

I can only stare at him and nod. I don't have any words.

Falk leans back, strokes my skin from my shoulders, over my breasts, down to my stomach, and back up again. He wraps his arms around my shoulders and lifts me to him. He slides one hand down to my ass and pulls me into his lap, my legs wrapping around his hips.

With his arms around me, he lifts me gently and slowly until I can feel just the head of his cock inside of me, then pulls me back down, burying himself. He does this over and over as his mouth and tongue move along my collarbones.

I stroke his shoulders and the back of his neck, reveling in the feeling of him inside me, his body wrapped around me. His forehead glistens with sweat as he presses his lips to my neck, his breath hot on my skin.

He pulls me down and holds me there, panting. He looks at me with those dark, intense eyes for a moment before he closes them and takes a deep breath. I reach for his cheek and stoke his jaw. I can't find any words to express to him what I'm feeling.

Falk raises himself up on his knees, slipping out of me as he lays me on my back. He keeps his eyes locked on mine as he balances himself on one hand and strokes my skin with the other. His fingers dance over me, and I can feel every touch in my throbbing clit, but it's his eyes that hold my attention. I can't look away.

He leans forward and kisses me, our tongues wrapping around each other as he tilts his head to the side. He moves his hand over my stomach and between my legs, pushing them a little farther apart as he caresses me. His thumb is on my clit, rotating, as he pushes two fingers inside of me. He moves them around in a circle, stretching me as I moan beneath him.

He withdraws his fingers, and I glance down to watch him grip his cock and center it against my opening. He presses forward slowly, filling me again as I wrap my calves around his.

Falk moves inside of me, slowly at first, alternating between stroking my pussy with his cock and stroking my lips with his

160

tongue. My entire body feels like it's going to explode with sensation with every movement. He shifts his weight, resting on his elbows with his hands coming up underneath me and gripping my shoulders. He uses my body for leverage as he nearly pulls out of me and then slams home.

I cry out and pull my thighs up so they're around his hips as he plows into me again and again. His movements are quick and deep, igniting every nerve in my body.

I wrap my fingers around his upper arms and hold on as he moves faster. I try to meet his strokes, feeling my already overly sensitive clit beginning to throb again. Each time he moves forward, his pubic bone presses against me hard enough that it's almost painful. All I can do now is hold on as I feel him swell inside of me.

Falk cries out incoherently as he thrusts one last time, burying himself deeply. I feel the warm rush as he fills me, and it's all I need to set me off again. My body shudders as I tighten my legs around him and push up against his body.

I sink into the bed—eyes closed, heart pumping—completely sated.

Three times. Three times in one round.

Falk stays poised above me. I can feel the heat from his body on my skin and the slight shaking of his triceps under my fingertips. I keep waiting for him to collapse on top of me, but he doesn't. I open my eyes and look up at him.

His eyes are still closed, his breathing still labored as I reach up and stroke the side of his face. He doesn't move, just holds himself inside of me, his weight on his arms.

"Are you all right?" I run my thumb over his bottom lip.

He opens his eyes and stares at me. He licks his lips, swallows, closes his eyes again and nods.

"It's been a long time," he whispers. "That was…incredible. I just need a minute."

"Take all the time you want."

161

He leans down and presses his lips to mine. He doesn't move—just holds them there for a moment before pulling away. I feel him slip out of me as he rises up and rolls to one side. He gathers me up in his arms and holds me to his chest.

Falk hugs me tightly against him and then slowly relaxes. I lean my cheek against his shoulder, and he kisses the top of my head.

"You okay?" His voice sounds rough and scratchy.

"Much better than okay," I tell him. "I'm positively elated and completely exhausted."

His chest shakes as he laughs softly.

"Good," he says, "because I don't think I'm going to be ready for another round of that for an hour, at least."

"An hour?" I glance up at him. "I'm not going to be able to walk tomorrow as it is."

"I don't want to leave any room for speculation," he says. "I can't think of anything sexier than seeing you hobble around all day."

"As long as I don't have to run from anything." I snicker, but the sudden tension in his arms alerts me. He doesn't find my joke humorous, and his tone becomes serious again.

"I won't let them take you," he says. "I don't know what they did with the others, but whoever they are, they aren't going to get you."

I place my hand on the center of his chest. His dedication is admirable but also concerning. I warm at his words, but I also know he won't always be able to protect me.

"You can't control everything," I say. "You shouldn't put all of this on yourself."

"I am." He kisses the top of my head again. "If I don't do it, who else will? You are in my charge, Ms. Savinski. I take that very seriously."

"I know you do," I tell him. "I just don't want you to think you're responsible for anything and everything that happens to me."

162

"I do think that," he says, "and that's not going to change. I have to do this. I won't fail."

He looks at me, his deep blue eyes intense and pleading.

"This is all I have left, Hannah. I've never bailed on a job because things got rough, and I'm not about to do that now. There's no fucking purpose for me except to make sure you're protected."

~~~~~~

I wake in Falk's arms.

He's wrapped around me so tightly, I have to duck under one arm and around the other before I can slide down and out of his grip to head to the bathroom. The air in the apartment is cool this morning, and I shiver as it hits my naked skin.

As I go into the bathroom, I catch a glimpse of myself in the mirror. My hair is everywhere and looks like a lion's mane. I quickly smooth it down and tie it back at my neck before I walk out to the kitchen and start a pot of coffee on a camp stove. The natural gas stove has long since stopped working. Falk said it was because the compressors that move the gas to the apartments need electricity to work. We're almost out of propane for the camp stoves, and I wonder if anyone found some during the last supply run. I'll have to go check the shed later.

When I come back to the room and dress, Falk's arms are still splayed over my side of the bed, giving me a wonderful view of his muscled arms and shoulders. He snores lightly as I pull on my clothes, which makes me smile.

With the coffee made, I head outside with a mug in my hand, wishing we still had some of the vanilla creamer and then being mad at myself for wanting something so frivolous. As soon as I start walking down the stairs, I can feel how sore I am between my legs and grunt slightly. When I get to the last step, I pause a moment, shifting my weight from one hip to the other, remembering the feeling of Falk's cock deep inside of me. My muscles clench at the memory, and I smile to myself as I continue to the common area.

It's early enough that no one seems to be around yet. There's still some dew on the grass and only the faint chirping of birds and chipmunks. I head over to the fire pit and stare down at the mess from last night. It will have to be cleared of mud before it will be useful again, so I might as well get started.

It's too big of a mess to do by hand, so I head off to the shed for the shovel, but it isn't anywhere to be found. I remember Falk was using it out by the well yesterday. He's usually very good about putting tools away, but I decide to go look for it there.

The area around the well is clear of tools. I sigh and look around the edge of the woods, but I don't see anything there. I try to think of where someone might have used a shovel recently and remember that Marco and Sam had been digging a trash pit back in the clearing where Falk had been teaching me to shoot. The group didn't like the idea of burning trash in the same fire pit where we cooked.

I head off into the woods, my mind wandering back to the lights in the sky last night. I glance upward, wondering if they are still there but not visible in the sunlight. I try to picture what they might look like, but all that comes to mind are the pictures I've seen all over the internet of grey-green creatures with large, oval eyes.

Maybe there is some truth to all those stories about Roswell and Area 51 or whatever it is called. Maybe some of those pictures were real, and we did capture some kind of alien spacecraft all those years ago. Could it just have taken this long for them to come back for revenge?

With my head full of aliens, I startle when I see motion between the trees in the distance.

I tense, wishing I had listened to Falk and brought a gun with me. My heart starts to race as I crouch to get a better look. I see a shape moving through the trees again and duck down into the underbrush behind a fallen tree trunk. I bite my lip and stare over the log and through the leaves, waiting to see if the invaders are actually green.

The shape moves again, and I hear voices.

"We just need to wait a little longer."

"How long?"

My held breath escapes my lungs. It's only Caesar and Brett. I press my palm against my heart, willing it to slow down. I'm about to stand and hope I don't appear a complete fool for being so scared, but I halt my actions when I hear the next sentence.

"We gotta take care of Falk before we can move on Hannah."

What did he just say?

I lower myself completely to the ground and continue to listen.

"We should be able to catch him off guard easily enough," Brett says. "He doesn't suspect anything."

"Don't underestimate him," Caesar replies. "That guy knows his job. It might be two on one at the moment, but I wouldn't bet against him unless I knew the odds were well stacked in our favor."

"The problem is, we don't have any support here." Brett stops walking and turns to Caesar. "Once he's out of the way, it will be easier. The others will fall in line."

"This isn't about whether or not we have support," Caesar says. He places his hands on his hips and looks down at the younger man. "This is about the future. Think about it, Brett. Yeah, the world has changed, and we're still struggling to figure it all out right now, but that won't last forever. We already know of one other group of survivors, and they don't have any women. At some point, we're going to have to start trading for what we need."

"And we have one thing that everyone is going to need."

"Well, two, really, but yeah. Fresh water hasn't been an issue yet, but it's going to be—food as well. Just our small group has managed to use up what's around here pretty quickly. When we come across other groups, we'll be fighting for necessities."

"But we have a major bargaining chip."

"Very major."

"It's not just about that, though."

165

"No, it isn't. This is also about retribution. She took from us, and Ty always said she was going to pay for it. I find it wonderfully ironic that she's going to be the first in a new industry."

Ty.

Ty as in Tyler.

Tyler Hudson.

My body goes numb.

"You don't have to tell me. I've been fighting hard to be nice to that bitch, and I still have the scar she left me with. I can't wait to get her under me without any chance of escape. I am going to fuck that bitch raw."

Caesar laughs quietly and reaches out to clasp Brett on the shoulder.

"You and me, both. That's the best part of all of this—we get unlimited access. Eventually, she's going to be our ticket to anything we want."

"So what now? We're back to plan A?"

"Plan A was to grab her at the airport," he says. "I don't think we had a post-apocalypse plan, but frankly, it makes the whole thing easier. We just need to get rid of Falk. Then we grab her and start collecting bids."

Oh shit.

Chapter 12

I place my hand over my mouth to hold in the scream that wants to come out.

Slowly, I sink down to the ground and into a deep shadow. I close my eyes, praying that they won't turn this way and see me. If they see me, they'll know I've overheard them. If they know, they're going to kill me on the spot.

No. No, they aren't going to kill me. What they will do is much worse.

"At least we now know for sure that a murder doesn't attract a lot of attention." I hold my breath and keep my eyes closed as I listen to their footsteps come closer and then pass me by. I open my eyes just a little to watch them continue off toward the common area, still talking.

"I'm still floored by that," Caesar says. "Once Beck was in the ground, no one said another fucking word about it. Even when I kept pressing the issue, no one seemed to care."

Did Caesar kill Beck? No...that's not possible. Beck was his friend. Beck was probably on his side. He wouldn't have killed Beck.

I hear their soft laughter as they move out of sight, but I can't move from where I'm sitting. All I can do is think about Brett's hand on my thigh and remember how it had immediately brought back thoughts of being in the van. It had felt familiar, but I dismissed it as my own paranoia.

But it wasn't. It was familiar because his hand had been on me before—holding me down, spreading my legs. The scar on his face is from where I hit him. He was the one on top of me—he was the one *inside* of me—when I fought my way free.

I turn my head quickly and throw up on the ground.

My stomach continues to retch for a full minute before I force myself to my knees and then to my feet. I can't stay here. I have to get back to Falk—back to safety. I stumble, wrap my arm around my middle, and look toward the apartment. I don't see any sign of Brett or Caesar.

I have to get there—get there and lock the door. I have to get one of Falk's guns and make sure it's loaded. If they come for me, I'm going to have to kill them.

I run across the common area and up the stairs, throwing the door open and then slamming it again behind me. I push my body up against the door, turning the deadbolt with a loud click, and then slide down to the floor, still holding my stomach and trying not to throw up again.

Falk rushes out of the bathroom at the sound.

"Hannah? Hannah, what's wrong? What happened?" He crouches beside me, reaching out to lay his hand on my shoulder.

"I…I heard them…them talking…about…about…." I can't catch my breath.

"Slow down," Falk says, gripping my shoulder and turning me toward him. "What were they saying?"

"They know who I am, Falk!" I cry. "They were talking about me. They're with Hudson!"

He grabs my face in both of his hands and peers down at me. "Who?" he demands. "Who knows?"

168

"Caesar and Brett."

"Tell me exactly what you heard."

"They were talking about getting rid of you and…and using me to barter with. Caesar said there was another group of people he already knows about."

"He never was shot at," Falk mumbles. "I thought there was something fishy about that story. What makes you say they're with Hudson?"

"They said they wanted revenge," I tell him. "Caesar said they were supposed to get me at the airport."

"They're the ones," Falk said quietly. "They're the ones in the reports I read." He slams his fist against the floor. "Motherfuckers!"

"Falk, what are we going to do? They're planning to kill you!"

I watch his eyes as they dance back and forth between mine. He glances over his shoulder, down to the common area and then back at me.

"Pack," he says.

"What?"

"Pack. Pack *now*. We're leaving."

Falk marches into the bedroom and starts opening footlockers. I follow, and he hands me a huge backpack from the closet.

"Fit everything you need in here," he says.

I nod dumbly and grab a pile of my clothes out of the dresser drawer.

"Where are we going to go?"

"Let me worry about that," Falk says. "Just get what you need."

"What about food and water?"

"Right here." Falk pulls out several small packages of premade food. "I've got water purification supplies, too."

"We'll need flashlights."

"I've already taken care of that." Falk stands and heads to the kitchen to grab the spare batteries from the drawer. "There are a couple of things I need from the shed. You stay right here. Don't fucking move, you hear me?"

"What if they come here?"

Falk halts for a moment before removing the gun at his hip. He checks the clip and the chamber, makes sure the safety is on, and places it in my hands.

"Shoot them."

My stomach turns over.

Falk is suddenly on his knees in front of me, cupping my face with his hands again.

"Don't hesitate, Hannah," he says. "If one of them comes through that door, you shoot to kill. You can do it."

I nod quickly.

"Promise me."

"I promise."

He stares into my eyes for a second before he presses his mouth against mine. The kiss is hard and brief.

"I'll be right back."

He's out the door, and I am alone. The entire exchange between Caesar and Brett flows through my head over and over again, and I stare at the gun in my hands, trying to remember not to put my finger on the trigger. I jump at every sound I hear outside, and I'm afraid I'm going to blow up the couch.

Relax. Breathe.

They've been here all this time, knowing exactly who I am, and I had no idea who they were. They've been watching me. Brett had his hand on my leg—the thought makes my skin crawl—and at the time, I had been angry with Falk for overreacting.

Now I wish he had gone ahead and shot Brett. Caesar, too.

I swallow hard and pace back and forth. Where is Falk? Shouldn't he be back by now?

I hear someone on the steps, and I look quickly to the door. There's a slight scraping sound, and my heart lodges in my throat.

They've come for me.

I back up against the wall on the far side of the living room, gun held in both hands and pointed at the door. I promised Falk I would shoot to kill, but I can't even imagine myself doing it. I'm not even sure I can hit the door from here.

Take the safety off!

A little squeaking sound escapes my throat as I turn the gun to the side and flip the safety off. My hands shake and the gun wobbles. How will I ever keep my aim straight? I try to breathe slowly, remembering that I should fire as soon as all the air is gone from my lungs.

Focus, Hannah!

I take a deep breath, look down the barrel of the gun, and point it at the door as it swings open.

It's Falk.

"It's just me!" He ducks quickly and holds out one hand. "It's just me, Hannah! Don't fucking shoot!"

I drop the gun, and cry out when it hits the floor. Falk is at my side, gathering me up in his arms and holding me to his chest.

"You're all right," he says. "It's just me. You're fine."

After a minute he pulls away, holding me at arm's length and looking me over.

"You all right?"

I nod quickly.

"Are we leaving now?" I ask.

"Yes, we are."

"Where are we going?"

"Away from here."

"But *where*?" I can't hide the panic in my voice.

"I don't know yet. I'll let you know when I find it."

Falk hauls one of the two backpacks over his shoulders and shoves an additional box of ammunition into his pocket along with a spare clip. He grabs a long rifle from the closet and straps that over his shoulder as well.

"What else should I bring?"

"Nothing," Falk says. "We'll find what we need somewhere else."

He reaches out and grips my hand.

"Trust me, Hannah," he says softly.

"I do."

As we exit the apartment, I look off to the right side to see a few people in the common area. They don't look our way as we head down the steps and then to the left, away from the group. Falk keeps looking behind us as he urges me forward, across the parking lot and around a broken gate. Just beyond is the main road.

"Just keep moving," he urges. "Don't look back."

The farther we get from the group, the more I relax. Falk, however, does not.

"There's another group out here somewhere," he says when I ask. "I don't know where they are or how much contact Caesar has had with them. If you heard him right, then he's been talking about trading with them. More specifically, he's talked about trading *you*. I'm not about to let my guard down now."

We keep walking, sticking close to the rubble of former houses, stores, and office buildings. Falk keeps a steady pace, and we don't stop for breaks unless we have to. We see and hear no one.

We end up finding a convenience store still standing, and take a look inside. Though the building is still in good shape, it's obvious someone has already gone through and taken most anything of value. The inside is a complete wreck.

"Someone's been here," I say.

"This place has been empty for a while," Falk says. "See all the dust on top of the footprints? No one's been here in some time."

"But someone was."

"Yeah."

"Not us."

172

"Definitely not us," Falk confirms. "We didn't come anywhere near this far away. All of our supply runs have been toward the university and the other nearby shopping areas."

Falk goes over each of the shelves, looking for something to salvage, but comes up with nothing. At least the water is still running in the bathroom, and I can fill my bottle.

"Let's keep going." Falk pushes the door open, checking to the left and right before going back outside.

I have no idea where we are when we stop in a neighborhood with one of the houses still standing. The outside of it is a wreck, but Falk thinks it's structurally sound. We enter through the broken front door and find a master bedroom with a king-size bed.

"Get some sleep," Falk says. "I want to put as much space between us and them before the end of the day tomorrow."

My body is definitely tired, but my mind is still racing through the events of the day. As I slowly take off my clothes, I decide to go with the best distraction available and climb into the bed naked.

Falk stares at me for a long moment before doing the same.

I wrap my arms around him as soon as he's beside me and plant kisses in the center of his chest. He coils his fingers around the hair at the back of my head and gently pulls me back until he can press his lips to mine.

He makes love to me slowly as we lie on our sides, my leg wrapped around his hip. Afterward, he holds me to his chest and runs his fingers through my hair.

"Falk?"

"Yeah?"

"What about Christine?"

"What about her?"

"They're going to do the same thing to her."

"Yeah, probably."

"She's my friend." I feel pressure building behind my eyes, and my throat tightens up.

173

"I can't think about anyone but you, Hannah. If the opportunity to get Christine out of there comes up, I'd only attempt it if it didn't jeopardize you."

"It's not right." I blink back the tears.

"I know it isn't," Falk says, "but if there was ever a time to be selfish, this is it."

I can't agree with him. All I can think about now is Christine and how she's the only woman in the group with people like Brett and Caesar there. She has no idea what kind of men they really are, and though I know Chuck would fight to the death for her, I don't think he would win.

I hardly sleep at all. Instead, I lie in the oversized, comfortable bed, stare at the gun Falk's left on the nightstand, and listen to his breathing as he holds me against his chest. Hours later, I watch the morning sun come up through the window.

Falk mumbles in his sleep and pulls me tighter against him. He's got morning wood, and it's pressing hard against my ass. I'm exhausted from my lack of sleep, but I press back against it anyway, and he mumbles again.

I press my lips together, trying to contain my smile, and push back again. Falk groans and he wraps his arms around my midsection. One hand comes up and cups my breast.

"God, woman," he mumbles. "That's a hell of a way to wake up."

"Part of you was already awake," I point out.

He finds my neck with his lips and nips at my skin as his fingers pull at my nipple. It's my turn to groan as he grinds into my backside and covers my shoulder with kisses.

"I want you on your hands and knees." His breath is hot in my ear.

I'm startled by his bluntness, but the words send tingles down my spine, and I move quickly to comply. Falk rises up and takes position behind me, pushing my knees apart with his hands.

He sighs softly as he enters me in one, swift motion. I feel his fingertips digging into my hips as he pulls me back against him. He's so deep, moving slowly in and out of me. I lean down on my elbows and push against him.

"More," I say with a grunt. "Please, Falk."

"You don't have to beg for that."

His rhythm increases, and he leans over my back to reach around and cup one of my breasts while his other hand still grips my hip, providing him with leverage. I grunt with each deep thrust, closing my eyes and focusing on the feeling of him inside of me.

He reaches around my hip and finds my clit with his fingers. I gasp as soon as he does and start moaning when he rubs the sensitive nub. He presses against it, rubbing in a circle as I push back with my ass to meet his thrusts.

There's a rippling sensation in my gut, which spreads down and through my thighs. I tense as the wave hits me hard and cry out. As my muscles clench around him, Falk gasps and slams into me rapidly

"Oh, fuck! Yeah!" He empties into me and then drops his head to my shoulder. He keeps his arm tight around my torso, holding me up as he delivers a final stroke.

He kisses my shoulder, leans back, and pulls out of me. My skin is instantly cold as the contact is lost, and I reach over to grab the blanket and wrap myself up in it. Falk lies beside me, holding me against his warmth, but it doesn't last.

"We need to move," he says. "Get yourself together."

He jumps out of bed, leaving me no time to argue any points about staying put for the day. I wouldn't win such a debate anyway.

After a quick rinse in the cold shower, dressing, and eating, Falk is anxious to get moving again. He lifts his backpack to his shoulders and grabs his rifle.

"So, where are we going to go?" I ask.

"I want to head toward one of the army bases in the area," Falk says. "Something outside the city. I think the chances of finding someone are better."

"How far is that?"

"Forty miles or so east," he tells me. "There's a National Guard armory in Monroe. If we keep up a decent pace, we could make it in a couple of days. Do you think you're up for it?"

"That's a lot of walking."

"It puts a lot of distance between us and them. We should be able to find enough supplies along the way to keep the load light."

I bite my lip and look out the window. Clouds have blocked the sun, and it looks like it might rain. This place isn't bad, and a part of me wants to just hunker down and hide here. Falk steps up and strokes my cheek.

"We'll stop when you need to," he says. "It really won't be that bad."

"What if there's no one there?"

"Then we go on to the next one."

"You want to head toward Washington, don't you?"

"Eventually, yes," Falk says with a nod. "I think we should make our way there. Survivors will flock to that area."

"I don't know if I want to 'flock' toward everyone else," I tell him. "For all I know, I'll be the only woman there. It won't be any different except there will be more people."

"Not gonna let that happen."

"All right," I say with a sigh. "Let's do it."

"There's a VA hospital close to here," Falk says. "I want to stop there and make sure I have all the first aid supplies we might need. We should be able to get water there as well."

In distance, the hospital really isn't too far. The problem is, I haven't slept at all. I've got a headache; I'm lightheaded and even a little nauseated. Falk's annoyed with how slow I am and keeps urging me to go faster.

"What the hell is the problem?" He's been patient, but he finally snaps at me.

"I'm tired!"

"It's not even ten o'clock yet!"

"I didn't sleep much."

He's perturbed but doesn't push it anymore. He keeps his hand on my lower back, pressing lightly to keep me going but doesn't mention it again.

We walk around a lake and to a trail that crosses a large creek. At least, the trail should have crossed it. When we get there, we see the bridge has collapsed. Falk debates crossing the water on foot but doesn't want the supplies getting wet, so we make our way around to the main road to get to the building.

What's left of it anyway.

The parking garage is still standing, but the building behind it is more rubble than structure. One whole side is completely flattened, but it looks like the building in the back is partially standing. Falk wants to check inside of it.

"If we're going to be walking the whole rest of the day, I'd rather just hang out here and rest for a little while," I say.

"Are you asking me to leave you alone?" Falk shakes his head slowly.

"I didn't sleep and I'm wiped out. If I can just rest a little while, we'll be able to get farther today. Besides, you can get in and out of there faster without me."

Falk stares at me hard. I know he doesn't like the idea, but we haven't seen anyone along the way, and we're miles from the camp where we started. It takes a little more convincing, and eventually I just sit down with my back against the concrete wall of the parking garage and cross my arms.

Falk sighs and scans the area.

"If you stay here between the parking garages and keep out of sight, I can be back in a half hour, tops."

"I'll do that."

Falk drops his backpack to the ground, rummages inside of it, and pulls out a handgun with a small hip holster.

"Take this," he says. "If you see anything, you use it."

"Okay." He helps me get the holster fastened on my hip and then spends a couple of minutes helping me get used to pulling it out.

"I'll be back before you know it." He kisses me quickly before running off in the direction of the hospital building.

I sit back down and close my eyes. My head feels swimmy. I lean my forehead against my knees, hoping to doze for a few minutes. If I can get in a power nap, maybe I'll be able to keep going a bit more.

I wake with a start. I have no idea how long I've been out. The sky is overcast, and I can't tell for sure how high the sun is. My arms and legs are cramped and sore from sitting too long, and I get up to stretch.

Falk is nowhere to be seen. I'm pretty sure I've been asleep at least an hour, and he said it wouldn't take that long. It's possible the building is in poor enough shape that he's had to dig for the supplies he wants.

I look all around the area and see nothing of interest. I pace a little near the side of the building, staying out of sight of the main road but still loosening my muscles up. I lean against the wall and stretch, looking back toward the hospital, but I don't see any sign of Falk.

I'm bored.

I lean against the cool wall and stare out past the flagpoles and across the street. A row of trees and hedges makes a barrier between the sidewalk and what I think used to be an apartment complex. It's just rubble now, but some of the greenery survived. The trees have turned yellow, and many of the leaves have fallen off the branches.

Behind a utility pole, just under the hedge but slightly visible, is a body. There's a lot of debris piled up around one side of it, but I can clearly see the legs sticking out from under the bushes, as if he might have dived underneath for cover. I scan the body and see one arm under the branches, grasping a collection of brown plastic bags from a supermarket. The bags flap around in the wind, and I wonder what might be in them.

I should go find out.

I hate the very idea of it, but I know if Falk was here, he'd get it himself. I consider waiting until he gets back but then decide I need to take some initiative. Being squeamish is no longer a luxury I can afford.

I walk out past the flagpoles slowly, checking left and right before running up to the edge of the street. Everything is quiet, so I venture farther out into the street, still watching. I place my hand on the handle of the gun on my belt just to be sure it's still there.

A sound from behind me catches my attention, and I look off to the side of the parking garage but see nothing.

It's your imagination.

I steel myself and head to the other side of the street and next to the body. I was right—there are three plastic grocery bags grasped in his hand. I crouch down and reach out to pull them away, but the man's fingers are coiled tightly around the bags.

Closing my eyes and grimacing, I give the bags a quick yank, freeing them from their original owner's corpse. The smell of decay hits me square in the face, and I stumble back a bit but manage to keep my grip on the bags.

Inside, I find a carton of broken eggs, which smell only slightly better than the body itself, a container of cottage cheese and another of yogurt. I push that bag to the side and open the other one. Three cans of soup and a couple of boxes of ready-to-eat meals are inside. The final bag contains hand soap and a box of bandages.

I shove the useful items into one bag and discard the rest beside the body before I stand to head back inside the store.

"Well, look what we have here."

I jump slightly before looking in the direction of the voice and then freeze.

A hundred feet away from me, coming out from the lower level of the parking garage, Caesar and Brett appear. Behind them is a large man with a stocking cap on his head and long, unkempt hair.

"I had a feeling we might find you nearby," Caesar continues as they all walk out into the street, headed in my direction. "Glad to see it didn't take long."

"Look at her!" Brett says with a laugh. "That's a deer in the headlights if I ever saw one!"

I drop the grocery sack, and the contents spill out onto the asphalt.

"Looks like running didn't help much," Caesar says with a smile. He reaches up and rubs his chin with his fingers. "A good chase always makes things more interesting though. What do you think, Mark?"

"I like a bit of a chase." The tall, chunky man nods slowly. He presses his lower lip with his tongue, making it look like he has a mouth full of chewing tobacco.

"I've had about enough of it myself." Brett folds his arms over his chest. "I'm ready for a little 'catch and release' personally."

Caesar and Mark chuckle, and at first, I don't understand the joke.

Release.

He definitely doesn't mean letting me go. I shudder and take a step away from them.

"What are you doing here?" I ask. Maybe if I can keep them talking long enough, I'll give Falk time to get back. I gesture to the other man with them. "Who's he?"

"Where are my manners?" Caesar says with a smile. "Hannah, this is Mark. We met a few weeks back and have been negotiating some trade with him and his group since then. Mark, this is Hannah. As you can see, she's definitely worth her weight in batteries."

My body goes cold. It doesn't matter how much Falk talked about what the others wanted from me. It doesn't even matter what I heard Brett and Caesar talking about in the woods. Hearing him actually tell someone else what my body was worth to them brings bile to my throat.

"You aren't touching me." I hope my voice sounds more determined than I feel.

"I'm gonna do a lot more than that," Caesar says. "Like it or not, you know this is gonna happen. Think of it as your duty to humanity if you want. It's not too soon to start thinking about how we're going to repopulate the planet, and we're going to need you to do that. You might as well get used to the idea."

"That's my choice."

"Not anymore, it isn't."

"If you touch me, you know what Falk will do." I back up a few more steps, looking to my left and right. The hedge is behind me, blocking much of the way, but there's an opening on the other side of the body, and I angle myself in that direction as I walk. I don't know if I can outrun them or not, and I may need a place to hide until Falk gets back. I know I can't fight three of them.

"Funny, I don't see him here," Caesar says. The sneer on his face makes him look like a completely different person. "Maybe he took a little nap or something."

"Or something." Brett snickers.

My chest tightens, and I move my hand slowly to my waist and pull out the gun. I hold it in both hands, my arms out in front of me. I don't know which man I should aim at and end up waving the gun between the three of them.

"Leave me alone!" I feel tears burning in my eyes, and I try to blink them away. I have to keep myself calm, or I won't be able to aim. Falk taught me that. Stay calm, breathe slowly, focus.

Falk.

What did Brett mean when he said "or something"? Had they already come across Falk before they found me? Did they hurt him?

Did they kill him?

I bite down on my lip, forcing myself to keep my thoughts on what is happening around me.

"Don't move!" I order as Brett takes a step closer.

He hesitates and glances at Caesar. Caesar nods, and all three of them step forward.

I back up several steps, keeping the gun leveled. I aim at Caesar since the others seem to be taking direction from him.

"That is one hot little ass."

I turn quickly, and three more men come at me from the opening in the hedge. One is an older guy with a bushy grey beard. The other two are maybe late thirties, clean-shaven, and stocky. I back up a couple of steps, looking over my shoulder at Caesar and Brett. They both have their arms outstretched, waiting to grab me.

Sidestepping to the left, I point the gun toward Caesar.

"Don't come near me!" I yell. My hands are shaking. I can't get a proper grip on the gun as I fumble for the safety. "I'll shoot!"

Brett laughs.

"I've seen you shoot," he says. "Somehow, I don't think you'll manage to hit any of us, let alone all of us, baby."

Breathe, Hannah. Breathe!

I take a step backward, trying to keep all of them in my vision at once. I wrap my finger around the trigger and bite down on my lip again. I want to come back at him with a clever retort of some kind, but my mind is devoid of words.

They start to spread out and move in on me. I swing the gun from right to left. I should fire. I know I should fire, but I just can't.

What good would it do?

Someone grabs my arm. The gun goes off. Caesar and Brett duck out of the way, but the bullet goes nowhere near them. There's a sharp pain in my wrist as my hand is wrenched to one side, and the gun falls to the ground.

I scream as another man steps up and grabs my free hand, twisting my arm behind my back. Caesar appears in front of me, grabbing me by the chin.

"I told you," he says, "it's gonna happen. You might as well get used to the idea. We're gonna take you back to Mark's camp now, and you're gonna cooperate, you hear me?"

"Fuck you!" I scream in his face, and one of the men behind me grabs a hold of my hair, pulling my head back painfully.

"I don't give a shit if she cooperates or not," a gruff voice growls into my ear. "I'm happy to smack some sense into her as soon as we get back there."

"I don't want to wait." Brett steps forward and shoulders his way past Caesar.

"What?" Caesar turns his head to look at Brett.

"I'm gonna teach her a little lesson right now."

Caesar snickers and grins.

"Suits me."

I kick and scream as I'm pulled backward and over to the grass next to the sidewalk, but there's nothing I can do to get my arms out of the tight grip on them. Brett is in front of me again, reaching out and gripping one of my breasts roughly.

Pushing back against the man behind me, I pull both knees to my chest and kick out, landing my heels firming into Brett's stomach. He doubles over, gasping for breath, and the hand holding my hair shakes my head hard enough to rattle my teeth.

Brett stands and catches his breath, glaring at me. All at once, he steps forward, pulls his fist back, and punches me in the side. I think I hear one of my ribs actually crack, and I scream again.

"Stupid little bitch." Brett reaches down and unfastens his belt. "Get her down on the ground."

I'm thrown forward, barely catching myself on my hands as they hit the dirt. The pain in my ribs is crippling. I can't catch my breath. Brett is on top of me, rolling me to my back. I try to pull my legs to my chest so I can kick him again, but his hands are on my thighs, and Caesar is pulling my arms up above my head.

I keep screaming and struggling, but there are hands all over me, pinning me to the ground.

"I'm gonna finish what I started, baby," Brett says with a laugh.

"It's gonna go easier on you if you relax." Caesar's hand comes around my chin and pulls my head backward painfully. "Just let it happen, and you won't get hurt."

Caesar's hand presses against my cheek, turning my head to the side and holding it to the ground. In front of me, there is a single dandelion. I stare at the tiny seeds clinging to the top of the stalk in a gossamer ball, waiting for the wind to carry them off and start new life somewhere far away.

Feet shuffle around me, and the dandelion is crushed under a boot, the seeds smashed into the ground. There's a rock poking my left ass-cheek. I focus on the slight pain as I close my eyes, trying to ignore the sound of a zipper.

"After what you did to Hudson, and after all this time hunting you," Caesar murmurs into my ear, "I can't think of a better way to start up our new enterprise."

Not again. Oh, please, God, not again.

Tears pour from my eyes as I focus on the crushed dandelion, trying to tally the seeds. The little tufts are so jumbled, it's hard to get an accurate count, but I keep trying. I keep my attention on the seeds and not the pain.

Oh, Falk. Where are you?

~End of Part One~

COMMODITY

Part Two

Chapter 1

I startle awake.

Trees loom over me, and drops of rain sneak through the branches to land on the mossy ground where I sit with my back against an evergreen. I glance around through the brush of the old forest, but I see nothing but my khaki backpack. I cock my head to one side, but there's no sound other than the dripping of raindrops and the chirping of insects.

Something woke me.

I reach for the gun holstered at my side, withdrawing it and holding it close to me. The weight feels good in my hand—it always has. With the opposite hand, I touch each of the four knives at my belt and find their presence there comforting.

Maybe the rain woke me.

I can't remember when it rained last. It's been at least two months since the last real rainfall. Finding fresh water while on the move is becoming increasingly difficult. The ground is still fairly dry under the trees, so it hasn't rained much.

My position against the tree trunk is less than comfortable, and my leg aches as I push myself up from the moss and leaves. I rub at the spot on my thigh, feeling the rough scar tissue under my jeans. It never healed quite right. At the time, I'd been too busy trying to keep from bleeding to death from my abdomen to worry about my leg. By the time I got to it, I went with the fastest way to sew up the wound, and my stitching has never been pretty. It kept me alive though.

Wasn't fast enough.

I shake my head at the thought. It doesn't help to dwell on it.

I walk slowly and silently toward the nearby outcropping of rocks that overlook the dry creek bed below. It's a good vantage point. I can see for a couple of miles. My gaze scans the creek, looking for anything large enough to have made the sound that woke me, but there is nothing to be seen. There are no foxes or deer in the area. There aren't even signs of a raccoon or squirrel. Many animals have migrated farther north in search of water.

I should do the same, but I won't. I won't leave until I've found them—the men that took her. All these months and there has been no sign at all, but I'm not going anywhere.

I swore to protect her. I failed.

Across the creek bed and off in the distance, the collapsed tops of skyscrapers are easily seen, but I can't make out any detail from here. I haven't ventured near the city limits in quite some time—it simply isn't safe there. However, I'm probably due a supply run.

The crack of a dry twig alerts me, and I turn quickly with my gun raised, but I see nothing through the trees. My skin tingles, and I've learned to rely on my senses.

There's something there.

I sidestep back to the base of the tree where I had been sleeping, press my shoulder against the trunk, and look farther into the woods.

Movement.

The hair on the back of my neck stands up. I swallow hard as I creep forward to the next tree and then the next, making my way closer to whomever is out there in the forest. I hold the gun low, pointed at the ground, and I creep around each tree. As I get closer, I hear voices.

"Can't fucking believe it!"

"It's like findin' Venus' tits!"

"Venus wasn't missin' her tits, asshole."

Pressing my back to a large tree, I peer out cautiously. Less than a hundred feet away, down in a small ravine, six men gather in a lopsided circle, crouching slightly to get a better look at something on the ground.

From this vantage point, I can't see whatever it is they are gathered around. I drop low to the ground and move to my left and behind a fallen log. I listen carefully to make sure I haven't been heard, then again look down at the group.

They have someone pinned to the ground, face down in the leaves. I can only make out dirty jeans and a pair of boots. The figure on the ground struggles fruitlessly, and I catch a glimpse of a soft, curved cheek and full lips within a blur of long, dark hair.

Female?

My heartbeat picks up.

I haven't seen a female in months and then only from a distance. There are so few left. I was starting to think I would never see another one.

A female. A real, live, apparently healthy female.

She continues to thrash on the ground, kicking at her captors, but she's completely pinned and grossly outnumbered. The group taunts her.

"You think she's a breeder? I bet she's a breeder."

"Looks fertile enough to me!"

"Only one way to find out!"

"We gotta take her back to camp. Gary's gonna want to see her."

My ears perk up at his words. They must have a camp nearby. It could even be the one I came out here to find. It's the perfect opportunity to follow them back and gather more information on the group before I make a move.

"If we have some fun first, we won't have to wait later. Won't have to pay for it, either."

"Good point, man! Tie her hands! Hold her legs!"

I glance away for a moment, silently shoving the rage down as far as it will go, boiling inside of me. I'm not about to get involved in this—not now. I need to follow them back.

The woman is rolled to her back and then hoisted up by her armpits until she's sitting. They wrench her arms up over her head and tie her wrists together with nylon rope. She struggles and kicks as her ankles are grabbed and held to the ground. One of the men starts fumbling at the top of her jeans.

I lick my lips and breathe slowly through my nose. I need to stay quiet and out of sight so I can follow them back. I can't watch what they are going to do to this woman, and I can't get in the middle of it, either. That shit doesn't concern me. Besides, it would be six against one. Getting involved in something that isn't my business is just going to get me killed. I can't risk that. I push myself onto my knees, planning to move a little farther out until they're finished with her. I stand slowly before taking a slight step back.

She must see the movement because her eyes suddenly lock with mine.

My stomach clenches as she stares at me. For my own sake, I should sneak away and pretend I never saw any of this. It's the tactical thing to do. I don't know these people. I have no quarrel with them. I only need to follow them and get my hands on their pack leader.

A woman's voice echoes in my head as her face flashes through my mind. If she were here now, she'd want me to do something about it. She would never let me just stand by while this happens. She knows what it is like, and I know what it did to her.

This woman isn't my problem.

188

Her eyes are still locked on mine, her expression pleading as a dirty hand covers her mouth and muffles her cries. The rage I'd been shoving into my gut resurfaces. I can't do it. I can't just leave this woman to her fate.

I raise a single finger to my pursed lips. The woman's wide eyes show understanding. She looks back to the men surrounding her and doesn't look in my direction again.

I scan each of the men in turn, searching for any weapons. The only obvious one is the assault rifle strapped around one man's shoulder. One of the others has a slight bulge under his arm. It could be another gun. The others have knives at their belts but no obvious firepower.

I've got nine bullets in the gun. I don't want to waste them all, but I need to increase the odds in my favor. The men are all thin, undernourished, and from the way they speak, uneducated. They are probably used to using their numbers to overwhelm adversaries and don't think about tactics.

If I take out three of them with the gun, I can handle the other three melee.

I can't take any chance of hitting the woman. I'm a good shot but not perfect, and she's far more valuable than bullets. If I aim for the men on the far side of her, I'll decrease the chances of a stray shot getting near her. I've also got to take out the guy with the AR. He's standing closest to me, which puts the woman right behind him. He needs to go first, and I'll need to go for the head shot. The second will be the one with the suspicious bulge under his left arm. My last distance target will be the one guy who looks like he could give me the most trouble physically. He's bulky and taller than the others by several inches.

Flicking my finger over the safety, I raise my arm and take aim. I breathe deeply, slowly exhale, and pull back on the trigger.

Five of the men in the group startle at the sound. The man with the AR falls to the ground as the back of his head explodes. I switch my aim to the right, targeting the guy with the bulge under his arm—he's reaching into his jacket—and shoot again before the remaining four men begin to scramble. As they dive for cover, they all look around for a moment before they catch sight of me.

I get one more shot off, but the tall man moves too quickly. I hear his scream and know I've hit him but only to wound. I fire again, and the shot goes wide to his right.

"Fuck," I mutter.

I aim again, following his movement in the sparse undergrowth. One more shot and I see his body drop to the ground. I only have four bullets left. I've wasted more ammo than I can afford. I shove the gun back in its holster and rush down the hill, drawing one of my knives.

I tackle the nearest adversary immediately, shoving the knife into his side and shoving him to the ground. He screams in pain as the other two take position, trying to flank me.

"I don't know what your problem is, bro," one of them says. "We ain't got no fight with you."

I don't reply. I stand at the ready, waiting for either of them to make a move.

"Hell, we can even share a little, if that's whatcha want." He motions to the woman on her back. She's pulled her hands up in front of her face and is trying to get her ropes untied. "We got other breeders, too. We got a whole camp nearby."

"Where?" I keep my eyes on both of them as I utter the single word.

"Not far. I kin show ya." His eyes widen just a little. He has no intention of showing me anything. There's a hint of fear, but it's not exclusively because of me. He glances up the side of the hill and then quickly back to me.

At least I know in what direction to begin my search.

I stand up a little straighter and move my hand to sheath my knife. I watch his muscles relax as he glances at the man beside him.

190

With one quick movement, I switch the knife to my other hand and draw out a shorter throwing knife. I flick my wrist, and it slams into his neck.

He drops to his knees, gurgling.

The younger man to his side stares open-mouthed for a moment. When the body drops the rest of the way to the ground, the young man takes off, running up the side of the ravine in the same direction the older man had indicated with his eyes.

"Don't move." I glare at the woman on the ground but don't wait for her to answer before I head off after the runner. They mentioned others, and I can't risk him getting back to his camp and warning them about me. I also can't risk anyone else knowing about the woman they found.

My thighs burn as I propel myself up the hill. The runner isn't coordinated enough to navigate the forest floor, and once I get to flat ground, I catch up with him quickly. I leap forward and grab him around his waist, sending us both into a patch of mayapples.

With a quick thrust, I jam my knife into his kidney. He screams and thrashes on the ground, but I press my weight into his shoulders and stab him again. Withdrawing the knife from his side, I grab hold of his hair and pull his head backwards to slit his throat, ending his cries.

As his head drops to the ground, his profile is clearly visible. My chest clenches slightly. He can't have been more than eighteen or nineteen. I exhale sharply out my nose, push off the boy's body, and head back to the ravine.

As I get to the edge and look down, the guy I had stabbed first is stumbling over to the woman on the ground. She's trying to simultaneously push herself away from him and tug at the knotted rope around her wrists.

One target left.

Turning my feet perpendicular to the downslope of the hill, I shuffle down as quickly as I can. The wounded man holds his side as he tries to keep his footing and lurches for the woman on the ground. I don't know what he thinks he's going to do; he's in no condition to haul her off somewhere.

I stride quickly to him, and he turns at the sound of my footsteps. He reaches for his belt and pulls out a long hunting knife. He crouches slightly, defensively, and grimaces against the pain.

"You think you can take me, you piece of shit?" His taunting has no effect on me.

I don't respond. I've been in this position far too many times, especially in the beginning. I discovered early on that my silence is more unnerving than any clever, threatening retort.

He tosses his knife from one hand to the other. I watch, still and silent. I'm not sure if he thinks his display makes him look more skilled with the weapon or if he's trying to make me think he has equal skill with either hand. If the latter is his intent, it doesn't work. I can tell by the way that he grips the knife that he's predominantly right-handed.

He lunges, but the wound affects his balance. I sidestep easily, catching his ankle with my boot. When he stumbles, I dive on top of him. We roll twice, and he knees me in the side, trying to gain the advantage. For a moment, he's on top of me, and he slams his elbow into my face.

I'm stunned just long enough to feel his blade at my throat. I twist my neck away from the cold metal and punch at his existing wound. He grunts, and the grip he has on the knife loosens. Wrapping my legs around his, I flip us both over and pin him to the ground.

His eyes widen as he feels my blade slip deep between his ribs. He grabs my shoulders with both hands, but his grip is weak. I twist the blade, feel the gush of blood from the artery I've severed, and he sags to the ground.

I stand, panting, with my heart still in my throat and blood trailing from my knife to my arm. I move my gaze from the last body on the ground to the face of the woman behind him. She's breathing quickly through her mouth as she grips the leaves on the ground with her shaking fingers.

She lean, but has color in her cheeks underneath smears of dirt. Her legs are long and clearly muscular. Her eyes are bright and intense though I can't tell what color they are from this distance.

I should ask her if she's hurt. I should tell her that it's all okay now and that I'm not going to hurt her. I should offer her some kind of comfort, but I don't.

I swallow hard past the lump in my throat.

I take a few steps closer to her, and she pushes with her heels against the dusty soil to move backward, but there's nowhere for her to go. I crouch and grab hold of her arm. Her eyes draw me in. They're dark blue and surrounded by thick lashes. Her lips are full and look soft. I look over the rest of her, taking in the roundness of her breasts under her thin T-shirt and the curve of her hips encased in tight denim. Her knees are still bent and her legs slightly spread.

My head swims. I barely see the actual person in front of me. Instead, I see another woman—beautiful and strong. She had soft lips and gorgeous curves. She challenged me, infuriated me, made me laugh, and made me care. She brought out every primitive, protective instinct inside of me, and I had failed her.

I inhale slowly, trying to slow my racing heart. I want the scent in my nostrils to match the memory. I want to smell her skin, but all I can sense is the thick scent of blood in the air. It brings me back to the present and the real, physical woman in front of me.

Barely a woman.

She's young. I'm not sure she's even twenty years old.

Glancing back to her face, I reach out and run my thumb over her cheek, rubbing at the dirt there. I only manage to smudge it, not rub it off. She's got that look in her eyes that I've seen way too often. It's the kind of look that reveals she's been through too much. She's on the edge. She could break at any time.

She could be mine.

The voice in my head has become louder and louder lately. It keeps telling me that my cause is futile—I'll never see her again. I would be better off joining one of the camps so I'm not constantly providing for myself and having to watch my own back. More importantly, so I wouldn't be alone.

Being alone has never worked out well for me.

This woman could change that.

I could take her back to the bunker. I could protect her from anyone else who might come along and find us. I could hold her at night and fuck her slowly. I could give into all those wants and desires like everyone else has. I wouldn't be alone anymore.

"Let go of me!"

Her voice startles me out of my thoughts.

She doesn't actually pull away as she makes her demand, but I release her arm anyway. My palm cools as I let her go, and I swallow again. I look around though I'm sure there is no one else in the area. That doesn't mean someone else won't come. If I'm found with a woman at my side, there will be no negotiating.

I have to get her out of sight.

"Get up." I stand and look around again, listening carefully to the sounds in the trees.

"I'm not going anywhere with you!"

I shift my gaze back to the woman on the ground, almost expecting to see the vision from my mind there instead. Her tone sounds similar.

I don't have time to argue with her. Her voice is already too loud. If someone hears her, they will be on us in a heartbeat. I'm tired and my head is pounding. I might even have a concussion. There is no room for debate.

I crouch again and grab her wrist. I speak slowly and quietly.

"You are going to stand, and you are going to come with me. No talking."

"Why?"

"Because those men have friends," I tell her. "Because those friends may be closer than you think. We need to get out of here before more of them come back."

She stares at me for a moment before she comes to her senses and listens. I watch her rub her wrists after she gets herself off the ground, but she doesn't appear to be hurt in any other way.

"Follow." I start climbing up the ravine where I first saw her. I need to get my pack, which I left at the base of the tree where I had slept last night.

I don't stand behind her or otherwise put myself in a position of protection, but I do listen to her footsteps to make sure she's keeping up.

I'm annoyed with myself.

I've spent the last seven months with one purpose and one purpose only. Find her. I haven't aligned myself with anyone unless doing so furthered my cause. Now I've picked up a hitchhiker, and I have no idea what to do with her.

I grab my pack and sling it over my shoulder and then start heading back south.

"Where are we going?" she asks.

"I've got a place," I tell her. "It's safe there."

She mumbles something I can't hear, but I don't bother asking. I've never been good with people in general, and I'm not used to talking at all anymore. I've never had a taste for idle chitchat, and I'm definitely out of practice now.

Very little else is said until we get to the entrance of my abode.

"What the hell is that?"

"A bomb shelter." I open up the hatch in the side of a small hill and pull it back. "Watch your step—the first part is steep."

I watch the woman grab the edge of the opening and carefully navigate her way down the steep stairs to the bottom, then follow her, closing the hatch behind me. When I get to the bottom, she's staring with wide eyes and an open mouth.

"Did you build this?"

"No, I found it."

The inside is small and probably intended for only one person. There's only one room, but whoever built it was smart enough to leave themselves two entrances. Apparently, they weren't smart enough to be here during the attack. The benefits of being underground include temperature control. Though it's late into the fall, it is still damn hot outside.

"It looks like something from the fifties."

"It's a lot newer than that."

"How do you know?"

"It's got fiber optic cable running into it," I say. "It doesn't work, but it's there."

"You mean to get on the internet?"

"Yeah."

"*Is* there any internet anymore?"

"Not as far as I know."

I go to the locker just below the small food prep center and grab two bottles of water. I hand one to her.

"Thanks."

I pop the lid off of mine and sit down on the twin-sized bed. There isn't any other furniture in the shelter—just the bed and storage.

"My name's Katrina," the woman tells me.

I don't respond.

"Are you going to tell me your name, or do I have to guess?"

"Falk."

"Falk?"

"Yes."

"That's unusual."

"It's German."

"Oh! Were your parents from Germany or something?" Katrina leans against the food prep area and sips from the water bottle.

196

"Grandparents," I say. I don't know why I'm telling her any of this. It's been weeks since I've talked to anyone. Even the sound of my own voice is strange. "It's a family name."

"How did you end up here on your own?" she asks.

"It's been a long year."

"I'll say!" She snorts out a laugh.

The food prep counter must not be very comfortable because she decides to sit on the floor. She places the bottle of water next to her and twists her fingers around in her lap.

"How did you survive?" she asks.

"I was underground."

"Oh yeah? I've heard others say that, too." She nods her head as if we magically understand each other completely now. "We were fishing up at Lake Lanier. Me, my dad, and my brothers—Seth and John."

She keeps glancing up at me. I should be friendly—engage her in conversation, ask her questions. That's what she wants. It's been too long though. I don't know what to say, and I don't want to hash through all the same shit again.

I was a bodyguard. I was protecting a woman. I failed at it.

"We were in a cove," she says when I don't respond. "There isn't much of anything around there, but we heard all the noise. A bunch of boats out in the middle of the lake were capsized. When we got back to shore, everyone was dead or gone."

I finish my water and toss the bottle in a nearby container. It's getting full. I'll have to haul the trash out soon.

"When the truck wouldn't start, we took the boat up the Chattahoochee River as far as we could go, all the way past where the ferries are. Walked into town from there."

I'm barely listening to her, but she goes on anyway.

"It was days before we found anyone. When we did, we wished we hadn't."

I glance over at her, but she's not looking at me. I wonder how old she is. If she was out with her father, she could be even younger than I thought.

"It started out all right," she says, "but when they kept finding more men, and I was the only girl around...well, Dad figured out what they wanted from me pretty quickly. He decided to get us out of there in the middle of the night. They came after us though. Dad stayed behind so we could get away. I never saw him again."

A sense of relief washes over me. I'm not sure if it's because she wasn't violated like I thought she probably was or if it's because I don't have to hear about it. She's chatty. She may very well have given me all the details, and I don't need to hear that.

"We've been in this area ever since then—me and my brothers."

"Where are your brothers?" Some part of her story is still missing. If she had family to return to, she wouldn't have followed me here so blindly.

"Seth got sick," she says. Her voice gets soft. "John went out to find some antibiotics or something, but he never came back. That was three weeks ago. Seth...well, he died in his sleep four days ago. I had to dig a hole big enough to bury Seth, and I waited around for John to come back. When the food ran out, I left. That was this morning."

"You haven't been on your own long."

"Just the past few days, really. Seth wasn't much of a talker at the end."

If they have been living out here, they probably got bad water. Her brother wouldn't be the first to die from it.

I kick off my boots and shove my feet under the blanket. I scoot back to the wall so there's enough room for her to lie down as well.

"Are you going to sleep?"

I close my eyes for a moment, sigh, and look back at her.

"It's late. I got a little beaten up saving your ass today. Yeah, I'm going to sleep."

She bites her lip and cringes at my sharp words. I should feel bad about it, but the lip biting reminds me of *her*, and my mood worsens.

"Where should I sleep?"

"There's only one spot big enough." I'm being a dick. I know I am, but I can't seem to stop myself.

I don't open my eyes as I hear her approach and then lie down beside me. I can feel her shuffling around to get comfortable on her side, facing away from me.

It's all too familiar.

Every muscle in my body is suddenly tense. Memories of *her* warm, soft body pressed against my chest and my arm wrapped around her, pulling her close against me and telling her she'd always be safe flood my brain. I try to swallow, but I can't. There's pressure behind my eyes, and I have to fight back the tears as my temples throb.

"Aren't you going to fuck me?"

The sudden bluntness of Katrina's question snaps me out of my own head. I can't even answer her—my throat is still too dry.

"You are, aren't you?" There's resignation in her voice.

"No." My tone is flat. I'm still too shaken from the memory.

"Why not?"

"Are you saying you aren't like the other guys? You don't want to fuck me?"

Her voice is far too clear in my mind. Fear and desire all wrapped up in one package. I wanted her more than anyone I'd ever wanted before. I just wanted her to feel safe with me, to *be* safe with me.

I fucked it up so bad.

"That's not why I brought you here." I finally spit out the words, but my head is still spinning.

"Why did you?"

199

I can't deal with this now. My head is still throbbing. I probably do have a concussion from that elbow to the face. I need sleep.

"Would you rather be out there alone in the woods?"

"No." She's quiet for another minute. "What are you going to do with me, then?"

"I haven't gotten that far."

"Are you going to sell me?"

"Katrina, shut up."

She tenses beside me, and I feel bad for being so harsh—God knows what's going through her head right now—but I can't take any more. I shove myself up from the small bed and climb over her. In a cabinet on the other side of the room is a bottle of vodka. I pull it out and take a big swig.

It's cheap stuff and burns my throat as it goes down. It warms my stomach and clouds my head, too, which is the desired effect.

"Who is she?" Katrina's words are barely audible.

"Who is who?"

"The girl." She sits up and looks up at me. "The reason you aren't fucking me now. What's her name, and what happened to her?"

I still as images rush through my head again but worse this time.

She was leaning against the concrete wall of a parking garage. Her hair was pulled up into a ponytail, but most of it had escaped, and the wind was blowing it all around her face. The last time I saw her—exhausted and so sure she would be fine—was when I glanced over my shoulder right before I entered the half-destroyed hospital building. I was supposed to be gone for only a few minutes.

I never should have left her.

"Hannah," I finally say. "She was taken from me."

Chapter 2

It's the first time I've said her name out loud in months. I don't even like to think it. Every time I do, I'm reminded of our first meeting when she told me to call her by her first name, and I had refused.

How could I have called her that? I'd been following her story since I read the first article about her turning in *the* Tyler Hudson for embezzling, kidnapping, and running a human trafficking ring. She didn't have just an inkling—she had tracked down solid evidence. She had enough on him that a prosecutor had to do something about it. Hudson was a king in both industry and politics, and some barely-out-of-college woman was willing to take him on. It was something no one else, not with money or power, had been willing to do. There was no way I could have referred to her in such a familiar manner—I was in awe of her.

"Will you tell me about her?" Katrina asks.

I take another long swig from the bottle, but I don't answer. There's gooseflesh appearing on my arms, and I can't seem to stop my right leg from jiggling up and down. I remember calling her by her first name when she would start to panic and how it would calm her. I remember whispering it in her ear as I made love to her. I remembered screaming it over and over and over again when she was nowhere to be found.

"She must be really important to you."

"She was. She *is*."

Katrina shifts on the bed, pulling one of the pillows into her arms and fluffing it. She props it up against the wall behind the bed and leans against it. She looks at me as if she's waiting for a bedtime story, but I don't have a "happily ever after" to tell her.

I remember when Hannah told me about Hudson's assault on her. It had taken everything in my power to keep myself calm and to stop myself from getting out of the bed and completely destroying the room. I'd asked her to tell me, and I knew I needed to keep my cool so she could tell me everything without breaking down, but I hadn't really been prepared for the look in her eyes. Afterward, she was drained, but she also seemed relieved and more focused.

I glance up at Katrina. She's still just sitting there, watching me. As far as I can tell, she's genuinely interested in hearing me tell my story.

Maybe I should.

"I was her bodyguard." Just the word makes my chest hurt. I can't believe I'm actually speaking out loud. I haven't told anyone exactly what happened. "I was supposed to protect her."

I slide down to the floor, bottle still in hand. Pulling my knees up to my chest, I lean my arms over them and take another drink. I put extra pressure on my right leg to stop it from bouncing around so much.

"I guess that didn't work out so well."

I shake my head.

"We had just gotten away from the group we were in. There were people there…men who wanted to hurt her. I got her away, but then…"

I feel the pressure behind my eyes again as the vodka works its way through my system.

202

"We stopped at a hospital to get a few things," I say slowly, focusing on my breathing and trying to remain calm. "Hannah was exhausted. She wasn't up for climbing through all the destruction to get to the supplies. She wanted to stay outside and rest. I didn't like it, but she…she had a way of convincing me to do shit I didn't want to do. She was always so confident and independent; it was hard to argue with her sometimes. I left her there while I went inside."

I let another gulp of cheap vodka burn my throat.

"I never should have left her alone."

"Did those guys take her? The ones you were trying to get away from?"

I nod before continuing.

"I was in a hospital building. We were running low on gauze and antibiotic cream, and I didn't know when we'd get a chance to find some again. The place was a mess, and though I found the storage area, I had to dig into it to find the supplies I needed. I was making a lot of noise throwing shit around—I was pissed it was taking so long to dig it out. I should have been quiet. If I had, maybe I would have heard them.

"I heard a sound behind me, and I knew exactly what it was. My back felt like I'd just been punched hard or maybe hit by a baseball that should have made it out of the park. I looked down. My shirt had a huge hole in it, and blood was seeping out. Then there was another blast, and I felt a sharp pain in my leg. I turned around and saw him—Caesar. He was the guy trying to get Hannah. He had a grudge."

I stop and try to catch my breath. All my words are coming out rushed, mimicking the way the thoughts are flowing through my head.

"There was another guy with him—Brett. I think he fired the second shot. I had the chance to kill him days before that, and I should have. I should have just fucking killed him the first time he touched her, but she…she wouldn't have liked it. She always thought the best of everyone, and she didn't realize what kind of person he was. Not then, anyway."

I shake my head.

"It doesn't matter now."

"What happened then?"

"I fell backward onto all the medical supplies. My whole side felt like it was on fire. I couldn't move at all for a moment. I think I knew I'd been shot, but it took me a few minutes to really comprehend it."

"He shot you?"

"Yeah. Right in the back. The bullet came out in the front."

I reach down and place my hand over my left side, sliding it down and grabbing the edge of my shirt. I pull the fabric up enough to show her the long scar between my ribs and my hip.

"Holy shit," she mumbles. "That's..."

"Pretty ugly."

"Yeah. At least. How did you even survive?"

"I'm getting to that." I breathe slowly, trying to say the words without actually reliving the experience, but it's not easy. "So I'm lying on all these boxes of bandages, pills, and ointments, just stunned. I could still see Caesar's face in my mind—he was smiling at me right before I fell—but I was having a hard time piecing together what had just happened. There was blood all over my shirt, and I also hit my head on something in the pile of supplies. I couldn't move at all. I don't know if it was shock from being hit, a concussion, or what, but I couldn't move for what felt like the longest time. He must have thought I was dead, because he didn't shoot again."

"What did you do?"

"When I looked down, my shirt was covered in blood, and I could feel it bubbling out of me. The box of gauze I had already set aside was still right next to my hand, so I grabbed it and ripped open the hole in my shirt even wider so I could see the exit wound. I nearly puked, and I'm lucky I didn't just pass out at that point."

I have to stop and take another swig from the bottle. It's strange how comforting the burning liquid feels. I've never been much of a drinker.

"I could see..." I stop again, taking a deep breath. "There was a lot of blood, and it was still seeping out, but there were also bits of tissue mixed in with the blood, and I could see part of my intestines sticking out of the hole."

Katrina gasps and places one hand over her mouth. Her eyes are wide, and she looks a little sick.

"I was sure I was dead. It burned so bad—like someone took a hot metal pole and shoved it right through me—but I couldn't...I couldn't *die*. Hannah was still out there, and he was going to go after her next.

"I pulled my shirt out of the way and used my fingers to push...to push everything back inside. I could feel everything shifting around in there, and I had to fight the urge to throw up. I used a wad of gauze to put pressure on the wound to try to stop the bleeding, but I knew it wasn't going to be enough. I could feel the blood seeping through even as I piled more gauze on it. I was trying to run through all the shit medics would do in combat, but I was getting lightheaded, and I couldn't think clearly.

"I felt pain in my back, too. At first, I thought I had landed on something that cut me, but then I realized it was where the bullet actually entered."

"That's good though," Katrina says. "The bullet wasn't still inside of you."

"No, it wasn't, but it was a hollow-point bullet. They're designed to do more damage coming out."

"Shit. What about your leg?" she asks.

"Give me a minute—I'll get there."

I reach to my thigh and rub at the scar before I go on.

"I'd been wounded before," I tell her. "When I was in Iraq, I was hit with shrapnel. Lots of small wounds but nothing like this. Actually, I'd never been shot before—seen it a lot, but it hadn't happened to me. All I could think was that I needed to stop the bleeding. I had to stop the bleeding and get back to Hannah, so I started looking around.

"I guess if you're going to get shot, get shot in the middle of a hospital supply closet. As I saw all the stuff lying around me, I started thinking a little more clearly, but I knew that wasn't going to last. I was losing a lot of blood. I had to crawl to get everything I needed, which made the bleeding pick up again, but I found a box of curved needles and suture thread."

"I don't know how you could even think after being shot," Katrina says, shaking her head.

"I had to get back to her." I look up at Katrina for a moment, wanting her to understand. "I knew they were heading for her and that they were going to hurt her. She was depending on me to keep her safe. I had to get back there. So I grabbed a bottle of alcohol and poured it over the wound, which made it hurt even worse. My hands were shaking, and it was hard to get the thread through the needle, but I eventually got it. I almost passed out after the first stitch though."

"You stitched yourself up?"

"I didn't have a lot of options. I was bleeding too much. Even if I could get the bleeding stopped with pressure, it would have started again as soon as I started walking. I didn't know if the bullet had hit an artery or a major organ or anything or if I was going to just keep bleeding internally. I knew I couldn't actually perform surgery on myself, and I did what I had to do to get myself moving."

"Shit." Katrina wraps her arms around her legs and lays her chin on her knees. "That had to have hurt so much."

"I don't think I've ever had anything hurt more," I say. "It was a big wound, and I had to use one hand to pull the skin together so I could get the needle through. I barely made it. Nineteen stitches total."

"Wow."

"Once those were done, I tried to reach around to the wound at my back, but there was no way. It wasn't bleeding as bad as the exit point, so I found some Dermabond and did my best to spread it around."

"Dermabond?"

"Glue."

"Glue?"

"Surgical adhesive, yeah. It's like superglue for skin. It's better for smaller cuts, but I couldn't stitch myself in the back, so it was the next best thing. I held it closed as much as I could, and spread the adhesive over it. After that, I got it covered with gauze and taped up both of the wounds."

I turned a little and lifted my shirt again. I can't quite see it myself, but I've looked at it in the mirror a few times. The scar is round and still a little red where tissue grew over the hole. It's ugly, no doubt about that.

"I tried to get up then," I tell her. "All I could think about was Hannah. I wasn't really sure how long I had been gone, and I was still a good five hundred yards from where I'd left her, and the whole area was covered in rubble. As soon as I tried to stand, I fell again."

"Because of your leg?"

"Yeah. Honestly, the belly-wound had me distracted enough I hadn't thought about my leg. When I looked at it, it wasn't bleeding much. The bullet grazed my leg pretty deep but didn't really penetrate. It burned and itched, but I didn't have time to stitch it up. I applied more glue, a bunch of surgical tape, and wrapped it as tight as I could. Wrapping it that tight made it hurt worse, but I could put some pressure on my leg then."

I rub at the spot on my thigh.

"Does it still hurt?" Katrina nods toward my hand on my leg.

"Sometimes." I take in a long breath and take down another long gulp of vodka. "Once it was taped up, I still couldn't walk well, but I was moving. However, I was stumbling and falling every

207

couple of steps, which jarred every wound. At that point, I didn't care about the pain. I was just pissed it was taking so long to get anywhere, and I needed to move faster."

"I found a crutch in the rubble. There was only one of them, and the end of it was broken. It wasn't long enough to use properly, but it was enough for me to pick my way through the rest of the rubble. I made it outside, and I could see the parking garage where I'd left Hannah, but I didn't see her anywhere.

"I kept telling myself that she was hiding inside the garage somewhere, that she had taken shelter in one of the abandoned cars. I was screaming her name over and over again, but I didn't get an answer."

I stop. I can hear my own voice echoing in my head, crying out for her and getting no response. I can feel the sense of dread and panic as it threatened to overwhelm me.

"Are you okay?" Katrina's voice pulls me back to the present.

"Yeah." I grip the top of the bottle but don't drink. I need to keep going. "Then I looked out into the street, and I saw these grocery bags. They looked weird just lying there, right in the middle of the concrete. I didn't think they had been there before, so I made my way over to them and found some canned food inside. I also saw some other bags near a body, and I think they belonged to the guy lying there. The stuff that had gone bad was left beside him, but the good stuff was what I found in the street. I figured Hannah had seen the bags and went to see if there was anything useful in them. That's when I saw…"

I have to stop again as the memory floods my head: the broken branches, the crushed grass, and all the footprints near the row of hedges. I remember the blood on the ground and the lingering smell of semen.

"There had…had been a struggle. I was too late. They already had her. There were footprints coming from the back parking lot of a different building, but they only led back to an alley.

208

They must have left by the road, and there wasn't any sign of them to follow."

Katrina nods but says nothing.

"I looked everywhere. For weeks, I barely slept. I searched anywhere and everywhere, finding more survivors than I ever expected to find, but I never found a trace of her. Every group I talked to was nothing but men, and none of them had even seen another woman since the attack. It wasn't until the second month that I found someone who thought he knew who Caesar was. In the end, he didn't have any idea where to look for him, though. I've found similar leads since then, but they all end up going nowhere."

"You're still looking," Katrina says.

"Yeah."

"It's hard to track someone after that much time."

"It doesn't matter. She was depending on me. I was supposed to keep her safe. I won't give up on her now."

"Well, what do you know for sure?"

"Only where she isn't. Groups are becoming less informative all the time, which makes me think they're protecting him now. Either that or everyone is becoming more paranoid of strangers. A lot of them seem to know who I am and what I'm going to ask before I say anything."

"Why do you think that?"

"Because Caesar's got what they want—a woman. He may even have more than one now. They'll protect him so they can…"

I can't finish the thought. Lifting the bottle to my lips, I take a gulp and swallow past the lump forming in my throat. The fact is, I haven't had anything that even remotely resembles a lead in months. The only thing that makes me think Hannah is still in the area is the lack of cooperation from the few people I have found.

"I'm pretty good at putting puzzles together," Katrina suddenly says.

I glare at her. The vodka is definitely hitting my head now. Everything is a bit swimmy, but her babbling pisses me off. I don't want to hear about her fucking hobbies.

"Well, if we come across a jigsaw, you'll be the first to know." I rub my temples with my fingers.

"I meant," she says, "maybe I can help you find her."

I stare at her, trying to figure out where she's going with this. I can't think of any way this young woman could help me unless she already knows something.

"How?" My suspicions are raised, but I haven't seen any signs that she's tried to deceive me so far, so what could she be thinking?

"We did some trading with groups in the area," she says. "Well, my brother did, anyway. I always had to stay out of sight. Seth was afraid if they saw me...well, you know."

"Yeah, I do. Do you think he talked to someone who might know where I can find Hannah?"

"I don't know," she says with a shake of her head, "but my brother kept records. He took notes on every group he came across when he was trading. He's got names, locations—everything."

For the first time since I dragged myself back to the parking garage of the hospital to find her gone, I feel hope.

Chapter 3

We wait until morning to leave, but I sleep very little. The thought of finally having a direction—somewhere to at least look for a clue—has my adrenaline pumping. By the time Katrina climbs out of the small bed, I've been up for an hour.

Katrina takes me to a ranch house on a flood plain right next to a river. The river itself is barely a trickle now, but the house is well sheltered by the valley and trees and seems to be in good shape.

I follow her up two steps to the front door and then inside. It's not a big place. It has that seventies energy-conservation vibe— small, compact rooms and windows barely large enough to crawl out of if you needed to. She goes straight to a desk in the main living area and pulls out a thick, spiral-bound notebook.

She's right—there are a lot of notes in her brother's journal. I glance through the first few dozen pages, and I'm amazed at the level of detail.

"How did he know to collect all this information?"

"Learned from my dad," she says with a shrug. "We were a big hunting and fishing family. Dad could track anything and taught us a lot about being quiet and on the lookout. Seth would stalk the

211

camps for days before approaching them. He'd get to know everyone's names and what they did for the group, if anything. He didn't meet them in person unless he was sure they'd be open to trade and that they would have something we needed."

"What did you have to trade?" I ask.

"Recipes."

"What?" I look at her sharply. I couldn't have heard that right.

"Recipes," she says again. "You wouldn't believe how many of these guys are just eating beans out of a can for every meal. They have no idea how to put foods together without a cookbook, and no one seems to be collecting those, but I do."

"You traded cookbooks?"

"Not the books themselves," she says. "I'd write down the recipes that use only things that are pretty easy to find. I found one that was from the Great Depression. All the recipes were geared toward rationing and such. I looked for ones that only included dry goods and ingredients that don't spoil. I kept the books to help me come up with new things to cook."

"And people want them?"

"They eat them up." She laughs at her own joke. "We could get batteries, lanterns, and propane for just a handful of them. The problem is, there are only so many. We had to keep finding new groups to trade with."

"And they're all in here?" I hold up the notebook.

"Should be."

I sit on the loveseat and start paging through the notebook, still impressed by the level of detail. It's the same kind of information someone would gather on a scouting mission in a warzone. There are hand-drawn maps with landmarks, names of the people in the group, and their relationships to each other. There's information on what supplies they have on hand, what seems to be in surplus, and what they might be interested in obtaining.

There are several notes in the margins of the pages about a larger, hidden group somewhere on the west side of town. Many of the people Seth talked with alluded to its existence, but there's nothing to indicate that he found it.

More than halfway through the book, a paragraph catches my eye.

It's a small group—only five altogether—and one is a woman. She seems to know what she's doing around a cooking fire. There's a guy with her who I think is her husband. He's got a wild red tip on the end of his beard. Passing this group up—they won't be interested in trading.

Chuck.

It has to be.

I go back to the previous page and check Seth's map of the area. If I'm right, and it is Chuck and Christine, they haven't moved far from where we were originally. They may have some idea where Caesar and Brett have ended up.

They could know where Hannah is.

"I have to go."

"You found something?"

"Yes."

"Well, let's go!"

"No." I shake my head. "Stay here."

"What?"

"You should stay here where it's safe," I tell her. "If people see you, there's no telling what kind of fight I'll have on my hands."

"You really think I'm safer here alone than I am with you?"

"I know it's more dangerous out in the open. They aren't as frequent now, but I saw the ships in the sky just three days ago."

"I can't live out the rest of my life being sheltered away!" Katrina snaps.

Her words sound so much like something Hannah would say, I'm caught a little off-guard. My muscles tighten, and I'm torn

213

between giving in—like I always did with Hannah—or insisting Katrina stay out of harm's way.

What's she going to do here?

If it is Chuck and Christine, and I'm almost certain it is, she might be better off staying with them. It's been a long time since I've seen them, but they were good people—I knew that from the day they joined us.

"I might not be able to protect you," I tell her.

"I didn't ask you to." She stands with her hands on her hips.

"Fine."

~~~~~~~

Following Seth's map, I find the location fairly easily. It is right next to Freedom Parkway and the Carter Center. There is a large stone wall separating the park from the road, and much of it is still intact, providing ideal protection. On the other side, one of the round buildings is still standing. There's also lots of tree cover and a lake nearby for water.

Nestled between the building and the lake, there's an area that looks almost identical to the common area shared by our original group. There's a fire pit in the center, cooking pots all around it, a lean-to full of kitchen items and a tub for washing, and lawn chairs scattered about. Despite the familiarity of the scene, I hang back and out of sight.

"What's wrong?" Katrina asks.

"Shh." I hold my hand up to keep her back and out of sight. "Just want to watch a minute."

She crouches behind me and looks over my shoulder into the distance. Someone has appeared near the edge of the common area, holding a compound bow. Even before I see the red beard, I know Chuck's stature. He moves around to the fire and sets a couple of dead animals near it. I think they might be rabbits. I snicker softly.

"What is it?" Katrina asks.

"Never mind." I shake my head and smile.

A moment later, Christine appears. She immediately starts yelling at him.

"Get those nasty things away from my pots!"

"We need the protein, babe!"

"And I said if you were going to cook them, you're also going to clean them!"

"That's what I was gonna do!"

"Not by my cooking pots, you aren't!"

They continue to squabble as Marco and Sam appear on bicycles. They ride up the sidewalk and then into the grass, propping the bikes up against the trunk of a tree. They both have backpacks and start to empty their contents into large plastic containers close to the building.

"I hope you found toilet paper!" Christine says.

"No such luck," Marco calls out, "but I got extra paper towels. They're the soft kind!"

"The skin of my ass is already falling off from the last batch you said was soft!" she yells back at him.

"Stop cooking so many beans," Chuck suggests, and Christine chases him and his rabbits off with a spoon.

Marco and Sam take a few additional supplies and duck inside one of the buildings.

"Hang back here," I tell Katrina. "I'm going to make sure everything's okay, then I'll call you down if it's safe."

"I thought you knew all these people."

"Not taking chances," I say with a stern look. "You stay put."

"Fine." She drops onto her ass and glares at me.

I make my way down the hill and around the side of the building. I stay at the corner, watching Christine for a moment, and then walk up to the fire. Christine is focused on her work but sees me a minute later.

"Falk?" Christine walks out from around the cooking fire, wiping her hands on a towel. "Holy fuck, that is you!"

215

She runs over and wraps her arms around my neck, practically choking me. I freeze for a moment, not sure what to do, then wrap one arm around her back and give her a quick hug. She pulls back, leaving her hands on my shoulders as she looks me over.

"Where's Hannah?"

I actually feel my organs drop lower into my body when I hear her question. I close my eyes for a moment and try to keep myself together.

"Shit, Falk," Christine whispers. "Is she dead?"

"I don't know." I take a step back, disengaging myself from her embrace. "I was hoping you might have some idea."

"I haven't heard anything about either of you since you left," she says. "Honestly, I thought you were both dead.

"Ho-lee shit!" Chuck jogs over to us and smacks me on the shoulder. "Never thought I'd see you again."

"You hungry?" Christine asks. "Dinner will be ready pretty soon. Let me get you something to drink."

She runs over to the kitchen area and Chuck looks me over.

"You look like shit, man."

"Thanks."

"They went after you, didn't they?" he asks.

I nod.

"What happened back at our original camp?" I ask.

"Well, when you two split," Chuck says, "Caesar and Brett said they were going after you. Said they were concerned for your welfare and all, but I called bullshit. Brett was pissed at you, and there was no way he could have given a rat's ass about your well-being."

"Good call."

"Caesar got all defensive, so I let it drop, but sometimes you just have a bad feeling, ya know?"

"Yeah, I know."

"They'd been gone a couple of days, and shit, we didn't know what happened to y'all. They came back, then left again. All

216

those times, they kept getting together in little groups and talking all hush-hush like. That shit made me nervous."

"Us, too," Marco says as he and Sam come around from the building to where we're standing, nodding their heads. "I never liked that Brett guy. I was pretty glad when you pounded on him."

"Yeah, that was sweet." Chuck laughs.

"Did they say anything to you?" I ask. "Before they left, I mean."

"They started coming up to me and asking why Christine and I didn't have kids," Chuck says. "I told them it was none of their fuckin' business, but they kept asking. Then Brian said something about sharing, so I popped him in the mouth. The next day, Ryan said he and Brian and the other guys were going off for supplies. The rest of us talked it over and decided to split. We took what we could carry and came here."

"Have you seen any of them since?"

"Yeah," Marco says, "a couple of times."

"Where?"

"Sam and I went back a few times looking for supplies," Marco says. "I saw Caesar and Brett there along with a bunch of other guys I didn't know, so I waited."

"How long ago?"

"Oh, that's been months. They cleared out of there just a few weeks after you two left. The last time I saw them, those spaceships flew by, so we took off. We probably could have gone back, but Chuck didn't want to chance it."

"Any idea where Caesar and Brett went?"

"None," Chuck says. "Marco is right though—they have a bunch of other guys with them now. Not sure where they came from, but they seemed like they were getting organized."

A bunch of guys.

I remember Seth's notes on a large group gathering somewhere. How many? Who are they? What has Hannah had to go through? My stomach turns.

"They got her, don't they?" Chuck asks.

"Yeah," I nod once, "they do."

"Shit."

"I've looked everywhere," I say, "but I haven't found any sign of them or her. I did check back at the apartments, but it had been cleared out by then."

"We don't see much of anyone," Chuck says. "When they started talking shit about Christine, I thought it'd be best to keep our distance, ya know? I'd fuckin' die for her, but I'm realistic, too. We focus mostly on making sure those ships can't see our lights at night. I mean, I can only do so much."

I swallow and nod. I know exactly what he means.

"Aw, shit, man," Chuck says as he snaps his fingers. "I should tell ya—I stole one of the guns out of your apartment—one of the shotguns. Never seen those ships land or anything, but I wanted to be prepared."

"That's okay," I tell him. "You keep it. I can only carry so many."

"I think Caesar swiped the rest of them. The ammo, too."

"Wouldn't surprise me." I take a deep breath. "I really thought maybe you'd know more."

"I wish I did, man."

Christine returns and hands me a cup of iced tea without any actual ice. It's still pretty good.

"Thanks."

"You're welcome, hon." Christine runs her hand over my arm in a motherly gesture. "I wish I had some ice for it."

"It's just fine like this," I tell her.

I drink the tea and confirm with Chuck that there are only the four of them there. He tries to get me to stay on at their camp, but I refuse—I have to keep looking for Hannah. Chuck informs me of two other groups they've seen that are located nearby.

"Never seen any women with them, though," Chuck says, "but like I said—we keep our distance. I would have noticed Hannah if she was there though."

"Poor girl," Christine says softly. "I wish we had known what those guys were up to sooner."

"She was worried about you," I tell her. "She didn't want to leave without warning you. That's on me. I wouldn't let her come back. I couldn't risk it."

Christine looks at me for a long time.

"It's okay," she finally says. "I get it."

"It's getting late," Chuck says. "Stay here tonight. Get some decent food in you. We'll see what we can spare to send you on your way in the morning."

"I got someone else with me," I tell him. "Is it all right if I bring her along?"

"Her?" Chuck raises his eyebrows.

"Yeah."

He keeps giving me the stink-eye.

"I just found her the other day," I tell him. "She was being harassed by a group of guys."

"What happened to them?" he asks.

"They met with an untimely end," I reply slowly.

Chuck laughs.

"Well, yeah! Bring her on over!"

I call to Katrina, and she's by my side a heartbeat later. I'm fairly certain Sam's eyes bulge out of his head. In fact, Katrina is kind of looking at him out of the corner of her eye as well.

I introduce her to everyone, and Christine heaps the plates full of food and passes them around. It's not long before she and Katrina are talking recipes. I enjoy the actual cooked meal and then steal myself off to the side of the common area for a cigarette.

Sam, surprisingly, joins me.

"I saw them," Sam says quietly.

219

I stare at him as he shuffles his feet. I'm pretty sure the kid has never uttered a word to me before.

"Who?"

"Caesar and Brett."

"When?"

"About two weeks ago." He looks over his shoulder at Marco. "I wasn't supposed to go over there."

"Over where?"

"Pretty much straight east of here," he says. "It used to be a pretty nice area, I think, but most of it's collapsed. There's a big sign that says 'FOX' lying in the street."

"The Fox Theatre?"

"Maybe." Sam shrugs. "Just a big sign—one that used to light up."

"You saw them there?"

"Yeah," he says with a nod. "I heard them talking, and I think they must be staying in a school nearby."

"Georgia Tech is near there." I think for a moment. "Why didn't you tell anyone?"

"I'm not supposed to go that far away." Sam looks over his shoulder again. "Marco's always watched after me, you know? I don't always do the right thing."

I take a slow breath and nod. Sam's not a stupid kid, but he seems a little slow on some things. Marco usually does his talking for him.

"You won't tell him I was there, will you?" Sam's face scrunches up, and he pleads with his eyes.

"I won't tell him, Sam," I say, "but I'm really glad you told me."

He smiles.

I grab Chuck and pull him off to the side.

"Sam thinks he may have seen them," I say.

"Sneaking around again, was he?" Chuck grins. "He's a good kid, but I think he's always had a short leash, ya know? He likes to explore."

"They might be near Georgia Tech. I need to go check it out."

"Pretty risky."

"I don't give a shit about the risk."

"You're gonna have ta play it smart with those guys," Chuck says. "I've seen you in action enough—you're gonna want to bitch-slap first and ask questions later, but they're too smart for that. If you rush into it, you're gonna get yourself killed."

"Maybe." I really don't care. If I have to die for Hannah, I'll be in a better place than I am now.

"I ain't bullshitting," Chuck says. He takes a step closer to me and points a finger in my face. "You got that rage look in your eyes. If she's still with them, and you get yourself killed, what happens to her? You gotta play this cool. Christine likes Hannah. Hell, I like her, too. I don't want her in that situation, but getting yourself killed isn't going to help her."

I pull a cigarette out of the pack and light it. I know he's right. If I rush in, I won't be able to get her out safely. I don't know who else Caesar has enlisted in his enterprise or what kind of people they are. Once I find them, I'll have to gather information before I make a move, and that's going to take some time.

I take another drag off the cigarette, letting the smoke burn in my lungs. Chuck is still staring at me, and I realize I haven't responded to him.

"I'll keep my cool," I tell him, "at least until Hannah is safe. I may need your help then."

"Anything you want, brother."

"Once I have her away from them, I'll need someone to watch out for her for a while."

We stare at each other for a moment, understanding one another.

221

"Gladly." Chuck holds out his hand, and we shake. "When are you going to leave?"

"You got room for Katrina to stay here? She's on her own."

"Sure." Chuck looks over to where Katrina is sitting with Marco and Sam. "Looks like she'll fit right in with the younger crowd. I swear, Christine thinks we've adopted the boys."

"I bet they appreciate that."

"Sometimes."

"You're going to have to make sure no one sees her."

"Yeah," Chuck says with a nod, "I was just thinking that. We've got decent cover here, but I'll rig up something to make it better. By the looks of it, I'll get lots of help from the boys."

"Good." I head back over to the fire, toss the cigarette into the flames, and crouch down in front of Katrina's chair. "I'm going to be leaving."

"Oh, okay." She stands up.

"You're staying."

"What?" She puts her hands on her hips, and Marco and Sam quickly excuse themselves.

"I've got a lead on them, Katrina," I say, "the first real lead I've had in a long time. I'm going after them, and you need to stay put."

"I'm the reason you have a lead," she reminds me.

"I know that, and I'm grateful. That doesn't mean you're going to continue along on this ride."

"I want to go!" She glares at me, and I almost expect her to stomp her foot in protest. She doesn't, but her hands ball into tiny fists.

I sigh and stand back up.

"Let me make this really clear to you," I say to Katrina. "I'm about to walk into a group of human traffickers. Not just people who took the opportunistic approach after all this shit happened, but people who used to make money off of it before the shit hit the fan. You aren't going anywhere near there."

"I might be able to help."

"You might just get in the way. Getting in the way is a lot like getting killed. I'm sorry, Katrina. You know I appreciate the help you've given me, but I want you to stay here."

"I don't even know these people."

"Well, I do. You'll be safer with them than you would be on your own. I don't even know if I'll make it back."

"Why do you say that?"

"Because if I can't find her, I'm going to kill them all."

Chapter 4

The hike to Georgia Tech is only about an hour, but I'm trying to keep out of sight as much as possible. That means staying off the roads. I don't see any signs of anyone as I reach the old Fox Theatre and its broken sign. The whole street is in ruins, much like the rest of Atlanta. This is the area where Sam said he saw Caesar and Brett, and though there are signs of looting, I don't see any signs of people.

I head across the highway and onto the grounds of Georgia Tech. The buildings are all flattened, making the campus look more like a collection of hills made of bricks and littered with pieces of the bleachers from the Bobby Dodd stadium.

Still no signs of people.

I stick to the outside of the campus, carefully checking around each pile of rubble for some sign of human habitation, but I find nothing, just more debris. I circle the area again, going farther to the center of campus, but again, there is nothing of note. It's getting late. I'm frustrated, and I'm about to give up completely. Maybe Sam was wrong about the location. Maybe he hadn't heard them right about a school campus. He's a simple kid, and for all I know, he wasn't anywhere near this area.

Maybe he even lied to me.

I don't really believe that. Sam doesn't even seem to be capable of lying, but these are strange times, and people no longer behave as they used to.

Looking up at the sky, I realize there are only a couple of hours of daylight left. I either need to find myself a place to sleep for the night, or I need to head back to Chuck and Christine.

I take one last look around the back of what I think used to be the old engineering building. There aren't any signs of people, but someone has definitely been through the area, looking for valuables. Many of the chunks of brick and concrete have been moved alongside the remaining building. There is also a small pile of wires coiled neatly off to the side. As I check them out, I hear something near the street.

I duck behind a brick ledge that once decorated the front of the building. Coming up the sidewalk are two men dressed in T-shirts with jackets tied around their waists. They each have a large pack on their backs, and one of them carries a canvas bag that looks heavy.

I don't recognize either of them. One is short and in his mid-forties, and the other is tall and lanky with a baby-face—definitely younger than the short man, but I can't determine his age. I keep myself out of sight as they go by.

"I just hope this is enough," the older man says.

"It's gotta be," the tall one replies. "Two packs of D-cells, boxes of ammo—that's all high demand shit."

"Yeah, but Caesar's prices keep going up."

"He's got the market cornered, and he knows it."

I lick my lips as my heart starts to pound. I can feel adrenaline rushing through me as I hear the older man speak Caesar's name. I wait for them to pass the brick ledge, then make my way along to the end of it, still crouching. I watch them continue their course up Bobby Dodd Way, heading between the buildings instead of turning left with the street.

I follow as far behind as I dare. I can't risk being seen, but I don't want to lose them either. They're both focused on the path ahead of them and their conversation, and they aren't watching what's going on around them, which works in my favor. I get up a little closer, but can't hear any more of their remarks.

They make their way toward a huge pile of rubble. I've been in this area before, but the destruction of the building is so complete, I hadn't gone close to it. As they approach a large pile of debris, I hang back, peering out from around a pile of broken cement.

The older man reaches into the debris near a piece of dull red cloth. I narrow my eyes as I watch him produce a cow bell on a string. He rings it twice, and the rubble begins to shift. A perfectly camouflaged door opens in the center of the pile. A bearded man with a shotgun peers out before motioning the two men inside.

I stand slowly as they disappear into the huge mound of debris. I blink several times, trying to make sense of what is before me. I look around the area in front of the mound and realize it's grassy, not concrete. This area wasn't a building at all, but a field.

They've constructed a camp out of trash.

I walk the entire perimeter, keeping myself out of sight. Now that I know what I'm looking for, I can see that the rubble all around the area has been moved from its original location and pulled up tight against the collapsed buildings to form a barrier. At a glance, it looks like any other building on the campus—crumbled and useless—but looking closer, I can see the deliberate placement of every item.

They've walled themselves in.

As I study the whole area closely, I find two other obvious entrances. The first appears to have once been the entrance to a parking lot. There are the remnants of a pay station and a gate. The actual entrance is hidden but not as well as the one in the front where the two men entered. I make sure I don't get too close. There are

227

several places around that look like they could be used to guard the entrance. I can't see anyone actually guarding anything, but that doesn't mean they aren't there.

It's the second entrance that has me intrigued.

The building was once a fast-food chicken place. It has been completely leveled except for the far wall, which butts up against the man-made wall of rubble. There is plenty of cover, so I can get a lot closer to it. I'm certain I'm in the cooking are of the restaurant, but none of the fryers or grills are in the wreckage. They've likely been pilfered and taken into the main camp behind the rubble wall.

That's where I find the other entrance.

It's not constructed, per se, but looks more like a leftover, as if those who grabbed the useful restaurant items and took them inside forgot to fill in the hole again when they were done. I don't see any signs of recent activity—the area is covered in dust but not footprints.

I move closer, gun drawn, and try to remain silent. The hole is about three feet wide and four feet tall—roomy enough to shove equipment through but not comfortable to walk. I step inside, bracing myself in case I run into someone, but I don't.

There's a short tunnel beyond the entrance—about six feet long—and then a sharp turn. I can't see beyond it, so I make my way slowly through the tunnel to look. On the other side, I pause. I'm blocked by stacks of crates. There's only about a six-inch gap between them and the tunnel.

On the other side, I see movement. I can't see their faces, but I can hear two distinct voices.

"We need to inventory the rest of the canned goods and the bottled water."

"I spent all fucking day yesterday doing inventory. Get someone else to do it."

"Everyone's got their jobs, asshole. This one is yours for now. Choosing day is tomorrow, so maybe you'll get something else. For all your bitching, you'll probably draw brown."

"I don't know why we're not allowed to trade."

"Because everyone would want to do the same things. Now stop with the butt-hurt and get shit done."

"This fucking sucks."

"Feel free to get the fuck out, then. You wanna try to live out there on your own again? You're welcome to it."

"Caesar thinks he can order everyone around."

"Caesar controls the pussy. You want pussy? Do your damn work."

My hands start to shake. I close my eyes and resist the urge to leap over the crates and beat both of them to death. Collecting myself isn't easy, and it takes me several moments to calm myself enough to focus again.

"There's a whole skid of canned goods out by the main entrance. Let's go get it."

The two of them leave, and I shove against the crate in front of me until the opening is large enough to squeeze myself through it. The large room is full of shelves, all stacked high with supplies. I look around briefly before heading to the door and peering out.

The storehouse opens up into a large green area. There's a fountain in the middle of it and small stations set up all around the fountain. There are water jugs at one of them, and two men stand there, refilling water bottles from the jugs. To the left of the water, there's a table full of canned goods. A man stands behind the table and collects something from each person who comes up to him—I can't tell from here what it is—and then hands them a variety of cans.

There are other stations—one for batteries and propane, another for paper goods. They circle the fountain and look much like the marketplaces I recall seeing in many small villages when I was overseas.

And there are men.

Dozens and dozens of them.

I've seen plenty of small packs of people as I've searched for Hannah but nothing even close to the number of people here. There have to be at least a hundred of them out in the open and who knows how many sheltered away in the surrounding structures. All men.

I still haven't seen any women. I look back and forth, but I still see nothing but men in the area.

Enough that I might not be noticed.

I step out of the door and into the common area, turn to the left, and walk with purpose. I look around with my eyes, but keep my head forward and my pace steady. I pass several people, but no one takes notice of me. There are several small buildings, made mostly of plywood, but they're well constructed and even have gutters with barrels to collect the rain.

"Right this way, gentlemen. The stable is just over here."

I know the voice immediately and have to resist the urge to draw my weapon. I slow my pace and glance sideways to see Brett walking with the two men I'd followed to the entrance. Changing my course slightly, I keep behind him as he approaches one of the small structures and opens the door.

"We have a couple options for you guys, so there's no need to wait." Brett leads them out of my sight through a door guarded by two armed men.

The front of the plywood building looks much like a house with no windows. The guards out front are the only thing that sets it apart from other, similar structures. I pass them by without a look and then glance around to make sure no one is looking in my direction before I veer off and head around the back of the building. I have to turn sideways to make it past the rubble wall behind me. I can't see or hear anything from the back, so I move slowly to the corner.

Around the side of the structure, there's light coming from a crack in the wall where two pieces of plywood don't quite line up. I check again to make sure no one is watching me and then duck behind a rain barrel and crouch low.

Looking inside, I can see the entrance and most of the main room. There's a large couch against the wall and an opening on the far side that leads into another room I can't see. There are two women inside in short, tattered dresses. One has long, dark hair and the other has closely-cropped brown hair.

Not Hannah.

Brett grabs one of the girls by the arm and pulls her close to the older man.

"How does this one strike ya?"

"She's fine...real fine." He makes a show of walking around her, running his hand over her backside and then up her arm. "Can I take her back to the barracks?"

"No, sir," Brett says as he shakes his head. "There's a couple of rooms right here. You can use one of those. Just remember there's always someone out front, so don't get too rough with them. You aren't the only customers tonight!"

He hauls the other woman over to the tall, lanky man, and both pairs head off behind the wall and into separate rooms. Brett follows. After a minute, he comes out dragging another woman.

He pulls her roughly over to the far side of the main room, giving her a shove toward a chair where she sits with her back toward me. She shifts uncomfortably. Her dress is longer but just as tattered as those of the other women. Her hair is long and unkempt.

I can barely see through the crack, but I know it's her. Everything about her is etched into my memory. I know the tilt of her head, the curve of her neck, and the shape of her shoulders all too well.

Hannah.

I reach out and press my fingers to the plywood wall. She's no more that fifteen feet away from me. Brett stands in front of her with his arms crossed.

"Next time we have visitors, I expect you to present yourself with the other girls, you hear me?"

Hannah's head bobs up and down in a silent reply. Brett pulls his arm back and smacks her across the face.

My legs straighten reflexively as my hands ball into fists. As Chuck's words scream in my head, I squeeze my eyes shut and force myself back down to a crouch. I can't give myself away, not yet.

"Fucking answer me!"

"I'm sorry." The voice doesn't even sound like her, not really. It's the same, but the tone is all off. "I wasn't feeling well, and Mandi said—"

"Mandi isn't in charge here, is she?"

"No."

"Then I don't give a shit what she says, and I certainly don't care how you're feeling!"

Brett pulls a bottle out of a cabinet on the wall and holds it up to his lips. He takes a long drink, staring at her the whole time.

"You're hardly worth it now, you know?" Brett says with a sneer. "Fat, ugly bitch. It's only watching you cry that makes it worth the effort."

I close my eyes and shake. I can take the two guys at the door, guns or not. Once I get inside and get my hands on Brett, I'd rip his dick off and shove it down his throat. I could grab Hannah, and then...

...and then I'd be surrounded by a hundred other men.

I squeeze my eyes shut and grind down on my teeth. I can't go after her—not now. There are too many of them, and they'd be on me in a heartbeat. I'd never get her out alive. I'd be dead, and she would be dragged right back and likely punished for the effort.

I have to wait.

Brett places the bottle back in the cabinet, steps up to Hannah, and runs his hand over her shoulder. She sits stiffly, looking off to the side until he grabs her chin and turns her to face him.

"I've got a couple more things to get done," he says, "but I'm gonna be back for ya later, darling. You just hang out, bent over that table with your legs spread until I get back."

He gives her chin a twist, laughs, and struts out.

I can't see straight.

I want nothing more than to yell out, letting Hannah know that I'm here and that I'm coming back for her, but I can't. I know I can't do that. Anything she said or did later could alert Brett to my presence, and I'd never get her out.

I have to wait.

I have to wait while they keep fucking her.

Pushing away from the wall, I stumble slightly before shoving myself back behind the building, next to the rubble. I make my way back to the other side, check around me quickly, and then head back to the storehouse.

There's someone inside, and I have to loiter around the outside for a few minutes, trying not to look conspicuous at all. No one seems to pay any attention to me, though. As far as they know, I'm just another of the many men at the camp.

As soon as the man exits the storehouse, I duck inside and head straight for the opening behind the crates. Shoving myself into the space behind them, I crawl into the tunnel and pull my knees up to keep myself hidden. I tuck my forehead down against my thighs and wrap my arms around my head. I can't keep the images out of my brain.

She's been here all this time. The guys here clean out latrines and divvy up cans of beans for a chance to rape her. How many times? How many times over the last seven months have they taken her? How is she even still alive?

My vision blurs, and the pressure behind my eyes becomes pain. I can't stop the tears. It's all my fault she's here. If I had insisted she stay with me, they never would have gotten her. She wouldn't be here now, preparing for another night of abuse.

I feel like I'm choking. I wipe my nose with the back of my hand and try to get my thoughts composed. I have to push all this aside. I can't think about it. If I do, I'm going to rush in there and seal her fate. If I can keep myself together, I can make a plan that will work, a plan that will get her far away from here.

When I look up, another man has entered the storehouse. He's an older man with a bit of a gut hanging over his jeans, a bald head, and a long, grey goatee. I hold my breath, waiting for him to get whatever he's come for and get out, but he takes a seat at a small table and opens up a large ledger book. I can see him fairly clearly through the cracks, but I don't recognize him. He jots down a few lines in the book, and then the door opens again, and two others approach him.

"Got a newbie for ya, Gary."

The man looks up from his ledger and eyes the scrawny, wide-eyed kid in front of him.

"What's your name?"

"Mike."

"Let me explain to you how our system works around here," Gary says. "Every three days, we get together at Kessler—"

"Kessler?" Mike asks.

"It's the fountain in the middle," Gary explains. "It used to be a big bell tower called Kessler Campanile, but that collapsed in the attacks. There's only the fountain now."

"Got it."

"We meet at Kessler, and everyone chooses a bracelet out of the pot." He holds up his wrist for Mike to see.

I have to shift to one side to get a look at it, but he's wearing one of those rubber bracelets around his wrist—the same kind people used to wear for various causes. The one on his wrist is red.

"People with red bracelets are the bosses, and we always have the same jobs." He speaks fluidly, as if he's made the same speech many times. "I'm in charge of work details and any labor disputes. Wayne and Ryan are responsible for supplies; Brian takes

234

care of the kitchen; Brett's in charge of the whores, and Caesar's in charge of everything."

"Tomorrow is choosing day," Gary continues. "If you get a yellow bracelet, you work for Wayne and help get everything inventoried and figure out what we're getting low on. That info goes to Ryan, and he figures out what we're willing to trade. Black means border patrol and guard duty; green bracelets are camp cleanup, and brown ones mean you're on the latrines. There ain't no trading, either. You get whatever you get."

"Okay." Mike nods. "And then after I do the work?"

"Every day, you'll get a voucher from your boss, based on what you get done. If you do your work, it's enough to keep you fed and provide you with whatever other necessities. If you do really well at your job—go the extra mile—you'll have enough left over at the end of the week. You can spend that on whiskey and whores or whatever else floats your boat."

"Okay," Mike says, "I'll be there. Where do I sleep?"

"There's a barracks set up on the northeast side," Gary says. "There are always a few cots available. If you do well, you move up in the ranks, and you could end up with a better place. Just put some effort into it."

"I will," Mike says. "Anything's better than being out there."

"Good attitude." Gary shakes Mike's hand and closes his ledger. "Meet by the fountain first thing in the morning. You'll meet Caesar and the other bosses then. Be patient—drawing the bracelets can take a little while. Some people like to complain, but don't be one of them. It takes long enough to get everyone their assignments anyway."

They'll all be in one place tomorrow morning, including Caesar and Brett.

That will be when I make my move. That's when I will get Hannah back.

Chapter 5

Outside of the rubble-enclosed compound, I fight with my desire to march right back in and drag Hannah out. I have to remind myself over and over again that it won't work—I'd be dead, and she'd be in the same situation.

Tomorrow morning.

One more night.

One more night of them doing God-knows-what to her.

My stomach heaves, and I swallow back bile. I need to focus, get my plan together, and get us both out of there alive. I only have a vague time frame—first thing in the morning. I'll have to be prepared before then, and that doesn't give me a lot of time.

It physically hurts to walk away from the compound. Hannah is closer now than she has been since she was taken from me, and I don't even want to leave the area, but I have to prepare. I need supplies, ammo, and an actual plan. I run back to the camp, formulating a plan as I go. Chuck greets me immediately.

"Any luck?"

"Yes," I say, panting as I try to recover from the journey. "She's there. They have her at Georgia Tech surrounded by walls of rubble from the buildings. They've built a whole fort there."

"Shit! How are you going to get her out?"

"I've got an idea," I tell him, "but I'm not sure if I can pull it off."

I explain my idea to Chuck, and he stares at me wide-eyed.

"Dude," he says, "that's like, right out of *The Hobbit*!"

"The what?"

"*The Hobbit*! J.R.R. Tolkien. *Lord of the Rings* and all that shit. Didn't you ever watch movies?"

"Not a lot, no."

"Shit, bro!" Chuck scratches his chin and shakes his head at me. "It's a classic! How could you not know about *The Hobbit*?"

I shake my head. It does sound a little familiar, but I have never been one for movies. When I watched television, I tended to fall asleep in front of it.

"You missed out on a lot," Chuck informs me.

"So, are you saying it will work or it won't?"

"It might. It worked for Bilbo, anyway."

"I have no idea what that means." I'm getting more than a little frustrated. I don't have time for this.

"It means that I don't have a better idea," Chuck says. "If you already got in there once without being noticed, you should be able to do it again. As long as no one sees you leaving with her, it should work."

"I hope so. I'm not sure there is another option."

Hearing Chuck's opinion makes me feel a little better. Maybe I have a chance of getting her out without Caesar or Brett catching on. If anything goes wrong, I'm going to be in a lot of trouble, but I can't think that way. I have to keep my mind focused on the goal.

"What are you going to do once you get her out?" Chuck asks.

"I've been taking refuge in bomb shelters over the past few months," I told him. "They're underground and I can use light without worrying about the fliers going overhead. When I found the first one, there was a map of other bomb shelters in the Atlanta area. I don't know if the original owner had a group of buddies or not, but I've found several of them. If you don't know what you're looking for, they are almost impossible to see. I actually fell over the ventilation shaft for the first one. Otherwise, I might have gone right past it. There is one less than two miles from here, and it would be the closest safe place to take Hannah."

"Who do you think built them?"

"No idea," I say. "Definitely people with some military knowledge, but there's no indication of who they might have been. I haven't run into anyone else inside any of the shelters, so whoever it was either didn't make it or wasn't in the area at the time of the attack."

"Keeping Hannah underground for a while is a good idea," Chuck says, nodding. "Safer if she's completely out of sight."

"It might not be a bad idea for you guys to think about moving farther away," I tell him. "Once they figure out she's gone, they may come looking for you."

"You ain't going at this alone," Chuck says. "I'm in it, too."

"Whoa!" I call out. "Wait a minute! This is my fight, not yours."

"Says who?" Chuck stands up straight and crosses his arms in front of his chest.

"Me," I respond. "You don't have to get involved. Hannah is my responsibility, not yours. You don't need to give those guys a reason to come after you."

"You think I don't already have a reason?" Chuck looks pointedly in Christine's direction. "You don't think it's a matter of time before they come after her, not to mention this girl you found?"

"That's not the point."

"That is *exactly* the point."

239

I try to form some kind of valid argument in my head, but I honestly don't have one. I hadn't even considered the idea of help from anyone and wouldn't dream of putting another soul in the crossfire. As I'm about to completely refuse the offer, the rest of them gather around me.

"I want to help," Marco says. "So does Sam."

Sam nods in agreement.

"I'm going to help, too," Katrina adds. "Don't even try to stop me."

"We're all in it," Christine tells me. "Hannah is one of us, and we'll all help get her out of there."

"I can't ask you all to do that."

"Who's asking?" Chuck claps his hand against my shoulder and gives me a big grin. "One for all and all for one!"

I can't come up with a viable argument. I need to save Hannah. The more help I have, the greater the chances of success. My initial plan had been me alone, but if I have help, my odds of succeeding are much better.

"All right," I say as I let out a long breath. "We'll do it together."

~~~~~

"You sure you got this?"

"I've got it, hon," Christine says. "Don't you worry about me."

I'm trying hard to believe her, and I have to admit her aim is pretty good, but I'm not used to handing my sniper rifle over to someone else to use.

"Just stay out of sight, and only use it if you have to."

"If I get a chance to nail one of those assholes after you are away, I might just have to take it." Christine smiles and winks at me.

"No," I say as I shake my head. "There are too many of them. There isn't that much ammo. You would just be putting yourself at risk."

"I'll keep her covered," Marco says.

"I can't have any of you getting trigger happy," I remind them. "This should be a quick in-and-out operation. Hopefully, no one will even know what's happened until it's too late. No shots fired, no bloodshed."

"Do you think that's likely?" Chuck asks.

"I think we're outnumbered," I say. "We have a serious disadvantage if we're discovered. Everyone will hear a shot fired in that area. They have two exits they use plus the one I found. We only have enough people and weapons to cover two of them. I'm still not sure I like the idea of any of you being involved."

"Cope." Christine looks at me pointedly, and I sigh.

"If you come with me, and something happens, you won't be able to come back here. They almost certainly know where you are."

"Sam and Katrina can get everything moved to another location," Marco says. "Just the essential stuff. If something goes wrong, we'll meet there."

"We can go to the house I was staying in with my brothers," Katrina says. "I don't know those guys, and they obviously don't know about me, or they would have grabbed me, right?"

I can't argue with her logic. Katrina gives detailed directions on finding the house—I don't want any of it written down to be found by someone else. Everyone seems clear on where to go if we're separated.

"The two of you move the essentials," I say, "and then meet up with the rest of the group only if there is time."

Katrina and Sam agree though Katrina's not happy about it. She seems to want to be in the potential thick of it.

"We'll meet up with everyone else before daybreak," she says with determination.

"Just be careful," I warn. "Don't be seen."

She salutes me with a grin.

"We're wasting time," Chuck says. "Let's get going."

~~~~~~

Christine, Chuck, and Marco take their positions around the camp. Christine has the high ground on the far side of Ferst Drive on top of a semi-truck trailer abandoned in the street, and Chuck is close to her on the ground. Marco is two hundred feet away, under cover of rubble and facing the main entrance. If I'm discovered, it's the most likely place people will exit, and it won't take Chuck long to join Marco if needed.

I take inventory of everything I'm carrying: two handguns, extra clips, a small crowbar, and my knives. Satisfied, I look to Chuck.

"Good luck," he says quietly.

"Thanks." I give him a grim smile. "I appreciate this—more than you know."

"Go get her," he says as he grins back at me. "I'll get Christine to cook those rabbits in celebration when it's all over."

"Like hell," she calls down from on top of the trailer.

"I'll cook them myself," I tell him.

"Deal!"

It's still dark as I approach the former fast-food place and duck inside. I have to walk carefully to avoid tripping over the debris on the floor as I make my way to the hole in the wall and the tunnel beyond. There's no one in the storeroom when I get to the other side, and I slip between the crates and make my way into the compound without anyone taking notice.

There are only a few people milling about outside. The water station I had seen the previous day now holds large percolators of coffee. At first, I think they have somehow managed to get a generator running, but then I realize the pots aren't plugged in. Someone is filling them from smaller pots heated on a cooking fire.

I keep close to one of the buildings between the Kessler and the shack where they're keeping Hannah. I can't see the front of the latter, but I assume the guards are still posted out front. As the sun breaks over the wall of garbage, more people enter the common area.

I pull the ball cap down a little, shielding my face. I haven't seen any sign of Caesar or Brett, but I don't want to be recognized if they enter the area, and I don't see them first. I scan the faces of the men as they pass me, recognizing only the two men who came to trade last night and the young man who had just shown up to join the camp.

"Come on. It's time for the drawing."

I take a deep breath and push off from the side of the building where I'm standing and walk at a steady pace against the crowd heading for the Kessler. No one seems to be paying attention to me as I make my way to my destination.

To Hannah.

Hold on a little longer. I'm coming.

There is only one guard at the door. I wasn't sure if these assholes would be included in the drawing or not, but one is better than two. He's sitting near the door, propped up against one of the support beams holding the shelter roof in place. He's smoking a cigarette and picking at dirt under his nails.

I walk past, not looking at him, and twirl the small, yellow bracelet around my fingers. He glances in my direction and then goes back to picking at his fingernails. When I step off to the side and around the back of the building, he stays in the same position.

Perfect.

I close my eyes briefly as I center myself. I ignore the fact that Hannah is just inside, only a few feet from me, and concentrate.

With one swift motion, I grab his head, pulling it back as I wrap my fingers around his neck and plunge the knife into his back. I turn and twist it, making sure the artery is severed. The rush of blood over my arm and his quick collapse tell me I'm successful.

Propping him up against the support post, I try to make him look as lively as possible before I jump back to the side of the building. I look around quickly to see if anyone has noticed, but everyone is still focused on the drawing and not looking in this direction.

Moving quickly, I pull the gutter away from the rain barrel and tip it to dump out the small amount of water at the bottom. I glance inside the container. It's smooth enough and shouldn't cause undue injury. There are rails on each side where Hannah will be able to brace herself. It will be a tight fit for her, but it's the best way to get her out unnoticed. Even if her absence is discovered before I'm out of the compound, no one will suspect she's inside the barrel.

Again, I check the group in the distance. A few of them are starting to move about, their tasks for the next few days determined, but none of them seems to be in any hurry. I pull the barrel back into the cover of the shrubs beside the building and peek through the crack in the wall.

There's no one visible inside the main room.

Quietly and quickly, I pull the small crowbar from my belt and slide it into the crack, wedging it securely before pulling back. The plywood is thin and cracks easily under the pressure. I pause a moment, making sure no one has heard the sound, but everyone is still far off at Kessler.

When I've made the opening large enough to squeeze through, I find myself inside the empty main room. I have no idea how much time I really have, so I make my way around the room to the other side of the building.

Beyond the wall, in the area I couldn't see from the crack, there are two small doors side-by-side. They look like stall doors from a public restroom. I can see underneath them well enough to tell that there isn't much inside other than a pile of blankets to make up a bed. To the side of the stall doors, there's another small cot.

Hannah is there, lying with her back to me, sleeping. I can see her shoulders shift as she breathes steadily. I check the door behind me as I approach and then lay my hand on her shoulder, shaking her gently.

"Hannah!" I call quietly. "Hannah, wake up! I gotta get you outta here!"

She doesn't respond though I sense her breathing change. I want to revel in the fact that she's right here in front of me for the first time in seven months. I can feel her warm skin under my fingers again, and all I want to do is hold her close to me and enjoy the moment, but I can't.

"Hannah! It's me! It's Falk! Now come on—I'm going to get you out!"

She still doesn't move, so I grab onto her shoulder and pull her toward me. Her eyes are open but dull and unseeing. Her hair drops off her shoulders in long, greasy strands. There's a bruise on her cheek and smudges of dirt on her neck and arms.

But that's not what alarms me.

When I look her over, I see her round, protruding stomach.

Oh fuck. Oh fuck, no.

I have to force myself to start breathing again. Hell, my heart may have stopped, too. My fingers are shaking as everything hits me at once. I know what they were doing to her—I've known it since the day they took her away—but seeing the evidence of what they have done is too much.

"Oh, shit, Hannah," I whisper. I run my hand along her arm, but she still hasn't uttered a word.

What the fuck am I going to do? How is she ever going to be able to live with this?

I consider smacking myself in the face to get my shit together. Everything else can be assessed later—I have to get Hannah to safety. I can't fall apart now.

"Come on," I say again. This time I grab her by the shoulders and haul her to a sitting position. She's dead weight in my

245

arms but stays up once she's sitting. I grab her legs and pull them over the edge of the cot, but I can't get her to stand up. She just stares into space without saying anything.

This is taking too long.

Out of options, I take a second to compose myself and then slip my arms underneath her. I'm going to have to carry her like a child—there's no way I can toss her over my shoulder with her swollen belly. Carrying her isn't easy. I have difficulty just getting her through the crack I made in the wall, and I have to force it farther open while holding on to her with one arm.

Outside, I look at the rain barrel and stop.

There is no way I can put her in there. She may not even fit in it at all, and even if she did, I can't roll her around in her condition.

There's a lot of movement off to my left. Everyone in the group is breaking up now, moving off to start their new assignments. The other guard could be back here at any moment.

"Not supposed to leave the stable." Hannah's looking left and right, but there's still only dim recognition in her eyes.

"I'm getting you out of here," I tell her, but she doesn't say anything else.

But how?

I can't just walk carrying a limp, pregnant woman without being noticed, and I have no other way to conceal her. Wrapping her up in a blanket or something like that would be equally suspicious. I wouldn't get ten feet without being questioned.

What could I say that wouldn't arouse suspicion? I need something that will be believable enough to allow me to get past whoever stops me without having to draw my gun. If I have to fight my way out, I'm going to lose.

Possible reasons I might be moving her to another location run through my head, but anyone who stops me is going to wonder why I would be moving her at all. It's not my job. Only one of her guards would be asked to do something like that.

246

The guard.

"Stay here," I whisper to Hannah. "Don't move, okay?"

I have to lean her up against the wall, telling her again not to move. She still doesn't respond to me, and I'm not even sure if she knows what's happening. She does stand in one spot at least, giving me the chance to get what I need.

Crouching down to stay out of the line of sight, I rush over to the dead guard. On his wrist is a black rubber wristband with a silver "X" on it. Slipping it off his hand, I place it over my own and roll up my sleeve so it can be plainly seen.

I get back to Hannah, wrap my arm around her waist to support her, take a deep breath, and then start walking purposefully down the path toward the storeroom.

"Come on, Hannah," I whisper in her ear. "You gotta walk with me. Just a little ways, then everything's going to be okay."

There are still a lot of people in the group near the Kessler, drinking coffee and complaining about their assignments. Others have broken off from their groups. The first two glance at me but say nothing. The third one is the man I saw yesterday leading the traders around the camp.

He narrows his eyes as he watches me walk closer to him. I can see the questions forming inside his head already. I beat him to the punch.

"Hey!" I call out to the guy who is eyeing me. "Where's Brett?"

"What are you doing with her?" he asks with a glare. "She isn't supposed to be out of the stable."

"Hey, I just got this job," I tell him as I hold up my wrist. "Brett said he wanted her brought to him and Caesar right away. I'm just trying to do my damn job!"

He continues to eye me suspiciously.

"Come on, dude," I plead with him, "I only got here last night. I don't want to fuck this up."

His face relaxes a little.

247

"They were headed toward the depot," he tells me. "Someone just brought in a new batch of toilet paper, and some fuckers are already fighting over it. It's on the other side of the main entrance."

"Cool," I say. "Thanks a lot, dude. I owe ya one."

"You'll be all right," he says. "Pretty nice duty for the first day!"

"I ain't arguing!" We both laugh, and I move quickly past him, heading in the direction he indicated.

When I'm sure he's not checking on my route, I veer off and pull Hannah over to the storeroom. I have to pull her close and balance her against my hip to pull the door open. Thankfully, there's no one inside. I shift her weight to my other arm to get her through the door.

"What the fuck?"

I glance over my shoulder and see Brett standing not twenty feet from me.

"Hey!" he screams at me, and I see his eyes widen in recognition. "Motherfucker! You aren't going anywhere with her! Caesar!"

Fuck!

I shove Hannah the rest of the way into the storeroom and slam the door behind me. I let her go, and she sways slightly but doesn't fall. I grab onto one of the shelves with both hands and pull as hard as I can, toppling the shelf in front of the door. I grab the table from the middle of the room and lodge it in front of the door as well.

"Move, Hannah!"

She's still almost completely non-responsive. I grab her arm and pull her to the crates near the opening. I have to drag the crate back farther to fit her through the crack and then shove her into the tunnel.

"Come on," I tell her. "You gotta crawl. Move with me, Hannah. You can do it! Move!"

248

I shove her ass to get her to go, and she moves a couple of feet. It's enough for me to grab the crate and pull it back, blocking the tunnel. I can hear scraping sounds coming from the door, along with a lot of yelling and cursing. The mess from the shelf won't hold them for long.

I shove at Hannah again, trying to get her to go, but she doesn't even seem to be aware of what's going on around her. I'm not sure if she's in shock or just shut herself down, but I don't have time to figure that out now. I keep pushing and encouraging her, and we finally get to the other side of the tunnel.

A shot is fired behind me, and I hear the bullet ricochet off the side of the tunnel.

"Go out the front entrance!" I hear Brett yell. "Cut them off before they can get out! I've got them from this side!"

"Goddammit, Hannah! Move your ass!" I scream.

I don't know if my voice or the shot spurs her on, but she moves faster. She gets out of the tunnel and stands up on the other side, turning and moving backward as I start to crawl out.

A hand grabs onto my ankle, and I'm pulled off balance. I fall forward and land in the debris on the floor, cutting my hand on something in the process.

I roll quickly, drawing my gun, but I'm not fast enough. Brett is on top of me, and I take a right hook to the chin. The back of my head bounces off the floor, stunning me for a second. Brett is straddling my chest, grabbing his gun from a shoulder holster and swinging it toward my face.

I slam my fist into his crotch. I don't have enough leverage to really make it count, but it slows him down enough for me to grab his wrist and twist it backward. The gun falls to the floor, sliding out of reach. I quickly punch up and into Brett's nose. He jerks back as blood spatters over my face.

Turning my hips, I dislodge him and pin him to the ground. With my knees on his shoulders, I land blow after blow into his face.

How many times? How many times has he hurt her?

I punch again. I'm fairly certain I've cracked one of my knuckles, and I don't care. I should have killed him when he first touched her. I wanted to. My gut instinct told me to, and I didn't do it. He's punching me in the side, bruising my ribs, but I don't stop.

A sudden, sharp pain in the side of my head sends me to the ground. I'm not sure what he hit me with, but Brett is now on top of me, wrapping his fingers around my throat. At first, I'm too dazed to respond. All I can manage is to grab his fingers and try to pull them off my throat, but it's no use.

I'm lightheaded. I can't be more than a minute away from losing consciousness. I have to move. I have to *think*, but the dizziness is getting to be too much. I can't loosen his fingers from my neck.

No. If he gets me, he'll get her back. Oh fuck, no!

With all my strength, I reach up and grab a hold of his shirt, wrapping it up in my fingers. I yank him down as I clench my stomach and pull myself up, slamming my forehead into his. It dazes me, but it also gets his hands off my neck.

I roll to the side, choking and gasping. Brett is on my back a second later, and we roll again through the rubble all over the floor. Something hard slams into my shoulder, halting the roll with Brett back on top of me. He doesn't grab for my throat again, though—he reaches for whatever stopped me.

The barrel of my Sig is pointed under my jaw.

Brett's eyes are wild as he grins maniacally down at me.

"You never should have come here," he says.

The blast rings through my ears. I wait for the pain, but nothing comes.

Am I dead?

There's screaming, but the sound is dulled in my ringing ears. I realize Brett's weight is no longer holding me down, and I roll to one side.

Brett is next to me, holding his shoulder and yelling at the top of his voice. I look toward the wall and see Hannah. In her hands is Brett's gun.

Holy shit! She shot him!

I look back to Brett, who is still rolling on the floor in pain. I grab my Sig from where he left it and waste no time shooting two rounds into his chest and another in his head. I stare at the body for a long moment, making sure there is no room for doubt before I clamber back to my feet. I stumble a little—my head is swimming and my ears are ringing—and make my way to Hannah's side. Slowly, I cover the barrel of the gun with my palm and take it out of her hands.

Hannah takes a step back, pushing herself against the wall near the broken glass door. She wraps her hands around her stomach, and tears start to run down her face. Her eyes are still blank, but she comes with me when I pull on her arm. Her other hand still reaches around her stomach, cupping the bulge.

Marco stares at her with wide eyes as I bring her out to the street.

"Where's Chuck?" I ask.

"He told me to come make sure you got out! He's at the front gate. There were a lot of guys coming out, but I think he was leading them the other way."

"They know I'm coming out over here," I say, shifting Hannah's weight on my arm. "I need to get her out of here. We *all* need to get out of here."

"Marco and Katrina are at the old Coke place."

"You go ahead," I tell him. "Get them ready to move out. We'll cover you."

Marco rushes off, and another shot rings out. I recognize the sound of the discharge of my rifle. I glance at Christine and then in the direction she's aiming.

Chuck appears from around the corner, firing shots as he turns and backs toward the truck.

"How many?" I yell out at him.

"Four armed!" he calls back. He fires again. "Make that three!"

There's an additional blast from the rifle.

"Just two!" Christine's aim is good. "I can see some others coming around!"

She fires two more shots as Chuck makes his way across the street, and two more men fall. I can hear the shouts of others coming around the bend, and I have no idea how we're going to get away without being seen.

"You're fucking awesome, babe!" Chuck yells as he grins up at his wife. His eyes are full of admiration, and he raises his arm to give her a thumbs-up. A sharp pop from near the building echoes off the wall of rubble. Chuck's expression changes suddenly, and he drops to his knees.

"Chuck!" Christine's scream is followed by her unloading the rest of the rifle's clip into the man at the edge of the street. His body jerks several times before he falls backward to the ground.

I pull Hannah the rest of the way behind the trailer.

"We gotta go!" I yell up to Christine.

"We can't leave him!"

"Come get Hannah!"

Christine drops from the top of the trailer, tripping slightly as she lands but manages to keep herself upright. She runs to my side and takes Hannah from my arms.

"I'll get him," I tell her. "You follow Marco. Get Hannah and yourself out of here."

Christine nods. I check the clip of my Sig and then step out from around the trailer, firing. There's a group coming out of the alleyway between the building and the wall of rubble, mostly holding blunt objects in their hands. Only one has a gun, and I take him out quickly before firing on the rest. They scramble, running back toward the main entrance.

252

Chuck is on his face in the street. I crouch down, gun still raised, and roll him over. He blinks at me a few times but doesn't speak. There's a trickle of blood at the side of his mouth, and his shirt is soaked in it.

"Come on, big guy," I say quietly. I glance up at the building, but all of the men have taken off, presumably to better arm themselves. In the distance, I can hear Caesar's voice, shouting commands, but I can't hear the actual words. "Let's get you out of here."

I loop my arms under Chuck's shoulders and drag him off the street. He's a big guy, and the dead weight isn't easy to haul, but I get him behind the trailer and check him out.

There's a huge hole in his stomach. He's losing blood so fast, I don't know why he's still conscious.

"Chuck? Can you hear me?"

He looks toward the sound of my voice, and I can tell he's trying to smile. He raises his hand slightly and gives me a thumbs-up. He opens his mouth as if to say something, but a bubble of blood comes out instead. His chest heaves, and I place my hand on his shoulder to try to hold him down.

There's nothing I can do.

"Fuck, man," I say quietly. "This wasn't supposed to go down like this."

Chuck closes his mouth and his eyes. He raises his arm a little more, thumb still extended, and then it drops back to the ground.

I close my eyes for a second and then push myself back up onto my feet. I can't take his body with me. I'll never be able to carry him and get away fast enough. Caesar and the rest of his crew could be out here at any moment.

"I'll try to come back for you," I whisper. "I swear. Thank you, brother."

Chapter 6

"We can't stay here."

The group looks at me. We're barely a mile from Caesar's compound, and we need to move fast. Everyone's face holds the same expression of shock as we stand one fewer than we were. Christine is actually more composed than any of the rest of them.

"I should have stayed," Marco says. "I should have covered him better."

"You were exactly where you needed to be." I step up to him and place a hand on his shoulder. "There is nothing—*nothing*—you could have done to change this. You can't go back. You can't 'what if,' and you can't blame yourself for that bastard getting Chuck. You trust me when I say I am not done with those guys yet."

Marco nods and wipes his eyes with the back of his hand.

"Falk is right," Christine says. She blinks a few times and dabs at her eyes. "Chuck…well, Chuck always wanted to go out in a blaze of glory like some comic book hero. I think he's satisfied with that. Now we need to get Hannah and Falk out of here to give Chuck's actions some meaning."

"I'll make my way back there when I can," I tell her. "If it's at all possible, I'll bring him back to you, make sure he gets a proper burial."

"He wouldn't want you to risk that." Christine shakes her head. "Go on. Get out of here. There will be a lot of days to talk about the dead. Get Hannah somewhere safe. We'll lead them off in another direction."

"They're going to come after you, too," I say.

"I realize that."

"I'll make sure they follow me and Sam," Marco says. "Katrina and Christine will head to the house, and we'll head back to our camp. I can leave a clear trail. They'll follow us, and the girls can get away."

"If they find you, they're going to kill you."

Marco's throat bobs as he swallows.

"I know," he says, "but they're not going to get Katrina. Christine, either."

I look over at Hannah where she sits on a large slab of broken concrete, staring at the ground. I've got a long walk ahead of me, and she's still practically comatose. I need to get her somewhere where I can make her feel safe again, but I'm not sure how long it will take if I have to carry her the whole way.

"Will she fit in the cart?" Sam asks quietly.

"What cart?" I ask, wondering if he's reading my mind.

"The one we use behind the bikes," Sam says. "Would she fit in there? It would be better than carrying her."

"She might." I think about it for a minute. If I head all the way back to the camp for the bike, I'll have wasted far too much time. I might end up at my destination faster, but I won't be far enough away from the camp. Surely Caesar and his group are gearing up to come after us. "There's no time to get it."

"I stashed it nearby."

"It's here?"

"Just behind the pile of cars, where the parking garage used to be."

"What made you bring it?" I ask.

"I thought if someone got hurt, they might need it." Sam shrugs. "It would be a lot faster than carrying anyone."

"Yeah," I respond with a nod, "let's get it."

I head over to where Hannah is sitting, kneel beside her, and place a hand on her shoulder.

"Sam's got some transportation worked out," I tell her. "I've got a safe place where we can hide out until this blows over, okay?"

She just stares.

I follow her gaze to a puffy dandelion growing between the cracks in the sidewalk. I can't get her to look at me or respond to my questions.

I've seen the same look far too many times in the eyes of the men who served under me—men who had seen one too many horrific acts for their minds to process. They were the ones to watch out for back at the base. If they weren't able to snap out of it quickly, they ended up putting bullets in their own heads.

Sam retrieves the bike, and we get Hannah loaded into the cart. It's actually fairly easy to get her to curl up and lay down. She continues to stare at nothing, looking so small despite the protruding belly, and my chest tightens up at the sight.

"In a week's time, assuming all is quiet, I'll head for Katrina's house," I tell them all. "If you aren't there, try to leave me some kind of sign that you're all right and where I can find you."

"My brothers and I had a code for that," Katrina says. "It's math-based using coordinates and easy enough if you know what to look for."

"Show me."

Katrina hands me a map of the city—one that shows the lines of latitude and longitude on it—and writes down the simple equation she and her brothers had used in the past, and I shove it into my backpack.

"I'll put it in that same desk where the notebook usually is," she tells me.

"Won't you need the map back?"

"I have another one back at the house," she says.

"Perfect."

"We need to move," Christine says again.

I make sure Hannah's all right on the back of the bike before I climb onto the seat. Marco and Sam gather up everything and start heading straight to their camp, leaving signs along the way.

Katrina and Christine are taking a long route to the house, backtracking a couple of times to hide their trail.

"Be careful," I tell them. "Don't take any chances."

"We'll be good," Christine says.

I nod and place my foot on the pedal to get going.

"Falk?"

I look back to Christine, and she stares at me with narrowed, serious eyes.

"You raise that fucking baby like it's yours."

I clench my jaw. It's not something I'm prepared to think about, but I understand her meaning. Hannah will need me now more than she ever has, and I'll have to do anything and everything to help her, regardless of how I may actually feel.

"Yeah," I finally say with a nod. "I will."

"You better."

~~~~~~~

The bicycle and cart work wonderfully. My legs are killing me by the time I reach my destination, and I'm sure I never would have made it if I had to have carried her the whole time. I ditch the bike and the cart between a collapsed house and detached garage, help Hannah to her feet, and then carry her behind the house and into a small wooded area near a man-made lake. I've only been to this shelter once, but I find it again without too much trouble.

This shelter is far larger and more sophisticated than the one I had claimed as my own early on. It has been designed for nuclear fallout. The hatch drops down to a sloping ramp that ends with an airlock. There are four small rooms inside: a main living area with a food preparation center, a table and two chairs, a bedroom, a storage room, and a generator room. Off the main room there is a small shower, a decent-size washbasin on the floor, and a toilet.

I seat Hannah on a chair before going around and turning on some battery-powered lamps. There are some supplies in the storage area but not a lot. I think the shelter was never completely finished. There's no fuel for the generator even if it would start up, which it likely would not. There's some food and a few bottles of water as well as some toiletry items and extra batteries for the lamps.

Hannah hasn't moved from the spot where I put her. She doesn't even look around the room. I have no fucking idea what I'm supposed to do. She's completely shut down. I've dealt with several guys in similar states but only long enough to get them some actual help. I'm not a therapist.

Start with the basics.

I get her to drink a little water, but she doesn't respond to anything I say to her.

She doesn't even look like herself, and it's not just because of the pregnancy. I don't know where the dress she is wearing came from, but I don't think it's something she ever would have picked out for herself. There are bruises on her arms and her cheekbone. She's smudged with dirt, and her hair is greasy and unkempt.

Hannah has always been very neat and orderly. She likes her clothes comfortable and her hair clean and soft.

I have some of her clothes back in the other bomb shelter, but they don't do me any good here, and they wouldn't fit her now anyway. Digging through my own things, I find a pair of sweatpants and a T-shirt.

She doesn't look at me as I pull the dress off of her, but she does start to shake. It's just a little but still noticeable. I speak to her quietly, reminding her that it's me and that I'm not going to hurt her, but I don't think she comprehends my words. When I finally get the dress over her head, I gasp at the sight of her body.

She has no undergarments at all, and though I've seen her body before, I hardly recognize it. It's not just her stomach though I have to swallow hard to force myself to look at the bulge and what it represents. I'm reminded of jokes about women swallowing basketballs. That's exactly what it looks like, and I wonder how far along she is or if she even knows.

It's the bruises that alarm me the most.

There are marks on her shoulders and upper arms. Her thighs are covered with discolorations ranging from dark purple to brownish-yellow. There are additional bruises on her breasts and rope burns around her ankles. She smells of old sweat and semen.

"Oh, fuck, Hannah." I look away for a minute. When I look back, there are tears in her eyes. I run my hand over her cheek and whisper to her. "It's over. They're never going to touch you again."

The tears leave streaks on her dirty face. With no response from her, I decide to get her cleaned up before putting clothes on her. I try to wipe her face off with a wet cloth, but I can tell right away that it isn't going to be enough. I won't be able to hold her up in the shower even if the water does work, which it doesn't.

I look to the large basin. It's not bathtub-sized, but she'll fit in it as long as she's sitting up. I decide to go that route and quickly warm water on the propane stove to fill the basin.

Coaxing Hannah to stand and walk over to the basin, I lift her over the edge and then lower her into the water.

"It's warm." They're the first words she's spoken since we got here. I watch her reach down into the water and let it cascade through her fingers.

"Yeah, it's warm," I respond. "I remember how much you complained when the shower water went cold."

I grab a cup from the food prep area and use it to rinse her off and wet her hair. I'm pretty sure she isn't capable of washing herself, so I grab some shampoo from the storage area and start working on her hair. It's grown much longer since I last saw her, and it's a tangled mess. I wish I had some kind of conditioner for it to help get the snarls out. I'm pretty sure there are other things that work as a conditioner, but I can't for the life of me think of what they are.

Hannah doesn't even seem to be aware of what's going on. She just keeps placing her hand in the warm water and watching it run through her fingertips when she raises her hand up again.

Once her hair is lathered up, I grab the cup and start rinsing the shampoo out. I can get most of it without her help, but I don't want the suds to run into her eyes.

"Lean your head back a little for me." I place my hand at the back of her head, and she tilts her head back against it. I carefully pour the water around her hairline to get the rest of the shampoo out while she stares up at me with the same dull expression.

"You look like him." She reaches up and touches the side of my face with her wet fingertips.

"Hannah," I say softly. "It's me. It's Falk."

She shakes her head.

"He's dead."

I don't know why I'm surprised to hear the words. Of course they would have told her that. They might have even believed it themselves. I put the cup down and place my hand on her cheek.

"I'm not dead, Hannah," I say. "I'm right here."

I feel the pressure on my palm as she leans into it. She smiles slightly and then shakes her head.

"It's a dream."

"It's not a dream." I reach up and push some stray hairs off her forehead. "I'm here. Brett's dead, and you're safe now."

"Safe." She huffs through her nose. "Simple word."

"You're safe," I repeat. "I'm going to get you cleaned up, get you into some comfortable clothes, and then you can sleep for a while. Okay?"

She doesn't respond, but she does keep looking at me. I take that as a good sign and start washing off the rest of her. I'm careful around her bruises and her belly, expecting her to cringe from my touch, but she doesn't. The only time her expression changes is when I wash between her legs. She looks away from me, and her eyes become unfocused.

"Almost done," I say softly. I grab the cup and pour water over her upper body before helping her to stand so I can rinse off the rest of her. The only towels in the shelter are small hand towels, and they aren't very useful, but I do my best. I dry off her body, but the water dripping from her hair gets her wet again. I know she used to wrap her hair in its own towel, but the ones I have aren't big enough for that.

I settle for draping one over her shoulders to catch most of the drips and then dress her in the sweats and T-shirt. The shirt stretches over her stomach, leaving a little gap where her skin shows, but it will have to do for now.

"Okay," I say, half to myself and half to her, "let's see what we can do about this."

I use a large comb, and I discover very quickly that I suck at brushing hair. I can't get the comb through the tangles at all. At first, I think it's just because her hair is so wet, but after drying it a bit more with the towel, I still can't get the teeth through the strands. I actually get the comb stuck in her hair.

Hannah reaches up and takes the comb from my hand. I sit back a bit and watch her twist it back out of her hair, then start combing the strands herself. She starts at the bottom, getting the tangles out there before moving up farther. It works much better than starting at the top as I had done.

I continue to watch her as I grab some of the first aid supplies from my pack and doctor up the few cuts and scrapes I acquired during my battle with Brett. She doesn't say anything, but she seems focused on the task at hand. It takes her a while to get through it all, and I just let her do her thing until she finally sets down the comb.

Standing from the edge of the bed, I head over to my pack and pull out my woobie. I take Hannah through the doorway into the small bedroom, climb into the bed, and scoot back toward the wall. Hannah tentatively lies down on her back beside me. She doesn't look in my direction, and her body is stiff.

I pull the woobie around my shoulders and cover her with it. I want to hold her close to me, but I'm almost afraid to touch her. I want to help her feel safe, but I'm not sure where I should put my arm. I could slide it between her stomach and her tits, but that seems weird to me—like my arm will be pinned between. If I put it around her stomach, it will be a constant reminder of what she's been through. I'm having a hard enough time trying not to think about whose child she might be carrying. I meant it when I told Christine I'd help Hannah raise the baby as if it were my own, but I can't help the thoughts that run through my head.

The baby could be Brett's or Caesar's. It could be the progeny of some other nameless, faceless man who abused her. How is she even going to be able to raise it? What if she doesn't want to? What if she refuses to?

"This is a woobie," Hannah says suddenly. She looks up at me with wide eyes, and her shocked expression makes me smile.

"Yeah, it's my woobie."

"Don't make fun of the woobie." Her tone is serious, but it makes me smile.

"Yeah, you better not." I chuckle.

She tightens her grip around the edge of the woobie and pulls it close to her shoulder. Settling her head against my shoulder, she lets out a long sigh. I tighten my arm around her for a second, but I don't want to put too much pressure on her belly, so I relax again.

"Falk had a woobie." Her voice is so quiet, I can barely hear her.

Her words make me feel cold.

"It's me, Hannah. It's Falk."

"I know," she whispers, "but this is a dream."

"I swear I'm real, and I'm here. You aren't dreaming."

She looks at my face and narrows her eyes a little. She reaches up, stroking a single finger from my temple to my jaw. She touches my eyebrows, the bridge of my nose, and then my lips. When she takes her hand away, she sighs.

"When I wake up, will you still be here?"

"Absolutely," I tell her. "I'm going to stay right here the whole time. I'm not going to let go of you. When you wake up, I'll be right in this spot."

"Okay." She doesn't seem completely convinced, but I feel the tension in her muscles wane as she rolls to her side, her back to me, and closes her eyes.

I listen to her breaths until I'm sure she's asleep. Pressing my chest against her back, I close my eyes. I'm mentally and physically exhausted, but I still can't sleep. There are too many thoughts running through my head, and I don't know what to do with any of them.

I need to get Hannah completely out of the Atlanta area. I have no doubt of that. There are too many men at that camp who know who she is. I could never recognize them all, and the likelihood of running into any of them again is too great to take that risk.

Somehow, I need to prepare for childbirth.

But before I can do any of that, I have to find Caesar and kill him.

~~~~~~~

I'm not sure how long I've slept, but I'm sure I've been in the same position the whole time. I shift my hips a bit to get comfortable, but it doesn't help. I'm not moving even though I have to pee. I told Hannah I'd be right here when she woke up, and I'm not about to go back on my word.

Settling back with my head just above hers, I hold her closer to me. I inhale, grateful for the clean scent of her skin and hair. I wish I had some of the fruity-smelling shampoo she used back at my apartment. I can't remember the brand, but I liked the smell. If she can remember the name of it, I'll try to find some later.

Hannah rolls slightly and digs her fingers into my arm for a moment. She grunts softly as she shifts her hips and reaches down to rub her stomach. She stretches, pressing her back against my chest, and her eyes fly open.

She jerks away from me, and I have to tighten my grip to keep her from falling off the bed. Her gaze darts from my arm around her to the woobie covering the lower half of us and finally to my face.

"I'm awake." Hannah looks from my face to the room around her and then back to me.

I'm not sure if she's asking a question or making a statement.

"You're awake." I try to smile, but I feel apprehensive. I have no idea how she is going to react.

"You're...you're still here."

"I'm here."

"You're real?" It's definitely a question this time.

"I'm real, Hannah."

"Oh, God!" She throws her arms around my neck, nearly strangling me.

She tucks her forehead against my chest and starts to shake all over. I wrap my arms around her back, holding her as tightly as I dare, and breathe a sigh of relief. I know this is far from over, but having her acknowledge that I'm here is huge.

"You weren't there." She pulls back and looks at me. Her eyes fill with tears. "I kept thinking you were going to show up, but you didn't. They just kept...they kept going, and you weren't there."

"I know. I..." I don't know what to say.

Hannah begins to sob as she buries her face back in my chest—huge, terrifying sobs that shudder through her body. Her grip around my neck tightens, and my ears burn with her cries.

I squeeze my eyes shut.   Every defense, reason, and justification for abandoning her jump to the front of my brain. I want to tell her I was shot in the back. I want to explain to her how it felt to look down and see my own intestines through that hole in my side. I want to tell her how much it hurt to grab my skin and hold it closed while trying to remain conscious enough to stitch myself up. I want to tell her that I'm not completely sure how I managed to survive and that I was trying to get to her—I just couldn't get there fast enough because I didn't have time to fix my leg properly. I want to tell her that I still walk with a limp sometimes because of it.

I don't.

It doesn't compare to what she's been through.

"God, Hannah, I'm sorry. I'm so sorry. I never should have left you alone."

I feel her tears soaking through my shirt. I remember the first night she was with me and how she had held me and cried then. I'd felt so awkward. I didn't know how to respond. I still don't know how to respond.

This is all my fault.

"I'm sorry. I'm sorry." I say it over and over again as if it makes some kind of difference. As if it takes away anything that's happened to her.

My eyes ache with my own tears. I just want to be able to take all her pain away. I want to erase it, but I can't. I can't change what's happened, and I can't do anything about the constant reminder she will have of what she's been through—the baby growing inside of her.

Slowly, Hannah's choking sobs diminish to raspy breathing and eventually quiet. I hold her to my chest as my own tears dry on my cheeks. My eyes burn and my head aches, but I don't move. We stay like that for a long time. I don't have any comforting words. I just hold her until she shifts in my arms and moves her hand from behind my neck to my shoulder.

She slides her fingers down my arm until she comes to my hand. She takes it in hers and then places it over her stomach. I close my eyes again as my throat tightens up. I wait for her to tell me it's my fault—that she blames me for this child she never wanted and will never be able to love.

All because of me.

"It's yours, you know," she says suddenly.

"What?"

"The baby—it's yours."

My heart flutters in my chest.

"How do you know that?"

"I just do." She shrugs.

She can't possibly know that. Even if she found out she was pregnant shortly after she was captured, she couldn't know for sure if it's mine. We've had sex exactly four times. There is no way I could have gotten her pregnant.

Is there?

We hadn't used protection. I remember seeing a box of condoms in one of the stores during a supply run and almost considered grabbing them. I wanted her, and I knew it, but it seemed in poor taste considering what she had already been through. It was simply too presumptuous, so I hadn't taken them.

"It is yours, Falk," Hannah says again, more emphatically this time.

I watch her eyes, but her expression doesn't change. I have no doubt that she believes what she's saying, but I'm not sure I can believe it.

Four times—that's it. Four times over three days. The last time was the morning before she was taken from me.

Swallowing hard, I reach down and run my hand over her stomach, caressing her slowly. Hannah places her hand on top of mine again and guides it down around and underneath the bulge. A moment later, I feel a bump move across my palm.

"Is that…is that the baby?"

"He's kicking," she says with a smile. "He's saying hi."

"Was that his foot?"

"I'm not sure," Hannah says with a shrug. "Maybe a knee or an elbow. It's hard to tell."

I've never felt anything like it. It seems completely unnatural and totally *right* all at the same time. I move my hand down a little more, trying to figure out just where the little guy went, and I feel another bump.

Looking back into Hannah's eyes, I can't explain how I feel. The idea that this child could be *mine* hadn't entered my thoughts before she said it. I hadn't considered the possibility at all. Now that I'm thinking about the very idea that this child could be exactly what she says—a son that comes out looking like a combination of Hannah and me—has my head spinning and my heart racing. I'm elated and excited, but there's also a hint of terror deep down inside of me.

If this baby is mine, then maybe she'll be able to put all of it behind her. Maybe she won't see the child as a constant reminder of what she's endured.

I stroke the side of her face and lean in close to her. I watch her eyes, not completely sure how I will be received. When she glances down at my mouth and her eyes close slightly, I close the distance between us and press my lips firmly against hers.

If Hannah believes the baby is mine, then I'll believe it too.

Chapter 7

Hannah and I stay in the shelter for several days. There are plenty of supplies to keep us going, so there's no need to go outside. I still exit twice a day—once in the morning and again in the evening—just to make sure there aren't any signs that someone has tracked us here.

I find nothing.

Hannah progresses faster than I could have imagined. She's not exactly herself, but every day she's a little closer. She has nightmares and cries a lot, but when that happens, I just hold her, and she calms down pretty quickly.

I have no idea how much of it is trauma and how much of it is pregnancy.

We sit down together and calculate the due date of the baby based on when we were last together. She's roughly six weeks away from giving birth, and I know we have a lot of preparation to do before that time.

"We should meet up with the rest of the group before you're due," I say. "The more help we have, the better."

"I don't think Christine ever had any children," Hanna says. "What about that other woman you said you found?"

"Katrina? I doubt it. She's pretty young."

"How much help do you think they're going to be?"

"Not sure," I say with a shrug. "I just know they'll be more help than I will."

"Don't you want to be there for the birth of your son?"

"You have no idea if it's a boy or a girl."

"You didn't answer the question."

"Of course I want to *be there*," I tell her. "I just don't want to be there *alone!*"

"I thought you were a big, bad military hero!"

"What the fuck does that have to do with babies?"

Hannah covers her mouth to hold in the giggles.

"We can use your woobie as a cushion."

"You mean, like…while you're giving birth?"

"Yeah."

"Oh, fuck no! You are not going to give birth on my woobie!"

Hannah bursts out laughing this time, and I scowl at her. Her mood swings are going to give me an ulcer. I check the time and figure it will be about ten minutes before she starts crying over something else. It's become the pattern.

She stands up on her toes and presses her lips to mine. I kiss her back, opening my mouth as I feel her tongue against my lips. She runs her hands over my chest, and I can feel the rest of my body—one part in particular—beginning to respond. I gently grab her hands and pull them down to her sides.

I haven't touched her in that way since I brought her here. It's not for lack of desire. Frankly, I'm terrified to attempt sex with her again. I have no idea how she's going to react, and I'm afraid I'll trigger something inside of her.

There's more to it as well.

I can't stop thinking about how long she was a prisoner. I have no idea how many men have been inside of her since I was with her or exactly what they've done to her. The bruises are healing, but the evidence is there. I know she was brutally raped multiple times. I know she was sodomized. I can't even imagine everything they may have done to her. I don't blame her for any of it, of course, but it's still in my mind.

There's also a tiny, completely irrational part of me that thinks the baby might grab on to my dick.

I know enough about anatomy to know the idea is ludicrous, but that doesn't stop me from thinking about it. I'm also afraid I'll do something that will hurt the baby, but more than anything, I can't stop the image from invading my brain of having sex with Hannah and then feeling a tiny hand grab on to the end of my cock.

Hannah stares at me, her expression confused. It quickly changes to anger as she rips her hands away from my grasp and stomps away.

"What?" I call out after her.

It's not like she can get very far from me in the small shelter. She's only twelve feet away when she reaches the other side of the main room and turns on me.

"Do you still want me at all?"

Shit. Yeah, I've fucked this up.

"Of course I do."

"So why won't you touch me?"

"I didn't want to…shit, Hannah." I stop talking and run my hands over my face. "I don't know what to do here. Yes, I want you. I want to pick up right where we left off, but I don't know how to do that."

"Because of everything that happened to me in between?"

"Yeah."

"Or is it because I'm fat?"

"Christ, Hannah, you're not fat. You're pregnant."

"Same thing."

"It is not!"

There is no way I can win this argument.

I rack my brain for the right words to say but come up with nothing. She's been through so much, and I can't take it all away. There's nothing I can do or say that will make any difference.

Tears start streaming down her face. I go to her, wrap my arms around her, and hold her against my chest. It isn't easy with her stomach in the way, but I manage. She leans into me, circling my waist with her arms.

"I'm fat and ugly," she says again.

"You're hardly worth it now, you know? Fat, ugly bitch."

Brett's malicious words to her echo through my head. I tighten my hands into fists. For a moment, I wish he was still alive so I could beat him to death again.

"*He* said that to you." I clench my teeth. "He did that just to break you down. You're beautiful, you're strong, and I'm still in awe of you."

She shakes her head but doesn't speak. I kiss the top of her head, hold her, and try to think of something clever to say. I've never been a wordy guy, and I don't think I can really start that now. I'd spent all that time looking for her and thinking about her, dreaming about her, but now I don't know what to say to her.

Maybe that's the answer.

"I spent all that time looking for you," I tell her. "Every day, I'd picture your face in my mind. I'd remember what it felt like to hold you. I'd hear your voice in my head, usually yelling at me about something."

She looks up at me and cracks a smile as I wipe the tears off her face.

"I'd remember how you smell and how your eyes would shine when you'd look at me. That's what kept me going. I knew you were out there and that you needed me."

"I thought you were dead," she says quietly. She sniffs and tightens her grip. "That's what they told me. They said they shot you dead."

"Nearly."

She pulls her hand around and presses it against the scar on the side of my stomach. She freaked out the first time I took my shirt off and she noticed it. She cried when I told her exactly what had happened.

"Now that is ugly," I say with a smile. "You used to ogle my abs."

"I did not!" She tucks her head against my chest again.

"Blushing, aren't you?"

She shakes her head vehemently.

"Liar." I place a finger under her chin and tilt her face up to look at me. Her cheeks are tinged with red, and she won't meet my eyes, but there is a hint of a smile. "Does it make me ugly?"

"The scar?" She narrows her eyes in confusion. "No, not at all."

"Do *you* still want *me* even though I'm not the same as I was before?"

"Yes."

"I have other scars," I tell her. "Not the ones you're thinking of. I've got scars you can't see, just like you have. Some of those scars…well, they changed me and not in a good way."

I take a step back and run my hand through my hair. I try to figure out what I need to say—how I can make it clear—and decide the beginning is as good a place as any.

"When I was overseas…" I stop in mid-sentence. I don't know how to explain this.

Hannah takes my hand in hers. She leads me over to the edge of the bed, and we both sit down. She doesn't let go of my hand. I stare down at our entwined fingers, take a deep breath, and start.

"When I was deployed, I saw a lot of shit. Horrible shit. Shit I can't think about even now. That got to a lot of the guys in my unit. Some of them never got over it."

"It didn't get to you?"

"Not in the same way." I shake my head. I'm already not explaining it well. I decide to just move on. "There was this…this kid in my unit. Eighteen years old. Went to basic right out of high school. Before we were deployed, I met his parents. It was a dinner function I didn't even want to attend, but I had to go anyway. He introduced me to them, and they were so proud of his decision to enlist, but his mother pulled me aside and told me how scared she was for him."

I take a long breath and slowly breathe it out again.

"I told her not to worry. I told her I would bring him back, safe and sound."

"He didn't come back, did he?" Hannah squeezes my hand.

I shake my head.

"We were on patrol. Lots of insurgents all around us. An IED exploded, and he…fuck."

There is a wall in my head that is threatening to crumble. Behind it are images of torn flesh and fragments of bone. There's a memory of gathering pieces together…trying to find those parts that were missing…

"No," I finally say. "He didn't come back."

There's more to the story—much more. Right after that, shit happened that I could never talk about, not even now. Some secrets are best left buried. Even though it involves our current situation, I don't think it matters anymore.

"I shut down after that," I tell her. "I became…emotionally closed. Just turned it all off. It worked. I completed my tour and went on to do another one after that. Took some shrapnel during the last one. They decided I'd done enough at that point and kicked me out. The thing is, after I was discharged, I couldn't turn that part of me back on."

It's close enough to the truth. Hannah doesn't ask questions. She just waits patiently for me to continue.

"Before I got into security, I did nothing for two years. I got a good pension from the army, and I lived off of that. Spent way too much time in bars. Had a lot of one-night-stands, but if a woman actually seemed interested in me…well, I couldn't handle that. I'd just stop talking to her. My sister would call to try to get together with me, but I always found some excuse. She finally stopped trying. Even once I started escorting executives and shit around, that didn't change much. I did my job, collected a paycheck, but none of it really mattered."

I remember sitting alone in my apartment between assignments, a glass of whiskey sitting on the table in front of me, right next to the bottle. I remember staring at the television but never actually watching a single show. I remember my phone ringing, glancing at the screen, and never answering the call.

"You changed all of that," I tell her. "I never thought I'd be able to turn that side of me back on, but with you, it was possible. I hadn't cared about anything since that happened, and I didn't think I ever would again."

"I was already impressed with you before I ever met you," I say. "I told you that before. But when I stitched up your leg—no pain meds or anything—shit, Hannah. I've never known anyone like you. Every time I turn around, you're surprising me. Everything you've been through over these past months, and even now, you're trying to comfort me over something that happened five years ago."

I close my eyes for a moment. The words are on the tip of my tongue. They want to come out, but I have no idea what will happen once I say them. I decide to take the leap.

"I'm in love with you, Hannah. I can't believe I'm fucking saying that, but I'm in love with you."

I feel her hand on the side of my face, and I open my eyes to look at her. She breaks into a big smile.

"I love you, too, Falk."

275

Capturing her mouth with mine, I try to pour everything I feel for her into a single kiss. Any words I use will be inadequate, so I try to show her with my lips and hands. I'm still terrified of doing something wrong, but I know I can't hesitate. I want her too much.

"I need you," I whisper against her lips. "I need you so much."

"Please, Falk," she whispers back. "Please don't wait any more."

I kiss her again as I reach down and grab the bottom of her shirt. I carefully pull it around her belly, break the kiss, and take it off. Hannah grabs my shirt and does the same, then runs her fingertips over my shoulders and chest. I stand quickly, release my belt and drop my shorts and boxers to the floor. I step out of them without ceremony and then help Hannah get her sweats and panties off.

I pull her down to the bed and lie down beside her, running my hands over her skin. Most of the bruises have faded to yellow, but as I brush one, I get concerned.

"Hannah…"

"Don't, Falk," she says. She places her hand over mine, covering both it and the bruise beneath. "I know what you're thinking, and you have to stop."

"I just…I can't imagine what you went through," I say. "It tears me up when I see that. I'm the reason they got to you."

"You're the reason I survived," she says, correcting me. "If it weren't for you, I couldn't have endured it."

"But…you thought I was dead."

She nods and closes her eyes. She grips my hand tightly with her fingers as she speaks.

"Every time they…every time someone came for me, I just closed my eyes and thought about you holding me. I thought about your arms around me, wrapping me up and keeping me warm. I didn't think about what was happening—I only thought about you."

"I'm not sure that makes me feel any better."

"Falk…" Hannah sits up, places her free hand on her face, and lets out a long sigh. "I don't want to go over this all the time. I don't want to have to think about it anymore. I need *you*. I need to feel *your* hands on me. I need to feel *your* cock inside of me. I need you to…to…"

Her voice cracks, and she lets out a shuddering breath.

"I need to feel *you* again so I can stop feeling *them*."

Pressure behind my eyes threatens to give way, but I blink it back. Hannah releases my hand, lies down again, and then runs her hand over my hip. She grips my shaft, stroking it slowly as I close my eyes and lose myself in the feeling. I reach for her thigh, and she wraps it around my hip. Running my hand up over her ass, I lean over to kiss her again.

My dick throbs in her hand, and I gasp into her mouth as she squeezes the shaft for a moment. She slides her fingers over my balls, sending tingles up my spine. I caress her back and then cup her face with my hand.

"Are you sure you're ready?"

"Yes."

"Please, tell me you'll stop me if you need to. I know I keep saying it, but I want you to be sure. *I* want to be sure."

"I will. Falk, it's okay. I want this so much. I *need* it."

Staring into her eyes, I find them dark and shimmering with desire. Her mouth is partially open, and the heat from her breath touches my skin. My pulse increases as I brush my thumb over her lips.

She really wants this.

I run my hands all over her. I don't want to leave a single square inch of skin untouched. I want to go down on her—feel her come on my face—but I'm honestly not sure how to do that with her stomach the way it is. I stay on my side and opt for another tactic. Reaching down between her legs, I slowly part her folds and slip a finger inside. She's warm and soft, so I add another finger as she groans and bites down on her lip.

Circling her clit with my thumb, I press my lips to hers, cradling her head with my free hand. Our tongues meet, and she grabs the back of my head to bring me closer and deepen the kiss. I feel warm everywhere as well as slightly dizzy.

I just want to give her everything.

It's been so long, and I can't wait any longer. I get up on my knees and look her over, trying to figure out what angle to use. I don't think I can kneel between her legs and hold her up without putting her in a really awkward position, so I drop my feet to the floor. I reach under her and pull her body to the edge of the bed.

Hannah cringes and twists her body. She pulls her knees up and stretches, but her expression doesn't change.

"Not working?" I ask.

"My back hurts," she says.

I should have thought of that.

"Roll over?"

"Yeah," she says, "I think that will work better."

I help Hannah get to her hands and knees, and then she crawls up to the head of the bed so I can get behind her. I run my hands over her ass, enjoying the view. My cock bobs up and down, as if it knows exactly what's in front of it. I scoot up closer, sliding it between her legs. I look down and half expect to see a little hand reaching out.

Don't think about it. Don't think about it. Nothing is going to grab you.

I slide in slowly, wanting to be as gentle as I can. She feels different—as if my cock is surrounded by a nest of silk pillows instead of gripped by a silk glove. My balls tighten up, and I nearly come in her immediately.

"Oh, fuck, Hannah! You feel so good."

"Please," she whispers, "more."

Leaning over her back, I reach around and cup her tits in my hands. They're so much bigger now, and her nipples feel huge under my fingertips.

I love it.

I pinch them gently, rolling them and pulling on them until I feel her clench around me with every stroke. With one arm still wrapped around her torso, I reach around her belly to her clit, slowly circling it—matching the movements of my thrusts.

"Oh, God!" Hannah pushes back against me, and I nearly lose my balance.

I pull back and shove forward with my hips, and she arches her back against my chest. Her breaths come in short gasps, and she digs her fingers into the blanket on the bed as she starts to shudder.

"Oh, yeah," I moan, "that's it! Come on…let me feel it."

Hannah lets out a high-pitched squeak and then a long groan as every muscle in her body tightens. She drops her forehead to the pillow, and I pick up speed.

I can feel her walls caressing my shaft, pulling me inside of her. There's nothing in my head but the sensation of being inside of her and the glorious pressure all around my cock.

I give up and let go. Waves of pleasure ripple through my body as I empty into her. I hold myself deep inside of her for a moment, but my arms are starting to shake with the exertion of holding myself up. I stroke in and out of her a few more times and then slowly pull out.

I flop over onto my back, eyes closed. I can hardly move. I haven't even masturbated since the last time I was with her, and it almost feels like the first time. I want to wrap her up in my arms and hold her against me, but I can't seem to make my arms work. I'm completely sated and in danger of passing out.

Hannah snickers, and I open my eyes to see her propped up on her elbow and staring down at me.

"Did you survive?" she asks, still giggling.

"Barely." I take a deep breath, but my heart is still pounding. "I hope that was good for you because my cock might not work for another week."

She strokes my stomach with her hand, letting her fingers outline the scar. I manage to move my arm just enough to wrap it around her shoulders, and she places her cheek on my chest. I close my eyes again and let the warm fog in my brain seep into me.

"Falk?"

I startle slightly at Hannah's voice, my mind still half asleep.

"Yeah?"

"Is your sister still...still alive?"

"I don't know." It isn't a topic I've wanted to consider. "She was living in California last I talked to her. That was...I guess Christmas before all this happened."

"Did she have a family of her own?"

"She married her girlfriend the day after gay marriage was legalized," I say sleepily. "Her wife had a kid from a previous relationship. His name was Garth, I think. I only met them once when he was about six. My sister was happy with the whole thing, though."

"Are...I mean, were your parents still around?"

"Not for a while now," I tell her. "My father passed away while I was overseas during my first tour—heart attack. My mother passed away from cancer a couple years after that. Both of my parents were only children, so it was just my sister and me left after that. We're seven years apart and were never very close."

"Do you think about looking for her? I mean, trying to find out if she's still alive?"

"Not a lot." I turn to look at Hannah and reach out to touch the side of her face. "I'm really only concerned about you."

Chapter 8

I pause in my evening patrol, lean back against the detached garage where I left the bike and cart, and light a cigarette. I bring the smoke slowly into my lungs, savoring it before letting it loose into the night sky. I close my eyes and take another draw. It calms me.

The air is still warm and dry. It's nearly November, and I'm not the least bit chilled by the night air even though I'm only in cargo shorts and a T-shirt. There hasn't been any rain since the night before I found Katrina.

Tomorrow I'm going to leave Hannah behind and head to the house where the rest of the group should be. If I'm lucky, I'll find them, and I'll be able to bring Hannah there before the baby is due. If they aren't there, hopefully they will have had time to leave me enough information to find them again.

I stare at the orange glow at the end of my cigarette as I finish it off and toss it down at my feet. I grind the butt under my heel to make sure it's out. The last thing I need is a fire near the shelter.

I must have burned my retinas because the orange glow is still visible to my eyes even when the butt has been extinguished. I blink a few times, but it doesn't disappear.

I'm immediately alert.

Crouching slightly, I peer at the bright orange glow through the gap between the trees on the far side of the demolished house. It's no more than five hundred feet from the entrance to the shelter. My muscles tighten—I haven't seen a light like that in weeks. I haven't seen a light like that on the ground since I was in Iraq five years ago.

I pull the rifle from my shoulder and hold it in front of me. Stepping slowly past the rubble and into the trees, I follow the orange glow. Just past the trees there are two additional houses, both flattened. Beyond that is a clearing, and in the clearing is a five-sided craft with two long, glowing shafts on either side. The craft itself is small, likely designed for only one or two occupants, but still takes up most of the area.

In front of the craft is an eight-foot tall, bipedal creature. Its arms and legs are rectangular with claw-like hands and feet at the ends. The body is neckless and bulky. It resembles the Transformers I played with as a child—the ones that shifted from a robot to a car or a truck.

I walk into the field, straight at the creature, until I stand face-to-face with the thing, my rifle raised to my shoulder. My heart is pounding, and I feel sweat trickling down the center of my back and into my shorts.

The creature shifts, and its arms and legs come together as if it's standing at attention. I hear a hissing sound as it moves, and it makes me think it runs on hydraulics. A claw-like hand rotates and the fingers open. There's a distinct hum, and a flickering image appears in front of the creature. It comes into focus and solidifies before my eyes.

The image is vaguely human. It's tall with thin arms and legs, and the hands are misshapen with two fingers and two thumbs,

282

mimicking the claws on the creature. The image is devoid of clothing though there are no sexual parts displayed—no genitals, no nipples. The image appears to have long hair, but there are no individual strands.

The face of the image though…the face is Hannah's.

"Greetings, Falk Eckhart." The voice is feminine but hollow. It's similar to voices heard on navigation systems and smartphones.

I slide my finger over the trigger and try to see past the image, well enough to determine the most vulnerable spot on the creature behind it, as a sense of déjà vu creeps through me.

I've been in this exact position before.

"You have questions," it says.

"A few, yeah." I can't hide my aggressive tone. I'm sure it doesn't understand the concept of sarcasm anyway.

"Ask, please."

The image's hand rises, its palm pointing upward as the head tilts slightly to the right. I swallow hard as I aim the rifle at the space between the creature's head and torso.

"Your high velocity projectile weapon will not impact me."

"That isn't you," I respond, nodding toward the huge metal contraption.

"You are correct," the image says. "My body is encased in a protective covering that provides suitable conditions to sustain my life. Your weapon cannot penetrate this protective covering."

"You said that the last time." I don't lower the rifle. I've believed this thing before, and I don't have any reason to believe it now, assuming it is one of the three I'd encountered previously.

"I am not here to harm you, Falk Eckhart." I tense as it speaks again. "You have questions, and I am willing to answer them."

"Are you Vole?" Images of a similar creature along with two companions fill my head. In the dim light coming from the craft, I can't be sure if the protective suit it wears looks exactly the same as the one I had seen or not. There is a symbol over the front of it that resembles an atom, and I remember seeing the same symbol before. The first time, they were in the desert near the border between Saudi Arabia and Iraq.

"I am."

"The image you're projecting is different."

"The image locks onto your psyche," Vole says. "At the time, the person in the forefront of your mind was a young man under your command, one who had been killed in an attack shortly before our encounter. Now, your focus is on your mate."

I narrow my eyes at Vole's choice of words but don't argue the semantics.

"You lied to me," I say. "You said you were going to pass us by."

"My exact words were, 'I see no benefit in further observation or interaction with your species,'" Vole says. "That is the information I conveyed to my superiors."

I'm frustrated by the inability to see the creature's face—observe its expressions, assuming I could understand them at all. Not knowing what it really looks like unnerves me. I want to know the face of my enemy.

"You said we weren't ideally suited for your needs," I say, not wanting to waste any time with this thing, "but you took the women and children. Why?"

"We were in need of vast labor forces," it says. "It was determined that the females and offspring of your species best fit those needs. They were deemed more likely to cooperate than human males. Your species is not ideal, and I did not see any benefit to its use, but we had deadlines to meet."

"Deadlines?"

"Our supplies were running low. There wasn't adequate time to locate another population."

"Where are they now?"

"Relocated."

"Relocated where?"

"The population was divided into three parts," the image says. "The first was sent to a Sulphur-rich satellite around one of your outer gaseous planets. The other two were directed to similar environments in other star systems."

I remember a book I had as a child, depicting various parts of the solar system—the sun, the planets, and the moons surrounding those planets. There was an artist's representation of the sulfur snow on Io, one of the moons of Jupiter or Saturn—I can't remember which. I have no idea why they want or need sulfur, and I don't care at this point.

"Why kill the men? You could have taken the women and children without harming the men."

"To create chaos," Vole responds. "The resulting turmoil will maximize the efforts your species would need to achieve to respond to the invasion. By the time you have reorganized into a civilized society again, we will be untraceable."

"What about the animals?"

"Sustenance for the workforce," Vole says. "We have found that labor forces are more productive when supplied with a familiar food source."

"What about the pets?"

There's a pause before the image responds.

"What is 'pets'?"

"The dogs and cats," I say.

"Sustenance for the workforce," Vole repeats.

My stomach flips over as I understand the creature's meaning. I decide not to ask any more questions about that particular topic.

"You didn't tell us that any of this was a possibility when we spoke the last time," I say. "You said you were looking for resources, not slave labor."

"We had no wish for conflict at that time," Vole says. "I was not aware of the proposed strategy behind the collection of the labor force. If it is any consolation to you, I voted against the destruction of the males. My research determined that your technology was too far behind our own to develop the necessary means to transport outside your own solar system. By the time you would develop such technology, we would have moved far beyond your reach. However, my colleagues voted against my alternative plan."

"Yeah, I feel much better about it all now."

"I'm pleased you understand."

No doubt—sarcasm is lost on it.

"What about the climate changes?" I ask. "No rain, high temperatures. It should be at least fifteen degrees colder now than it is."

"I'm afraid the extraction process had some unforeseen effects on the atmosphere," Vole says. "I've corrected for the problem, and it should not occur again. Eventually, the atmosphere should return to its previous condition."

"Eventually?"

"I would estimate between thirty and forty years. The damage was minimal."

"Minimal!" I snort and shake my head. "So, are you here to kill off the rest of us?"

There is a pause before the image responds.

"No, Falk Eckhart. I am a researcher –a scientist, not a soldier. I am merely taking my final readings of the progress of your society before I return."

"And what have you found?"

"Your culture has behaved within the statistical deviations of my research," it tells me. "You have formed factions that now war against each other. It will be decades before you recover enough to begin advancing your technology again. I am about to transmit my final report. Earth is deemed of no further use to us and not a threat."

"You're leaving, then? All of you?"

"The military forces left the surface nine days ago," it says. "They are in orbit now but will evacuate when my report is complete. They have no reason to return."

"So, you won't be coming back."

"There is no reason to do so."

"You're just going to leave us like this."

"You will rebuild in time." The head of the image tilts to the left. "It may not be in your estimated lifetime, but eventually. Already you begin to reproduce."

I narrow my eyes. It says the words as if Hannah is prepared to have this baby—as if she really wants it or would have let her pregnancy get this far if she'd had a choice. Everything Hannah has been through is directly the result of me not giving the order to attack these things when we first saw them. Maybe we wouldn't have been successful. Maybe they would have annihilated us in a second. They could have also then decided we weren't worth the effort, and Hannah would be fine.

Fuck this thing.

I pull back on the trigger and hear the blast followed by a sharp, metallic twang.

Vole doesn't move.

"Has your curiosity been satisfied?" it asks.

"Fuck you." I lower the rifle and take a step backward. I'm not surprised by the lack of effect, but it would have been nice if it had just fallen backward or something. I take a deep breath and then shout at it. "If you're done, then go on! Get out! I've got nothing more to say to you."

"I don't understand your animosity, Falk Eckhart. Are you not better off than you were before?"

"What the hell is that supposed to mean? In what way am I better off?"

"You were alone," it says. "You now have a companion—a function. You protect and provide for her, and you will protect and provide for her offspring. Your life has direction."

I can't respond. The creature's words hit far too close to home. I've thought the same thing myself—more than once. I had no purpose in my life before, and now I have one. I have Hannah, and I have the need to keep her safe. It gives my existence meaning.

If none of this had happened, I would have escorted her to Washington. She would have testified and hopefully put those bastards on death row for what they had done. Afterward, I never would have seen her again.

"A pretty high cost for the sake of my happiness," I mumble.

"But a benefit, still," Vole says. "Do you have any further questions?"

"No." I would have to be able to wrap my head around what I've heard before I could ask anything else.

"Then I shall take my leave."

I give the thing one last stare, toss my rifle back over my shoulder, and then turn on my heel to head back into the trees.

"Falk Eckhart."

"What?" I turn and glare at the image and the creature behind it.

"The child in the female's body is constructed of your DNA."

I tense, and I can't take in a breath. Part of me thinks Vole is just saying what I want to hear, but there's no reason for a lie. I hadn't asked the question; it hadn't even occurred to me.

"How do you know?"

"I analyzed the scan of the female's incubated offspring when preparing the projected image."

"You know for sure?" I have no real doubt of Vole's technological accuracy; I just need to hear the words.

"You were scanned during our initial encounter. The match is certain."

I nod. I'm not about to thank the creature for the information, but it does set me at ease.

"Why are you telling me this?"

"I understand now that you considered my words at our last meeting to be intentionally inaccurate. If I give you information you consider important, you will be appeased."

"You want to appease me?"

"I did not desire the destruction that has occurred. If you are appeased, I can add that information to my report, and the mission will be considered a successful effort."

"A successful effort!" A single burst of laughter erupts from my throat. All of this is nothing more that some paper-pushing alien trying to make their quota and get their bonus.

I consider firing the rest of my anno into it, but I know it will do no good.

"You want to appease me?" I yell at it. "Go have your military flatten those fuckers over at Georgia Tech. Destroy the bastards who fucked over Hannah. Maybe then I'll be *appeased,* and you can add it to your fucking documentation!"

"Do you have the precise coordinates?"

What?

My body chills despite the warm night air.

Is it…is it offering to…?

"Yeah," I say. My voice is barely a whisper, and I have to clear my throat to continue. "Yeah, I do."

I fish the city map out of my pocket as my heart begins to beat faster. I double check to make sure I've got it exactly right and then read the numbers off to Vole.

"I'll dispatch the message immediately."

"You're serious."

There's a pause before it answers.

"I don't understand. Why would I interject humor at this point?"

"Never mind." I shake my head. "I'm just surprised you're willing to do something for me."

"As I stated, Falk Eckhart, I find it necessary to make amends. I was not in favor of our actions, and you impressed me at our initial encounter."

"So, you're going to blow them up?"

"The vessels have already been dispatched." The creature behind the image shifts, and I hear the hum of hydraulics again as it turns its head skyward. "I must return now."

All I can do is nod. My brain is on overload.

The image returns the nod and then shimmers and blinks before disappearing. The creature that stood behind turns and heads back to its craft, and I head back into the trees. I return to the spot where I had been smoking earlier and have another one while I try to compose myself.

I replay the conversation in my head as the orange glow rises into the sky and quickly disappears over the horizon until there is nothing left but stars.

I stare into the darkness for several minutes before I see another orange glow descending from the heavens. At first, I see one light, but as it approaches, I realize there are three of them. They come down low, circling the city once in perfect formation.

There's a deep hum that seems to shake the air around me, and the three crafts separate, move around to form a tight circle, and then pause in the air to the west. The flash of light is so bright, I have to look away. There is an incredible explosion, and a ball of fire rises into the air.

"Holy shit!" I stare open-mouthed to the west as the ships rise back into the night sky and disappear. There is a pillar of smoke rising into the sky but nothing else.

"Falk!"

"Over here!"

I stomp out my cigarette and take off toward the shelter at a slow jog.

"Did you hear that?" Hannah stands just at the entrance, wrapped in my woobie. Her stomach is sticking out, and her hair is all over the place.

She's incredibly beautiful.

"Yeah," I say, "I heard it."

"What was it?"

"Dunno." I point off in the direction of Georgia Tech. "Came from over there. Looks like a fire or something."

"Do you think it was them? I mean, Caesar and everyone?"

"Maybe they blew themselves up," I reply with a smile. "Come on. You need to get back inside."

I'm not going to tell Hannah what I saw any more than I'm going to tell her about my original encounter. I really don't know how she would react, and I don't care to find out. I haven't forgotten about the other women held prisoner in that compound and she won't have either. She's under enough stress with the move to Katrina's house and the baby nearly ready to be born. She doesn't need additional heartache.

The invasion has passed us now. It's time to rebuild.

I lean in and kiss Hannah softly, then turn her around and take her back into the shelter.

Tomorrow we can start a new life.

~~~~~~

"What happened to those little flavoring packs?"

"Which ones?" I look over at Hannah's ass as it sticks out of the storage room door while she rummages through the shelves. I like the way her ass wiggles when she moves.

"The ones for water!"

"We might be out of them." I know damn well that she used them all up, but the idea of going over there with the pretense of helping her look and then ending up fucking her on the floor of the storage room is really tempting. Unfortunately, there isn't time.

"Dammit!"

291

"Don't worry about it," I say. "We can look for more along the way."

It's been nine days since I parted ways with the rest of the group, and I told them I would check back with them in a week. We really need to get going, or we won't make it there before dusk.

I had initially planned to make the trek without Hannah, but I just can't. I can't leave her alone for that long. Besides, the longer we wait, the harder it's going to be for Hannah to travel. She's already starting to waddle a bit, but I value my balls, so I don't mention it.

She's still fucking around in the supply room.

"Really, Hannah, we have to go! We're going to run out of daylight before we get there."

"Ugh! All I want is a fucking iced coffee!" She slams whatever she's been holding against the bottom shelf and pulls herself up to her feet.

I have no idea where the iced coffee thing is coming from. That's a new one.

"Isn't coffee bad for the baby?" As soon as I start to speak, I know they're the wrong words to say. Her icy glare nearly throws me against the wall.

"Are you ready to go?" she asks, ignoring my comment.

"Yeah, sure." I've been ready for hours.

The trek to Katrina's house isn't that far. We could have used the bike and cart, but that would mean sticking to the roads, and I don't want Hannah out in the open for that long. I could have made it there on my own in a couple of hours, but we have to keep stopping so Hannah can rest. I'm nervous each time, constantly watching in every direction each time we stop and wishing I'd gone with the bike anyway.

I keep telling myself that Caesar's camp was destroyed—I went to check it out the day after the fire. There was nothing left of it, and I have no reason to believe anyone survived. However, I've learned to trust my instincts. I don't exactly feel like we're being watched, but something doesn't feel quite right either. It takes six hours to reach our destination, and I never quite shake the feeling.

The house is dark and quiet as we approach. I look around for the other bicycles or signs of a cooking fire, but I see nothing.

"Stay here," I whisper to Hannah.

She nods and presses herself up against a row of hedges at the edge of the yard.

I creep up to the side of the house and look in the window but see nothing. I head around to the back and find the remnants of a cooking fire, but it's cold.

"They aren't here," I tell Hannah. "No one else appears to be here either, so let's go look inside."

Once inside the house, I go straight for the desk in the living room. There's a notepad in the middle of it, and I pick it up to page through it. About a third of the way inside, I find a single page with numbers on it.

I grab the paper Katrina had given me with the formula on it and recalculate the coordinates.

"All right," I tell Hannah, "I know where they went."

"Are we going to go now?"

I look outside. It's not dark yet, but there are only about two hours left of daylight. I don't like the idea of traveling at night, and the location Katrina left me is about two miles away. Hannah isn't very fast in her condition, and there's no way we'd make it there before nightfall.

There's also a reason they left this location.

"I don't like it," I finally say. "We should leave. Do you think you're up for it?"

"How far?"

"Not far."

"Every time you say that, we end up walking for hours." She sighs and leans against the couch with one arm wrapped around the underside of her belly and the other pressed against her back. "Couldn't we just stay here for the night?"

My stomach is all knotted up. They must have gotten out safely since they left the note, but it still doesn't feel right.

"I'll carry your pack," I tell her. "I know you need the rest, so we'll take a few minutes, but I'm not comfortable staying here."

For a moment, it looks like she's going to argue with me, but she looks closely at my face and nods instead.

"Just give me a little time," she says softly.

Hannah sits on the couch. She looks exhausted, and I consider changing my mind for her sake, thinking I am just being paranoid.

Always trust your gut.

I drop down on my knees in front of her and take her shoes off. She leans back and practically purrs as I rub her feet.

"God, Falk, that feels so good!"

"That's the same thing you said last night." I grin.

"I'm not sure if you're better with your hands or your cock."

"I'm not sure if I should be insulted or not."

"Not." She smiles down at me. "I think you should keep doing that. Maybe I'll come."

"Don't tempt me." I release her feet and slide her shoes back on. "We need to go."

I grab both her pack and mine and hoist them onto my shoulders. Hers is much lighter, and it's left me off balance, but it will still be more comfortable for her if she's not carrying anything.

"I'm anxious to see everyone again," Hannah says as we walk. "It feels like it's been forever since I've had someone else to talk to."

"Do I bore you?" I grin and adjust my speed yet again as she slows. I'm trying to get a couple of steps behind her, but she seems to want to walk at my side.

"You are not the greatest conversationalist." She glances at me out of the corner of her eye.

I shrug. I can't argue the point. Conversation is distracting, and I need to be on my toes at all times. I scan the area again, that niggling feeling still in the pit of my stomach.

"Tell me about Katrina," Hannah says.

"I don't know that much about her." I reach up and scratch the back of my head. "She's pretty feisty, like you. I'm interested to see if she has taken a liking to either of the guys. They're all about the same age, and Marco and Sam were both eyeing her."

Hannah laughs softly and then cringes.

"What is it?"

"I don't know," she says as she takes a deep breath. "I think it's just all the walking. My back is still killing me, and my feet are threatening to strike."

"Not much farther, I promise." I'm lying. At the rate we're going, it will be another hour before we reach the coordinates Katrina provided. Hannah has slowed down again, and I sigh as I shorten my stride and move a little to her right.

We only get a few blocks farther before Hannah has to stop. She wraps an arm around the underside of her belly, supporting it.

"What's wrong?" I ask.

"Maybe it was something I ate," Hanna continues. "I feel like if I could just get out a good fart, I would feel better, but I can't."

I laugh.

"It's not funny!"

"You saying 'fart' is funny."

"It hurts!"

I reach out and rub the small of her back.

"When we look for those flavor packets, we'll find you some Gas-X, too," I tell her.

"I may need it. It really does hurt."

Hannah leans against a retaining wall near an alley. I can't get her to sit even though her feet are hurting. She's afraid she won't be able to get back up. I take a quick run around the area, hoping maybe there are the remnants of a drug store around, but I find nothing. I'm not familiar with this part of town. I'm nearly back to the retaining wall when I hear Hannah scream.

My body turns cold. My legs suddenly feel like they can't keep me upright, and I can't take a breath.

Hannah is still next to the wall. Behind her, Caesar stands with his arm around her neck and the barrel of a gun pressed against her temple. There is no doubt that Caesar didn't escape the destruction of the compound without injury. His face and neck are badly burned, and his left ear is gone, likely burned off. He must have been caught in the explosion but somehow managed to get himself away in time.

How did he survive?

"Did you really think I was just going to stand by while you steal my property and blow up my camp?" He shakes Hannah roughly.

She cries out again, one hand still under her bulging stomach and the other gripping Caesar's forearm. I can see the tears on her face from here as she stares at me.

Caesar pulls the gun away from her head and aims it at me.

"I've officially had enough of you," he says.

Oh, fuck.

Chapter 9

Even though I know there's a gun pointed straight at me, the only thing my brain can register is that he has his hands on her.

That motherfucker has his hands on *my* Hannah.

I'd promised her that would never happen again. I said I was going to keep her safe, and there is no way in hell I'm going to let that asshole get in the way of my promise.

He is going to die.

My body calms. My heartbeat slows, and my vision sharpens.

My gun is at my hip. I know Caesar is a good shot—I've seen him practice often enough. I also know I'm better, but I'm at a disadvantage. His weapon is drawn, and mine is not. By the time I pull out the gun, he will have had plenty of time to fire.

I'm thirty feet away from them. If I stand still, he will definitely hit me. If he hits me, the chances of saving Hannah are drastically reduced. I have to move fast and unpredictably. I also have to get her away from him as quickly as possible. Speed won't be enough—I need cover.

All of this races through my head in a split second.

The only cover in sight is a faded blue Ford in the street, and I dive forward and roll toward the front tire. I hear shots fire and Hannah screaming, but I reach my destination without being hit.

"Get your ass out here, Falk!" Caesar yells. "If you don't, I'll put a fucking bullet right in her head!"

"You aren't going to kill her," I call from around the tire as I reach for my gun. "You're out of women. You need her alive."

"Maybe so," he says, "but I sure as fuck can hurt her. Maybe that's what I'll do. Maybe I'll just fuck her in the ass right here while you watch. Then I'll put a bullet in your skull."

I'm not about to fall for that shit.

"I'm the one you want," I remind him. "I'm the one who took her from you. Now why don't you let her sit off to the side, and we can settle this between the two of us."

"Is that how you think this is going to go down?"

I take a deep breath and force myself to think for a moment.

Caesar was obviously caught up in the explosion. He's also obviously alone, or he'd have his backup hauling Hannah off while he took care of me. That means he's the only survivor of that attack, and he was badly hurt. Hell, he might have completely lost his mind over the whole thing.

A little psychological warfare is called for.

"So tell me something," I say, trying to draw him into another line of thought. "When your little base blew up, was your brother there? Did he burn like the puffed-up marshmallow that he was? That's a shit way to go, dontcha think? I bet he screamed a lot. Did you hear him? Did you hear him screaming while he burned?"

"Motherfucker." His voice is low, but I still hear the curse.

"I bet you wonder how they found you, huh? I'll tell you how."

"What the fuck do you know?"

"I ordered that attack," I tell him. "Yeah, I got my little contact on the other side. Bet you never suspected that, did ya?

298

Aliens came right to me, asking me if there was anything they could do to help me out. Thought to myself, 'Ya know? There is this little batch of fucktards over there by Georgia Tech. Why don't you just bomb the bejesus out of them for me, huh?' Their only question was to ask for the precise coordinates. Nearly took ten minutes."

"Get out here, you fucker," Caesar yells. I can hear his footsteps as he moves toward the street. If he's moving toward me, he's moving away from Hannah. I only hear the footsteps of one. "You wanna put the guns down and fight this out? Because I'd be happy to just go ahead and fuck you up."

"That sounds pretty ideal to me," I reply. "Put the guns down and fight it out, man to man."

"Sure."

He's lying; I can hear it in his voice. He's just hoping to draw me out, but I don't have a lot of options. If I can't get to him, we'll be in a stalemate, and that doesn't get Hannah to safety.

I step out from behind the Ford with my gun hanging at my side. Caesar stands the same way with his finger on the trigger. He's got a nasty smirk on his face—overconfident and just a little bit crazy.

I drop as soon as I see his arm flex and hear the blast just afterward. The ground is abruptly in my face, smashing my nose. There's a sharp pain in my right arm when I land on it, and I can't take a breath as the wind is knocked out of me.

Did he shoot me?

I don't feel any pain like I did when I was shot before. All the pain is in my arm, but it doesn't burn.

"I knew I should have put a bullet in the back of your head as soon as I saw you! That's what Beck wanted from the beginning! Kill you and fuck this stupid little bitch sore!"

The words send waves of red-hot rage through me. I shove as hard as I can with my left hand as I roll myself over onto my back. I look up to see Caesar's face, and his gun is pointed right between my eyes. I don't have time to think.

I kick at his legs, and the gun goes off again. I feel chips of cement hit the side of my face as Caesar falls beside me. I flip over, grab one of his arms and pin it to the ground as I throw a leg over his torso. I slam my fist into his face as he knocks me in the side of the head with the butt end of the gun.

The hit stuns me, and the next thing I know, Caesar has me pinned to the ground, punching my face. Hannah stands a few feet from me, her arms wrapped protectively around her middle. Caesar glances over at her and sneers.

"I told you to get used to the only thing you're good for," he says. "You had your little break. It's time for you to get back to work!"

Caesar slams his right fist into my face again.

"You killed Beck, you motherfucker." He puts all his weight on his knee, driving it into my gut. I can't breathe right, and my right arm is still pinned painfully by his other leg. "I know you did."

"Stop!" Hannah screams. "Please, stop!"

"Wait your turn, sweetheart," Caesar calls to her. "Believe me, once I'm done with him, I'll be taking a turn on that sweet ass of yours. Just be patient."

I jab my left fist into his kidney, and we roll together across the concrete. I can feel rocks and bits of debris scraping my skin as we go, and another shooting pain runs up my arm. Caesar kicks out at me, separating us, and we both jump to our feet.

"Yeah, I killed Beck," I yell at him. "Wrapped my hands around his neck and squeezed the life out of him. Watched his eyes bulge out and his face change color. It takes a long time to kill someone like that, you know? A lot longer than you think. Movies and television never get it right."

Caesar's jaw flexes and his free hand balls into a fist.

"Cried like a bitch when I cut him, too. I noticed you didn't tell anyone about that. Figured you were waiting for me to slip up, but I'm not that stupid."

"I knew it was you," Caesar says with a growl. "I knew it the whole time."

"Damn, did he make a fuss about getting cut, too." I let out a laugh. "You served with him, right? Was he kicked out for being a milk-toast-gumming beta? I can't see special ops holding on to a pussy like that."

He raises his gun again.

We're close enough to each other that I dive at him, rolling forward quickly. I hear the blast right behind my head. I jump to my feet and rush at him, wrapping my arms around his waist and tackling him to the ground before he can get off another shot. Shooting pain surges up my right arm, and I can't get a good hold on him. We roll, and I lose my grip as Caesar's gun scrapes across the concrete.

We both jump up at the same time, and I reach to my belt and draw my knife. We stand facing each other while we both catch our breath. Caesar looks at the knife in my hand and then glances down at the gun. It's only a yard away from his feet.

"You are going down," Caesar says with a growl.

I say nothing and I don't move. I can hear Hannah behind me, her breath coming in staccato gasps. I have to subdue and kill him before he has the chance to go after her.

"Almost caught you back at that house by the river," Caesar says. "I must have missed you by about five minutes. Tracked you for a mile, lost the trail, but then I heard Hannah yapping. Of course, I recognize her voice. I've heard her screaming often enough."

He's trying to distract me, but it's not going to work. I clear my mind, keeping my sole focus on him and him alone. Caesar glances at the gun near his feet, and I grip the knife tighter in my left hand. I'm less than twenty feet away from him.

Twenty-one feet. I don't recall his name, but I remember the instructor at the security training center saying that twenty-one feet was the golden rule. It's the distance a running person with a knife in his hand can cover before someone can draw a gun from his holster. None of us believed him, and we all had to try it.

The guy with the gun failed every time.

As Caesar goes for the gun, I race for him. My knife is in his gut before he can get a good enough grip on the gun to bring it around. He gasps, and I pull the knife out, feeling his blood spurting onto my arm.

I jab the knife into him again, and the gun falls back to the ground. He drops backward, and I go with him. I raise the knife up and slam it into his chest, feeling the resistance of bone. I twist it to the side, and shove it between his ribs.

Caesar's eyes go wide and his mouth hangs open. I stab him again.

And again.

Blood pours from his mouth. He reaches up and grabs the edge of my shirt fruitlessly as I pull back and lodge the knife in his neck.

Blood spurts out of his carotid, spraying my face, and I finally sit back on my heels.

My chest burns as I shove off of him. I cringe when I put a little weight on my right hand in order to stand up. At least there isn't a bone sticking out of it. I take a couple of stumbling steps away from the body and turn to look for Hannah.

She's up against the retaining wall, sitting with her arms wrapped around herself. I wipe the blood from my face with the tail end of my shirt and grab both the guns. I take one last look at Caesar's body before I go to her.

"It's okay, Hannah," I say as I crouch down next to her and lay my hand on her shoulder. "It's over. He's dead."

"Are you sure?" she suddenly screams at me. "I mean, for God's sake, Falk! Stab him a couple more times!"

She bursts into tears and grabs onto my neck at the same time.

"It's all right," I say. "You never have to worry about him again."

She pulls back and looks into my eyes. I can see it in her face—she isn't worried about him anymore; she's worried about me.

"I will always protect you, Hannah," I whisper. "No matter what."

She looks over to the body on the ground.

"So much blood," she whispers.

"Don't look." I take her face in my hands and turn her to face me. "Let's just get out of here. We'll get to the others, and you can rest for as long as you want, okay?"

Hannah wipes her eyes, sniffs, and nods. She winces as I help her to her feet, her arm still around her stomach. I wrap my arm around her waist to support her as much as I can. I'm fairly certain my right arm is broken, but I'll just have to deal with that later. I don't know if Caesar had anyone else with him or not. I don't think so because someone would have come to his aid before now, but it's still possible. It's getting dark, and I need to get Hannah out of here.

"Can you walk?"

"I think so." She's shaking all over.

I give her a minute to collect herself. She keeps looking over at Caesar's body, so I stand in her line of sight. She looks up at me and scowls. She knows exactly what I'm doing.

"Let's go," I tell her.

"What happened to him?"

"I killed him."

"I mean, what about all that shit you said about aliens and bombing the camp? What happened?"

"Later. We need to get moving."

"Falk!" She yells at me, her eyes narrowing.

"Not now!" I run my hand through my hair out of habit and then cringe as pain shoots up my arm. "We can't stay here. We have to get going. I'll explain it all later."

303

She continues to look at me sideways as we finally start moving again. She's trying to keep up a good pace, but she doesn't last long. We stop again, and she grips her stomach with both hands.

"Falk?" She looks up at me, her voice barely a whisper. Her eyes are wide and full of fear.

"What is it?"

"I think…I think I might be in labor."

No. No, that can't be.

"I thought you said it was gas?"

"That's what it kinda feels like," she says, "but not quite. And the pains are getting more frequent."

"You're not due for weeks, Hannah." I shake my head. There is no way this is happening, not now.

"This isn't an exact science, you know!"

"But the baby will be too early, won't it? You can't have it yet." I don't believe it. Maybe if I don't let her believe it, it won't be true.

"I don't think I get much of a say in the matter!" She cries out then, doubling over as I grab her arms to keep her upright.

"We have to get to the new camp," I tell her. I look around quickly, not even sure what I'm trying to find. There's nothing. I look back to Hannah. "I think…well, I think my arm's broken. I'm not sure I can carry you. Can you keep walking?"

"Do I have a choice?" she growls through clenched teeth.

I support her as much as I can, stopping every ten or fifteen minutes as another contraction hits her.

"How much farther?"

"A half mile, tops," I tell her.

"I don't think I can make it."

After everything else we've overcome, this can't possibly be happening now. I don't know that much about pregnancy or babies, but I know newborns that arrive too early need a lot of help. They need extra oxygen. They need incubators. They need someone who knows what the fuck they're doing.

304

I'm not even sure getting her to the rest of the group will make any difference, but I know the chances of having a successful birth in the street are right about nil. I have to get her moving.

I move in front of her and place one hand on her belly and the other on the side of her face.

"Hannah Savinski," I say, "I've seen you do shit the most alpha guy in the world would balk at. You've endured what would cause most people to give up—put a bullet in their skulls. You are the strongest woman in the world, and you can do anything if you set your mind to it."

Her chest rises and falls rapidly as she stares at me. The fear is still in her eyes, but there's something else as well—the determination I've seen from her so many times before.

"We're going to make it to the group," I say. "We're going to keep going, and we'll stop when we need to, but we're going to make it."

"Okay," she says, nodding quickly. "We're going to make it."

"That's right."

"There's something you gotta do for me though."

"Anything," I say.

"Tell me what you meant when you said all that shit to Caesar," Hannah says. "Tell me all of it."

"Not now."

"Yes, now!" she yells at me. "I need the damn distraction, and I have the feeling I'm going to be furious at you! That's as good a distraction as any!"

I glance at the dark sky. We need to move, and I don't have the time to argue with her.

"All right," I say, giving in. "I'll tell you."

"Damn right you will."

We start walking, and she glares until I start talking.

"When I was out patrolling a few nights ago, I found one of them."

"One of the aliens?"

"Yeah."

"What did it look like?" she asks in a whisper.

I don't know why she's whispering or who she thinks might hear us, but I lower my voice as well.

"I have no idea," I say. "It was wearing a suit—like a big metal robot covering up what it actually looked like. It said the suit provided the right kind of atmosphere so it could breathe. It was also bullet-proof."

"You shot it?"

"Yeah, but it didn't do any good."

"But you talked to it?"

"Yeah," I say with a nod, "for a while."

"What did it say?"

"A lot of shit," I respond. I'm not prepared for this conversation, and I have to sort through the discussion I had with the alien to figure out what I want to divulge and what I want to keep to myself.

"Like what?" She starts to say something else but has to stop as a pain hits her. Once it passes, and she catches her breath, she berates me to continue.

"I asked it what happened to the women and children," I tell her as we start walking again, "and why the men were killed."

I tell her most of the story, leaving out anything that might hint that I'd spoken to the same creature years ago.

"You told it to kill everyone there?" Hannah asks when I finish.

"Honestly, I didn't really think the alien was serious," I tell her. "I had no idea it would actually call down ships to bomb the whole place. I just...I just said what was in my mind. I wanted Caesar and all the rest of them dead. I didn't expect them to annihilate the place."

"Those other girls were still there," Hannah says in a low voice.

"I know." I take a deep breath. "That wasn't my intent—you know it wasn't."

"What about the rest?" she asks.

"The rest of what?"

"*Did* you kill Beck?"

I swallow hard. I should have realized she would eventually find out. I should have prepared some kind of statement, but I haven't.

"Yeah, I did."

"Christ, Falk!"

"He fucking deserved it!" I stop and turn to her. "You know he would have been the first in line to rape you. Tell me you believe otherwise, and I'll consider apologizing for killing him before he had the chance."

"You don't know that." She looks away from me, and I know she doesn't believe what she's saying.

"He told me he had you cornered. He laughed and said you needed to get over it. So yeah, I lost my shit. I punched him; he punched me. I hit the table, and we struggled. I ended up on top, and I choked the life out of him. I'd do it again, too. I only wish I'd done the same thing to Brett when I had the chance."

Hannah doesn't look at me. Instead, she stares at the ground in front of her feet as she walks. I'm not sure if I've made her angry or if I've frightened her.

"We don't live in the same world anymore, Hannah," I say. "It's not like you can call the cops and get someone arrested if they fuck with you. Yes, I killed Beck. Not only would I do it again, but if anyone else threatens you, I'll going to kill them, too."

She looks over and stares at me, wide-eyed.

"Get used to it," I finally say when she doesn't respond. "It's how it's going to be."

We start walking again, and Hannah remains quiet for several minutes. I'm still tense. I feel like I've outed myself. I might as well confess my part in the death of every human being who has ever died at my hands—in war and otherwise.

Yeah, Hannah—you were escaping from a bunch of violent men, and your only protection is a killer. Sorry about your luck.

"Falk?"

"What?" My tone is harsh. I'm expecting her to argue some point about how we need to hold onto our humanity or some other bullshit, but she doesn't.

"The pains have stopped."

I look her over. She's breathing easier now, and though her hand still rests on top of her belly, she isn't clenching her abdomen like she was before.

"You sure?"

"It's been a while, hasn't it?"

"Yeah." I look at my watch. It's been more than half an hour, at least. "Can you keep going? If we can keep up this pace, we'll be there soon."

"I never believe you when you say that."

"Ten minutes. I promise."

"I'm going to hold you to that."

Twelve minutes later, we reach our destination. It's a small neighborhood just to the east of the bypass that surrounds Atlanta. We cross a bridge over a small creek that still has some water in it and make our way to the coordinates.

I can smell a fire as we approach.

"It smells like Christine's cooking!" Hannah says with a smile.

"Let me check it out first," I say. "Stay back here for a—"

"Falk?" Hannah grabs my arm, halting my words.

"What is it?"

"Please don't leave me alone." There are tears in her eyes as she speaks, and I nod before giving her a hug.

"I won't," I tell her. "But we're going to go in quietly, okay?"

"Okay."

I hold Hannah's hand as we creep through the edge of the neighborhood, sticking close to the trees. Locating the exact house is pretty easy—we just follow the smell from the fire. As we get close, I can see the smoke rising from the back yard of a huge house. Around the fire, Marco, Sam, and Katrina are all sitting in lounge chairs. Christine appears a moment later with bottles of wine in her hands.

"Aren't they underage?" I ask as Hannah and I step out of the trees.

"Falk! Hannah!"

They all run up to greet us. There's a lot of hugging, which I put up with for a moment before letting Hannah take center stage while I back off for a cigarette. I close my eyes and lean against a tree, just watching.

Caesar's dead—for sure this time. Hannah is with friends, and she'll have more help besides me when the baby decides to really come. I don't know what the future will hold for us, but for the time being, I'm going to allow myself to relax.

Just a little.

Chapter 10

"Hey! Check this out!"

Inside the storage unit, I stand and walk across the small open space to Marco. He's pulling a cardboard box from a large, plastic storage bin.

"What is it?"

"It's a portable DVD player!" he says. "Runs on batteries, and there are a bunch of movies with it, too. We got a *Star Trek* movie, *Tron*, *Aliens*, and even the *Charlie Brown Christmas Special*!"

"Looks like a waste of batteries," I respond.

"You are no fun." Marco holds the DVD boxes to his chest as if I'm going to try to steal them from him.

"I am practical."

"Morale is important." He grins up at me, and I roll my eyes.

"You seem to be getting plenty of 'morale.'" I raise an eyebrow at him, and he actually has the decency to blush.

I had initially been concerned there would be a fight over Katrina—both Marco and Sam were obviously interested. Katrina could have gone either way, or she could have been disinterested in both.   What I didn't expect was for the three of them to all be…well…*together*—or sharing, at least.

"It works for us," he says with a shrug. "Beats fighting over her, and I'm not sure she would have liked having to choose."

"She seems pretty happy with the whole arrangement."

"She is." Marco wiggles his eyebrows at me. "In fact, yesterday morning—"

"No details, *please!*" I cut him off, shake my head, and go back to the other side of the unit as Marco chuckles to himself.

Finding a nearby storage facility with most of the units undamaged has been a godsend. A lot of what we find I would have considered crap before all this happened, but now I see uses for almost everything we come across.

We gather up our haul for the day and head home. I push the shopping cart with my left hand and rest my splinted-up right arm on the handle while Marco carries the backpack. As soon as we get back, Marco heads into the living room to show everyone the DVD player, and I head into the first-story master bedroom where Hannah and I have been sleeping.

Christine insisted on it. She said she didn't want Hannah climbing the stairs.

"Any luck?" Hannah asks as I walk in.

"Not really." I drop the pack on the table. "I found some of the things on the list but none of the medical supplies. I did get you some more clothes."

"That's a bonus."

"Hope they fit."

"Nothing *fits!*"

Ah shit—here we go again.

Hannah is due any day now and absolutely miserable. I've done everything I can think of to help her be more comfortable, but all the things that used to work on her just don't anymore. She can barely sleep at night, so she's exhausted all the time, and she's driving me crazy.

I don't mention the latter.

"I have to pee!" Hannah suddenly cries out as she runs for the bathroom.

Hannah has to pee every fifteen minutes. Thank God the toilets in the house continue to flush. I can only hope they'll last a while longer.

Grabbing my backpack, I pull out the box of shotgun shells I found in one of the storage units. It's been a while since I've been able to stockpile some ammo. I don't have anywhere near enough, but at least I'm making progress. I wish I had found the actual shotgun, but there was no sign of it. Marco was too excited about the DVD player to convince him to go through one more storage unit, so I'll probably head back there tomorrow. Maybe Katrina would like to get a look inside one of them.

Hannah comes back into the room, her face pale.

"What is it?" I ask as I go to her. "More of those Braxton-Hicks?"

Katrina has looted every book on pregnancy and childbirth she could find and has been educating all of us on the topics. She even found a book on home birth, and we've found all the supplies listed. The whole thing scares the shit out of me, but it's not like there's a choice.

"I don't think so." Hannah grips her stomach and scrunches her face for a moment. "I think the baby's really coming this time."

"You thought that before."

"Yeah," she says, "but my water just broke."

~~~~~~

"Breathe!" Christine yells. "Come on, now! It's not that bad!"

Not that bad?

I hold my hand against my chest and wonder if I'm having an actual heart attack. I've never felt such pain before and almost wish I were just sewing up another gunshot wound.

313

I'm going to be a father.

"I...I...I can't!"

"Goddammit, Falk!" Christine pulls back and slaps me across the face. "You get your shit together, man! That baby is going to be born any minute now!"

The shock of her hitting me has the same effect as being shocked with a defibrillator. My heart starts beating again, and I finally draw breath.

"I can't handle this shit," I tell her.

"You get your ass in there, Falk Eckhart!" Christine hauls back, this time with a closed fist.

"All right! All right!" I head back into the bedroom where Hannah is on all fours with Katrina poised behind her like a World Cup goalie.

"Almost there, Hannah," Katrina says softly. "Just a few more times!"

I can see the baby's head, and I almost throw up. I start to turn and run out, but Christine is right there, a fist at the ready.

I go back to the foot of the bed where Hannah is kneeling and crouch down beside her. She looks over at me, her face red with sweaty hair hanging in her eyes. I push a few of the strands off her forehead.

"I love you, Hannah," I say softly.

"I kinda hate you right now," she replies. She squeezes her eyes shut and her arms begin to shake.

"One more big push, Hannah!" Katrina calls out. "Come on!"

"You got this, Hannah." I lay my hand on the back of her neck. "You're the strongest woman in the world."

She shifts her hand and places it over mine on the floor, gripping it tightly. She takes in a big breath, holds it, and her face practically turns purple.

A moment later, I hear a cry.

"Oh my God! Oh my God!" Katrina is squealing. "It's a boy! Hannah, you have a little boy!"

Holy fuck, she was right!

"Is he okay?" Marco and Sam ask in unison.

"He's perfect." Christine kneels next to Katrina with a pair of surgical scissors to clamp and cut the cord. "Falk, give me that blanket."

He's got all his fingers and toes.

He's wrinkled and streaked with blood and yellow mucus. His eyes stay closed, but he keeps opening and closing his mouth. The cries that come out of him are barely audible.

"Falk—the blanket!"

His ears are pointy.

"Here you go." Sam hands a receiving blanket to Christine, and she wraps the baby up.

"He's kind of a mess," Marco says.

The baby stops crying once he's swaddled in the blanket, and Katrina takes him from Christine's arms and lays him across Hannah's stomach. Hanna is still breathing hard, and tears are running down her face, but she's smiling.

I have a son.

"He's beautiful," Hannah says with a sniff. The baby opens its eyes and stares up at Hannah's face though he doesn't seem to be able to focus very well. "You see, Falk? He looks just like you. He even has your eyes."

He's healthy. Hannah's okay.

Christine takes the baby, and Katrina helps Hannah get back up on her hands and knees to deliver the placenta. I lean back against the bed and stare into space until Christine sits down beside me.

"Come on, Falk, you big dork! Hold out your arms so you can hold your son."

I do as she says, and Christine lays the baby in my stiff arms. My throat seizes up. He weighs practically nothing. He's so, so tiny. His fingers aren't even as long as one of my knuckles. His nose is so small, I'm not convinced he can breathe out of it. He proves me wrong almost immediately as he lets out a strange cry.

"Did I fuck it up?" I ask.

Christine laughs.

"No, you did not 'fuck it up,'" she says. "Just relax a little."

I take a deep breath and try to relax my arms, but the baby keeps crying. I have no idea what I'm doing, but Christine is obviously wrong—I am fucking it up.

I hold the baby while Christine takes a sponge and cleans him off, but he keeps crying no matter what I do. Once the afterbirth has been delivered, Katrina gets Hannah onto the bed and propped up with a bunch of pillows.

"I already suck at this," I tell her.

"It's okay," Christine says. "You just need a little practice to get used to it."

"I'm not sure I'll ever get used to this," I admit.

"You will." She sounds so confident, so sure of her words.

I just shake my head.

Christine takes the baby back from me, and he quiets almost immediately. She lays him on a pillow draped over Hanna's stomach, and he immediately goes right for her breast. I push myself to my feet and stand beside the bed. All I can do is stare at the two of them while Marco, Sam, and Christine start cleaning up the rest of the room.

"It's good to get him nursing right away," Katrina says. "I read that."

It takes several tries, but eventually the baby gets a good grip. Hannah winces a little when he latches on, but then they both settle down. I slowly sit on the edge of the bed, and Hannah smiles up at me.

"Come over here," she says, nodding to the spot next to her.

I scoot up next to them both, and Hannah leans over and kisses my cheek.

"Well," she asks, "what do you think?"

"I don't know." It's the only phrase I seem to be able to utter.

"Are you okay?" Marco asks.

I just shake my head.

"Daddy's a little overwhelmed, I think." Hannah giggles. She reaches over and wipes tears off my cheek.

I didn't realize they were there.

Daddy.

"Come on, all of you." Christine puts a hand on Marco's shoulder. "Everyone out. Let's leave the family in peace for a while."

"Just yell if you need anything," Katrina adds, and they all walk out, closing the bedroom door behind them.

Grateful for the sudden serenity, I press my forehead to Hannah's shoulder and look down at the baby. His eyes are open, and he sucks furiously at Hannah's breast. He looks so serious about the whole thing, and I can't help but smile.

Yeah, bud—I like them, too.

"Chuck is a nickname for Charles, isn't it?" Hannah turns her head and nuzzles her chin in my hair.

"I think so."

"So…can we name him that? Charles?"

Pressing my lips together, I fight against the memory of the image of Chuck lying dead behind the truck. Instead, I focus on remembering the look on his face when he'd show up at camp with some rodent on the end of an arrow, begging Christine to cook it.

"Yeah," I finally say. "I think Charles is perfect."

Little Charles closes his eyes and his sucking motions slow and finally stop. Hannah strokes the top of his head gently, careful of the soft spot.

"Does all this scare you?" she asks.

I look from her to the tiny, new human being in her arms.

317

"Hannah," I say seriously, "I've had insurgents surround me and start throwing grenades. I've had IEDs go off and kill the guy next to me. I've had dozens of assholes chasing me while trying to get you to safety, and I've shot at an alien."

I turn my head so I can look her right in the eyes.

"This scares the ever-loving shit out of me."

Hannah tries to hold in her giggles so she doesn't shake little Charles awake. I reach over and stroke his cheek. He's lost his grip on her nipple, but as soon as he feels my touch, he starts making little sucking motions with his mouth.

"Thank you, Hannah," I whisper.

"For what?" she asks.

"For giving my life purpose again."

Epilogue

I'm awake but only barely.

The bed is warm and comfortable. My arm is wrapped around my wife and son, who both sleep peacefully. It's Sunday. It's still early, and I'd promised Hannah she could sleep late this morning.

She wants everything to be normal, and apparently, that means sleeping in on Sundays.

Charles is not always cooperative, so occasionally I open my eyes just to check on him for a moment, but I soon close them again when I see he's still sleeping. Once he wakes, I'll get him up and give Hannah another hour or two to rest.

My mind recounts the events of the previous day.

"Do you, Falk Eckhart, take this woman to be your wife?"

I glance sideways at Hannah before answering. She's giving me the stink-eye, and I have to admit that I like to rile her up.

"Yeah, sure," I finally say, and she elbows me in the ribs.

"Say it right!"

"Marco's not a priest! What difference does it make?"

"Falk!" She purses her lips and glares as I let out a long sigh.

"I do."

"You may kiss the bride!" Marco announces with a big grin. "Slip her some tongue!"

Katrina giggles, and as I place my lips on Hannah's, everyone cheers except Charles, who starts to cry instead.

I smile at the memory. It hadn't been my idea, but I was okay with it. It made Hannah happy. Next to keeping her and Charles safe, that is my primary function. I even danced while Marco wasted battery life playing some music he'd found in a storage unit. It felt like tenth grade all over again—my dancing skills haven't changed much since then—but Hannah smiled when I twirled her around and laughed when I nearly fell on my ass in the attempt.

Movement next to me causes me to open my eyes again. Charles is awake and kicking his little legs. Katrina says he'll start crawling pretty soon. He's already rolling himself all over the floor when given the chance.

I push back the blankets and scoop him up. He smiles and makes little cooing sounds as I carry him out of the room.

"Hey there, hot stuff!" Christine looks over at me from the couch in the living room.

I glance down, realizing I'm just in my boxers.

"Sorry," I say. "I didn't want to wake Hannah."

"Who says I'm talking to you?" Christine raises an eyebrow at me, stands and takes Charles from my arms. "How's my handsome little man today?"

I take the opportunity to grab a cup of coffee and head outside.

The front porch of the huge house is the perfect place to hang out in the morning, but I bypass it and walk off into the yard to loiter under a tree. I lean back, light a cigarette, and watch the community in front of me come to life.

Katrina and her boyfriends come out of the house first, hand-in-hand-in-hand. They've started talking walks in the morning together, claiming they're trying to get in some daily exercise. I have no doubt they're getting their cardio in, but I don't think walking is what's keeping them in shape.

I nod as they wave at me, hiding my smile behind the smoke.

A door opens across the street. Hugo and Frank emerge, also holding hands. They joined our pack a month ago. Katrina has the idea that we should seek out couples to join our group, believing they will be less likely to represent a threat to the rest of us. I'm not sure I buy into her philosophy. I only agree to these guys because they're gay.

Does that make me a bigot?

Katrina's been talking to an older man and woman who have been hiding out in a campground near Stone Mountain and wants to bring them here. I'm still suspicious, still cautious, but I agreed to go meet them. There's nothing altruistic about it—Katrina says they have working solar panels on their motorhome and that the man is some kind of scientist.

Both might be useful.

There are still packs of men out there hunting women. No one as organized as Caesar and Brett's group, but they're around. Hannah has talked about rescuing the women they're using for barter, but we haven't made any attempts.

I'm torn on the whole subject.

It's the right thing to do, or at least it would be if we didn't live in the world we live in. This is a selfish world, and I'm a practical person. Anyone we try to rescue puts the rest of us in danger, and I'm not ready to put my family in the line of fire. Maybe that makes me an asshole. I don't really care.

Hannah's perspective is different. She feels for each and every woman she knows is out there. At some point, it's going to become a bigger issue for her. Right now, I keep her distracted with

Charles, but he'll grow, and her need to bring peace to those women's lives will grow along with him.

I stomp out the cigarette and erase the thought from my mind. It's a topic for another day. I head back inside briefly to dress and grab my rifle before I do a quick patrol around the neighborhood. It's quiet today, and I see nothing of concern. When I return, Hannah is on the porch with Charles lying across her lap, sucking away. I head up the steps and lean over to kiss them both on their heads.

"Did you sleep well?" I ask.

"I did, thank you," Hannah replies with a smile. "Did he have you up early?"

"Nah, he believes in Sundays, too." I return the smile and run inside to make some breakfast.

The day passes quickly and quietly like Sundays should. Katrina's trying to make a solar oven by spray-painting a cardboard box black and lining it with tinfoil. I don't have a lot of hopes for it, but she's got a book on the topic, and she's determined.

As evening approaches, I make my last patrol around the neighborhood. When I get back, Hannah has a blanket spread out on the lawn with Charles in the middle of it. He's rolling back and forth, trying to grab anything he can reach and stick it in his mouth.

I sit down on the blanket just as he gets to the edge, reaches into the grass, and grabs a fluffy dandelion. Reflexively, I grab his hand and pry it from his tiny fingers before he can get it into his mouth. He screams at me but is quickly distracted by one of his teething toys.

"They're edible, you know," Hannah says. "Katrina puts dandelion leaves in the salads all the time."

"He doesn't need a mouthful of those seeds," I say. "He'd scream about that for hours."

"True."

"I'm surprised you haven't gone all wifely on my ass yet and demanded I get the weeds out of the yard. We're in the burbs here. Aren't we supposed to have a perfectly manicured lawn?"

Hannah shrugs, and a small smile crosses her face.

"I like them, actually." She reaches over to another dandelion and runs her fingers gently over the fuzzy white tips. "They're survivors. Just when you think they're dead, they plant little seeds everywhere."

I give her a look. She's trying to make a point, but I don't get it, and she doesn't seem to care to elaborate. I don't push it, but it does make me wonder.

I kiss her cheek, tickle Charles' stomach, and head inside to clean up. Once I'm thoroughly washed, I lie back in the bed with the hopes of catching a few minutes of sleep, but it doesn't work out that way. Shortly after I lie down, the door opens.

Hannah saunters over to the bed, climbs in next to me, and straddles my waist. I raise an eyebrow at her, and she leans over to press her lips to mine.

"Where's Charles?"

"Actually," Hannah says with a sly grin, "we have a babysitter for the night."

"Oh, really?"

"Christine is keeping him with her. I managed to get that manual breast pump thing to work just enough to get him through the night."

"So, I have you all to myself?"

"You do."

"Hmm…" I reach up and tap my finger with my chin. "What are we going to do? Checkers? Parcheesi? Oh, I know! Marco found a copy of *Escape to Witch Mountain* on DVD. Let's watch that!"

She swats at my chest playfully and then leans in for another kiss. I open my mouth and search for her tongue as my arms wrap around her. She feels so good against me—so right and perfect. It's as if she is meant to be right here with me, and everything that happened to get us to this point doesn't matter anymore.

Hannah breaks away from me and sheds her clothes quickly as I push my boxers down my legs and kick them to the floor. She's back on top of me a second later.

"Eager, aren't you?"

"I've been thinking about this since Christine's offer," Hannah says. "I want you inside me. Now."

"No argument here." I grab my cock by the base and Hannah rises up on her knees above me. She slowly impales herself, and we moan together as her warmth embraces me.

It's been a while, and I feel like I should take my time, but Hannah has other ideas. As soon as I'm all the way inside her, she starts grinding her hips into me. I hold her ass with one hand and use the other to explore her body. I slide my fingers up her side and over her breast, cupping it and enjoying how full it feels.

Hannah lets out a moan that goes straight to my cock. It pulses inside of her, and I have to close my eyes and grit my teeth to keep from letting loose immediately. Hannah starts to rock faster, and it takes all my control not to lose myself in her.

I hold tightly to her hips, pulling her down over me as her body clenches around mine. She makes the most beautiful squeaking noises as she tries to muffle her cries. She keeps herself balanced by gripping my shoulders tightly with her fingertips while I push up with my hips. It's not long before I feel the tension building in my thighs and stomach.

I try to keep my groans in check as I shove up into her one last time. My balls tighten, and I grit my teeth as I explode inside of her. Hannah drops down on my chest, her fingers still clinging to my shoulders.

I close my eyes and lean back against the pillow as I run my hands up and down her back. After a minute, Hannah sits back up and rolls off of me and onto her back. I move to my side and wrap an arm around her. I run my hand over her stomach. It's still bouncy and fleshy from pregnancy, and it jiggles when I poke at it.

"Stop that!" Hannah covers my hand.

"Why?"

"You're playing with my fat," she says.

"It's not fat," I tell her. "It's just soft. I like it."

"You're weird." She shakes her head at me. "Now let me go to sleep. It's the first time I actually get to sleep all night without worrying about Charles waking up and wanting to be fed."

"Love you," I whisper as I kiss her softly on the lips.

"Love you, too," she responds. She runs her fingers down the side of my face, rolls over, and presses her back to my chest.

I lay there for a long time, just thinking. I can't seem to close my eyes. I'm completely on edge, but I'm not sure exactly why. Everything is quiet. I've just had a massive orgasm, and I should be dropping off to sleep immediately, but I'm not.

The bed's too empty.

I swallow as I realize the reason for my discomfort. Charles is supposed to be here with us. Though I trust Christine unconditionally and implicitly, I can't protect him if he's not here. I need my son with me.

"Falk?" Hannah whispers in the dark as her hand creeps up to my chest.

"Yeah?"

"I miss Charles."

"I'll go get him."

Christine is sitting up in bed with a book, and Charles is sleeping peacefully in a laundry basket lined with my woobie. Christine grins widely and doesn't look the least bit surprised to see me at her bedroom door.

"I had a feeling you wouldn't make it through the night," Christine says, chuckling softly.

"Hannah misses him," I say with a shrug.

"Right—just Hannah."

I glance over at Christine, give her the finger, and then pick up the basket.

"Goodnight, Falk."

"Goodnight, Christine, and thank you."

I tiptoe back down the stairs with the basket in my hands and return to our room. Hannah sits up in bed and holds out her arms. Charles wiggles a little when I transfer him from the basket to his mother, but he doesn't wake.

Hannah runs her hand over Charles' head, and he lets out a quiet sigh.

"Do you think we should have another one?" she asks.

"Already?"

"Not right now or anything," Hannah says. "I mean eventually."

"I think eventually it will end up happening," I say. "Rhythm method has never been that reliable."

"What I mean is, would you want another one?"

I think about it for a minute.

"If we did, and it was a girl, it would scare the shit out of me."

"You would be a pretty fierce daddy bear to a little girl."

"I'd fucking kill anyone who came near her," I tell her. "Maybe it's not a good idea."

Hannah lays her head on my shoulder. A few minutes later, she's asleep, but I'm still thinking about her question.

I don't care much about repopulating the planet. I just don't care to think that globally. I don't even know what there is out there beyond the Metro Atlanta area, but it's likely more of the same. What kind of life is that for kids?

What kind of life did I have before?

Before all of this, I had my job and my memories. The job was just something I did, and the memories haunted me. My most intimate actions involved a bottle or surfing the internet on my phone. Now I have Hannah and Charles. I have a reason to exist in this world, so maybe I shouldn't judge it too unfairly.

I don't know what kind of future Charles will have. Hell, I don't know what the future holds for any of us. But I know we're alive, and we have each other. One way or another, we're going to make a life for ourselves in this new world.

I coil my arms around my family and listen to their slow, steady breaths.

In a world where everything was accessible with a few clicks on a smartphone, I had nothing. In a world of chaos where we have to fight for our very existence, I have everything.

I feel fine.

I feel needed.

I'm whole again.

~~*The End*~~

Author's Notes

Sometimes, a story just worms its way into my head, and there is nothing I can do but write it. *Commodity* wasn't planned. It wasn't on my list at all of things to write this year, but I'm not always in control of what goes on in my mind, and sometimes I have to just go with it.

People always ask me where I get my book ideas, and I don't usually have a straight answer. *Commodity* was sparked by a single event that took place in early September, and I couldn't get the scene out of my head. I was walking with a friend late at night, and he suddenly grabbed me and pulled me over to the other side of him as we walked between a group of guys. Afterward, he said he'd done it because he'd determined that there was a certain level of threat from the group and needed me on that side of him so he could take out the most threatening person first.

Nothing actually happened, but his quick thinking and understanding of a potentially dangerous situation intrigued me, and I couldn't get it out of my head. We talked more about his experience as a bodyguard, and *Commodity* is the result.

How does alien invasion fit into all that?

Hell if I know.

Artistic license!

Until next time – keep on reading!

Shay Savage

Other Titles by Shay Savage

Evan Arden Series:

Otherwise Alone

Former Marine Lieutenant Evan Arden sits in a shack in the middle of nowhere, waiting for orders that will send him back home—if he ever gets them. Other than his loyal Great Pyrenees, there's no one around to break up the monotony. The heat is unbearable, but he makes do with the little he has. He's accustomed to harsh conditions and simply exists as best he can. The tedium is excruciating, but it is suddenly interrupted when a young woman stumbles up his path.

She's lost; she's cute, and he can't resist the temptation of luring her into his bed. Why not? It's been ages, and he is Otherwise Alone.

Otherwise Occupied

Evan Arden is a hit man for a Chicago mob boss and moves through life with darkness in his soul and a gun in his hand. Those who know him for what he is fear him, and those who find out the hard way never get a chance to tell anyone else. The few people who get a glimpse inside his head wish they never had. A merciless killer, his only loyalty resides with his employer, the man who calls the shots that rain from Evan's weapon.

As a POW of the Gulf War, Evan spent months in captivity, and the memories of his confinement combine with thoughts of the woman he left in Arizona. He lives his life day-to-day with little more than the company of his dog, Odin. As insomnia overtakes him, he seeks comfort from an unlikely source, but will confiding in her be his undoing?

He's struggling to forget his past and to keep himself Otherwise Occupied.

Otherwise Unharmed

After Evan Arden was imprisoned by the enemy for a year and a half, he returned from the desert as a military hero. He'd suffered some minor injuries during his captivity, was discharged from the Marines with a touch of shellshock, but was considered otherwise unharmed. Now he wonders how he ended up where he is—incarcerated in Chicago's Metropolitan Correctional Center for using his sharpshooting expertise to take out the neighborhood park with a high-powered sniper rifle and multiple rounds of ammunition.

Lia Antonio, the woman he rescued from the desert heat the previous year, is the only person who can bring him out of his sleep-deprived psychosis and mounting PTSD. When she does, Evan knows he can't just let her go again. He's never considered leaving the business before—who retires from the mafia?—but he's determined to get both Lia and himself out of harm's way.

Evan faces overwhelming forces from multiple directions as a deal to get him out of jail turns more dangerous than he imagined. With a mob war on the horizon and the feds holding evidence over his head, Evan has no choice but to throw himself into the middle of another warzone.

In his efforts to make things right, Evan crosses the wrong man and finds himself on the business end of the crosshairs. With his acute perception and intelligence, he tries to stay a step ahead of his former co-workers, but this time, it isn't just his own life on the line—he's got to protect Lia from the man who once called him son.

Isolated

Improvise, Adapt, and Overcome. The mantra is good enough for the Marines; it's good enough for me. Improvise . . . Near the top of the world, I fight for my life against my opponent, Sebastian Stark. He has the upper hand in strength, but I have the cunning to turn the tables on him. I battle the elements, my demons, and him until Stark and I manage to strike a deal to ensure freedom for us both—and the women we love.

Adapt . . . Being alone comes naturally to me. I've spent most of my life alone. Sharing my experiences, opening up to another human being, developing a relationship—all these things are foreign to me. Sometimes I wonder if it's even meant to be.

Overcome . . . I've been away from Lia for far too long, yet I still have commitments I must keep. When I make my way home, I will tell her I have decided to end the life I have led and move on to become the man she needs. I can overcome my demons; I must. But will Lia be willing to wait?

Irrevocable

Have you ever made a mistake?

A big one?

I'm back in Chicago and back in business with my boss, Rinaldo Moretti. So much for my run at a normal life. There are some new faces in the organization, and someone's been cooking the books. Personally? I think they're after more than a just little cash. If I have any hopes of flushing out the traitor, I'm going to need to find a good hooker to help me sleep at night.

As the bodies pile up, I find solace in Alina. There's something about her, something different. She understands me without asking a lot of questions. It's as if she's known me for years, yet we've only just met. If I weren't so distracted by business, I'd try to figure out her story. She's the only one keeping me grounded as my world spins out of control.

I'm going to lose the one man who has ever meant anything to me – the only man to ever call me son. I want to deny his request, but there is no avoiding what awaits me. I never wanted any of this, but I'm out of options, and time is running out.

Some choices have unforeseen consequences, and some choices are simply irrevocable.

Uncockblockable

Nick Wolfe is famous in Chicago—or is that infamous? He's not only known as the illegitimate son of Mafia boss Rinaldo Moretti, but also as an unstoppable ladies' man. He always seems to get the girl in the end, even when everyone around tries to plot against him. He's a party guy, doesn't work, and spends all his time picking up women and making notches on his headboard. He's the ultimate ladies' man...or is that man-whore? However, his days of infamy come to a startling halt when he meets *her*, and she turns the tables on him.

Surviving the Storm Series:

Surviving Raine

As the captain of a schooner catering to the elite on the Caribbean Seas, Sebastian Stark does his best to avoid any human encounters. Interacting with people isn't his thing, and he prefers the company of a bottle of vodka, a shot glass, and maybe a whore. There's no doubt he's hiding from a checkered past, but he does well keeping everything to himself...

...until the night his schooner capsizes, and he's stuck on a life raft with one of the passengers.

Raine's young, she's cute, and Bastian would probably be into her if he wasn't suffering from alcohol withdrawal. As the days pass, DTs, starvation, and dehydration become the norm. Even the most closed person starts to open up when he thinks he's going to die, but when she realizes their traumatic pasts are connected, it's no longer the elements that have Bastian concerned.

He has no idea how he's going to Survive Raine.

Bastian's Storm

Sebastian Stark just isn't cut out for normal life with a girlfriend in the hot and humid city of Miami. All in all, he'd rather be back on the island where it was just the two of them, and he could keep everything in balance. The bar down the street tempts him daily, but he's determined to remain strong. Adjusting to normal life is difficult, but Bastian is doing his best to keep himself together and the nightmares away. Raine's happy, and that's what matters to him the most.

But not all nightmares can be driven away.

When Bastian's former mentor comes into the picture and presents him with an ultimatum, Bastian slips into old habits. Though he wants to shield Raine from the truth, the shady circumstances of his past form into a hurricane he can't control. In an effort to protect her, Bastian has no choice but to throw himself back into his old job—death match tournaments—just one last time.

Dropped into the arctic wilderness with weapons loaded, Bastian has to compete against representatives from major crime lords all over the states. He's studied his competition, he knows their weaknesses, and he's ready to battle for the woman he loves. There's only one opponent in the mix that causes him any concern. In order to guarantee Raine's safety, Bastian will be pitted against the key hit man for Chicago's largest mob family—a guy who's known as one hell of a shot.

A guy named Evan Arden.

Caged Trilogy:

Takedown Teague

This is not made for TV. This is the raw, brutal underground of no-holds-barred combat. Inside the cage there is nothing but me and the pain I inflict on those who dare enter. In the cage, I never have to worry about anyone but myself. Yet, when she began standing outside of the cage, everything changed. I was no longer fighting for the money or the glory – I was fighting for her.

Trapped

Bizarre rituals on a remote island in Maine.

My crazy neighbor lying naked in the produce section of a grocery store.

The sting of a knife as it slices through my flesh.

Now I know why they say life is never easy.

The soft touch of Tria's hand against my chest is the only thing that keeps me going, but there are consequences. As a fighter, I should be able to deal with anything life throws at me, but there is one circumstance I simply can't handle.

I only have one coping mechanism: a tube around my arm and a needle in my vein.

Released

Oblivion is a sweet, sweet place.

No pain. No disturbing thoughts of the past. No guilt from my recent actions.

Deep down, there is still a part of me that knows how screwed up I am. I don't see a way out, not now. Tria's gone, and the possibility of her forgiving me in my current state is exactly zero. I know I have to pull myself together, accept my responsibilities, and try to make amends, but I have no idea where to start.

No job. No apartment. I'm living on the streets with the other junkies. As little as I had to offer Tria before, I have nothing to give her now. The only way out is to come clean and tell Tria the truth about my past, but the idea of reliving the memories is so painful, I can't think about it long enough to figure out a solution.

I've hit rock bottom, and I don't even know which way is up any more.

Stand Alone Novels:

Transcendence

It's said that women and men are from two different planets when it comes to communication, but how can they overcome the obstacles of prehistoric times when one of them simply doesn't have the ability to comprehend language?

Ehd's a caveman living on his own in a harsh wilderness. He's strong and intelligent, but completely alone. When he finds a beautiful young woman in his pit trap, it's obvious to him that she is meant to be his mate. He doesn't know where she came from, she's wearing some pretty odd clothing, and she makes a lot of noises with her mouth that give him a headache. Still, he's determined to fulfill his purpose in life—provide for her, protect her, and put a baby in her.

Elizabeth doesn't know where she is or exactly how she got there. She's confused and distressed by her predicament, and there's a caveman hauling her back to his cavehome. She's not at all interested in Ehd's primitive advances, and she just can't seem to get him to listen. No matter what she tries, getting her point across to this primitive but beautiful man is a constant—and often hilarious—struggle.

With only each other for company, they must rely on one another to fight the dangers of the wild and prepare for the winter months. As they struggle to coexist, theirs becomes a love story that transcends language and time.

Offside

I have to be the best. I *am* the best. I'm quick. I'm strong. I'm smart. I'm the star keeper of my high school soccer team, and I've got major leagues scouting me. As their captain, my teammates will do anything I say—on or off the field. Girls practically beg to be added to my list of conquests. As long as I manage to go pro for the best team in the world, I won't have to worry about my father's wrath.

I'm Thomas Malone, and I've seen to it that the world revolves around me.

There's a new girl at school, and it's just a matter of time before she gives in to my charm. This one's just a little more stubborn than most—she won't even tell me her name! She's smart, too. Maybe *too* smart. I can't let her in. I can't let anybody in. I'm not too worried, but even I have to admit she's interfering with my focus on the goal.

Dad's not going to be happy about that.

Did I mention I love Shakespeare? Yeah, I know. I'm a walking contradiction. According to the Bard—"some are born great, some achieve greatness, and some have greatness thrust upon them." Somehow, I got all three.

Now how is anyone supposed to live up to that?

Worth
An injured Roman Tribunus finds comfort in the touch of the slave commanded to tend to his wounds. As a slave, her value is measured as a couple of coins, but as Tribunus Faustus learns more about her, he begins to understand her true worth. Still, a man of his station can never acknowledge feelings for a slave, and she is already owned by another man.

Alarm
Safe and comfortable. That about sums up Chloe's life. Meeting a tall, dark stranger covered in tattoos is not in her plans. Bad boys just aren't her type—even if they are gorgeous and built like a brick wall. Her internal alarms warn her that Aiden Hunter is definitely on the list of men her mother told her to avoid, but she doesn't listen. Instead, she finds herself drawn to Aiden and the excitement he promises.

Near the beach in Miami, he occupies her days with thrills and her nights with passion she's never experienced before. She knows he's hiding something from her, but Chloe pushes away her concerns and embraces this new way of living.

As Aiden teaches her to live life to the fullest, Chloe battles the internal warnings that tell her to be wary. By the time she realizes her fears may be justified, it's too late.

Aiden's past is catching up to him, but is he the hunter or the hunted?

About the Author

Shay Savage lives in Cincinnati, Ohio, with her family and a variety of household pets. She is an accomplished public speaker and holds the rank of Distinguished Toastmaster from Toastmasters International. When not writing, she enjoys spending her weekends off-roading in her bright yellow jeep, watching science fiction movies, masquerading as a zombie, and participating as a HUGE Star Wars fan and member of the 501st Legion of Stormtroopers. When the geek fun runs out, she also loves soccer in any and all forms - especially the Columbus Crew, Arsenal, and Bayern Munich. Savage holds a degree in psychology, and she brings a lot of that knowledge into the characters within her stories.

Website - http://www.shaysavage.com/

Twitter - @savage7289

Made in the USA
San Bernardino, CA
01 November 2015